The Azure Crown

The Azure Crown

Book One of the Dreamers Saga

Elizabeth Bird

ISBN: 979-8-9913364-4-4

Art by Taylor Schoonover

Illustrations by Taylor Schoonover

First edition 2024

This book is dedicated to anyone facing their own dragons. It'll be okay, love. We got this. Straighten your crown, grab your sword and let's go!

And for Evelyn and Charlotte.

Do good recklessly. I love you always.

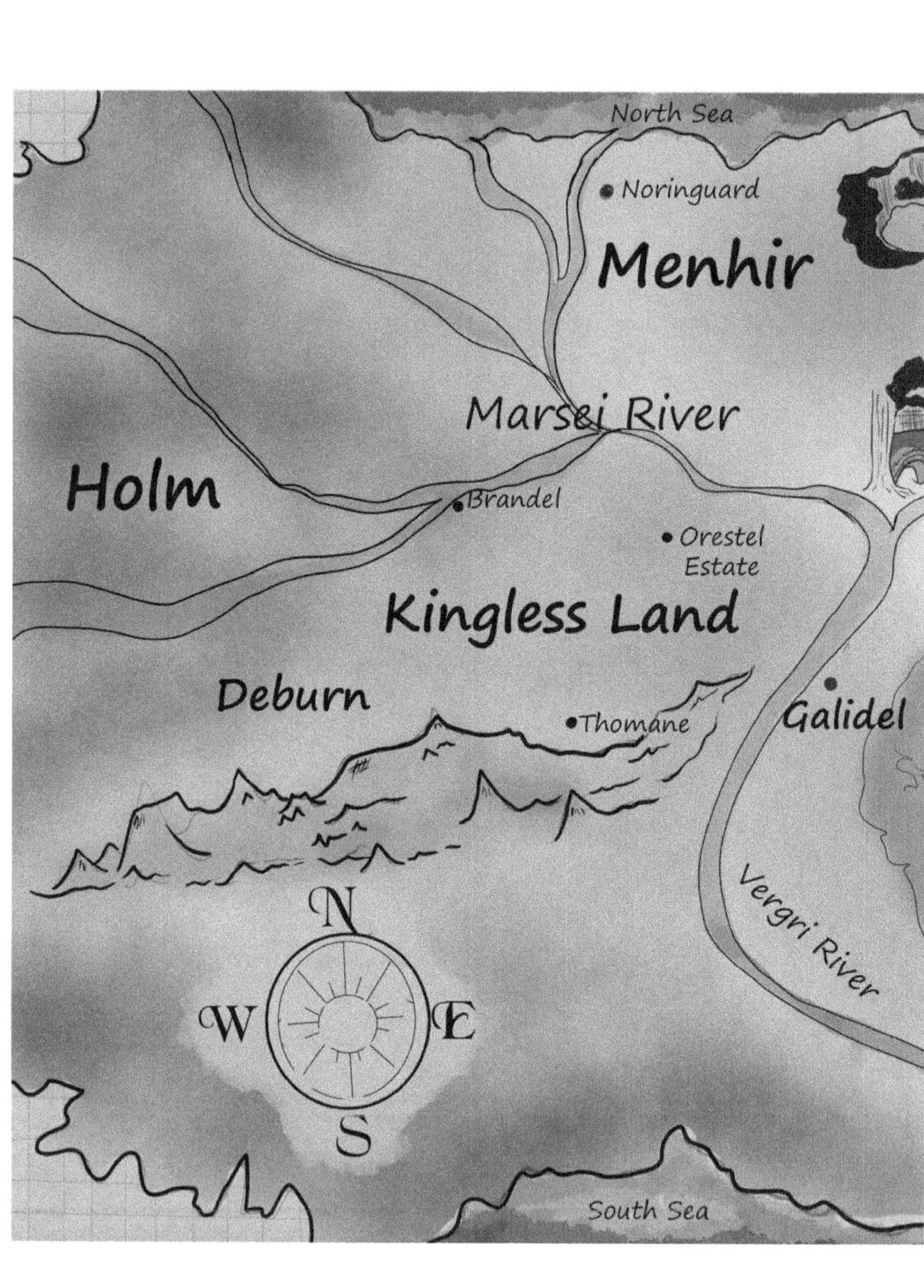
North Sea
Noringuard
Menhir
Marsei River
Holm
Brandel
Orestel
Estate
Kingless Land
Deburn
Thomane
Galidel
Vergri River
N
W
E
S
South Sea

Avani
Angori River
Dwarmin Hill
Erwani
Daradir
Alaron
Dark Wood
Vaylis
Aresti Woods
Calebrir

Chapter One

Never Trust A Good Cosplay

Remain calm. Nessa had to remember this was something she had prepared for. She could do this.

Nessa Everette had realized a long time ago that she had very little control over her own life. One could only do so much. For all the planning in the world, something unexpected was always bound to happen. She tried not to let those things get to her. Worrying only meant you suffered twice, after all. No amount of anxiety could change the weather, nor would it prevent a history professor from deciding to be cruel during finals week. She knew this from many canceled picnics and several vindictive history enthusiasts. There was simply no controlling the other people in her life.

She could, however, control her own facial expression when speaking to Mr. Lane.

"What is a 'caramel latte?'" The elderly man leaned over the counter to see the menu better, his bushy eyebrows knitting together as he adjusted his glasses. Nessa's smile tightened when she heard Maria snicker behind her. Of course, Maria had good reason to feel self-satisfied. She was usually the one who had to wait on the infamous Mr. Lane, but today Nessa had somehow gotten roped into it.

She was less than thrilled. If she tightened her smile any more, her lips were bound to split. *Just keep smiling. Get a tip. Buy more books*. Buying food probably wouldn't be a bad idea, either.

There were forty-three different drinks on the menu of Ollie's Coffee House, ranging from drip coffee to smoothies to milkshakes masquerading as coffee, and in the last fifteen minutes, Mr. Lane had inquired about the contents of thirty-seven of them. This was a daily ritual. None of this information was new to Mr. Lane. And yet, he still managed to look pensive and uncertain about his choices, day after day.

Why hadn't Nessa hidden in the bakery when she'd had the chance? Oh, that's right. Melissa I'm-Head-Of-The-Book-Club Jones just *had* to order eleven separate drinks. She also had eleven separate cards to run and of course Lydia had to change her order twice. All this drudgery had stranded poor Nessa at the register when Mr. Lane made his appearance.

Everyone had a breaking point. Nessa was almost at hers.

"It's steamed milk with espresso and caramel flavoring, Mr. Lane." Nessa's forced cheerfulness made Maria's head pop up like a meerkat. She could see the other barista's reaction in her peripheral vision. Maria, and Ollie for that matter, had come to know that tone of voice. Nessa was only able to produce it when she smiled so hard her lips couldn't move and her jaw ground her teeth together.

She was nearly finished with a double shift that had included both the Sunday brunch *and* lunch crowd. She'd had a frat boy drop a chair on her foot, a child fling syrup on her apron and whipped cream squirted in her face by a high school girl who didn't know how cream-in-a-can worked, all before noon. Then there was the local book club, currently heading into hour three of sulking in their usual corner. They were like children, in that they cried or screamed when they wanted attention or were bored.

Maria and Ollie shared a look. Ollie pursed his lips and nodded — and then, distracted by his silent exchange with Maria, managed to pour scalding hot coffee directly into the lap of Melissa I'm-Head-Of-The-Book-Club Jones. She shrieked, and Ollie began apologizing profusely.

Nessa wasn't quite sure what Melissa's middle name was. It might actually have been Jones, since she introduced herself every week as, 'Melissa Jones, I'm head of the book club.' Nessa, being a halfway intelligent girl, did not need the reminder.

The bell over the door chimed happily, and Nessa let out a soft puff of air to reset her smile into something more natural and less murderous. Bells were *good* things. Their happy little chiming meant the arrival of someone — or, depending on what religion and superstitions one belonged to, some*thing*. Nessa liked the bell over the coffee shop door because it normally meant a person she liked was here. Most frequently it was her best friend, Liv. But today had been such a whirlwind that Nessa had stopped taking notice of the tinkling bell. It had been hours since the shop was quiet enough to hear it.

She glanced at the door and froze solid.

Who in the Blessed name was that?

Nessa's blue eyes widened as her jaw went slack, all feigned friendliness forgotten. A young man towered in the doorway to the shop, casting a long, threatening shadow across the floor. His appearance alone was enough to silence the entirety of the book club. All eleven of the suburban housewives were gawking open-mouthed at him.

The menacing young man looked back at the glass door, smiling slightly from under uneven dark scruff. He looked like he was trying to grow a long beard, but hadn't fully hit puberty yet. His eyes traveled up to the bell, and he gave it a playful flick before turning to survey the coffee shop with sharp eyes and an amused smirk. He had to be at least Nessa's age, or maybe slightly older, with darkly tanned skin and faint wrinkles around his eyes. The boy could have been one of those hipster types, complete with man bun and beard oil, but that description didn't quite fit. For one thing, there wasn't a scrap of flannel in sight; instead, he was decked out in leathers and furs. The strange look was completed with tunic, boots, and an air of misplacement.

A glint of silver caught Nessa's eye. Was he wearing a sword? Yep, that was a sword, alright. Who wore a sword to a coffee shop? There was no way that thing could be real. The campus police would have tackled him to the ground the instant he so much as breathed in their direction. Then again, Nessa's faith in the generally overweight and out of shape campus law enforcement was only slightly stronger than her belief that she would pass her Calculus midterm. Was there a Renaissance fair in town, or some sort of Game of Thrones reenactment happening? She shook her head, attempting to clear the muddled thoughts from her brain.

Her stomach clenched as she shuffled her feet slightly, her back going ramrod straight. When had she started clutching the edge of the counter? She forced her fingers to relax and felt the muscles in her wrists strain from tension. Why couldn't she get a full breath? Air was suddenly coming to her in quick, shallow gasps; none of it would stay in her lungs. The already soft lights of the store seemed to dim even further as Nessa ripped her eyes away from the strange boy.

Don't stare, she told herself.

"Isn't he odd?" Mr. Lane grumbled from the other side of the counter. Nessa didn't hear him.

Syracuse was a college town, so she shouldn't be surprised by a little oddness. College was a time to experiment, and some people experimented differently, so strange things happened all the time.

Then why? Why had a thrill of fear settled in her stomach? He was only some whack job who dressed funny. She had survived Shark Week with frat boys who thought they were God's gift to women, even avoided crazy religious zealots preaching about how she was going to hell for getting an education as a female. Both kinds of troublemakers had been forcibly removed from campus. This boy hadn't even opened his mouth yet; he couldn't mean them any harm…could he?

That sword at his hip looked like evidence to the contrary.

Her fingers flew to the pendant at the base of her throat. Something was off. The air in the coffee shop had changed from friendly to foreboding with his arrival. How could one boy silence an entire room just by walking in?

A shiver ran down her spine.

"…Hmmm?" She jumped, realizing suddenly that Maria had been speaking. Blinking a few times to clear the cobwebs from her mind, she shuffled a little too clumsily over to Maria. The other girl was staring at her.

"I said, Ness…" Maria put a gentle hand on her arm, the gesture snapping Nessa back to Earth. Maria raised two perfectly sculpted brows at Nessa, a slight smile on her red-painted lips, and moved her attention to Mr. Lane. The older man's response was to roll his eyes and Maria's smile flashed briefly to a sneer. She snapped back to Nessa, the sweet smile returning. "Ollie needs you. I'll finish checking out Mr. Lane."

"Sure." Nessa's jaw unclenched, and she nodded. She moved along the back counter toward the door, the pads of her fingers skimming along the cold stone counter. She felt as though there was some memory just out of her reach. Something was stuck in her mind that she should remember…she should…

She shook her head once and everything fell into place with a snap. She had to focus on work. Get paid, buy food, pay tuition, become a famous author and literature professor. She was so busy focusing that she nearly ran straight into Ollie's chest.

Ollie reached out to steady her and Nessa reflexively grabbed his muscular arm, blinking up at him in surprise. The world came back into focus for the second time in five minutes. She *had* to get it together.

"You alright, kid?" Ollie lowered his head to get a better look at her face. Nessa wasn't exactly short, but Ollie was close to seven feet tall; *everyone* was short compared to him. "Your whole back went rigid as soon Jon Snow hit the door."

"Yeah, he threw me, is all."

Nessa was making an effort to not even look at the wild boy, much less notice that he was prowling around the perimeter of the shop like a caged animal, his eyes scanning the room. The pads of her fingers skimmed over the smooth surface of the clear, deep blue stone at her throat, following the intricate silver swirls of the setting. Her breath started to come slower and deeper the moment she felt the cool crystal and silver metal under her palm.

They both turned to see the book club still staring at the strange boy. She had *never* seen those women silent before, let alone for any length of time. Perhaps there was a silver lining to this weirdness after all.

"I'll kick him out if he tries anything, okay?" Ollie pulled the rainbow bandana from his head, his massive pile of dreads falling loose, and wiped it down his face. He let out a long breath.

"I know, Ollie." Nessa gave her boss a brave smile. With Ollie's past as both bartender and doorman, she had no doubt of his ability to enforce the threat. It wouldn't be the first time Ollie'd had to 'help' someone out of the shop for harassing her or Maria, usually for the safety of the poor, misguided Neanderthals. Maria had been known to slap a few customers with wandering hands, and while Nessa had considered the idea herself, she was generally far too timid.

Today, however, might be a good day to reconsider.

She chanced a glance over at the dark, wild boy and found his eyes flitting between her and Maria at the register. Every time Maria caught him looking, her scowl deepened. His eyes landed on Nessa again and she took a step closer to Ollie, who put a hand on her shoulder and angled her away from the boy's gaze, staring down the scruffy Jon Snow look-a-like on behalf of his skittish waitress. Nessa swallowed hard.

"Something wicked this way comes," she muttered under her breath.

The bell over the door rang again. Nessa turned a little too quickly, her heart already running away in her chest. A young woman with flowing white-blonde hair stepped through the door, her bright green eyes scanning the shop before they settled on Nessa. Nessa felt the tension in her shoulders melt the instant her blue eyes met green, and she smiled. Livia Aeris smiled back, giving a little finger waggle of a wave to her best friend.

Nessa took a deep breath for the first time since the strange boy had entered the shop.

Backup had arrived.

"Did you know Liv was coming in when you said that?" Ollie quirked a brow at her, trying — and failing — to hide his smile.

"No." Nessa's bow-shaped lips stretched into an amused smile of her own. "But she's got the best timing."

She took the coffee pot from Ollie and went to fix Liv her usual, watching out of the corner of her eye as the oddly dressed mountain man took a seat directly in the middle of the room. Liv placed herself in her usual spot in the back corner, settling herself near the counter Nessa currently occupied so Nessa could stop to chat in between running orders. This seat also allowed Liv see the entire shop. Nessa had noticed that Liv seemed to have a problem sitting with her back to a door, but she was never sure if this was a conscious decision on Liv's part or not.

"Ness?" Maria had come over, and Nessa turned her sky-blue eyes to the curvaceous other woman. "What do you think of Legolas over there?"

Nessa's pretty pink lips twitched. "Legolas was the elf, Maria. He's more Boromir than Legolas."

"Didn't Boromir die?" Maria asked, leaning her luscious backside on the counter beside Nessa.

Nessa nodded and blew a piece of chestnut hair from her eyes, trying to focus on the movement of her hands and not the eyes she could feel drilling into her back. Hot water, tea leaves, splash of lemon…where was the giant green mug?

"Yep," she replied, popping the end of the word with her lips. She glanced over her shoulder again, unable to help herself. She didn't like taking her eyes off the strange man for long. Something about him made her skin crawl.

Had she ever seen him before? No, of course not. The only burly mountain man she was interested in was Strider, and he was fictional. She pinched her lower lip between her teeth to bring herself back to reality. She had to focus on work, not on carefully crafted fantasy sagas.

Maria arched a dark brow at her. "Think he'll hit on you?"

Nessa snorted. She knew she was cute at best. Both Liv and Maria were prettier than she was. Liv was tall and long and Maria was a perfect hourglass, while Nessa was somewhere in-between, falling more on the boyish side. She felt nothing about her was particularly distinctive except for her blue eyes. Liv had an elegant face with high cheekbones and snowy skin, while Maria's copper skin glowed in the sun like a jewel. Nessa wasn't curvy and exotic like Maria, nor tall and elegant like Liv. She thought she was just … sweet.

"Not with you in the room." Nessa nudged Maria playfully with her hip.

Maria's red lips parted in a wicked grin. "Jon Snow isn't exactly my type."

Nessa rolled her eyes as she took the coffee pot and Liv's usual giant mug of tea out to the front of the counter, stopping by Liv first to postpone meeting the wild boy for as long as possible. Liv stretched her long legs out in front of her and crossed her feet at the ankles, an expression of forced calm on her beautiful face.

"Hello, Nessa." She smiled up at her friend.

Nessa smiled back as she set Liv's tea in front of her. "Hey Liv." She felt her shoulders relax a little further.

Liv glanced around Nessa at the scruffy boy, a perfectly groomed blonde brow arching toward her hairline. No one could arch a brow like Livia Aeris. In fact, Nessa was certain her current expression could make whole armies think twice before invading. There was a sharpness under Liv's sympathetic air that let you know she was not a woman to cross. Now, she settled back in her seat with both hands wrapped around her mug, her face a calm sea: beautiful and serene with a fierce riptide just below the surface.

"When did he appear?" Liv's cool voice tinkled like silver bells. She took a delicate sip of her tea.

"About sixty seconds before you came in." Nessa shrugged, refusing to look back at the boy. She could feel him staring at her, though, his eyes burning a hole in her neck. Her fingers flew to her pendant again.

She told herself to be a big girl and just get it over with. Liv was here. Liv always had her back. She glanced toward the back counter, where Maria and Ollie were standing side by side, arms crossed and glaring at the boy.

"I'll be right back," she told Liv, plastering a forced smile on her face as she approached the Jon Snow doppelganger.

He looked up at her and the air stuck in her lungs. She had read plenty of novels where something like this happened, a stranger entering someone's perfectly normal life. No good ever came of it.

"Can I help you?" Nessa's years of waitressing took over. *Smile, be polite, earn tips to pay for books.*

"I'm looking for someone," he answered in a strange, thick accent Nessa couldn't place. It wasn't German or French but sounded like a mix between the two, some lilt of western European. Obviously, he wasn't from Syracuse, or even New York. Nessa herself was from San Francisco and people still claimed she had an accent. This was a vicious lie, of course; everyone here sounded like they were from New York while she spoke normally.

"You look lost." She set the empty mug in front of him and began to fill it, keeping her eyes firmly on her work instead of him. She had chosen one of the smaller mugs on purpose, hoping that once he was finished with his drink, he would leave. "And fair warning, pick-up lines like that don't work on me."

"What?" He blinked up at her. "Pick-up lines?"

"Flirting." Nessa nodded to Liv in the corner. "My friend over there is a master of mental warfare, and she's protective."

Liv's green eyes were burning into the pair. When she saw them looking over at her, she smirked with a joy that didn't reach her eyes and gave another little finger-wiggle wave. Her fingers could have been mistaken for dancing blades, her expression a thinly veiled threat. The ferocity of the angry sea was barely being kept in check.

"I see." He looked back up at Nessa. "I'm looking for a girl."

"Men usually are," Nessa almost snapped.

Good Lord, was he another creeper? Chances were high; men like that came in all the time. They would order coffee, make small talk, and then try to do what they called flirting, and what Nessa called borderline assault. Though that happened less and less the more Liv was around. And anyway, what sane man walked around carrying a sword?

He narrowed his eyes. "A girl named Nessa."

Nessa nearly dropped the coffee pot.

Fear settled in her belly, her teeth clamping down on her lower lip to keep her gasp inside her chest. *Don't look at him. Just don't*, she thought frantically.

Some sixth sense was telling her it would be a bad idea. Her hands trembled. and she clenched them around the coffee pot till they hurt. She glanced over at Liv, who had straightened in her chair, her mouth a grim line. Her friend's gaze had turned cold and calculating. She looked ready to pounce.

Nessa swallowed hard, forcing herself to breathe. The boy's scrutiny had turned to Liv in the corner, and Nessa was pretty sure the entire coffee shop could feel the murderous vibe radiating from her usually serene friend.

"...Why?" She willed herself to appear calm, arching a brow at the boy as he turned back to her.

He grinned up at her. "Only to speak with her about her family."

Nessa swallowed down a squeak along with her lunch. Her family? What about them? This strange boy couldn't possibly know her, or her parents. Cold fingers ran down her spine and she clamped her mouth shut to keep the bile down. Her parents were teachers. Lilly and Albert Everette had adopted her before she was even two years old. They had lived a very simple and loving life in San Francisco. There was nothing to talk about.

Could he mean…?

No. Not even her adoptive parents knew who her biological parents were, though it certainly wasn't for lack of trying. But no matter how hard they'd looked, nothing was ever found. Three private investigators later, not one single clue had turned up. They couldn't even find Nessa's original birth certificate.

So how could this wild boy possibly know anything about them? That had to be what he was implying, right? Or was he threatening her? Trying to bait her? This had to be some sort of scheme. What did he want? Money?

Heat flashed through her stomach and her vision. She may have only been nineteen, but Nessa was no fool. She set the coffee pot down on the table with more force than necessary and straightened to her admittedly unimpressive full height.

Liv's attention immediately snapped to Nessa. The boy's response was to quirk his lips in a way that made Nessa's stomach drop into her toes. She turned to look at Maria, who nodded.

Great. She had backup.

"Why don't you enlighten me?" Nessa gritted through clenched teeth. "Then I can tell you if she would even *want* to speak to you."

"I'm afraid it is a private matter."

He leaned toward her and her heart jumped into her throat at the definitely-not-threatening posture. Seeing this, he grinned cruelly. "...Your Highness."

The words made Nessa's chest freeze. She swallowed, pointing to the door. "Then I'm afraid you must get out of my shop."

Your Highness? What kind of psycho crap was that?

The boy leaned back in his chair as though it were a sunny day at the beach, that wickedly smug expression still on his face. He looked her up and down.

"That's a lovely pendant you have…"

"I said, get out!" She raised her voice but kept it firm, hoping he wouldn't notice her hands trembling.

Liv leaned forward in her chair as Ollie suddenly appeared next to Nessa. Ollie might have been lean, but he was still more intimidating than Nessa's relatively petite five-foot-six frame. He crossed his arms over his chest and took a step forward so Nessa was half behind him.

Snow looked over at him, both eyebrows shooting up.

"Is there a problem here?" Ollie more stated than asked.

A dark grin appeared on the boy's face, his eyes sparkling with something that made Nessa's skin crawl. How could a man manage to look pleased and malicious at the same time?

The strange boy rose, turned away, then paused and turned back to Nessa.

"My lady." He gave a low bow, his eyes lingering on the terrified waitress. Then he turned on his heel and left the coffee shop.

Nessa didn't take a breath until the door closed behind him.

She swallowed hard, feeling like she was going to collapse into a puddle on the floor right then and there, when Liv, tea in hand, materialized at Nessa's side along with Maria. Her friend's hand found its way to her shoulder, the mug of tea appearing like magic in front of her. Nessa took it with trembling fingers as Maria let out a low whistle, voicing what they were all thinking.

"That is one crazed-up fruit loop."

Chapter Two

Deep Fried Carbs Always Help

The night was quiet and cool, the trees casting deep shadows. A biting breeze rustled the golden leaves, which appeared almost alight with the flames that stood out in stark contrast to the inky black of the night sky. Every turn of a leaf sent new sparks spiraling into the black, the scent of smoke hanging heavy in the air. Black silhouettes huddled around the flames, captivated by the light and warmth. The group wore leathers and furs that seemed almost familiar.

Crisp, excited words floated on the breeze. The mountain boy was standing at the center of the circle, speaking adamantly to a large, darkness-shrouded being that could have been either a man or a bear. The language was odd, seemingly a mix of German and French, though no words were familiar. The boy gestured to his throat as he spoke, and as he did, the bear-man's lips spread into a horrible grin...

***

Nessa shot up with a gasp.

Her heart pounded for a moment as panic set in. Where was she? This wasn't her dorm room.

Her body relaxed when she recognized Liv's simple guest room, and she collapsed back onto the dark blue sheets to stare at the ceiling, arms splayed wide. Her breathing began to slow, but she could still feel her heartbeat wracking her body, her sweat-slick skin sticking to the sheets. What a horrible nightmare!

What had she been dreaming about? There was a light in the darkness and then…the sky? No, a person? No, that wasn't right, but she couldn't remember. She closed her eyes and tried to concentrate, but the image kept slipping through her fingers. It was like trying to grab smoke; in fact, she could almost smell it.

Her hand went to her chest, the steady, quick thumping of her heart pressing against her fingertips. Cold perspiration covered her face. Why was she so scared? It was only a bad dream.

What would Liv say to help calm her down?

Tea. Tea will help.

Nessa threw back the covers and padded over to her duffle bag to retrieve a sweatshirt, hoping something that smelled like her mother's dryer sheets would help ground her back into reality. She threw the blue hoodie on as she walked down the short hall to the kitchen, blinking at the unexpected light.

Apparently, Liv was already up.

"Can't sleep?" Liv offered Nessa the mug of tea that was already in her hand. Liv always had impeccable timing. Whenever Nessa needed her, it was as though Liv would magically materialize.

Nessa nodded gratefully as she took the tea. She was beginning to think Liv was secretly psychic.

"Thanks." She took a sip of the chamomile tea as Liv poured herself another cup. "How did you know I was awake?"

"I heard you tossing. I supposed it was only a matter of time." Liv shrugged. "Do you want to talk about it?"

"There's nothing to talk about." Nessa rested her hips against the counter as she sipped her tea.

Yes, she was awake at two-thirty in the morning. Yes, that was unusual. Yes, she was scared, and no, she didn't know why. She had a few guesses, though, and they all started with the wild boy.

After the incident at the coffee shop, Liv had insisted that Nessa come stay with her for a while. The strange wild boy had made both of them nervous. Nessa had tried to argue that she had two roommates who would look out for her, but Liv had pointed out that Nessa's dorm was on the first floor and it wouldn't exactly take a genius to break in through a window.

Nessa had conceded fairly quickly after that. For some reason, the thought of Liv as her protector felt more comfortable than two early-childhood education majors.

Only seconds after her shift ended, Liv had accompanied Nessa back to her dorm to gather her things and tell her roommates where she was going. Aisha had agreed that the guy sounded like a total creeper and promised to tell Jess what was going on when the other girl got back from class.

It had all taken less than twenty minutes. Nessa had only grabbed the essentials: toiletries, some clothes, her school bag and six books before Liv had not-so-subtly rushed her out the door. Liv hadn't started to calm down until the door to her apartment was securely locked.

Thankfully, Liv's quaint apartment was as homey as it was secure. The little room above the eclectic secondhand bookstore had once been the owner's apartment until his husband passed away, and Liv had moved in not long after and made the place her own. It may have only been an apartment, but with all Liv's plants, most from the store below, there was more green here than in all the city parks combined.

Nessa knew this was the safest place she could be right now. The only way in was through the back room of the store, which meant there were two different sets of locks and security systems between a potential stalker and herself.

Liv tilted her head at Nessa, who was gently tapping her thumb against her warm mug. The fingers of her other hand were once more at the pendant at her throat, gently tracing the intricate silver patterns.

"Do you even remember what the dream was about?" Liv lightly touched the smooth stone at her own throat, which could vary in color from a green so dark it was nearly black to the color of sunlight through a spring leaf. The setting of Liv's stone was far more practical than Nessa's own, with dozens of gold loops around the edge holding the stone to a delicately twisted Y-chain. The gold chain looped around Liv's throat twice, the stone resting just above the rise of her bosom. Most of the time it remained tucked away under her clothes. Though the settings were vastly different, Nessa often wondered if they had somehow managed to get their stones from the same place.

"...Hmmm?" Nessa's eyes snapped back from a thousand yards away. Only then did what Liv had asked register. "Oh, no. No, I don't...well, I can't really seem to remember what the nightmare was about. Dollars to donuts it was Jon Snow's evil twin."

Liv's brows knitted together. "Who?"

Nessa sighed heavily. She knew Liv was incredibly intelligent. Nessa had seen her gobble up books about history and mathematics. She'd seen Liv twirl chopsticks around her fingers like she was a drummer in a heavy metal band. She'd even seen her move faster than any quarterback she knew, but when it came to pop culture, Liv knew about as much as a hermit.

"That wild mountain boy from today," Nessa clarified. "He just felt..."

She had to pause to find the proper word.

"He felt wrong."

"I did not care for him either." Liv's tone could have sentenced the boy to the guillotine.

Nessa smirked in the face of Liv's narrowed eyes. "No stabbing innocent people, Liv."

Her friend looked shocked, putting a hand on her chest. "I do not stab the innocent, Nessa."

Green eyes flashed mischievously as Liv grinned and Nessa smiled into her tea. The innocent were indeed safe from Liv's wrath — for now. Nessa could only imagine what she would do to the guilty. Liv was very creative.

Liv may have had the face of an angel, but she had the wicked streak of a fae. It was probably the shock of near-white hair. Nessa had seen the trickster in Liv rear its ugly head only twice thus far, but she would never forget either time. There had been a lot of forging signatures involved.

"Breakfast?" Nessa asked. "I'm never getting back to sleep now."

"Yes, please."

Nessa popped over to check the fridge, but she already knew what Liv had by way of groceries. She was over so often that they usually just went shopping together, which came with the wonderful added benefit of Liv being fed.

Constantly.

Lilly Everette had tried her best to keep her girl fed and happy over the years. After Nessa joined the cross-country team, combined with a massive growth spurt in her freshman year, it had taken everything poor Lilly had just to keep weight on her child. She'd finally relented and taught Nessa everything she knew after finding Nessa baking cookies at one in the morning. Again.

Nessa liked to bake when she was stressed. Or tired. Or had had a bad day. Or simply felt like it. Liv's little apartment was forever filled with cookies, brownies, cakes and every kind of sweet imaginable, far more than was good for either of them. The chocolate chess squares Nessa had whipped up to deal with midterms were still eyeing them from the counter.

"How's French toast sound?" Nessa asked.

The noise of bliss that came from Liv's mouth was nearly inhuman and Nessa allowed herself a small smile. She grew all warm and fuzzy when she was able to take care of her people. That included feeding them.

Liv watched Nessa scurry around the kitchen as she drank her tea, a soft, thoughtful smile playing around her pink lips.

Nessa saw it, and raised an eyebrow. "What?"

"Oh, nothing." Liv shook her head gently. "You are so much like…"

"Like what?"

Liv sighed and shook her head, her smile resetting into something else. "I am glad you are okay."

Nessa let out a clipped laugh with no real feeling in it. "So am I. I thought I was going to get dragged out the door by Robinson Crusoe."

Her fingers tightened around the spatula, and she exhaled hard through her nose as she flipped the French toast over in the pan. She couldn't get those eyes out of her head. They'd been dark and cold, though she couldn't seem to quite remember their color, with absolutely nothing behind them. When he looked at her, he didn't see a person, he saw a trophy. It was the same look a hunter would wear the moment before they shot a lion. She didn't like feeling like prey.

Why had he said anything to her? Why had he brought up her biological parents? It was obvious he'd wanted to get a reaction from her. He had relished in it. Each word had been calculated and mocking.

Everything except…

"Where'd you go, Ness?" Liv's voice cut through her racing thoughts.

Nessa jumped. "What? Oh, just thinking." She handed Liv a towering plate of French toast.

Liv picked up the top piece with her hand and began to eat. Nessa shook her head, but smiled all the same. Liv had some odd tendencies, but Nessa tried not to question them.

"About the boy from earlier?"

"Yeah." She kept her head bowed over her work. Perhaps she could find some divine French toast intervention.

Why was this bothering her so much? Why did her stomach drop into her toes every time she thought about it? She was fine, nothing had happened to her. But what if something *was* happening? She couldn't shake the foreboding feeling in her gut.

"He was so…weird." Nessa shook her head. "He called me *Your Highness*. How crazy is that?"

Liv went absolutely still, a bite of French toast halfway to her mouth. "He said what?"

"Your Highness." Nessa forked her French toast onto her plate. "And he said he wanted to talk about my family. It had to be some sort of con, right? I mean, my parents are teachers, Liv. There's nothing special about them. And Lord only knows where my biological ones are. This whole thing has just put me so far off my balance it's ridiculous."

Silence hung in the small kitchen for a few moments as Nessa rummaged through the cabinets. Hadn't they gotten syrup the last time they were at the store? She could feel Liv's eyes on her as she moved, but pretended not to notice.

"Did he call you anything else?" Liv's voice chilled like water dripping from an iceberg. She had straightened, returning her fried carbs to the plate, and now sounded much older than the twenty-something she was.

Nessa shook her head. "No, nothing…"

Come to think of it, how old *was* Liv? Nessa had never asked. The ever-present wine in the fridge indicated she had to be at least twenty-one. Then again, maybe not. Why had she never thought to ask?

Nessa paused, a bite of syrup-covered French toast half-skewered on her fork. She stared at it for a moment without seeing before her eyes focused again.

"What is troubling you?" Liv stepped toward her friend, her brows drawing together.

"Nothing, just…" Nessa paused again. *My lady*. He had also called her 'my lady' and bowed. No one *bowed.* He could have been mocking her, but no, that didn't seem right. He had bowed while holding her eyes; he had never looked away from her. Not once. Could he truly have thought she was royalty?

Nessa shuddered.

"You remember when he bowed?"

Liv nodded, her sharp green eyes drilling into Nessa's own.

"Well…when he bowed, he called me 'my lady,' as if he was following an old custom." Nessa shoved a bite of French toast into her mouth, hoping the carbs would settle the nerves in her stomach. "I think he really believed it."

"You do look like a princess." Liv's lips quirked up on one side. "Like in one of those cartoon movies you showed me."

Nessa snorted. "I swear too much for that," she replied around a mouthful of crispy bread.

Liv gave a delicate laugh. There was always something delicate about her, in the same way a newly honed knife was delicate: beautiful, sharp and possibly deadly. She had never showed any proclivity towards the latter, for which Nessa was profoundly grateful.

Now Liv smiled to herself as she took a long sip of her tea. "True."

Nessa took a deep breath, the smells of tea, eucalyptus and French toast surrounding her. She loved the smell of home.

Familiarity and warmth settled around the two girls in the kitchen. She and Liv had spent most of the past summer in these rooms. There had been countless movie marathons; Nessa had been astonished to learn Liv had never heard of James Bond, Indiana Jones, or even Star Wars. As a decent friend, this was a problem she had rectified immediately.

The only trilogy they'd marathoned more than once was *The Lord of the Rings*, and Liv had been ecstatic to learn the tale was told in books as well as moving pictures. They'd read through Tolkien's entire catalog of work together in three days, and now Liv never seemed to be without one of them.

Nessa's eyes fell on the stacks of second-hand books around the sofa. Between the two of them, they'd read every single one at least once. There had never been a book long enough or a cup of tea large enough to suit either of them. They'd spent hours on the floor wrapped up in blankets, discussing their latest book, and these literary discussions often led into talks about the events of the day: the tests, the boys, the friends, the coffee shop. Eventually, those everyday conversations would become ideas and fears and tales of old that Liv had learned from seemingly nowhere.

There are people you meet and then there are people you've known your entire life. Liv was someone Nessa had known before she ever set foot in her bookshop.

"You refrained from giving him your name, I hope?" Liv asked.

Nessa's head shot up. "No, I didn't tell him."

She glanced back down at her empty plate and shook her head again.

"He knew it already."

Chapter Three

Coffee Makes A Surprisingly Good Weapon

It took two pots of coffee for Nessa to make it through her morning classes. She hadn't been able to sleep after her strange dream, but she did manage to sneak in a nap around lunch. College, she'd observed, appeared to be a series of choices between sleeping, eating, passing classes and participating in social activities. And she had begun to suspect she could only have three out of four.

Her phone had pinged multiple times throughout the day, usually her mother or father. Lilly and Albert texted every day. Nessa glanced at her phone. Albert was desperate to know if she had gotten her 'care package' yet. She couldn't help but smile.

Ever since she'd learned to read, her literature professor adoptive father had taken his daughter to every yard sale they could find. He would always say they were searching for treasure, and they would come home with boxes and boxes of books. Nessa knew her dad would be damned if he let the tradition die, and sure enough, two days ago she had found a huge box of second-hand books waiting on her doorstep. There had also been a warm scarf from her mother in the same shade of sky blue as Nessa's eyes. Her mom always worried about her baby being cold in New York.

Nessa hadn't told them about the strange boy from the day before. Her parents worried enough about her as it was; there was no need to scare them over something so silly. She did wear the blue scarf around her neck, though. It was still a little too warm outside for such a thing, but it smelled like home.

When Nessa entered Ollie's Coffee Shop that afternoon, the bell above the door made Ollie and Maria snap to attention, and they both rushed over to tell her why she should have stayed home, or with Liv, or gone literally anywhere else. Nessa assured them that she was fine and they were being unreasonable. They were in public, Liv was going to come by for emotional support once she got off work, and Nessa had a secondhand Taser in her purse. Between Maria's 'fight me' spirit and Ollie's imposing figure, Nessa was certain she was safe.

When she'd moved to Syracuse for school all those months ago, Ollie had been the first person she'd met. He'd taken in her thin frame, tired eyes and half-finished enrollment forms and given her a job on the spot. Maria had been so grateful for the help that she'd crushed Nessa in a bear hug the second they were introduced, and from that day on, Nessa knew she had found her people. Her shoulders relaxed every morning as soon as she smelled the cinnamon and sugar from the bakery, the smell of coffee, pastries and vanilla helping to soothe her nerves. And Maria cursing at the dough as she baked never failed to amuse her.

Plus, Maria's cursing always meant one thing.

Cinnamon rolls. Hot, gooey and the size of your head.

Maria truly had a gift for baking. The woman could bake a used flip-flop and Nessa would probably eat it.

And if she wasn't here in the coffee shop, she was at Liv's apartment. Nessa's roommates often joked that they were the only tenants, and she was simply that one random friend who kept half her stuff there. Jess had even taken over Nessa's desk to use as a make-up counter, but Nessa didn't mind. Half of her things were over at Liv's and she certainly didn't need the desk space. She felt more than welcome in her dorm, but the smells were all wrong. There were no piles of books, or warm coffee, and no sweet aromas of baked goods and fresh tea. She didn't belong in her dorm, not the way she belonged here.

Ollie finally stopped hovering over her shoulder after the first hour, though not before informing Nessa about the shotgun he kept behind the counter, and Maria even offered her the switchblade that lived in her back pocket. Nessa's eyebrows shot up at that, but Maria's only response was a saucy wink. Nessa silently wondered if she should ask, then wisely decided to keep her mouth shut. Her main concern was Ollie and that shotgun; she was pretty sure the city boy had never been hunting in his life.

Oh well. At least they were prepared in case someone stormed the castle.

Nessa kept her mother's scarf close while she worked, often playing with the white lace around the hem. But her cheeriness to the customers felt forced, her smile too bright. She could already feel the strain in her cheeks and temples, and a throbbing ache was forming behind her eyes.

Maria kept glancing at her out of the corner of her eye and most of the regulars had asked if she was feeling all right. But Nessa only smiled and said, 'Of course.' She hated to admit it, but every time the bell over the door rang, she nearly jumped out of her skin, her heart pounding until she saw who it was. Only after Jon Snow failed to appear could she breathe again.

This was already shaping up to be very long day.

The dinner rush hit with a vengeance, and the Syracuse Sisters Reading Society made their inevitable return, Melissa I'm-Head-Of-The-Book-Club Jones seething at its head. Ollie usually refused to have anything to do with the group of gym-going, yoga-pant-clad super moms, but today he gave them a free bottle of Merlot to make up for his coffee mishap the day before. Once he'd placated their anger with wine, Ollie quickly made himself scarce.

Maria cast the first volley in a silent war of expressions with Nessa over who had to serve the ridiculous women, the looks devolving into childish faces and finally outright vocal slander until Nessa pointedly reminded Maria of her age. Nessa had only turned nineteen the week previous and was not yet old enough to serve alcohol due to Ollie's rules. Maria, quickly approaching thirty, was.

Anyway, the book club was the least of their problems. Every inch of the shop was crammed full of people. Seriously, someone might have been sitting on shoulders. Everyone's parents had come from out of town for a ritual known as a 'football game,' and there were Syracuse sweatshirts as far as the eye could see.

Football, as Nessa understood it, involved people watching muscular young men move a ball around a long rectangular field for three hours. The only thing she really enjoyed about the sport was watching the handsome boys in their tight pants, but with such pleasant sights to take in, she cheered proudly for her alma mater.

Football season and the bite in the air warned of the impending winter. Autumn had settled firmly into the northeast, and more and more students were cramming into the shop every evening to avoid the cold and their responsibilities. Happy chatter and the whir of the espresso machine filled the small space; it looked like every seat was full. Ollie finally had to bring out folding card tables and chairs from the back, and even those filled quickly. Nessa winced as her hip banged into the third table corner in the last five minutes.

"You could vault over the table," Maria called from behind the counter. "Pull out some of those Matrix moves you keep hidden."

Nessa ignored the other woman's cheeky grin. "I don't have the space to make the jump!"

The sweet ringing of the bell over the door had been so constant that she wasn't even paying attention to it anymore.

That was, until the shop went silent.

Nessa looked over her shoulder, her eyes going wide.

Five men stood in the center of the shop. An absolute giant of a man spearheaded the group of strangers, the other four fanning out behind him. All were dressed in dark leathers and furs. The leader must have been at least seven feet tall, with wiry black hair streaked with gray and a long, braided beard hanging from his chin. If Nessa hadn't known better, she might have mistaken him for a large black bear, though the angry scar that ran down the left side of his face was far from cuddly.

Jon Snow's evil twin stood behind his left shoulder.

His eyes fell on Nessa, ice filling the air between them, and Nessa's stomach twisted as the ground dropped from beneath her feet. Suddenly, she felt hands on her arms. Maria was next to her, holding her upright. Ollie was already running interference, an unpleasant set to his jaw as he approached the interlopers.

Snow was still staring at her; she could feel his eyes crawling across her skin. She thought she might be sick. She felt like prey being studied before the attack.

"Oh, hell no. Not this whacko again." Maria shuffled Nessa behind her, and Nessa's heart began to pound as she dove under the counter for her bag.

"Phone…phone…phone…." The words were half search and half prayer. Her trembling hands couldn't get a grip on the zipper of her bag, the cool metal slipping through her fingers.

The sounds of the coffee shop faded away. Even the clinking of cups and cutlery had stopped. All Nessa could hear was the steady thumping in her ears.

"I'm sorry, gentlemen," Ollie began, a little too loudly. "There isn't any room for you here tonight."

The voice that responded was dark and gravelly. "We do not intend to stay."

Nessa huddled around her bag, her fingers ceasing their movement as cold fear ripped through her body at the words. She forced a deep lungful of air into her chest, then another until her vision stopped spinning.

She could do this. If Frodo could walk into Mordor, she could damn well get to her phone.

"We only came for the lady."

"I will not tolerate anyone harassing my employees." Ollie's tone was fierce.

Nessa's arm was elbow deep in her bag before her hand finally found her phone. She yanked it out, dumping her homework all over the floor in the process, and had it ringing in half a heartbeat. Glancing up, she saw Maria on her phone as well, her hand gripping the blade in her back pocket.

"Hello? Ness?" Liv's voice came through the phone after the third ring.

"*He came back...*" Nessa's voice shuddered. It wasn't what she had meant to say, but it was the only thought filling her mind.

She heard shouting behind her and a wall of noise suddenly crashed into her ears. Chairs squeaked and clattered across the floor, the panicked ringing of the bell on the door sounding over the *smack* of wood on tile. Metal clashed amid the tinkle of breaking glass and shrieks of terror as the door slammed repeatedly into the wall, the poor bell ringing and ringing until Nessa ground her teeth together at the noise.

Were they leaving? *Please, let them be leaving.*

"Nessa?" Liv's voice came from far away.

"Put him down!" she heard Maria roar from above her.

Nessa turned and straightened in one quick move, feeling Snow's eyes snap back to her the second she popped up from behind the counter. The other three minions were intimidating people out the front door by overturning tables and chairs, and she winced at the loud *clank* of wood against tile.

The screams of the fleeing customers filled her ears as she watched them race out the emergency exit, the alarm shrieking every few seconds. The emergency lights flashed erratically, temporarily blinding her, and the strangers shouted demands no one could understand as cutlery and china shattered against the floor.

The bell over the door rang one final time, and blessed silence fell at last.

Nessa spun to survey the scene. The once calm and peaceful shop lay in ruins. Drinks flooded the cracks in the tile, while pieces of everything that made the shop a home littered the floor: trampled cups, wooden splinters of chairs, shattered glassware, shards of china and broken wine bottles. The soft, secluded corner the book club had previously occupied was torn to shreds, stuffing erupting from the furniture. A stain covered one of the seats, a deep red liquid that dripped ominously to the floor.

Nessa swallowed hard. *Please be wine.*

A gurgling sound behind her caught her attention. The bearlike man was holding Ollie up by the neck, while Maria had taken the shotgun out from behind the counter. She was pointing it at the intruder as Ollie's legs kicked fruitlessly in the air.

Nessa's jaw fell to the floor along with her phone. She was screaming before she could stop herself.

"Stop it! Put him down!"

The huge man turned his gaze to Nessa. She felt like throwing up the second their eyes met, but she swallowed down her fear — and vomit — with some difficulty. No. She wouldn't be scared.

Slowly, she raised her chin, their eyes remaining locked. If she did the courageous thing, perhaps actual courage would follow. She took a few brave steps to stand beside Maria before she even realized what she was doing. Maria snarled at the men, and the loud metallic *click* of the shotgun echoed through the now-empty coffee house.

"As you wish." The menace in the bearlike man's voice, though quiet, made Nessa shudder. "My lady."

Suddenly, Ollie was flying across the room, and Nessa and Maria didn't even have time to scream before their boss collided with one of the display cases, glass shattering down around him. All that was visible was his legs, dangling limply out of the case.

They weren't moving.

"No!" Nessa leapt over the counter to reach her friend.

"Ness!" Maria called after her, but Nessa didn't listen. Ollie was completely still, his eyes closed.

No, he had to be all right. He couldn't be…

Her arm was suddenly yanked back so hard she screamed, and she spun to see one of the minions holding her wrist. Nessa planted her feet and pulled with all her might, Maria materializing at her side to put an arm around her shoulders. They both pulled and twisted, but were still unable to free Nessa from the man's grip.

Like lightning, Maria's switchblade slashed across the man's wrist, and he recoiled just enough to let Nessa slip through his fingers.

"Nessa, go! Get out of here!" Maria pushed her toward the bakery door. Nessa stumbled a few steps before she took off running, with Maria right beside her, pushing her forward.

She yelped as she suddenly felt searing pain rip across her skull, her eyes watering in agony. Without a thought, her fingers wrapped around the closest thing she could reach, and she swung the weapon around with all her might. The heavy glass coffee pot shattered against her captor's thick head, scalding coffee and broken glass raining down on minion number two. He growled and swore, but released his grip on her hair, and Nessa danced out of his reach with a squeak, teetering dangerously off-balance. Her back collided with something solid, and strong arms wrapped around her, pinning her arms to her side.

"Let go!" Her legs kicked wildly in the air, and she managed to plant her feet on the counter before she pushed back as hard as she could, sending them both sprawling across the tile floor. Nessa's shoulder collided with the ground hard enough to make her see stars, a damp trail of what she hoped was spilled coffee trickling down her arm. Ignoring the bruise she would surely have, she rolled to the side, clawing desperately at the smooth tile to get to her feet.

Before she managed that, however, her wrists were seized in a viselike grip, and she was unceremoniously yanked to her feet. Her back pressed against an unyielding chest as she was spun around and restrained, her arms crossed over her body to pin her in place.

"Let me go!"

"Quiet, quiet…" Snow pressed his lips against her ear, and Nessa shivered, unable to breathe. Her eyes flew to the door.

She saw Maria, lying unmoving in a pool of red.

"No!" Ice shuddered through Nessa's body, and she gasped desperately for air between screams, her chest aching. Her feet scrabbled against the tile floor. Maria! She had to get to Maria. The other girl had to be okay. She just had to be. Hot tears stung Nessa's eyes.

"Shhh. Shhhh." Snow held her firm. Nessa didn't listen, but the rest of them were on her before she could do anything other than scream. She kicked out at the three minions before her as one swept her feet into his arms.

"No!" Nessa shouted as loud as she could, but to no avail. She thrashed, rolled, and kicked, but nothing got them to put her down as the men carried her, literally kicking and screaming, out the back door. And honestly, she thought, even if they did drop her, could she actually outrun them? The pounding in her ears grew louder. What could they possibly want?

Keep fighting. Don't make it easy. Maria didn't.

Oh God…Ollie and Maria! Were they…

Burning tears escaped from her closed eyes as she screamed every insult she could think of at the men. She didn't want to watch whatever they were going to do to her.

Suddenly, she fell, letting out a shriek before her back collided with hard earth. All the air flew from her lungs, and she coughed as she rolled to her knees, looking up to meet the eyes of the bearlike man. She wanted to calm her heart rate, but couldn't seem to get her lungs filled.

Snow stood to her left while the three other minions surrounded her, forming a tight circle. There was dirt and grass under her knees, and she could see a thin dusting of young trees behind the bearlike man and Snow.

The park… They had dragged her to the park behind the coffee shop. Her eyes fell back to the leader. Nessa wanted to rise to her feet, to be eye-to-eye with the despicable man, but her knees wouldn't hold her.

"Who the hell are you people?" She tried to keep her voice steady even as she wiped her eyes. When had she started crying? "What do you want?"

Bear grinned down at her, a look of dominance, madness and rotten teeth that made Nessa's stomach churn. Slowly, he knelt next to her, his dark eyes never leaving hers. Nessa ground her teeth. *No. Don't show how scared you are. Don't give this* thing *the satisfaction.*

Bear reached out to her, and Nessa flung herself back, landing on her rear.

"Don't!" The word was out before she could stop it.

Bear grabbed the jewel at her neck, pulling her closer with a rough yank. It was a miracle the chain didn't break. Nessa's air would only come in deep gasps; her heart was nearly humming, it was beating so fast.

Bear looked at the pendant, then at her.

The word that left his lips sounded like a curse, though Nessa didn't recognize the language. He turned back to Snow, speaking again in the same odd tongue, and they all laughed, a joyful chorus that made Nessa shiver in horror.

"Where is your portal?" Bear asked. Nessa only blinked at him.

Did he just…

"My…my what?"

"Your portal, my lady." His words clarified nothing. "I'd rather not waste more blood and magic if I don't have to."

"Magic?" Nessa's eyes grew wider. *Magic?* Oh, now she got it. These guys were insane! "What…I have no idea what you're talking about!"

"Now, now." Bear's growl grew dangerous. "Be a good girl."

"I. Don't. Know." She spaced the words out so her voice didn't shake. "I have no idea what you're talking about! You are out of your mind!"

Yeah. Great idea, Ness. Piss off the guy who possibly killed two people you cared about in less than five minutes. That's a great survival tactic.

Bear's expression stayed blank, then suddenly he had ahold of her arm and a knife was pressed to her throat. Nessa gasped as she tried to lean away from the madman, shivering hard against his horrible grip. He leered at her, leaning close enough for her to gag on his rank breath.

"When did your visions start?" he growled.

The words and her heart caught in her throat. "My—my what?"

"Your visions!" he roared, and Nessa felt the cool metal of the knife press against her flesh. She closed her eyes against the sting.

"I—I don't know what—what you mean."

"Then where is your portal, Your Highness? Surely your Guard would have told you about it in the event of his death."

"My Guard? I don't know what you're talking about." Nessa swallowed hard. "Really."

Her heart felt like it was going to leap from her throat, her tightening stomach threatening to make her sick. She felt a sting on her collarbone and winced, a small, pain-filled gasp escaping her lips. Bear's eyes flashed from the blade to her face, and his expression spread into the most horrible grin Nessa had ever seen. His tone was astonished, but also smug and triumphant.

"You were never told, were you?"

Nessa wanted to ask what he meant, but thought better of it. She bit her tongue to keep from speaking and kept her eyes steady on the monstrosity, refusing to show him how scared she was.

What did he know about her? Why was he talking about magic? Why did they even want her? She had to be brave. Or at least fake it.

Her courageous façade almost collapsed when Bear threw his head back and laughed.

"Don't fret, Your Highness. We'll take good care of you."

He lunged, and before Nessa knew it, she was hoisted over his shoulder like a sack of potatoes. She braced herself against his back to keep from falling as the stench of body odor, sweat and death assaulted her nostrils, and she swallowed down bile. Perhaps if she kept her hands over her nose…? Nope. Didn't help. She rammed her knee into his shoulder, but the blow had no effect. Really, she hadn't expected it to do much. He was so much bigger than she was.

The mountain men carried her further into the park, but instead of sticking to the picturesque, paved walking paths, they took off into the brush and trees, carefully avoiding every lighted lamppost. They all seemed to know where they were going without even a word. Had they scoped out the route beforehand? How long had they been planning this?

This was insane! She had to escape! But even if she got the man to drop her, how would she get away? Run? Fight? It would be five burly outdoorsmen against one petite college waitress; the odds were hardly in her favor. Running could maybe work; she might find help…but could she outrun five men?

It wasn't like she had another option.

Would they kill her? No, they could have killed her in the coffee shop if they wanted her dead. They knew her name and had been looking for her, so whatever they wanted her for, they needed her alive. Was that enough to keep them from killing her if her escape attempt failed?

"Hello, Nessa."

Nessa's head shot up the instant she heard Liv's voice. Well, technically it shot *down,* since she was currently hanging upside-down, and she saw Liv standing before them, calmly taking in the scene around her. Only her slightly raised brow indicated any interest in the unusual situation. And to be fair, these men were not exactly Nessa's type.

"Are you well?" Liv tilted her head, and Nessa's eyes widened. No, Liv had to get out of here! These men would surely kill her. One of the men started toward Liv, and her narrowed green flashed suspiciously to him for a half a heartbeat.

Liv clasped her hands behind her back, arching her brow at Nessa. Gods, was she really just going to stand in front of these murderers and wait for an answer? Did she really need one?

"It's been a trying day," Nessa finally groaned. Her head spun, and she could feel her ears growing warm as she fought to pull herself upright, certain she looked like a flailing starfish. Bear jerked her roughly to the side and Nessa let out a squeak that made Liv's jaw flex, her eyes snapping to Nessa's busted lip and the cut dripping down her collarbone.

Her jaw clenched tighter.

Bear barked an order at his brute squad. It sounded like something along the lines of 'Oh, just kill her and be done with it.'

The heavily armed murderers descended as one on the single girl standing in the wood.

They didn't stand a chance.

With a twirl of Liv's fingers, a blade slashed across the throat of the closet attacker. A second lunged at her with a sword, but she clamped down lightning fast on his unprotected arm and spun. Nessa heard a sickening *crack*, and the minion roared as Liv used the spin to sling another blade from her fingers, the metal flying straight into the chest of the third man. Bear and Snow both took off running before their compatriot even hit the ground.

Nessa hurled her weight to the side, tumbling free of Bear only to land on top of Snow. A hand clamped down on her wrist as she clambered to her feet, and Snow yanked her into him. She used the momentum to ram her elbow into his gut and Snow doubled over, all the air leaving his lungs.

Nessa danced out of his reach, scooping up rocks as she raced back towards the coffee shop. She didn't have anything else.

Suddenly, she was thrown to the ground as a fist wrapped around the back of her shirt. Bear stood over her, something dark sparking in those black eyes, and Nessa shivered in horror. This man would kill her, prize or no.

With a groan of effort, Nessa slammed a rock into his head. Maybe she could outrun him if she got him disoriented enough. He let out a yell, his back arching at an inhuman angle, and as he fell to all fours, she could see the blade sticking out from his back. She scampered backward madly; whenever her fingers touched a stone, she chucked it at the Bear.

Bear turned his eyes on her, that burning madness becoming an engulfing flame, and Nessa stumbled onto her side as he bared his teeth at her, blood staining his mouth. She felt bile rise in her throat. She couldn't breathe.

Then he did the unthinkable.

He started to crawl toward her.

Nessa could only stare in horror. Blood was seeping through the front of his shirt; it dripped from between his lips. He should be dead. He should have stopped, but he was too unwilling to release his quarry.

Nessa whimpered.

"Come here, girl." The words gurgled from his throat and she sprang to life, fumbling backwards blindly as her nails dug into the earth below her. She couldn't move fast enough. Her back slammed into a tree trunk, and she held on so tight her nails left marks in the bark as the rest of her threatened to shake apart. There was nowhere else to go. Air came in deep gasps, but she never had enough to scream. She couldn't take her eyes away from the madman; she was trapped. And still he came for her.

A blade suddenly slashed across his throat, and Nessa winced as the Bear's eyes bulged. He gurgled in rage as he fell to the ground, blood pooling beneath him, and Nessa stared at the body with wide-eyed horror. That blade…it was dark and rough, as though it were made of iron, not steel. That wasn't one of Liv's, yet Liv was the one standing over him.

Nessa gulped down air. What had just happened? What was going on? Her mind was so busy spinning that it couldn't be bothered to get her body to work. Her brain refused to even begin processing what was happening, let alone what she thought of it. The only thing she could manage to do was to shake.

There was a dark liquid pooling under the body.

No, don't look. She closed her eyes.

"Nessa!"

Liv shook her abruptly from her thoughts, and Nessa blinked. Liv? Her friend Liv was here. Liv had saved her. How? She worked at a glorified plant shop. She ate too much Chinese food and was obsessed with succulents. How had Liv taken on those horrible men? No, Liv had *killed* them. Her best friend had killed people who were seemingly *trained* to kill and hadn't even blinked or broken a sweat. The thought made Nessa stiffen.

Liv had known what she was doing.

The terrifying thought spurred Nessa into action, and she took off into the park, refusing to look back. Liv was trained, and trained well; she knew how to fight, how to kill. She wasn't just some kind girl in a weird little shop.

Was she even Nessa's friend? After all, Nessa was valuable somehow. Who was to say their acquaintance was coincidence? Had everything been a lie? Had everything they'd shared been a tactic to get her guard down so Liv could take her instead? Why did anyone even want her?

"Ness!" Liv was after her instantly. Nessa kept running.

She had never run so fast in her entire life. How had Liv done that? And those men? What had she done to them? She flew over the uneven ground, sliding on the dead leaves that seemed determined to make her fall. It was difficult to keep her balance when she couldn't even control her heartbeat, her mind moving faster than her feet. She just had to keep going. The only clear thought she had was *get out and get out now*.

The trees grew thicker as the park ended and the forest began. The branches clawed at her skin, ripping her clothes and flesh, but her fear kept pushing her forward. Liv wasn't a killer. She couldn't be, right? But Nessa had only known her for a few months, so what did she really know about the other girl?

The terrain had become less level, the ground's dips and hills seeming to grow like waves as she ran. The land finally reached a peak before a sharp decline nearly sent her tumbling down. She'd almost missed the drop due to the water in her eyes.

She had to breathe. Why couldn't she breathe?

She managed to catch herself on a tree and whirled, panting, to check whether she was alone. The forest was quiet and calm, with no sign of her apparently crazy friend, and her heart finally began to slow for the first time since this whole thing had started. Dear gods and angels, what was going on? She put her face in her hands.

Calm down, she told herself. *You have to calm down.*

"Nessa?"

She jumped when she heard Liv speak. The other girl was standing right next to her, a little over an arm's length away. Nessa stumbled away from her friend.

"You killed them." Her voice cracked.

"I did not mean to scare you." Liv's voice was quiet and calm as she held her hands up, palms out toward Nessa to show she meant no harm. She appeared unarmed, but Nessa now knew that those daggers could appear seemingly out of nowhere. They were silver death that flew through the air.

"Nessa…"

"How can you do that?" Nessa pressed her back against the tree to stay upright. She wanted to run, but couldn't make her feet move. Gods, she wanted to go home.

"Ness, I know this is going to be hard, but you are going to have to trust me." Liv tried again since her first attempt at soothing her friend had failed, but Nessa was already backing away from her, getting ready to run again if she could. She had no idea what was happening, but she was going to do her best to get as far away from the crazy as possible. Nothing remarkable ever happened to her, nothing! So why was it all going wrong now?

"What is going on, Liv?" she demanded, her mind trying to make sense of everything that had just happened. How could Liv be a trained killer? She seemed so nice and sweet. She read a lot, shared tea, always took care of her little plants, hoarded chocolate… And she looked so delicate! How…

"Calm down, Nessa." Liv's voice was calm and crisp like an autumn afternoon as she placed her fingertips on Nessa's arm. Nessa grabbed the sides of her head, burying her fingers in her hair. Calm down? Was she joking?

"Calm down?" she squeaked. "You…you just…"

"Do you want to live?" The words spilled abruptly from Liv's mouth. The phrase was cliché, but it made the wheels in Nessa's head kick into gear. Live? Of course she wanted to live. Was Liv threatening her? Was that what she meant?

"What?" Nessa blinked at her.

"Nessa, those men have allies who won't be far behind," Liv explained, her voice taking on a tone well beyond her years. "And I doubt they will be as kind. They will try to take you."

This couldn't be happening. Nessa was barely nineteen years old; she hadn't done anything wrong. She was a college student! Nothing more! Her parents were teachers! Her family hadn't done anything so why was she suddenly so important? She was only a waitress!

"You are my charge. I will take care of you, I promise." Liv's voice, calm and soft, cut through her racing thoughts once again. "Just please, trust me. We really need to be going."

Nessa looked up at her friend. Liv had just killed a squad of men with ease. She could have done the same to Nessa, but she hadn't, though she'd certainly had more than enough opportunities in the past few months.

Besides, the men she'd killed probably would have killed her. Did that make it self-defense in advance? For all Nessa knew, they may have wanted to kill *her*, too. Liv didn't seem to want that, at least not at the moment, and Nessa knew she stood no chance on her own when said reinforcements came.

"Promise?" Nessa asked.

"You have my word."

"Okay." She nodded once, her voice small and uncertain. She could trust Liv for a little while, at least until the immediate danger had passed. Liv gave her a small, reassuring smile, but it vanished again in a heartbeat.

"Thank you. Are you hurt?"

Nessa shook her head *no* as Liv's eyes fell once more to the cut on her lip, then to the one on her collarbone. The elder girl made a face, a slight tightening of the jaw that would normally have gone unnoticed, and the angry sea behind her eyes roiled. Still, she seemed to satisfy herself with that.

"Good." Liv gently grabbed her hand and began leading Nessa back to town. "We have to find a car to steal."

Maybe trusting Liv hadn't been the best idea.

Chapter Four

Ew, Wet Socks

Liv made Nessa drive.

The car they had commandeered belonged to Maria. At least, Nessa hoped it still did. She couldn't stomach going back into the coffee shop; she didn't want to see if her friends…

She tried not to think about it.

Maria always left the car unlocked because she kept the keys in the sun visor. After all, she claimed no one would want to steal this car. It was a beat-up old minivan that had been through all four of Maria's older brothers, and all the seats were missing out of the back, along with part of the right bumper. A speedy getaway car it was not.

Nessa didn't feel right about stealing it, but what else could she do? Liv said she was trying to protect her, but she didn't see how stealing Maria's van was keeping her safe. She supposed she just had to put her faith in Liv. Neither of them spoke, save for the directions Liv was giving her.

They left town behind in a matter of minutes, the forest around them becoming denser the further from civilization they drove. Liv kept glancing over at Nessa, but refused to speak on the thoughts that were causing said looks of concern. Perhaps she was waiting for Nessa to have another breakdown, but Nessa was determined to keep herself together. Her death grip on the steering wheel was enough to keep her grounded in reality; plus, it helped to hide her shaking hands.

It didn't take long for her to realize where they were going.

Lover's Bend was a secluded spot in a small valley not fifteen minutes from the edge of town, though Lover's Bend was not its true name. The actual name for the place was boring and wholly unremarkable, but the valley had become infamous for its privacy and romantic atmosphere. Hence, the change in moniker.

Though it was close to town, Lover's Bend was completely isolated, making it a wonderful place for the local lovestruck youth, though Nessa herself had never utilized the valley for such a purpose. There were too many murder mysteries that started with horny teenagers in the woods for her to find the idea romantic.

The spot in question was a quiet clearing where two small rivers came together to create a larger one called Shadow Creek. Nessa knew Shadow Creek well. It formed the eastern border of the campus, which seemed like poor planning as the river had a tendency to flood in the spring. Canceled classes were guaranteed.

...Perhaps the planning hadn't been so poor after all.

Lover's Bend usually flooded as well, but once the waters receded, the valley was filled with every flower imaginable. And at the moment, it was dry and open for use, the summer flowers having been replaced by tall grass and golden leaves. The valley formed a nearly perfect semi-circle, bordered by the now-colorful trees, and a small path led down to the bank, just large enough for a small car to pass through. Frankly, Nessa was surprised she managed to maneuver the minivan down there at all, the way the path wound and curved.

Liv had her stop the car as soon as they passed through the treeline, and was out in a flash, pulling Nessa behind her so quickly she didn't even have a chance to shut the door. Nessa was beginning to silently question what exactly Lover's Bend had to do with mercenary Westeros lookalikes. Then again, this had been hands down the most unusual day of her life. Why not add a little more crazy to it?

Liv sprinted to the edge of the water. Nessa assumed she would stop when she met the river, but Liv hardly even slowed down. Instead, she dashed straight in, spraying water around her.

Nessa herself elected to stop at the bank. She didn't have any apprehensions about the water itself; she was perfectly fine swimming in lakes and that sort of thing. In fact, she was a strong swimmer. No, she stopped because she didn't have any idea what Liv was doing, and she was tired and scared and really didn't feel like adding cold and wet to the list. Her trust in Liv was beginning to wane.

Liv was knee deep in the river before she realized Nessa wasn't following her. She turned, her face expectant.

"You have got to be kidding." They were the first words Nessa had spoken since agreeing to follow her friend. Liv looked slightly appalled, as if *Nessa* were the crazy one. Her expression settled into one of determination.

"Nessa, we do not have the time to argue." She sounded like a stern mother.

"I'm not getting in the river, Liv," Nessa told her sharply. She'd thought they were trying to escape from the terrible men chasing her, and at the moment, she didn't see how getting in the river was going to help the situation.

Liv seemed to realize she wasn't going to win this one. The slight cock of Nessa's right eyebrow clearly expressed her belief in her friend's insanity.

The couples who had come for some nice, quiet necking were now staring wide-eyed at the two. Well, one couple who already had half their clothes off was still very much occupied with one other, but for everyone else, the girls made quite the spectacle.

With a slight sigh of exasperation, Liv waded out of the water toward Nessa, who jumped back once again. She wanted to live and she knew, for some reason, that she had to trust Liv in order for that to happen. However, that trust was working better in theory than in practice.

"Come on now, it's all right." Liv spoke as though she were trying to soothe a spooked horse. And to be fair, Nessa really did look like she was prepared to bolt at any moment.

Liv gently took her by the elbow and began easing Nessa into the river, while Nessa just let her feet move, forcing her mind not to interfere. She could hear the splashing of the water and felt the slippery rocks below her boots. She nearly fell, but Liv steadied her easily.

Nessa swallowed hard. "W—why are we walking into a river?"

"Because it is where the Veil is thinnest," Liv answered, as though it were obvious.

"The Veil?" Nessa glanced up in confusion, gasping when water rushed over the top of her boots. It was *cold*. Besides, she hated the feeling of wet socks. The water began to rise until she was soaked up to her knees. "Is that what those deranged Vikings were looking for?"

"Mercenaries."

"Yeah, whatever." Nessa gulped in a slight panic. Mercenaries, Vikings, for all she cared they could have been goblins! Whatever or whoever they were, they were after her and she wanted to stay far away from them. That was all she was really able to process right now. She stumbled again, but Liv held her steady.

The current was gentle as it swirled around Nessa's thighs, the water cold even for early autumn. The chill began to seep into her legs, working its way slowly up her spine, and she shivered. She failed to see how this so-called Veil was going to help them — or where it even *was*. Perhaps it was across the river, hidden somewhere inside the forest. It was a kind of portal, after all; it most likely would not be difficult to find.

Liv finally stopped in the middle of the river, a peculiar spot where the two creeks came together to form a point. Nessa could feel the two currents mingling, each trying to pull her body in a different direction. The water was a little over waist high, and she was having trouble keeping her feet under her.

"L—Liv?" Nessa looked up at her friend, confusion and fear on her face. She was not accustomed to not understanding a situation or being unprepared; she was a curious girl, and if a question needed answering she would find the answer, somehow. She was always in control, be it of her space, her studies, or herself. But she had no control over this, or even a vague notion of what she had just been pulled into. She didn't even know what had made her a target to begin with.

Liv grabbed her hands, squeezing them tightly, and Nessa noticed they were trembling. At first, she assumed it was her own hands shaking, but the tremors were out of sync with hers. For the first time since the entire ordeal had begun, Nessa realized Liv was probably just as scared as she was.

Liv's chest rose as she took a deep breath and slowly released it, her green eyes fluttering closed.

"Please, try to stay still." Liv's voice was smooth and calm, completely contradictory to the signs of concern her hands were giving off. Nessa felt her friend's grip tighten, and to comfort either herself or Liv, she squeezed back.

"Whatever you do, do not let go."

Nessa swallowed, hard. "Yeah, no worries there."

Liv began muttering under her breath, something Nessa couldn't understand, though the consonants were crisp and the vowels round and distinct. She thought it was gibberish until she realized it must be a language, though it certainly didn't sound like any language she knew of. It sounded like it could have been a mix of Latin and French, but softer and more delicate, like the chime of the bell over the coffee shop door.

She felt the water begin to race past her, the rush of the current becoming stronger, and she held tighter onto Liv. Glancing down, she saw the water beginning to foam and swirl around them, as if an unseen river monster was circling them. The vortex was only around the two of them, the rest of the water seemingly untouched, and Nessa's fear settled into her chest. Was Liv doing this? There was no way she could be, right?

The water began to swirl around them faster and faster, becoming angrier, rougher, the crests of the waves growing larger with each pass. Nessa wanted to close her eyes so she wouldn't have to watch, but she couldn't bring herself to do so, her hands beginning to tremble along with her body. What was going on?

"L—Liv…?" Her voice wavered.

Suddenly, the water flew up around them, forming a cyclone, and they were swallowed by it so swiftly Nessa didn't even have time to scream. She tried to duck on reflex, feeling Liv squeezing her hands to make sure they didn't get separated, and Nessa felt her feet lift off the rocks as the water whirled around her and Liv.

Holding onto Liv for dear life, she closed her eyes in terror. Was she going to die, to drown here? Hadn't Liv said she meant her no harm? Then again, what people meant and what actually happened weren't always the same thing. She wanted to scream, but was too petrified to open her mouth.

Suddenly, she felt herself being pressed down by the water, the pressure growing until it felt like her lungs were going to pop. Then all at once her feet hit rock and the water let go, falling lifelessly back into the river in a great rush. The abrupt release knocked her down, her already shaking knees buckling.

The current was harsher here, doing its best to push the two girls over, and it took advantage of Nessa's clumsiness to sweep her away. She barely managed to catch a breath before she was pulled back underwater, the angry river ripping her from Liv as she desperately tried to hold on.

"Nessa!" Liv screamed, trying frantically to catch the other girl. But Nessa was already out of reach.

Nessa struggled to get her head above the water as the current tossed her violently around. Finally, she broke through to the surface, gasping for much-needed air. The river was in fact shallow enough for her to stand if she could manage to get her feet under her, but the current was so fast it wasn't allowing her. She barely heard Liv call her name before she was sucked back under.

Nessa flailed, trying to keep herself upright and knowing it was a fight she was losing. She had learned to swim when she was a child, but this was different. This wasn't the local city pool, with still water and lifeguards supervising. No, this water was pushing and pulling her in every direction, and she had no idea how to correct for it. She managed to make it to the surface once more, filling her lungs with air before going back under.

Suddenly, she felt a heavy pressure on her arm, and realized she must have hit something. Whatever it was, she grabbed onto it for dear life, looking up to see Liv. Her friend was soaked, her hair dripping onto her clothes, but her expression relaxed to one of relief when she saw Nessa grasping her arm.

"I told you not to let go."

Liv's attempt at humor was half-hearted at best as she pulled a half-drowned Nessa from the river. Nessa shot her a look that told Liv just how tedious she found *that* little comment, coughing mouthfuls of river water onto the bank as Liv patted her shoulder gently.

Nessa was sure she looked like a drowned cat. *Everything* was dripping, from her hair to her clothes and even her fingers. Wherever she stepped, she left large puddles in her wake. She brushed her hair from her face, her eyes wide as she stared at Liv.

"Liv, what was—"

She froze solid as she finally took in her surroundings. The trees were taller than any she had ever seen, a mix of pines and white-barked trees that seemed to stretch all the way to the sky. They were in the middle of an enormous forest, the trees forming a thirty to forty-foot bank on either side of the massive river. The bank faded from grass to the white rocks the two girls were currently perched on.

In shock, Nessa moved a few steps forward on wobbly legs.

This was *not* Lover's Bend.

Chapter Five

Definitely Not Kansas

The wind ripped across Nessa's skin, goosebumps rising on her arms as a shiver wracked her spine. Her wet clothes stuck to her frigid skin, rubbing and dripping in awkward places, but it did nothing to distract from the sight before her.

The trees were just…wrong. They could have been maples, except for the white bark and the rigidity of their trunks. Leaves that should have been golden with autumn instead glistened a healthy green.

She slowly turned to look at Liv. She had to stay calm, had to keep her head, even if right now it was spinning like a top and felt impossible to catch. Her lungs constricted in her chest.

"Where are we?" Nessa licked her lips uncertainly. They tasted like river. Glancing upward, she saw a dusty pink sky chasing away dark blue. Was it dawn?

"I cannot be quite certain yet." Liv appeared unbothered as she wrung river water from her own pale hair, and Nessa watched the droplets fall onto the white stones at their feet. Liv tossed her hair back over her shoulder to survey the still-very-wrong trees. "I do not know where we came through."

Nessa could only stare at her in utter disbelief.

"Came through *what?*" Her voice squeaked slightly, and she swallowed, fighting for some semblance of control over her next words. "What *was* that, Liv?"

Liv looked her over as Nessa wrapped her arms tightly around her middle, which did nothing to stop her trembling. She wasn't quite sure whether it was from the cold, adrenaline, or shock, but she decided she would just shake until she figured out the answer.

She took in their surroundings once more, mostly so she didn't have to meet Liv's eyes. Even the idea made her stomach twist uncomfortably. She had never seen a forest like this before. The closest she could think to compare were the forests in movies and photographs. The trees huddled close together and she couldn't see more than fifty yards into the woods; after that, her vision became a foggy mess of dark greens and browns. It could have been the forest belonging to a witch in a fairytale.

Liv's eyes looked up at the sky. She didn't bother to respond, her eyes turning to the forest around them, and Nessa huffed quietly. Perhaps if she looked pitiful, Liv would finally answer.

When she still didn't, Nessa tightened her grip around her middle, water droplets rolling down her spine. Liv was just as soaked as she was, but her friend didn't seem bothered by anything. Her bright green eyes were alight with thought.

Nessa watched her friend quietly, unsure of what to say or do next. What had that thing been? Where were they? What…

Her thoughts came to a screeching halt.

Something was wrong with Liv's profile. But what? She looked the same as she always had, aside from being dripping wet. She still had the same high cheekbones, though they suddenly appeared a little more pronounced. Her skin was still pale, but her green eyes shone a brighter green than before, her hair alight with pearlescent flame. She appeared to be more…*Liv* than Nessa had ever seen her. It was as if she had only ever seen a reflection of Liv in a mirror and now she was meeting the living person for the first time. The air about her was different, too. She suddenly seemed much older than her early twenties.

…And her ears tapered to fine points.

Nessa blinked, thinking there must be water in her eyes. Perhaps she had swallowed some river water that was causing her to hallucinate? Yeah, river water.

But the sight didn't go away. No matter how long she stared, Liv's ears remained elegantly tapered. They weren't overly long or large; they could have passed for normal if she hadn't been looking closely.

She only knew of one species with ears like that.

…But that was impossible.

She stared, wide eyes glazed in shock, her jaw slightly slack. What in the world? Pointy ears, water vortexes and mysterious forests were making her mind implode. On top of that, there had been the stalking, attempted kidnapping, *and* attempted murder, all in the last twenty-four hours. She simply couldn't take in anything else. Why was everything spinning?

Suddenly, she found herself within arm's reach of Liv, and twiddled her fingers to disperse the desire to touch her friend's ears. That would just be weird, and she'd had enough of *that* for one day, thank you very much.

Liv was speaking, but Nessa couldn't hear the words. Liv paused as she took in the other girl's expression, arching a questioning brow as she glanced sideways at her charge.

"Nessa?" She reached out to lightly touch Nessa's shoulder, and the world stabilized. Had she been swaying?

Liv held Nessa's eyes. "Are you with me?"

"You—your ears…" Nessa couldn't stop the words. "They…have they always been like that?"

"My ears?" Liv reached up to touch them, gently following the line of her earlobe to the very point. A bright, joyous smile slowly spread across her lips, and her eyebrows shot up, her eyes glittering with something Nessa had never seen. Liv was *happy* that her ears had changed? She self-consciously touched her own ears to make sure they hadn't changed as well. Nope, still normal Nessa ears.

Liv's expression was composed when she looked back at Nessa.

"Yes…and no," she began. "I'll explain once we get under some cover."

"But…"

"I know this is scary, and you've done so well, but please, just trust me a little longer, Nessa. Please."

Nessa chewed her lower lip. Trust Liv? Well, what choice did she have now? She didn't know where she was, or…when she was? She didn't even know what the right questions were. Liv at least knew that much, pointy ears or no.

Slowly, she nodded, and Liv's shoulders relaxed.

"Thank you."

And Nessa could tell she meant it.

Liv took Nessa's hand, guiding her into the woods, and Nessa let her, her shoes squishing as she walked. Ugh, wet socks. To top off her weird, terrifying day, there had to be wet socks.

The forest floor was covered in dry grass and fallen leaves. She might have expected some low-lying shrubs or flowers, but there were none, only the monotony of green and brown, with an eerie silence shrouded overtop it. With the light of the sun gone, Nessa shivered violently.

The trees continued to be wrong. The bark was white and flaky, but the trunks were far too large to be birch trees. Plus, the leaves were too dark, and the branches swayed and curved oddly, despite the rigidity of the trunks. It was like the strange trees wanted to reach out and grab her.

Where was this place?

She saw Liv's eyes dart around the forest. Was she searching for something? Nessa glanced over her shoulder. Were other mercenaries coming after them? Her stomach tightened painfully at the thought.

What if they were found? What if they took her away this time? To where? What did they want? Would she ever be free again, would she ever go home? What if the backup was here waiting for them; what if those men were hiding here, waiting to pounce? Her lungs heaved, gathering air she couldn't seem to use, her heart bashing against her ribs as if it wanted out.

Breathe, breathe.

Nope.

The world tilted before her eyes as the ground rushed up, and Nessa managed to catch herself against a tree, her knees shaking.

"Nessa?" Liv turned to her. "Are you well?"

"I…uh…" Nessa wasn't sure what to say to that. Yes, physically, she was going to recover just fine. Well, probably. But her mind? She shook her head, hating how the world shook with her.

"Liv, where are we?" She reminded herself not to bite her lip, which had finally stopped tasting of warm, sticky copper. "This isn't Syracuse."

"No." Liv shook her head, looking around. All that could be seen was dense forest. She sighed, lowering herself to a fallen log, and Nessa stared at her for a moment as Liv refused to meet her eyes. She seemed to find the ground below her feet captivating. Nessa held onto her pendant, her fingers following the swirling setting as warmth seeped into her skin. The longer Liv remained silent, the louder Nessa's thoughts became.

If they weren't in Syracuse, then where were they? Had they been swept downriver? Very far downriver? Her stomach flipped and twisted, her last meal threatening a reappearance. No, something was telling her that they were nowhere near Syracuse. But how could that be? How had they gotten here, wherever *here* was? And how was she going to get back home?

"Liv?" Nessa kept her voice quiet, worrying that if she spoke any louder, Liv might hear the fear laced within her name. Liv's head snapped up, the usual serene waters of her gaze rocking and swirling uncertainly. Nessa held very still as Liv's eyes examined her from head to toe.

Finally, Liv sighed, defeated.

"We are just south of the northern border of the Kingless Lands, west of the Marsei River."

Nessa blinked. West of the what?

"I understood like sixty percent of what you just said." She shook her head. "Where is the Marsei River?"

"Avani. We are in Avani."

Avani? That sounded like something from a video game. What was an Avani?

Something tickled in the back of her mind. A world. Avani was this world. Why…why did she know that? Her thoughts began to whirl.

She rested her back against the tree and slid to the ground, her vision swaying. She had to remind herself to breathe. *Breathe!*

Liv was speaking again.

"Nessa, we are not on Earth anymore."

Nessa's unseeing eyes flew wide, and everything seemed to stop for a full heartbeat as static roared in her ears. White flashed before her eyes. Not on Earth?

Reality smashed into her all at once, the world tilting roughly to the side, and she was on her hands and knees before she knew it. Her breath tried to settle her burning throat, her face blazing hot, but her stomach lurched with an aching heave and half the river spewed from her mouth. She gasped, but her stomach wasn't finished. Her lunch left her next.

Suddenly, Liv was on her knees next to her, gently rubbing Nessa's back until she stopped dry heaving. Finally, she pushed her friend away, resting back on her heels as she wiped her wet eyes, ignoring the twinge behind them that ran all the way to her temples. The cool air felt good on her overheated cheeks. Different world. Not Earth. How? Why?

"Liv?" Nessa gulped deep lungfuls of air, her stomach churning violently again. She swallowed down what tasted like bile. "Why…I don't understand. How did we end up in another world? How do we get home?"

"Nessa…" Liv patted her knee as Nessa wiped at her wide, damp eyes. She seemed to have expelled most of her fear along with the contents of her stomach. Her hands didn't shake, she didn't cry. She was too tired to cry anymore. Instead, her body tingled and slumped as if each muscle was weighed down and drained. She needed answers and she needed them now.

"I will answer all of your questions, but later," said Liv. "Right now, it is not safe, We are too close to the Menhiran border. Can you please trust me a little bit longer?"

Nessa bristled as she looked over her shoulder, expecting to see those men running into the forest after them. Her heart pounded wildly against her ribs. Taking a deep breath, she forced herself to think. She had survived a near-kidnapping, a near-drowning and being dragged into another world, all in the last six hours.

Another world! Who knew what creatures roamed this wood? Werewolves? Mermaids? The boogeyman? She had no idea. She didn't know anything about this land, its rivers or whatever creatures lurked hidden in the forest.

Liv at least knew where they were, and she might know more. Which meant Liv was her best chance for survival. Anyway, with her current luck, on her own she'd stumble across a hungry bear or into a ravine.

And that was if she was lucky.

"Okay." Nessa nodded. "But can you please explain your ears?"

Liv gave her a small, pleased smile.

"I am an elf."

Nessa blinked. Her best friend was not only a trained killer, but also not human, apparently. Nessa's lips set into a thin line. Perhaps strange and weird was just going to be her life now. For a while, at least.

"Of course you are," she deadpanned.

Liv tried to give her an encouraging smile. "You are taking this rather well."

Nessa grimaced, her voice cracking. "Am I?"

They headed south. Liv didn't hold onto Nessa as they ran, but she kept hovering within arm's reach, and Nessa suspected Liv was considering putting her on a tether like one of those rowdy toddlers at the mall, just to make sure she didn't bolt. Liv kept eyeing her, waiting.

Nessa, thankfully, was a little smarter than a toddler.

...She hoped so, anyway.

Though the sun kept climbing in the sky, the forest remained cool. The canopy above them wove together, each leaf greedy for sunlight. Nessa glanced up, but could see nothing but green. No sun, no blue sky. Only leaves and branches and shade.

Her clothes didn't stop dripping for hours, and there was no fixing the wet socks. She couldn't recall ever being so exhausted; she was cold, soaked to the bone, and hadn't slept in over twenty-four hours. An all-nighter for a test was one thing. Running through unfamiliar woods for her very life was another. She barely had enough air to keep up with the spry Liv, let alone ask all the questions spinning through her head. Plus, all Liv's focus was on the task of navigating, though she clearly knew the terrain. She only had to stop to check her bearings twice.

The ground slowly became less rocky and more even, though Nessa only noticed because she didn't have to mind her footing as much. The trees grew gradually broader, and far greener than she could have ever believed. It was mid-October; everything should have been amber and gold and red. Was it a different season here? In Avani?

It was mid-afternoon before Liv paused again. She glanced over at the huffing and puffing Nessa, whose cheeks were red, her brow covered in sweat. Nessa was a fit girl, but travel like this was hard. There were hills, hidden rocks, and logs to jump over, not to mention the constant threat of being discovered by mercenaries that one just didn't get from a run on a treadmill. Nessa wasn't sure why they'd stopped, but she was grateful to have a chance to gasp for breath. It didn't help the tremble in her hands, though.

The edge of the wood was finally in sight, sunlight dotting the forest floor ahead of them. Beyond the young trees, a line of stones stretched to the horizon. Liv had frozen in her tracks at the sight, her emerald eyes fixed on the stones, though her expression remained blank otherwise. Nessa knew that look. She swallowed.

"What is it?" She finally found the air to speak as Liv shook herself out of her reverie.

"It is nothing." The elf's voice was quiet. "We can slow our progress for the time being. We should be far enough ahead of anyone trying to follow."

Nessa nodded as Liv began to stroll toward the line of stones, taking a deep breath for what felt like the first time in nearly two days. The air smelled like dust, grass, and sunlight.

She followed Liv, dancing here and there to place herself into every patch of sunlight she could find. The warmth contrasted with her cool skin, and she relished in it. No matter where you were, sunlight was sunlight. At least that hadn't changed.

The trees eventually faded away, drenching the two in light, and Nessa paused as warmth washed over her. She closed her eyes and turned her face upward, the last of the river water evaporating away. It was finally warm. She would take whatever comfort she could, and being dry would have to do for now. Liv's lips twitched upward and she nudged Nessa with her shoulder as Nessa blinked.

"Come on," she urged gently, and Nessa quickly fell into step with her.

"Liv?"

"Yes?" Liv arched a brow, and Nessa bit her lower lip. Something had been bothering her all day. Well, really a lot of somethings, such as river portals, mercenaries, that kind of thing.

"You're an elf," was what came out of her mouth instead.

"Yes."

They passed the line of stones, finding themselves in an open meadow, and Nessa blinked at the sudden intensity of the light. There were no trees here as far as she could see, only tall grasses dotted with blooms of various colors. The grass brushing her knees had turned slightly golden. She expected it to be rough, but it was quite smooth against her palm. She ran a blade between her fingers to keep from looking at Liv.

"There aren't any elves on Earth, are there?"

Liv pursed her lips.

"Not that I know of," she answered finally. "Very few can actually travel through the Veil, and even fewer choose to make the journey."

"The what?" Nessa's head popped up.

"The Veil," Liv supplied, and Nessa was reminded of Lilly Everette's tone of voice when she taught basic math to her students. "It is the separation between our world and Earth."

Nessa's mind wandered back to the swirling vortex of water that had nearly drowned her. Had that been the Veil? How had Liv known about it? She readied herself to ask another question, but the other girl beat her to it.

"I am from here, Nessa." Liv turned her face to the warm sun, a contented expression on her face. "Avani is my home."

Nessa nodded. Somehow, she had already known that was the answer Liv was going to give.

"Then what were you doing on Earth?" She tilted her head at her best friend, pausing as her hand reached out to lightly brush over the long grass. The soft tips tickled her palm, the sun helping to soothe her troubled nerves. Everything here was, well…she wasn't sure *what* it was. But she could feel a tether somewhere in her and she wasn't sure where it was from or what it was attached to. She only knew that something deep inside her was finally settled.

"Nessa." Liv licked her lips, her eyes flicking back to her friend. "Avani…*all* of Avani…is at war. Almost one hundred years ago, the kingdom of Menhir sought to extend their empire. The king's desire for power had become too great, so he decided to take it. By any means necessary."

"Menhir?" Nessa asked. "That is the kingdom we, uh, *arrived* near?"

Liv nodded. "The men you encountered were Menhiran mercenaries."

"You were on Earth to avoid the war?" Nessa shook her head, but it made a lot of sense. She'd grown up in San Francisco, after all. How many people had fled to her home to escape violence and persecution? It was what America had been founded on, after all. Liv shook her head slightly, then paused, apparently changing her mind.

"In a way." It seemed like she decided which words to say as they left her lips. She stopped and turned to Nessa, who paused quizzically at her friend's side. Liv opened her mouth, closed it again, then repeated the cycle once more, the struggle for words appearing too great. She sighed, seemingly at herself.

"Ness…" Liv gently placed a hand on her arm. "I was on Earth to look after *you*. You are of Avani blood."

Nessa blinked. Her? From another world? Liv had to be joking. There was nothing special or important about her. How could she be from Avani? She had no memory of this place, or the Veil. She definitely would have remembered the Veil.

"Me?" she breathed, her heart beginning to pound again. "I—I can't be from here. I don't even remember it!"

"You were not even two years old when your parents sent you through the Veil." Liv's calm tone helped to soothe her nerves. She squeezed Nessa's arm to steady her swaying. "Their only thought was for your safety."

"My parents?"

The words were a prayer. Her biological parents had always been such a mystery. She had tried to find out who they were when she was twelve years old, had even asked her adoptive parents about it, but they knew nothing.

The Everettes had adopted her when she was almost two. They had become friends with a woman calling herself Nessa's aunt, and said aunt had very much approved of the idea. She had only one condition: that Nessa keep her given name. The Everettes had happily agreed, though Nessa's mysterious aunt had refused to tell them what happened to her real parents or even what their names were.

Later, when the Everettes had attempted to track down this so-called aunt of Nessa's, a three-year search revealed the woman had never officially existed. No legal documentation of her survived, if there had ever been any to begin with.

After that disappointing blow, Nessa had decided maybe it was better if she didn't know. But it hadn't stopped the curiosity lurking at the back of her mind.

"My parents can't be from another world. Liv, all of this is crazy!" She flung her arms out in exasperation. Liv tried to calm her again, but Nessa swatted her away, heat rising in her face. Her eyes stung. Why did her chest hurt so much? "I'm from San Francisco! My parents are *teachers*, and…"

"You must believe me." Liv's tone was calm but firm. "I know it is difficult to believe, but it is the truth. It is as simple as that."

Nessa ran her hands over her hair. She had to think. She took a deep breath, in through her nose and out through her mouth, until the sting left her eyes. Logically, what Liv had told her made perfect sense. Those Menhiran mercenaries had been after *her*. One had even asked for her by name. They hadn't been searching for Liv.

"Okay, okay." Nessa's voice was quiet as she took another breath. *Survive now. Get answers now. Freak out later.* Her entire body felt numb, her head buzzing.

"Let's just say I believe you." She had difficulty even getting the words out; Nessa was honestly surprised her brain was still functioning at all. "That I'm 'of Avani blood,' and all that. Why were those mercenaries after me? I'm not special or important. I didn't even know Avani existed until now."

Liv's lips set into a thin line, her brow furrowing gently. Nessa took a step away from her to stand in the sunshine again, the warmth on her back feeling like the comforting embrace of a familiar friend.

"Nessa, your parents—" Liv paused to search for words. "Your father is a very successful general for Calebrir and a powerful Guard of Avani. He is one of the greatest weapons we have in the war against Menhir."

"Is?" Nessa cut her off, her heart fluttering in anticipation. Her legs felt like gelatin. "My—my father is still alive?"

Liv nodded. "I certainly hope so."

Nessa couldn't take it anymore. Her body slid down into the tall grass before she even realized what was happening.

Her birth father was still alive. After years and years of searching, she finally had some answers as to where she'd come from.

Liv knelt beside her, lightly placing a hand on her shoulder. Nessa's light blue eyes were staring and seeing nothing. Her father…her father…she had a family…from another world…family…

"Nessa?"

Nessa blinked, snapping back to reality upon hearing her name. Liv was watching her carefully, worry dancing in her green eyes. Nessa tried to smile, but it only came out as a small quirk of the lips.

"Sorry." Her voice was quiet.

"This is a lot to take in so quickly. Do not apologize." Liv smiled at her warmly, and Nessa's quirk grew closer to a smile. Assassin or not, Liv was still genuinely her friend. She at least had one person she could trust.

The revelation gave Nessa the strength to push herself back to her feet. She gave Liv a slight nod, and the other girl squeezed her shoulder affectionately. They continued on.

A path of yellow flowers swayed in the breeze next to the ruins of a wall of stone, and Liv lightly brushed her fingers over them. Nessa plucked one, twirling the blossom between her fingers.

"My father…" She had to stop to compose herself. She couldn't believe she was actually saying the words. "My father guards Avani?"

"In a manner. He is a Guard, as am I."

"What is a Guard? Is it a military rank, like a general?" Nessa brushed her fingers over the flowers, the yellow blooms seeming to brighten at her touch. Liv let her eyes linger on them a moment too long before her gaze flicked back to Nessa.

"No." Liv shook her head slightly. "A Guard is someone who looks after all of Avani, who does what is best for the whole of its people, not just one country or kingdom. Our allegiance is to peace and understanding, regardless of the national borders. It is a highly revered position."

Nessa arched an eyebrow at her. Peacekeepers? "So, you are like Gandalf…or the Doctor?"

"Now you see why I prefer Tolkien."

"It's almost like he knew," Nessa joked. Liv gave her a sly smile. The look gave Nessa pause. Wait…did Liv mean…

"Yes, a Guard's role is very similar to Gandalf's, but none of us are wizards. Wizards are exceptionally rare here, and the few we do have are not quite so levelheaded."

"And you're a Guard?" Nessa clarified, her eyebrows jumping. "That's how—uh, *why* you are obviously trained in combat?"

"Yes." Liv turned to face her. "Becoming a Guard takes mastery of many things, including combat. We study history, diplomacy, cartography, anything to help us keep the peace. The apprenticeship usually begins in childhood."

"You sound more like Jedi," Nessa pointed out with a small smile.

"We do not have the Force." Liv sighed sadly. "I never understood those films."

Nessa almost smiled again at that.

So, Liv and her father were part of the great peacekeepers of Avani. That made sense, she supposed. If he were a Guard, and a prominent general, it would follow that Nessa would be a target for the enemy. She'd been sent away, with Liv as a bodyguard, for her own safety…and her father's, by extension.

"Why would my father…" She trailed off as Liv tilted her head at her. Nessa bit her lower lip, looking away.

"Your father would have burned the world for you, especially if it meant saving you or your mother." A heaviness tinged Liv's words, and her voice grew quiet. "We all would have."

"What happened to my mother?"

"Your mother was lost when Menhir took the border city of Daradir," Liv said softly. "She stayed behind to help the evacuees through the hidden pass beside the eastern gate. It was not long before Menhiran forces overtook them. No one survived."

Nessa's heart turned to lead and sunk with a clatter to her toes. She had suspected her parents were gone after so many years of no contact and no paperwork, but *knowing* it was another thing entirely. She would never know her birth mother, would never know whose eyes she'd gotten, or where her lip chewing habit had come from or if they even liked the same things she did.

The weight on her chest was something akin to grief. It was strange to mourn for someone she'd never met. It was like a hole in the fabric, a missing something that had never been there to begin with. Now it never would be. All because of a war she hadn't even known about before today.

"What started this war with Menhir? How has it gone on so long?"

"The war became more intense around twenty-five years ago, but it has gone on long enough to destroy entire kingdoms. We believed we were close to peace once, but Gaough of the House of Remont, the current Menhiran king, destroyed that hope. The war renewed, with a displeased and desperate Menhir with something to prove. They have been nearly unstoppable ever since."

Liv turned her eyes to the land around them. Nessa followed her gaze, though she knew she could never see what Liv was seeing. To her eyes, there were only a few spots of brightly colored flowers and a few trees planted in neat rows. The tall grasses swayed softly around them.

"This was once the land of Brandel, a free kingdom of men." Liv's words sliced through the silence.

Nessa stared at the field, a sudden rush of cold coming over her that the gentle sunlight did nothing to prevent. She saw it now, the flowers carefully planted before the fallen stones. The homes and people were gone, but the gardens remained. The bobbing flowers were ghosts, carrying the memory of how things once were.

"Brandel?"

"The best leather in all the Five Kingdoms," Liv answered. "Menhir either conquers or destroys completely. There is no in-between."

"But why?" Nessa gasped. Her chest tightened as her mind spun. "Surely, it can't justify..."

Her eyes fell on the other ghost gardens. Who had planted those light blue flowers? A wife? A mother? Had they had a family and a home? How many other homes and families were gone because of this war? Nessa was only just beginning to understand what she had lost. She had lost her home and her family when she was sent through the Veil, but what was that compared to those who'd had no escape?

"Nessa, Avani does not work the same as Earth," Liv began.

Nessa blinked as Liv removed the yellow bloom from her hand, watching in amazement as the leaves began to bob up and down in the other girl's palm. It could have just been the breeze, but the leaves were dancing separately, one going up and the other down. Nessa's jaw dropped. Was *Liv* doing that?

"There is magic here," the elf said. "Powerful and ancient magic."

"Magic?" Nessa's ears perked up. "Like fireballs, magic missiles and spells?"

"Only for wizards. Avani's is a subtle magic." Liv took a moment to think as her deft fingers spun the stem of the flower. "Avani's power comes from the world in which it exists. There is magic in everything you see; life itself is energy. Every plant, every bit of sunlight, every ounce of starlight is its own kind of power. Avani has its own pure power as well, but very few are able to access the pure power of Avani. Once it finds a way into an outlet, the power is twisted to suit that outlet."

"Outlet?" Nessa asked. She scrunched up her nose in thought. "So...you're saying anything with energy has magic, and that magic comes from Avani itself? And it's like electricity? Where, once it's put into something, like a lightbulb or a microwave, it becomes something else, like light or heat?"

"Yes." Liv smiled. She might have been a little proud of her pupil, but Nessa would never make that assumption. "Say the magic was to manifest in the wind, that would be air magic, or in a flower, then it is plant magic. These elements of magic are tied to life and the life is tied to the magic in a cycle. Life creates power and pain creates corruption, in a sense. Everything here has memory. When Avani's magic is filtered through that memory, things can become complicated."

"So, everything in Avani is connected to the land through its power?" Nessa tilted her head.

"In a very subtle way, yes." Liv nodded. "Each race has a preferred place, a *fisilmiri*. These are where they feel the most at home, or the most connected to Avani. It is a place where each race can…recharge, so to speak. The elves have the wood and the dwarves draw their power from the earth below, while wizards feel most comfortable practicing under an open sky."

"What does fitz…um…filmsi…" The word that Liv had said so delicately grew clunky on Nessa's tongue.

"*Fisilmiri?*" Liv asked with a slight quirk of her lips.

"Yeah!" Nessa smiled at the offered relief. "What does that mean?"

"It is Vaerin, the ancient language of the elves. In Common, it translates to *power home*."

Nessa nodded.

"And each race has a proclivity for a certain element? Like fire, or water?" Nessa took the bloom back, watching the petals fall still again.

"In a manner, but there are more than four of them. This magic can help each race subtly manipulate their environment, or control part of their craft."

Nessa bit her lip, her brow furrowing. "How? I don't understand."

"Well, elves are excellent trackers because the wood will tell us things it will tell no one else. Dwarves are the finest of smiths because they understand the elements of the earth. It is something that helps in our work."

Nessa continued to chew her poor lower lip. This magic didn't sound like anything she'd ever read about. She let the words form on her lips as she thought them. "And each race draws from this elemental magic, like a flower drawing life from sunshine? To help them live? It's not like fireballs being tossed around or water bending?"

"Exactly." Liv beamed at her student. "Every race has a connection with Avani this way. We call them our places of power."

"Will—will there be any side effects if you, say, leave for a very long time?" She glanced at Liv out of the corner of her eye, and Liv gave her a small, reassuring smile.

"No." She was still smiling. "These places of power are simply home to us. Leaving does not affect our connection."

"So, if every race has a place of power, what is man's?" Nessa blinked up at her. Would she have to go to a cave to recharge? Or a lake? Would she be called to a home on top of a mountain?

"It was lost, long ago." Liv shook her head gently, letting out a deep sigh. "It does not mean that the actions of man do not affect the magic here. The land knows all."

In the attic of Nessa's mind, the light suddenly flicked on.

"Kind of like stone tape theory?" She tilted her head and pointed at her friend. "You said the land has memory. So, if something bad happens somewhere, like a battle with a lot of death, the land would suffer? All that badness is absorbed?"

"Precisely. This is why Menhir seeks land elsewhere." Liv gestured to the desolated land around them.

"Because their land is dying?" Nessa clarified.

"Menhir is a militaristic kingdom. Their ways are ruthless." Liv glanced down at her feet. "That kind of violence and bloodshed leaves a mark."

Nessa glanced down at the spots of blue, yellow, and pink dotting the tall grass. The stones grew darker behind them, the lines of color and grey stretching to just short of the horizon. How many people had lived here? How many lives had been destroyed in one kingdom's pursuit of power?

"I can see that."

Chapter Six

Let It All Out

They didn't stop for the rest of the day. Nessa's brain was too full to ask any more questions. She'd been born on a different world, one full of magic she barely understood, her best friend happened to be an elf and her biological father was still alive. And not only was he alive, but he was the reason an entire militant kingdom was after her. A war that had been raging for decades was destroying entire territories; lives were being ruined and torn apart. The ruins of Brandel had left her too melancholy to broach any other topic.

What was the word for a military kingdom? Nessa had read it somewhere. Stratocracy, that was it. Menhir sounded like a terrible stratocracy. They were certainly determined. The Menhirans had conjured up enough magic to find her on the other side of the Veil; were they truly that desperate to get to a father she had never met? Surely Menhir wasn't on the losing side of this war? Not with the destruction she had just seen. What else had been destroyed in this world? What else had been lost forever?

Nessa thought about what she knew of Earth's history. In Europe's mad dash for resources, the cultures they destroyed meant nothing. How many cultures were gone here? For what reason? How many good men and women had died in the name of greed? Of pride? So much had been lost without any magic to help it along. The idea made her shudder.

Her head began to pound, her stomach grumbling as the sun sank to the opposite end of the sky. She was panting heavily when Liv finally stopped in a small valley nestled between two green hills. Nessa found her legs quivering even as she stood still, hands clenched into trembling fists.

Gratefully, she positioned herself in the welcome shade of a nearby tree, glancing up at the sunlight dancing through the yellow-green leaves. Small white blooms dotted the limbs forming the canopy above them. The tree's branches bowed like those of a willow tree, but it was far too tall, its branches much sturdier. Even an ancient oak would have grown too wide and tired to hold up such branches. Nessa ran her fingers over the leaves to watch the branches sway.

"There's nothing for it," Liv said suddenly.

"Hmm?"

Nessa watched her friend for a moment. The elf had her arms crossed over her chest, a finger tapping at her lips. Her eyes were distant.

Nessa sank to the ground, her legs applauding in relief as her fingers skimmed over the branches again, and the tree seemed to sigh contently. The leaves were cool under her fingertips, the petals of the blooms soft. Every movement of the branch sent a soothing aroma into the air, similar to jasmine, but spicier.

"Nessa?" Liv looked down at her, an edge Nessa couldn't place in her tone. Her expression softened when the exhausted waitress arched a brow up at her, and she smiled softly at her charge instead. "How are you doing?"

"Honestly?" Nessa's face scrunched up. "I'm exhausted."

She leaned her shoulder against the tree trunk, every muscle in her body melting into jelly and throbbing all at once. Could jelly pulse? She hadn't felt like this since their last hiking trip together, which had lasted two and a half hours longer than expected.

Nessa snorted. "Now I know why you like hiking so much."

"It *is* more difficult without three square meals and a bed," Liv agreed. "I'm afraid even I became accustomed to it."

Nessa rested her head against the bark. The tree wasn't the softest thing, but her head was getting far too heavy. Perhaps it would ease the steady thumping against her temples.

It didn't.

"We are not going to get much farther without supplies," Liv began. "I was hoping to find some in Brandel, but…"

"But it's not there anymore," Nessa finished for her. The other girl's eyebrows jumped as she nodded in Nessa's direction.

"Your hair looks atrocious." Liv adjusted herself to sit behind Nessa. She tapped her shoulder, and Nessa's neck muscles twitched as she raised her head obediently.

"That's what happens when you fall in a river." Nessa was nearly too tired to snark. That was not, however, going to stop her from trying.

"Which would not have happened if you had held on like I told you to."

Nessa closed her eyes as Liv began to finger-comb her hair. With her eyes closed, she could pretend they were back at Liv's apartment. Many a long night had been spent on Liv's floor with mountains of books and blankets surrounding them, a cup of tea never far away. Nessa's pile of dark locks always fell in the way when she read, but she normally became so engrossed in her story that she didn't even realize Liv was playing with her hair until the style was done. If Nessa was given a book, she would happily live in the author's world until she was rudely ripped from the pages.

She focused on the soothing strokes in her hair instead of the insane twist her life had taken, taking first one deep breath, then two. Would she ever experience those soothing times again?

"If my memory serves me correctly, and it always does," Liv said, "there should be a trading outpost just over the next hill."

"Okay." Nessa bit her lower lip and reminded herself not to nod since Liv still had hold of her hair. Right, she was still in crazyland instead of home. Her chest began to ache.

"Nessa, it might be best if you stay here." Liv tied off the end of a long French braid. "You might attract attention."

Nessa glanced down at her Florence and the Machine t-shirt, muddied jeans, and boots.

"And will you? Attract attention?" Nessa asked.

"I can avoid being seen if I wish." Liv patted her shoulder. "I just need you to stay here. Please, just stay out of sight."

The elf's jaw clenched, the hand on Nessa's shoulder a little too tight. Nessa gnawed her lip again, knowing Liv would have a better chance of being discreet alone. She herself knew nothing of this place, the customs, the language. Her temples throbbed harder.

Her mind flicked back to the mercenaries and her blood ran cold. She wouldn't be able hold her own against them. Not without Liv. She didn't want to be left alone, but what choice did she have? She might expose them both if she went with Liv. No, she had to be brave. She could handle this.

"Okay." Nessa nodded. They weren't going to get much farther without provisions. This was the smart thing to do.

…Yeah, the smart thing.

"Nessa…"

"Really, Liv? Where would I go?" Nessa flung her hands out, sounding a little panicked. "Mordor?"

Liv eyed her sideways.

"Nessa…" Her friend sounded older and more tired than Nessa had ever heard her, and Nessa softened ruefully.

"Really, Liv. I'll be here. I promise."

This whole world was strange, and the only thing Nessa knew for sure was that it was dangerous. If she wanted to survive, sticking with Liv was the only smart thing to do, so she'd do it. Well, there were always the mercenaries, but Nessa suspected they probably wouldn't be interested in seeing her home safely…or alive.

"Okay," Liv agreed. "Stay out of sight. Do not say anything to anyone, and most importantly, do not tell anyone your name. Names have power here." She paused, as if to continue on the subject, but didn't. "I will be back in a few hours."

Liv turned and dashed off before she could make a different decision. Nessa saw her turn back a few times, likely trying make sure the other girl was still sitting under the would-be willow tree, but Nessa only sighed heavily, cradling her head in her hands. Her aching temples cheered. What in the world was she going to do now?

She rested her back against the tree in defeat, a flood of emotions crashing into her chest. Fear sat heavy in her lungs while anxiety tore through her mind. Exhaustion slammed into her consciousness and her body, a constant, harsh sting pressing behind her eyes. All the heat drained out of her toes, and she finally let herself shake.

There was no one to hold it together for, not now.

She looked down at her mud-covered jeans. Her cardigan wasn't in much better shape, so she tore it off in frustration. She didn't need it anymore, she supposed; it was warm here, maybe even spring from all the odd flowers she could see.

Placing the garment in her lap, she inspected it for damage, finding a hole in the sleeve right by the elbow. She stuck a finger through the hole, wiggling it, and felt her heart drop out of her chest, though she wasn't sure why. It was just a sweater. She'd gotten it on a shopping trip with her adoptive mom.

Her adoptive mom…what did Lilly Everette think had happened to her? Or Albert? Surely someone had told them about their daughter being carried off by murderers. They would be heartbroken. And she didn't have any way to tell them she was alive and safe. Well, moderately safe, anyway. Would she ever see them again?

She hugged the cardigan as she drew her knees up close to her chest, lowering her head to become a small ball. The knit smelled like sweat, river water and sunlight; she couldn't make out the smell of her detergent anymore. She used the same soap Lilly did so her clothes would always smell like home.

Now, home had never felt further away.

A desperate desire for her mother slammed into her chest, and her breath came in shuddering gasps, her eyes closed tightly against the burn. She wanted her mom to hug her and stroke her hair. She craved the smell of her perfume.

She would never have that safety again.

She cried until she knew no more, before finally falling into an exhausted sleep.

***

"Nessa!"

A squeak escaped the startled girl and she scrambled to sit up, eyes wide and heart racing.

Silhouetted against the golden light was Liv, smiling down at her, and Nessa felt her heart settle as she shifted to rest her shoulder against the tree. Yawning, she rubbed her eyes. Now that the terror was over, she could calmly shake off sleep.

"Yeah?"

Liv attempted to hide her smile and failed. "Did you rest well?"

"Uh, not really." Nessa rubbed the side of her slightly aching head. "I didn't mean to fall asleep."

The light had shifted from honeyed yellow to amber and gold, the sun just barely peeking over the horizon through the leafy canopy. The air had turned from humid to cool, and the branches above her head swayed gently in the breeze. It was beautiful, but it would have been more so if the threat of kidnapping wasn't looming over her head.

Nessa blinked one more time to ensure she wasn't seeing things. Liv looked different. Her modern clothes were gone, replaced with a green shirt, tall boots and breeches. Brown leather armor covered her torso, with matching bracers on her forearms. She had a large bag flung over her shoulder, while a bow and a full quiver of arrows rested on her back; the perfect image of an elvish warrior. She set the bag beside Nessa and knelt next to her.

"You needed the rest. It has been an…" Liv searched for the right words. "…Unusual day."

"Has it only been a day?"

Nessa rolled her neck. It felt like a lifetime since she'd last gone to work at the coffee shop. Had that only been yesterday? Or was it technically this morning? It felt like a week.

She wondered if anyone had told her adoptive parents where she'd gone. But of course, they couldn't have. And what about Ollie and Maria? Were they okay? No, she couldn't think about that now.

"Eat." Liv put a large block of cheese into Nessa's hand. "You will feel better."

Nessa heard her stomach growl greedily. She didn't hesitate. The cheese was simply there one moment and gone the next.

Liv laughed a little. "Did you even taste it?"

"Yesh." The food in Nessa's mouth hindered her speech, and she swallowed. "It's good."

She looked down at the single bit of cheese left in her hand. How had she eaten so much, so quickly?

Oh no! Was she supposed to share? Was that supposed to last the week? She felt a blush creep over her cheeks. "Sorry. I, um…do you want the rest?"

"I already ate." Liv smiled, pulling something from her bag that might have been an apple, if not for the dark plum color. A small knife appeared in her hand with a little twirl.

"I got us some supplies, clothes," Liv told her as she split the fruit in two with the blade and handed half to Nessa. "And a little water. I also sent a message to some friends I should have nearby. They will help us get you somewhere safe."

The fruit tasted sweet and crisp, and Nessa licked the juice from her lips. Liv cut a small slice from her half, using the flat of her blade to slide it into her mouth. Nessa studied her for a moment. Never mind where that little knife had come from. She tried to spot any others Liv might have on her, but wasn't particularly surprised when she couldn't see any.

"How did you manage to get all that?" Nessa arched a brow at her friend.

"You do not need to worry about that."

Liv rummaged in her pack and started to pull out various garments. There was a white shirt, dark breeches, some kind of dark blue leather bundle, and a pair of boots. Nessa felt her mouth go dry as the pile increased.

Liv tossed Nessa a silver coin on a black cord. Nessa made a swipe to catch it, missed, and watched it land in her lap before picking it up and turning the medallion over to let it catch the light. The coin had strange markings all over it. They weren't Anglo-Saxon runes, or even alchemy symbols, but hard, sharp, and straight lines, with a few perfect circles overlapping the symbols.

"Put that on. Do not ever remove it," Liv instructed.

"What is it?"

"Peace of mind."

Nessa glanced uncertainly at Liv, whose expression had turned serious. She draped the coin around her neck, her eyes falling back to the colorful heap beside her. As she pulled it apart, the dark blue bundle revealed itself to be a short cloak with a corset-like vest tumbling out of it. There were two other leather pieces with laces, but Nessa had no idea what they were.

"Um, Liv?" Nessa tried to untangle a small, triangular piece of leathery material, succeeding only in snarling the cords into a bigger knot with her fingers twisted together in the middle. "What is…uh…"

Liv chuckled. "Let me help you."

As Liv untangled her friend, she explained that the material served as a kind of lightweight armor. It was made similarly to Earth leather, but apparently it was made from some massive Avani land creature and not a cow.

The overly large shirt wouldn't sit straight on Nessa's shoulders (though surprisingly, her light purple bra didn't show through the fabric), but the vest helped keep her top in place. She only got stuck in it once, and Liv rescued her by pulling it down hard over her torso to free Nessa's trapped head and arms, before helping her with the laces. The panels came together on the sides and down the front, while the triangular pieces of leather she had inspected earlier were bracers for her forearms.

"Do you feel like you are at one of those period fairs?" Liv settled herself behind Nessa as the other girl fought with the laces on her boots.

"Sort of."

Liv began to comb Nessa's hair with her fingers, and Nessa shut her eyes for half a moment. Like this, she could just pretend they were at one of their many sleepovers, surrounded by pillows and blankets on Liv's floor. It was a tempting illusion.

Liv twisted a pale blue ribbon into Nessa's dark locks, using it to tie off the end of an intricate braid, and Nessa glanced down at the armor. It was strong and stiff, but what had she been expecting? It was armor, not a t-shirt. She tried to stretch her back and felt very little give.

"How am I supposed to breathe in this thing?"

"It is better than a true corset," Liv replied flatly.

Nessa let out a despairing puff of air. She didn't even want to think about having to wear one of those. Casting a longing glance at her discarded jeans and tee, she wrapped her mother's scarf around her neck. She knew it was silly. If she wore her old clothes, she would stick out like a sore thumb. The Menhirans would spot her from a mile away.

Liv squeezed her shoulder. "We can take them with us."

Nessa leaned gently against her friend, feeling suddenly exhausted.

"No," she sighed mournfully. Near-death experiences apparently made her practical. "It'll just be one more thing to carry."

"We will take them with us."

And that was the end of the discussion.

Nessa plucked one of the white blooms from the tree and twirled it between her fingers as she studied it, frowning. She didn't feel like herself anymore. She was *there*, but it wasn't her, not really. It was some other girl in her head. One who also had no idea what to do. New worlds, long and costly wars, magic, elves.

Just keep going. If she stopped, she'd have to think about everything that had happened. So she couldn't stop. Not now, anyway.

Her stomach suddenly twisted into a tight knot, and her head shot up to look at Liv, who stood as soon as she saw Nessa move. Nessa wanted to jump up, but she felt like she'd lose everything in her stomach if she did.

"Something is wrong," Liv stated.

Deep, angry voices reached them from over the hill. Nessa didn't know what they were saying, but she recognized the language of Menhir. Ice crept through her bloodstream. How had they gotten so close, so fast?

Liv helped Nessa scramble to her feet. The voices grew louder.

"*Come on!*" Liv yell-whispered. "*Run!*"

The two girls dashed into the setting sun.

Chapter Seven

Great First Impressions Rarely Involve a Stick

The path quickly grew narrow and steep under Nessa's feet, and she stumbled a few times, her legs screaming at her to stop and rest. Her arms pumped, her lungs ached, and her heart cried with every beat. Still, she kept going, her limbs forgetting their quaking when she moved, though they felt heavier than ever. She could barely force herself to move fast enough, her body fighting against her will for survival — but finally, her will began to win out and she started making progress.

Liv kept glancing over her shoulder, a move Nessa had no courage for. She didn't want to see how much ground they must be losing. Suddenly, the elf snatched hold of Nessa's arm, yanking hard on the frightened girl, and Nessa nearly toppled over as an arrow went wide over her head. She didn't even have the air to squeak.

Liv pulled her into the thick mass of trees, and they dodged between the trunks and patches of light, leaping over fallen logs. Nessa slid on the loose dirt, wobbling as she settled back into a sprint. The air tasted hot in her mouth, and she panted as they made their way up the steep ground, her calves burning with every step. She ground her teeth against the pain and pushed on.

From the peak, there was only a sharp and unsteady path down, which proved to be no path at all. Nessa swallowed, taking only a beat to catch her breath. *Don't think. Just move.* She steeled herself and went for it, chasing after the more athletic Liv.

Two steps down, the ground gave way, and Nessa swallowed a shriek. She teetered as she slid, arms thrown out for balance she couldn't seem to find and heart stuttering every time she wobbled. Small stones and branches whacked and bounced painfully against her ankles as they followed the pair down into the valley, and Liv's hand clamped down on Nessa's shoulder, steadying her. Thankfully, it was enough. Nessa swallowed down a curse she had no air for when she finally hit the base of the incline.

Gasping for breath, Nessa looked up the hill. She didn't see anyone, but she could still hear them. Would the Menhirans follow them down? Her stomach clenched and heaved. Yes, of course they would, but maybe not the way she and Liv had come. Was there another way down? Nessa's body groaned at the idea of moving another inch; her mouth tasted acrid, and spitting didn't help. Her speeding heart, however, was ready to run.

Suddenly, Liv shook her shoulder, pointing down into the valley.

"Go. Run!" she ordered.

Nessa, however, had never been one to follow orders blindly. Instead, she stared at her friend. "What about you?"

"I told you to run!" Liv's already-cold voice turned frigid, her words coming fast and crisp; a torrent of waves on sharp rocks. "There is an estate half a day's walk to the south along this path. Once you reach the stream, head due east. Ask for Belara. I will meet you there."

Nessa's thrashing heart jumped into her throat and stayed there. She knew Liv had proven herself to be a force to be reckoned with, but this? What if there were too many? What if they were both taken? The Bear flashed across her mind's eye; she could still see the happy gleam in the mercenary's eye as he threw Ollie into the glass counter.

She clenched trembling fingers into clammy palms. Mercy did not occur to men like that.

"Liv…"

"Go!" Liv's eyes widened as a cutting edge crept into her command. She drew her bow.

Nessa shuddered, the world spinning about her head, and squeezed her eyes closed for a moment. She didn't want to be frightened. She didn't, but she very much was. She needed to stop shaking.

Stop. Shaking.

Finally, she bolted down the path, leaving Liv behind.

Nessa couldn't let herself think twice and turn back. She felt like such a coward. No, she had followed orders. Liv was going to be all right. She'd fought six mercenaries by herself and hadn't even broken a sweat.

What was her limit? Ten? Twenty? Could Liv handle an entire legion of Menhiran solders by herself? What would happen when they got to Nessa?

She'd escaped last time by pure luck. She knew if Liv hadn't been there, she'd be dead. Maybe their luck had just run out.

Her legs grew heavier, weighed down by the piles of leaves and debris that littered the ground, her body resisting her every movement. Each step proved a fight, every breath came with a fresh ache. Her lungs caught fire, but she kept going, her heart feeling like it had escaped her ribs to rattle around her ears. If those men made it through Liv, she didn't stand a chance. She would be taken, maybe even killed. She couldn't do anything to help Liv. She couldn't even help herself.

So she ran.

Nessa yelped as the ground abruptly disappeared from beneath her unsteady feet, her shoulder colliding hard with the dirt. Stars flashed behind her eyelids.

Breathless, she rolled across the ground until she finally settled onto all fours, gasping. She had to get to her feet. Her knees shuddered as she pressed her hands into the muck to force herself up.

The sound of shouting male voices reached her ears, and Nessa spun to look behind her. All she saw were trees, which seemed to sway along with her.

"Liv…"

What had they done to Liv? She wanted to yell for her friend to see if she was alright, if she was going to be okay, but she stopped short, swallowing her cries. Yelling would only give her away. The voices were so close.

She shook fearfully, but no, she couldn't do that. Before she realized it, she was running again, her aches and fatigue forgotten. She had to stay away from the Menhirans. Stay free and safe. Get home.

Get. Home.

Nessa heard a shout, this time closer than before, so she poured on all the speed she had left. Eventually, she jumped off the path to run alongside it, ducking and dodging behind the trees as the ground rose and fell haphazardly, making her stumble. She wiped away the sweat dripping into her eyes, bouncing off the trees to stay upright as she had once bounced between tables at the coffeeshop. The trees at least gave her someplace to hide, but the terrain was forcing her to move more carefully.

The voices grew louder.

Nessa swiped up a fallen branch as she sped by. It was no sword, but it was better than nothing. A kid with a slingshot had brought down Goliath, after all. Who knew what a feral waitress with a stick could do?

She could hear the hurried footfalls gaining on her. In terror, she glanced over her shoulder to see dark forms suddenly appearing from behind the trees. They were almost on her.

Nessa collided hard with something solid.

She stumbled back with a squeak, but managed to stay on her feet. A tall, lithe man with red-blonde hair was standing before her. At her appearance, he looked confused, then shocked, blinking at Nessa as she blinked back at him.

In a flash, his bow was up and drawn, the arrow-tip pointed directly at Nessa's face. Panicking, she swung her mighty stick hard, and the branch collided with his head with an almighty *THWACK!* The man fell to the ground with what sounded like a curse.

A sharp word cut through the air, and she screamed as someone pulled her behind a large tree, her back slamming into a hard chest. She tried to struggle, but whoever held her quickly covered her mouth and pushed them both down to their knees until Nessa was enveloped entirely.

"Bryn!" a deep baritone voice called, right in her ear.

The man she'd struck spun to a kneeling position, his bow poised to fire. Three arrows flew before she could even blink.

Just like that, three Menhiran soldiers fell.

The arms around her disappeared, and she stumbled forward. She came out swinging her stick with a white-knuckle grip, spinning first to point the stick at the man she'd collided with, then the one with the bow, then back again. Who was going to come at her first?

The flimsy weapon trembled in her too-tight grip.

"Move!" the archer commanded, arrow aimed right at her.

No, not at her. Past her.

Oh, right.

Nessa fell to her knees as she spun, swinging the stick around as hard as she could. The blow went wide, the wood colliding with a Menhiran soldier's knees with a loud, agonizing *crack*. He spat a curse as he fell, reaching for Nessa, but she was too quick. She brought the stick down hard on his head as he swore at her again, and her heel collided with his face as she let out a little scream, more of terror than battle rage. Two arrows flew into his back, and he stopped moving.

She kept her eyes on the body, holding her stick aloft like Excalibur as the wood shuddered in her hands. The air she was gulping tasted of dirt, sweat and blood, but she gasped it down anyway, staring at the unmoving soldier. She half expected him to wake, to come for her again. If she saw even the smallest twitch, she would swing. Hard.

Someone grabbed her and hoisted her to her feet.

"Don't!" Nessa screamed in panic.

"Calm, little one."

The bowman turned Nessa to face him, but she was already swinging for the fences. The stick *thwack*ed him in the face.

"Ouch!"

He rubbed at his temple as Nessa, panicked and wild, wound up again, ready to give him another good whack — but a hand caught the stick mid-swing. It was the man with the baritone voice. He was taller than her, with dark hair and thick scruff on his chin and jaw.

"Whoa, calm down. We won't hurt you."

Nessa trembled as she yanked the stick from his grip, and the man looked at her, his brow furrowed as if he was wondering if he'd left the stove on. Nessa, defiant, met his gaze. Finally, he actually *saw* her, and gasped.

"Sweet Arelen!"

Nessa bravely held her stick aloft, trembling as the man took a step toward her.

"Who—"

"Don't come any closer!" She took a swipe with her wooden weapon. It did nothing except make a very impressive *whoosh*ing noise.

Light footsteps reached their ears and Nessa spun around, then back so she could keep the men in her sights. The first man drew his bow, and a sword flashed in the other man's hand. Wordlessly, they both closed ranks in front of Nessa.

Liv appeared at the top of the hill.

Nessa felt her shoulders drop and suddenly, her limbs couldn't hold her up any longer. She slumped, staying upright only by the grace of her trusty stick. She felt like jelly, but alive, and relieved. She had never seen Liv smile the way she was now: open, happy, and completely unguarded.

Then, everything happened all at once.

A streak of white-blonde flashed before Nessa's nose, a high-pitched squeal echoing through the air. It took Nessa a moment to realize that the earsplitting noise had come from Liv, as her friend tackled the bowman in a ferocious hug. He dropped his bow, spilling arrows onto the ground to catch her, then the sight before him seemed to finally catch up to his brain and he burst into bright, bubbling laughter. The archer crushed Liv to him, lifting her off her feet, and spun her around like a helicopter, speaking rapidly in a language that flowed like crystal water. Liv shone like a star as he spun her around and around and around.

Nessa could only blink at the pair.

The dark-haired man raced over and wrapped both of them up in a tight hug, the crystalline language tripping from his excited lips like a child attempting a rapid tap dance they didn't quite know. The trio hopped up and down, everyone talking over each other at once.

Nessa stared in astonishment. She had never seen Liv 'hop' before. Liv was not the kind of the person to 'hop.' It was something Nessa had assumed Liv just didn't do. It was a little like the time Albert Everette, literature professor, with his thinning hairline and slight paunch, had gone roller-skating, elbow pads and all, on disco night. Not only that, but he had done it backwards. The questionable shorts he'd worn were burned by Lilly Everette shortly after the incident.

The two males spoke over each other, each growing louder in an attempt to gain dominance. Liv's hands fluttered around her head, and she said something with a laugh. The dark-haired man blushed slightly and brushed at the gray at his temples, not meeting her eyes. Liv rubbed his head affectionately, though the man had to lean down to let her.

Nessa gawked. Liv must have gone completely mad. Nessa had seen Liv animated before, but this was different. The sense of familiarity between the three of them left Nessa realizing that she hardly knew Liv at all, and Avani suddenly felt like a very lonely place.

Amidst all the chatter, Nessa suddenly heard her name.

The two males abruptly stopped talking. In tandem, their heads popped up and swiveled to look at her, not dissimilarly to prairie dogs — and their expressions were just as blank. Their wide eyes fell on Nessa and stayed there.

Nessa's cheeks grew hot. She looked at them, then at Liv, then back at them again. Sheepishly, she held the stick behind her back and let it drop to the ground, the weight of their eyes forcing hers to her feet.

Nessa had been to many parties with a friend only to discover the friend she'd come with was the only person she knew. She would stay close to them all night, desperate not to make a fool of herself, or worse, be forced to make small talk with the terror that was new people. This felt exactly like that, except her friend had gone and left her to the wilds.

"Uh…" she began eloquently.

Suddenly, the archer rushed straight at her, and Nessa squeaked in surprise, only to be scooped up into a tight bear hug.

"Welcome back!" He spun her around, chuckling happily. "Look at you, love! You're huge! In a good way, of course. You barely passed as a paperweight last time I saw you, and now look at you!"

Nessa tried to get her thoughts together, feeling it would help if the world would stop spinning and she didn't have to fight to keep her lunch in her stomach. Still, she couldn't be rude.

"Uh, can—can you put me down, please?" she asked. "The spinning…"

"Oh, right."

He gently placed her back on the ground with a guilty half-grin as Nessa blinked, grateful to be back on solid earth. And she would be even more so if it would just quit wobbling. She braced her hands on her knees and closed her eyes.

"Thank you."

"Sorry about that, love."

"I'm fine."

She wasn't.

"Be gentle with her," Liv scolded, rubbing calming circles on Nessa's back. "You are an acquired taste, after all."

"Okay." Nessa swallowed and straightened. The earth had settled and so had she. "What, exactly, is going on here?"

Who were these men? She felt like a cat who'd been given a Swedish Fish instead of a real one. Things were familiar, but something was very different and very off and she wasn't sure if she liked it and if she got any hotter, things were bound to get sticky.

Liv made the introductions. "Nessa, this is Bryn. My brother."

All the color drained from Nessa's face, and her jaw fell open as her hands flew over her mouth. Oh no! No, no, no!

"I hit your brother in the face with a stick!"

...Were the words she had not actually meant to say.

"Really?" Liv's face broke out in a wide grin.

"Twice," Bryn confirmed proudly.

"Thank Vaeril!" Liv laughed. "You probably deserved it."

"I have never done anything wrong ever in my life," vowed the elf who had surely done plenty wrong before breakfast today.

"Liar," accused the man behind him, who looked as though he already had the list prepared.

Bryn waved off the other man's words with an airy gesture as Nessa hid her face in her hands. Perhaps the ground could just open up and swallow her whole; maybe then she could successfully hide her blush. Gods and angels, what a terrible first impression! She finally met someone Liv cared about, her family no less, and what had she done? Hit him with a stick. Who knew what Bryn thought of her now? Probably that she was some mad, stick-happy freak.

Don't trust her! Especially not with a stick. She groaned mentally.

"Liv?" the dark-haired man asked, and Nessa saw him incline his head toward the side of the path, his eyes flitting between her and Liv. Liv patted Nessa's shoulder and followed him off to the treeline.

They leaned in, heads close as they spoke, their hushed, tense voices flying over one another. Liv stood proud and calm, while the man looked to be having an existential crisis.

"Oh, don't mind them, love." Bryn playfully nudged her shoulder, and Nessa blinked at the familiar gesture. She had just met him, plus she'd assaulted him with a piece of dead tree. Twice. How could he possibly be so cheerful?

Well, his sister *had* finally returned after being gone for nearly twenty years. And strangely, he seemed to genuinely like Nessa too. Though she had no idea why.

"Liv has decades worth of lectures to get through. She'll come up for air soon."

"I'm sorry I hit you," Nessa supplied sheepishly, unable meet his eyes as she said it. Her ears burned hotly.

"Don't be!" Bryn flashed her a proud grin. "You have a wonderful swing, *lebiet*."

"Li—what?"

"It means little bird," he explained. "You looked like one when you were a baby. Now, well, now you look like your mother."

Her chest tightened at the thought of her mother; she'd always imagined what the woman who birthed her might be like. The longstanding ache tingled like an old scar and the familiar questions tasted stale on her tongue. As usual, she swallowed them down, despising the taste.

She fell silent, her eyes turning back to Liv and the dark-haired man. He was running his hands down his face, Liv looking as though she had little sympathy for his plight. Apparently, the lecture was not going well for him.

Liv flicked the man on the arm, hard, and Nessa flinched just watching it. The dark-haired man pursed his lips, his expression set as if he were going into battle, and Liv, appearing displeased, shoved him toward Bryn and Nessa. He stumbled and glared at Liv, who waved him on, unbothered.

"Uh…" The dark-haired man winced. "Hello."

Nessa chewed the inside of her lip until she tasted blood. The man was staring at her so intently she felt the pressure of it on her chest. He eyed her searchingly, taking her in with an expression caught somewhere between hope, awe, and absolute terror.

"Dagorn. House of Callei." He bowed then, his fist over his heart. "Nessa, I…I never thought I'd see you again."

Nessa flushed, her eyes flicking to Liv for much needed reassurance, but Liv gave her none, leaving her to awkwardly flounder in the seas of uncertainty.

"Um." Her breath caught in her throat. What was wrong? Why was her heart pounding? "I'm sorry, but I don't know who you are."

Or who you are to me, she thought. Dagorn gave her a smile that seemed so sad, it shattered her heart.

"That's all right," he told her gently — and strangely, it was. "You were so small when your mother…" He choked on his words, swallowed, and powered on. "When your mother and I sent you through the Veil. I don't expect…"

Your mother and I.

Nessa blinked at the man before her, not hearing a word as he continued to speak. Him? *Him?*

Her stomach turned cold and twisted painfully, her hands going to her knees. It did nothing to ease the acrobatics of her stomach. Each nauseating flip pushed more air from her suddenly-too-small lungs, her vision swimming with heat and salt water.

Your mother and I.

The world tilted below her feet, and everything stopped, off-kilter and silent. All feeling ceased, even as her skin broke out in goosebumps. Heat swirled around her temples, her lungs forgetting their purpose.

Time was a funny thing. Everyone always talked about how strange time could be, but only when a Moment happened. A Moment like finding true love, or a tsunami disaster, or both at the same time. In those storied Moments, time simply stopped, the Moment suspended in time for much, much longer than a simple moment.

Now, Nessa found herself unlucky enough to discover what happened after.

The suspended Moment came crashing down around her ears as air flooded into her lungs too fast, leaving her gasping painfully with the force. A trembling hand flew over her eyes as the sunlight scorched her retinas, and she tasted anxiety, acidic and burning, in the back of her throat.

"Breathe, Ness."

Nessa followed Liv's order only for the air to get stuck on a sob.

"Again."

"L—Liv?" she whispered between heaving, panicky breaths, each wave of lightheadedness pulling her further and further out to sea. A hand found a way to her back, the light pressure anchoring her in place.

"I'm here. It's alright. Just breathe."

Nessa gasped fruitlessly.

Bryn cocked a brow at his sister. "Do you think she'll faint?"

"Bryn!"

"What? I'm very good with swooners."

Nessa's breathing turned shallow and erratic as she devolved into laughter reminiscent of a madwoman. Liv's gentle hand, which had been rubbing large circles on her back, stilled.

"Sorry," Nessa gulped, wiping her eyes as her crazed laughter finally died down. She tried to glance over at Liv and failed. "Your brother is an ass."

Slowly, she righted herself, still wiping at her cheeks, and Liv gave her a proud, gentle smile, a steadying hand still on her shoulder.

"It worked, didn't it?" Bryn gave Nessa a warm grin, but her eyes slid past the smile to Dagorn. He looked pale and stiff as a corpse, except he had too much worry written across his brow. His callused hands were twisting and trembling in a manner that seemed too young for hands so careworn.

Dagorn took a step towards her, then retreated again. "Are you…Nessa, are you alright? I'm—I'm sorry…"

Nessa felt her cheeks heat all over again. Over a decade of imagining this moment, picturing smiles and fear and light and answers and she'd done none of that. In actuality, it was hot and spinning and damp and just a little sickening. She'd always pictured this meeting being cleaner, somehow.

"Yeah," she answered. It was only half a lie. "I'm sorry. I wasn't expecting any of this today."

Nessa's face could have been sunburned, though Dagorn's appeared to be just as red. He rubbed the back of his neck, his shoulders finally collapsing.

"It's going better than I thought it would," he admitted. "Honestly, I expected a lot more shouting."

"I'll shout at both of you if we don't get going." Bryn (as usual, Nessa would learn) destroyed the touching moment completely. "Those scouts will already be missed."

Right. Enemy army. She'd forgotten.

Bryn scooped up his bow and arrows, taking the lead with Liv at his side. Dagorn hovered slightly behind Nessa's shoulder, his hand resting on the hilt of his sword as Nessa trotted into the trees after the elves. Her mind, still alight with questions, couldn't focus on anything better to do.

Bryn considerately slowed his pace once he saw that Nessa had much shorter legs than him. Then again, the only thing with longer legs than Bryn was probably an ostrich.

"How did you manage to find us so quickly?" Liv asked.

"We were at the estate to resupply," Dagorn replied. "Your timing, as always, is remarkable."

Liv flipped her hair. "Always is."

Liv then slipped into that flowing crystal-like language, leaving Nessa's thoughts to whirl a little more. She kept chancing glances at Dagorn. She wasn't sure what she'd been expecting when she pictured her biological father, but it certainly wasn't this. Nessa had thought he'd be more like her adoptive father: balding, a little pot-bellied, possibly bespectacled. Instead, Dagorn had a full head of dark hair and a neatly trimmed beard. Even so, something about him made him appear to be in a perpetual state of unkempt.

If he had been just a little younger, he would have made the perfect romantic hero, with his strong build and sharp jaw. Each step he took spoke of confidence and controlled power. Nessa could tell his nose had been broken a time or two, but it only added to his rough-and-tumble air.

She had clearly inherited none of that, neither the sureness of self nor the jawline. Their hair was a similar color, but it seemed like that was where the physical similarities ended.

Liv tossed a casual comment back to Dagorn, who chuckled and sent back a nervous reply. Bryn, with a mischievous grin, threw in a comment of his own, and the three of them laughed. Dagorn's eyes glittered when he laughed.

Nessa had gotten his blue eyes.

She wasn't sure how she felt about that yet.

Dagorn was watching her too, she saw, and Nessa's hands found the end of her braid, her fingers flying faster than the questions in her mind. She had so many, they clogged up her throat trying to all get out at once, so nothing emerged. The silence between them deepened.

"What do you think of Avani?" Dagorn asked her gently.

"It's…uh…different." One corner of Nessa's lips twitched up. "There's no magic on Earth. Well, that we know of."

Was this starting off easy? Small? Nothing about this felt small. The only thing that was small in the world was Nessa herself. After nearly twenty years, she was finally talking to her birth father. He was right there, within arm's reach, and she could think of nothing to say.

"I'm afraid you haven't exactly seen the best of it," Dagorn said.

"Been a bit busy not getting killed," she quipped.

"That's understandable."

"I have a lot of questions," Nessa began, though she still couldn't think of one.

"Take your time." He attempted to give her an encouraging smile. "I have a few of my own, though they all seem to have left me at the moment."

The little puff of air that left Nessa's lips might have been mistaken for a laugh if one was being exceptionally optimistic. She glanced at Liv, then Dagorn, then back to Liv.

"Can I ask? How do you know Liv?"

Nessa mentally cringed, deciding then and there that she was breaking off her friendship with her brain. It was the only logical choice since they appeared to no longer be speaking to one another.

"I am a Guard, like Liv," Dagorn answered. "She and Bryn assisted with my training and have known me since boyhood — unfortunately."

Nessa let out a heavy sigh, glancing up at Dagorn and the streaks of gray at his temples. How old *was* Liv? If she'd helped train Dagorn, she certainly wasn't in her early twenties. After all, she was an *elf.* She could be thousands of years old! Nessa shoved that idea back. She didn't have the strength to consider that right now.

"Oh."

"We were surprised to hear that you'd both returned." Dagorn bit his lower lip, searching for the right words. "I admit, I am very happy to see you again. I always wondered…" He trailed off, eyes gazing into the past. "…And you were so small."

"I'm still kind of small." Nessa had to acknowledge that she was the shortest of their party; the top of her head only reached Liv's temple and Dagorn was half a head taller than Liv. Bryn, of course, towered over them all. Nessa could have asked him how the weather was up there.

Dagorn chuckled. "Not that small."

"Was I even supposed to come back?"

A pit had opened up in Nessa's stomach. Dagorn chewed his lower lip for longer than she liked before answering.

"If the war finally ended, Liv was to give you a choice: to return with her or remain where your life was." Dagorn's throat bobbed. "I hoped you would choose to return, but I suspect these particular circumstances were, well, less than ideal."

Less than ideal. Nessa would call an attempted kidnapping less than ideal, yes. Would she ever have come back if that hadn't happened? Would Liv? This war sounded like it had already dragged on for decades. What were the chances of it ending in Nessa's lifetime? Her back went rigid when she thought of Jon Snow's evil twin, how he had gotten her here. Was this where Menhir *really* wanted her? Her hot face grew cold.

"What's the matter?" Dagorn's hand flew to the hilt of his sword again. "What happened? What is it?"

"Uh…" Nessa felt her chest tighten, her heart beginning to pound against her ribs. She took a deep breath, but it didn't help. The words kept slipping off her tongue. "It's nothing. Just, how I got here, found out about all this, was a little, uh, traumatic. I was at work and then this mercenary showed up and…uh…"

She couldn't get any more words out, but she swallowed hard and tried again. "Maybe I should let Liv explain it. She might understand it better."

Dagorn's brows knitted together as he looked her over. "Are you alright?"

"Oh! I'm fine!" She was not. "Liv scared the hell out of me, but I'm fine."

"You are in one piece," Liv defended herself. "I did what I had to."

"I'd never seen anyone pull six knives out of thin air before, okay? While being held upside down," Nessa shot back.

"Liv?" Dagorn's suntanned face grew pale.

Liv answered in that strange fluid language, Nessa's name peppered in amongst the unfamiliar words. She sounded as lax as a dog in a sun patch. Dagorn replied in a slightly manic manner, and Bryn cut in over him, clearly holding back laughter.

Dagorn's face grew even paler, and there was some back and forth as he made a few wild gestures. Liv remained perfectly calm while Bryn actually looked shocked at a few parts. At least, Nessa thought so. His eyebrows rose slightly, but that was the only real indication.

After a few moments, Dagorn let out a long puff of air and ran a hand over his hair, his shoulders slumped in defeat. Nessa looked up to see him trying to smile at her, but the expression looked more exhausted than genuine.

"It sounds like quite an adventure."

"What language are you speaking?" Nessa asked. She had decided changing the subject might be a better idea. All thoughts of Menhir made her stomach twist and her chest hurt.

She tried to think of home, but her chest grew tighter, her eyes burning. She hated both feelings, so she decided to avoid the subject altogether. Dagorn currently looked as bad as she felt, so it was perhaps wiser to simply change the topic.

"It's known as Vaerin, the language of the elves."

"Vaerin." Nessa tried the word out on her lips. It flowed easily like clean water. "Do all elves speak it or just a few?"

"Liv and Bryn know the history better than I do," Dagorn admitted. "Vaerin is the main language spoken in Kirivicl, the only elvish settlement to survive Menhir's advances. There are other dialects, of course, but it's the most common."

Nessa shook her head. "You're not an elf."

"Well spotted."

Nessa's lips twitched upward at Dagorn's teasing grin. "But you speak Vaerin?"

"Yes." Dagorn's smile only grew. "My mentor ensured I had a proper education."

"My parents did that too." Nessa shrugged to ease the ache in her chest. She'd been gone only two days. Two days and it already hurt this much? Would that twinge ever go away, or at least ease? What if it only got worse? She refused to follow her thoughts down that particular rabbit hole. "Though I don't think French will help me here."

"Is that a language?"

Nessa snorted. Right, there was no need for French without a France. Her spirits sank a little lower into her stomach.

"Thank you for proving my point."

"I'm sorry," Dagorn offered. "I didn't mean to offend."

"You didn't."

Was everything she'd ever learned now obsolete? She didn't even know the powerful kingdoms here, or the main religions. What was whatever she was speaking now even called? It definitely wouldn't be called English; there was no England in Avani, just like there was no France. Everything was different now. No indoor plumbing, no Chinese food, no more soda…

She was growing desperate. "Do you have coffee here?"

"Something like it," Liv answered over her shoulder.

"Oh, thank God."

Nessa almost fell over in relief. She would take her victories where she could get them, and coffee was at least a start. Heck, at this point, she would take three square meals in one day as a luxury. A bed wouldn't be a bad idea, either.

"Were you happy? Back on Earth?" Dagorn's quiet voice cut through her thoughts.

"Yeah," Nessa answered wistfully. "I was going to school…university? What do you call it here?"

"University," he supplied with a nod. "What were you studying?"

"Literature. I love reading so it seemed like a good fit." The words were tinged with longing for her lost life. "I was going to specialize in English Literature and hopefully get a teaching position at a college on the coast… I was working, too. It wasn't anything special, I was just a waitress, but…"

Nessa's throat swelled closed. She thought of Maria and Ollie, who had been so kind and loyal. They had only known her a few months, but they still put themselves in harm's way for her. In her mind's eye, she could see the blood seeping across the tile floor as the panicked screaming echoed in her memory. Grief crashed into her chest.

She'd lost everything.

The thought slammed into her hard and fast, nearly knocking her off her feet. Gone. Everything she knew was gone.

Ice enveloped her lungs, the world growing dimmer and dimmer until she could only see a small pinprick of watery light. A little hiccup escaped her mouth as her eyes burned. She blinked rapidly and came to a sudden halt.

Air, she needed air. She couldn't breathe!

"Nessa?" Dagorn put a hand on her shoulder, his brows knitting together.

Focus on the contact. Her family was lost to her. She had to focus on Dagorn's hand. Her father's hand. It was large and heavy and gently rubbing her back.

The slight breeze cooled her hot face. *Breathe.* The air smelled like moss, dirt, and wood. Her mouth tasted dry.

"I'm okay." Distraught, she waved his hand away, telling herself to just keep breathing. It was okay. She was okay. She inhaled, counting to four, held for seven and exhaled to eight. After two repetitions, she could see the world again.

The grass below her was greener than anything she'd ever seen. The tips came to slight points, fading to a lighter shade of emerald. She resisted the urge to touch it.

Liv moved to Nessa but stopped when Nessa held up a hand. Taking a deep breath, she forced a smile that was more exhaustion than ease.

"Sorry. It's been a long couple of days."

Dagorn gently rubbed her back, and Nessa found she didn't mind. It reminded her of her adoptive father. Albert had done the same when she was little, and terrified of the lightning outside. It wasn't the same, but it was close enough.

Dagorn's voice sounded equally gentle and unhappy. "I can only imagine."

"You have us now," Bryn added with a carefree grin. "We'll keep you safe."

Her lips twitched upward at her new friend's words. "Unless I piss off Liv."

Bryn grinned knowingly.

"She could take us all," he agreed solemnly, his eyes crinkling slightly at the corners.

Nessa's eyes fell to Bryn's. His intense blue eyes were soft, something shining in them that she couldn't place, and she believed him. She was safe with this ragtag group of Guards.

Her breath came just a little easier.

"Blades are faster than arrows," Liv called back, preening like a peacock to make Nessa smile. It only worked a little.

"Not by much," Dagorn pointed out.

Liv waved a hand like the queen she was. "You're just a sore loser."

Nessa's melancholy mood had lifted enough for her shoulders to relax. It wasn't much, but it was something. How strange that joking around about weaponry had helped her to feel better.

This had been a very strange week.

Nessa followed the Guards down the leaf-covered path, and Liv, Bryn and Dagorn kept her talking. Dagorn wanted to know everything from her favorite color (blue) to what her adoptive parents had been like (wonderful), and Nessa found it easier to answer than to ask. She told him of her adoptive mother, a woman whose patience had been constantly tested by teaching second grade, and how she had taught Nessa to bake. Saturday mornings were for pancakes and reality television.

It took poor Nessa a long time to explain television to Bryn and Dagorn, and she finally settled on 'moving pictures in a box.' She told them stories of her adoptive father, of the two of them waxing lyrically about Edgar Allan Poe around the campfire and their weekend 'treasure hunts' for lost books.

"Your mother loved to read," Dagorn told her regretfully. "It wasn't uncommon for her to jump between books because she wasn't sure which one she wanted to read first."

"Really?"

Nessa hadn't expected the little flutter in her heart. Her mother. The thought twisted her insides.

"It drove her father mad," Dagorn added, laughing slightly.

"I read like that sometimes." Nessa smiled. "Three or four books at once."

"She does," Liv confirmed, looking annoyed.

Dagorn beamed with pride. "What's a favorite story of yours?"

That particularly dangerous question led to a long moment of silence and intense thought. Finally, she answered, and Bryn requested she tell them the tale, so, somewhat reluctantly, Nessa began to weave the story of a homely creature pulled into an adventure with thirteen dwarves by the will of a wizard.

Bryn didn't care for dwarves much, a sentiment he made clear every time the dwarf leader did something stupid — which was often — while Dagorn was more intrigued by the magic ring. Liv grinned like a loon during the entire tale, interjecting what she could remember from her numerous rereads.

Nessa supplied fifteen voices, including the narrator. She couldn't quite make her bright-toned voice majestic enough for the dwarf king, but no one seemed to mind. Her audience listened, enthralled.

Once the company in her tale had escaped the frying pan and the fire, Bryn forced her to pause, guiding them off the road in the direction Nessa believed the sun was setting. The path quickly grew unstable and overgrown; in fact, there didn't seem to be a path at all. She had to focus on her footing instead of her story, but promised, after much lamenting from Bryn and Dagorn (mostly Bryn), to finish it as soon as she could.

The trees grew thicker and thicker as they journeyed deeper into the forest, and Nessa could feel her spirits wane as the sun set. She didn't much care for the dark at the moment; it held too much she couldn't see. Anything could happen here: trolls, giants, or perhaps even a wild hobbit would appear. Though she wouldn't mind meeting a hobbit.

...She was raving.

"Where are we going?" She spoke instead of following her wandering thoughts.

"The estate." As he spoke, Bryn bent a branch up for her so she didn't whack her head. Nessa glanced up at Liv, who nodded her agreement.

"That's not really an answer," she pointed out.

"Our destination is not exactly someplace that officially exists." Dagorn shrugged, failing to hide his grin. "Not to the outside world, at least."

Liv affectionately nudged Nessa's arm. "Meaning the Menhirans don't know about it."

Nessa relaxed a little. She had never felt so tired before. The closest she had ever come was during midterms, when she hadn't slept in two days despite Liv brewing buckets of chamomile tea and nearly forcing it down her throat. She'd passed out for fourteen hours after her last test.

Now, she felt like she could sleep for a week.

In the dim light, she spied a slight dip in the landscape. Or at least, she thought it was a slight dip until Bryn disappeared. Blinking, she opened her mouth to ask Liv what had happened, but Liv was already gone.

Nessa trotted up to the dip in question to see a long ravine stretching below her. The slope was steep, but Liv was sliding down effortlessly.

Nessa swallowed.

Dagorn appeared at her side. "It's not as bad as it looks."

She didn't believe him. The line between her brows deepened as she considered her options. She could just stay here. No, that wouldn't do. Her best ally was already at the bottom and currently staring expectantly at her. The only thing to do was slide down, possibly face first, which would then turn into a tumble that would break her neck.

She didn't like that option either.

"I'll help steady you, if you wish." Dagorn held out a hand, and Nessa's brows rose as her wide eyes turned to him. Her father simply smiled.

"Uh, okay."

She glanced over the edge, feeling her stomach twist further into knots.

"Just remember to bend your knees."

Dagorn took hold of her hands as Nessa nodded, and together, they stepped over the edge.

Immediately, they started to slide. Nessa wobbled and Dagorn squeezed her hands, helping her to stay upright. She did her best to bend her knees as the ground dropped below her, keeping her eyes on the base of the ravine. Her knees knocked even as she tried to keep them steady.

Nessa's front foot slipped, her knee giving way, and she squeaked as her heart leapt up in her throat. She nearly tumbled forward, but Dagorn held her up.

"I have you," he told her. "It's alright, I've got you."

Nessa nodded, steadying her nerves.

Relief washed over her when they finally reached the base of the ravine, and she released Dagorn to brush herself off, looking up at Liv with a deep sigh.

"Nice job." Liv patted her arm. "I know you are not in favor of heights."

"They're not my favorite thing," Nessa agreed with a sigh, as she and Liv began to follow Dagorn and Bryn. There was only one direction they could go. The ravine sealed off behind them in a towering wall of mossy rock.

Nessa eyed the darkening sky, snuggling into her adoptive mother's scarf. It smelled like wind and sunshine instead of dryer sheets. Ahead of them, Dagorn and Bryn looked to be having an intense conversation.

"We are almost there," Liv assured her. "Then we can get some sleep, and some food."

"I don't know which one I want first." Nessa tried to smile at her friend. It was weak and shaky, but the attempt was at least made. "I don't think I've ever been this tired."

Liv smiled. "You have done very well." She pursed her lips suddenly, releasing a deep sigh as her eyes traveled from Nessa's head to her toes.

Nessa knew she looked like a complete wreck. She could practically *feel* the weight of the bags under her eyes, and her hair probably would be standing on end if she released it from the braid Liv had made. Not to mention she still got a whiff of river whenever she turned her head the right way. Her mouth tasted of something disgusting, she felt like she had cotton balls stuffed in her cheeks, and the scratch along her collar bone itched fiercely. She was trying to avoid shrugging to prevent it from reopening.

She had definitely seen better days.

Still, she was alive. She would take that gladly.

"I owe you an apology," Liv blurted out.

Nessa blinked.

"Why?"

"I never wanted any of this for you." Liv deflated. "If you were ever to come to Avani again, it was not supposed to be like this, not sudden and terrifying. I was to have prepared you. Menhir was never supposed to know about you. I cannot regret what I have done, but I wish things had been different…"

"Liv!" Nessa's eyebrows shot up as she gave a snort. Sure, killing an entire group of mercenaries and soldiers was a little drastic, but it had kept Nessa out of their hands. There truly wasn't anything else Liv could have done.

How was Liv supposed to know that the Menhirans were coming after her? They had been completely removed from Avani for almost twenty years. It wasn't like Liv could receive word through the portal, or Veil, or whatever that thing had been, and anyway, Dagorn and Bryn, who were *in* Avani, hadn't appeared to know that Menhir had found her. If no one in Avani knew, how could Liv have known a whole world away?

Nessa shook her head at her friend. "I wouldn't be here with you if you had done anything differently."

Judging by the slight tightening of her lips, Liv wasn't wholly convinced.

"Liv, I'm alive because of you," Nessa pointed out. "Don't be so hard on yourself, okay?"

"I am never hard on myself." Liv's tone of voice could have tossed her hair over her shoulder. She tried and failed to hide the slight upward twitch of her lips.

"I'm not going to lie," Nessa began, a hint of a tease to her voice, "this whole situation is insane, as in 'we the jury find the defendant' kind of insane. In reality, I'm probably trapped in a padded room waiting for my daily pudding allowance."

"Has it truly been so horrible?"

Nessa looked up at Bryn and Dagorn. Dagorn glanced back at her, smiling.

Her eyes traveled to the trees up above her, seeing the splashes of pink and violet sky peeking between the dark emerald leaves. Little wildflowers dotted the grass around the massive white trunks, sudden bursts of color in yellow or white bobbing their floral heads as they passed. Nessa held a hand out to brush the lush foliage, the black and green branches soft as velvet. It felt strangely peaceful.

She smiled. "No, not really."

Liv smiled now. "Aside from the mercenaries, swordfighting and constant threat of death?"

"Yeah, besides that."

Liv gave a broad smile and wrapped her arm around Nessa's shoulders, giving her friend a little squeeze.

And the trees parted before them.

Chapter Eight

Sanctuary

They had arrived at the edge of a clearing. Gentle green hills dipped and rose before them, a small stone cottage perched perfectly atop the crest of the foremost incline. Nessa couldn't tell what color it was in the twilight, but the creeping vines around the windows looked either deep green or black against the vibrant golds and violets of the sunset sky. A small creek curved around the front outside a low stone fence, the trickling water twinkling in the evening glow. Moss-covered wooden shingles made up the roof, and a small stone path led toward them from the house, fading into the grass just before it reached their feet.

"It's not much," Dagorn began, sounding uncertain. He let out a deep breath and glanced down at Nessa, whose jaw had dropped.

"It's so cute!" She covered her mouth with her hands.

She turned to see Liv smirking sardonically at her.

"Yes, it is adorable," the elf agreed flatly.

"It is what remains of the great estate of Orestel," Dagorn said. "It used to be a simple hunting cabin on these vast lands. Now, it's the only undamaged building left."

Nessa finally spotted what she had at first assumed was a pile of stone behind the cabin, hidden by a small line of trees. That must have been the stables, at one point. Two hills over, a massive structure loomed, outlined black and square against the setting sun. Upon closer inspection, she noticed windows, and steps, and collapsed pillars, all ornately carved. That must be the manor house.

...Of course it was. She knew that.

How did she know that?

Bryn elbowed Dagorn playfully. “That’s what happens when its lord goes traipsing across Avani in search of adventure, riches and lovely women.”

Dagorn pointed at him reproachfully. “Mias abandoned it first.”

“Who’s that?” Nessa asked.

“The man who raised me.” Dagorn’s face turned thoughtful. “I’ll explain more once you’ve had some rest. I suspect today has already been enough.”

Nessa allowed herself to breathe more easily. She was grateful she didn’t have to worry about one more thing, even if it was just for now.

They reached the small creek well before the light had faded, and Nessa surveyed the stepping stones warily as Dagorn jumped easily from stone to stone, turning to wave her on once he reached the other side. She glanced at Liv, who was grinning like a mischievous older sibling. Nessa gave her a stern glare before turning back to the stones.

She took a careful first leap, the landing turning all her muscles to jelly. Shaking and wobbling, she flung her arms out to try to steady herself, then leapt to the next one, bobbling when her knees buckled under her weight.

Nessa took a deep breath. Her calves screamed at her to stop, but she leapt to the next stone instead, ignoring her understandably whiny muscles. The momentum caused her to stumble forward as she landed, and she slid right up to the edge of the stone. Her arms wheeled around, trying to stop herself, but she had no choice but to jump.

She knew already she wasn’t going to make it.

Suddenly, Dagorn appeared, snatching her up seemingly out of thin air, and she gripped his arms tightly to keep from falling flat on her face. Her body trembled wildly, her hands locked in a death grip.

“Are you alright?” Dagorn’s brow furrowed.

“Yeah,” she answered, sounding only a little breathless. “Just a little tired.”

Well, maybe more than a little.

The lithe Bryn and Liv both crossed in two effortless leaps, of course; Nessa was certain she even spotted pointed toes, ballet-style. She wanted to hit them, but that would have involved things like moving, and effort.

“Stop right there!”

Nessa turned to see a tall, curvy woman approaching from the cottage with a determined stride, a bow and arrow pointed squarely at Bryn’s chest. Dagorn quickly pulled Nessa behind him, and Liv closed ranks as Bryn stepped forward towards the newcomer.

She was the most beautiful woman Nessa had ever seen, with high cheekbones and shining golden eyes, her dark skin practically glowing in the twilight. Even her fingers appeared long and elegant as she held her weapon aloft. Her hair she kept cropped close, but Nessa could make out tight coils of dark hair in the fading light. Even the slightest breeze caused the woman to glisten and shimmer. She could have been made of obsidian dipped in gold dust.

"We come with open hearts and empty quivers…" Bryn began. He clearly meant to continue, but was cut off by a sublime voice.

"Bryn Aeris!" The woman lowered her bow with a hearty laugh. "It's only you. I didn't recognize you without your long hair." She laughed again, and it was lovely. "My Lord Dagorn, are you two not yet wedded?"

"I have better taste than Bryn, Bel."

Nessa held back a snort of laughter, a hand over her mouth, as the woman opened the gate to allow them in. Bryn gave her a little bow before entering, and Dagorn did the same, fist pressed to his chest. The woman gave a small curtsy to each of them as they passed, Liv mimicking Dagorn's bow as she followed.

"Livia of the House of Aeris, at your service."

"Belara Baerin, at yours." The woman gave a nod. "I've heard much about you, Miss Livia. I'm sorry you have the misfortune of being related to that one." She tilted her head in Bryn's direction.

Nessa's eyes fell on Bryn, who was too busy being offended that Dagorn wouldn't take him as a husband to notice the fresh insult. He was currently protesting that he would be an excellent lover, to which Dagorn agreed, but pointed out that he preferred women closer to his own age over ancient elven Guards.

Nessa watched Belara's golden eyes roll to the top of her head before they fell on her. Her beautiful features went slack for a brief moment, but she quickly returned to her previous swagger, her eyebrows shooting up.

"Come on, little one. Don't just stand there gawking."

Nessa jumped, blinking to allow her brain to reset.

"Uh, hi." She approached the gate warily, giving Belara a lopsided smile. Before giving her name, she glanced at Liv, who shook her head slightly.

"I'm Alice…Alice Liddell." It was the first name that popped into her head. Why she'd decided to be the girl who fell down the rabbit hole, she had no idea. She tried awkwardly to bow her head, but suspected she'd managed to mess it up, judging by the smile Belara gave her.

"Belara Baerin, young Miss Alice."

Nessa was a little uncertain about the manner in which Belara said her alias. There was a little too much emphasis to it.

She froze solid when Belara suddenly straightened, flinching away slightly as the woman reached for her. Belara stopped, her hand hovering by Nessa's cheek, and clicked her tongue.

"What have these heathens done to you, poor child? You look like a wildling!"

"Uh…it's Bryn's fault?" Nessa tried with a pained grin.

Belara's head fell back in a full, round laugh, and even Dagorn put a hand over his broad grin, earning him a slight shove from the elf in question. Liv had never looked prouder.

"Oh! We'll get on just fine, dear. Come on in. No one else has arrived, so you'll have the run of the entire Guard's quarters."

As Belara led them into the cottage, they passed gardens bursting with all sorts of colorful fruits, vegetables and greens Nessa had never seen before. The plot of wildflowers bowed as they passed, and she lightly ran the tips of her fingers over the soft violet petals. They almost smelled like gardenias. She could see Dagorn and Liv eyeing the blooms suspiciously.

"When was the last time you saw another Guard?" Dagorn asked Belara.

"About fourteen months ago," she sighed. "No one will venture this far north unless they are on the run south. It's been mostly refugees from Erwani."

Dagorn nodded solemnly. "Our spies believe Menhir will break their treaty with them soon, to take over the trades."

"What?" Liv sounded horrified.

"We have lots to inform you of, Li Li," Bryn said.

"*Li Li?*" Nessa grinned like the cat who got the canary.

"Do not repeat that again."

"Oh, I'm *so* repeating it again."

Bryn smirked. "Don't push her, *lebiet*."

Nessa, sensibly, stuck her tongue out at Liv. Liv, being far more mature than Nessa, responded in kind.

"My lord." Belara cut them off. "What trouble have you gotten into now?"

"How do you mean, Bel?"

"Menhir has doubled the price on your head. Raised it two days ago."

"They always do," Dagorn answered with a shrug.

Belara arched a brow in his direction. "Isn't coming this close to the northern border a huge risk for a wanted man such as yourself? I know it's your land, but your lack of caution…"

"Duty calls the loyal soldier." Bryn grinned as he nudged Dagorn's shoulder. Belara only arched her brow higher.

"What does Elvar want you two knuckleheads to do now?"

Even Liv tilted her head to hear the answer, and Nessa blinked, brushing another flower with her fingertips. Who was Elvar? Belara had said his name strangely, as though she both revered and hated the man. But she didn't think now was a good time to ask.

Dagorn already sounded exasperated. "Fetch Alaron. We are in dire need of his assistance and advice, especially at Galidel. The old fortress is not as sturdy as it used to be."

Belara laughed again, shaking her head. "Good luck. I wasn't aware Alaron still had all his marbles."

"If we're lucky, there may still be a few left," Bryn added hopefully.

Belara scoffed. "We could all use a little luck right now. Honestly, I'm lucky Menhir hasn't found the hidden entrances to the estate yet."

The semi-joyful mood popped like a bubble on a cactus, and Nessa's stomach dropped at the mention of Menhir. Her aching legs nearly gave out, but she swallowed hard and carried on. It didn't stop her from moving a little closer to Liv, however. Noticing that she had suddenly gone pale, Dagorn moved to flank her.

"Is something wrong with the protection spells?" Bryn asked, brows raised.

"No, they still work, but the stone wards Papa made are starting to fade."

"Stone wards?" Nessa couldn't stop herself this time. *Magic*. Avani had magic, something she had only ever read about. She wanted to know everything.

Belara only smiled.

"My papa was half dwarf. He knew how to work the stone and the earth like no human ever could. When the war started to get bad again, he placed protective wards all over our land. So far, they've held up."

Half dwarf? The top of Nessa's head barely came up to Belara's nose. Perhaps being only a quarter dwarf didn't affect height? She shook her head, vowing to figure that one out later. Right now, she was only a few steps away from a bed. *Focus on getting to the bed.*

Belara swept open the door and showed them into a small room, furnished simply with a fireplace at the far end. The hearth blazed merrily, a cast-iron pot bubbling over the flames. To their right sat a large bookcase, which she pushed aside to reveal a narrow set of stairs.

She gestured imperiously. "You know the way."

Bryn raced up the stairs two at a time. Watching him made Nessa even more tired.

Exhausted, she used the handrail to help push her lethargic body up the steps, her legs twitching painfully with every movement. Liv stayed close behind her, possibly in case Nessa collapsed right there. Her white-knuckled grip on the railing may have given her away.

The top of the stairs gave way to a small sitting room with another fireplace. Layers of well-worn rugs and pillows covered the floors, while four chairs that didn't match sat around a low stone table covered in angular carvings. A door was set in each of the dark wood walls to either side of them. Both stood open to reveal smaller rooms.

Nessa poked her head into one and saw two small beds, each with a nightgown laid out on the quilt. Each bed was built into a small alcove, with curtains to shut out the light. She peered into one and found a small window overlooking the rolling green pasture. They were eye level with the middle of the huge trees, which must have reached at least twenty feet above the cottage roof. No wonder no one had ever found Belara or the estate. It was extremely well hidden.

"Belara has helped us for quite some time." Liv entered the room behind Nessa, dropping her pack. "Her husband was one of us, back in the day, so I hear. And she grew up with your father. She is only a few years his junior."

"Oh." Nessa *thunk*ed her head on the alcove's ceiling and swore, rubbing the soon-to-be-bump. "Was her husband a human or a dwarf?"

"Human, I believe. Human and dwarf relationships are rare, but they do happen."

Liv walked to a trunk at the end of the room. Lifting the lid, she held a bundle out to Nessa. It was a pair of breeches and a shirt.

"Give me your clothes. We will get them washed."

All the gods and angels! A bed *and* clean clothes? That settled it. This place was heaven. Now if she could only find some food, she'd die happy.

Nessa instantly started fighting with the laces on her bracers. After a few moments of failing, she looked up at Liv, attempting to look as pitiful as possible. It was not difficult.

"You'll have to help me."

Liv smiled teasingly. "Only if you do the same."

By the time the two emerged holding their soiled clothes, Bryn and Dagorn were lounging by a roaring fire. Dagorn looked much calmer, sitting back in his chair with his feet up and a long pipe between his teeth. He had removed his leather armor, leaving him in pants and a dark shirt, though he still wore a belt with a small blade at his hip. Bryn had also removed his armor, but his shoes were gone as well. His feet made no noise on the old floor, though it creaked every time Nessa took a step.

She glanced down to see that Liv was barefoot like her brother. However, unlike Bryn, Liv was wearing a small dagger at her hip. And knowing Liv, more blades that Nessa couldn't see were probably hidden somewhere on her.

A wonderful aroma wafted into her nose, and her stomach growled loudly. She watched as Bryn set four plates down on the stone table, anticipation flooding her chest. Could it be?

"Supper!" Bryn called with a smile.

Nessa was at the table in less than a second. She didn't recognize a thing on the plate, but ate ravenously nonetheless. Bryn raised both eyebrows as he watched her. He looked at Dagorn, then Nessa, then back to Dagorn.

"'orry." She tried to get the words out around a mouthful of food. "It's been a while since I've had a full meal." As she ripped into the bread on her plate, she could have happily melted into a puddle then and there.

"Coffee does not count as a meal," Liv pointed out as she handed Dagorn a plate.

"Neither does tea," Nessa shot back, making a face at her.

"I never said it did."

Nessa ate until her plate was empty. Some extra food may have found its way there, likely due to Dagorn's trickery. She finally noticed after her third piece of bread, but she still swallowed down the extra food along with her pride.

Once she'd finished, she plopped down on the rug by the fire with her empty plate on her stomach and her arms flung wide, her entire body cheering. Falling back onto the floor, she let out a deep breath.

"Better?" Liv asked, smirking around her tea.

"Yeah." Nessa nodded, and it was.

Dagorn smiled, tilting his head upside down in order to look at her.

"Whaaaaaaaat?" Nessa drew the word out as long as she could, even though it ended in a tired moan.

"Enjoying yourself?" He arched an eyebrow at her.

"I'd rather be in Liv's apartment with a giant pot of tea and a Doctor Who marathon on TV, but this isn't too bad."

Silence.

"I understood only half of what you just said," Bryn muttered, bewildered.

Nessa couldn't help it. She burst out laughing, though she wasn't sure why. *Bryn* didn't understand what *she* had said. *Welcome to the club*. She hadn't understood anything since before she'd gotten here; everyone kept using words she didn't recognize. The absurdity of her situation slammed into her, but there was nothing else left to do. She laughed until tears streamed from her eyes.

"Well, that's good to hear!"

Nessa sat up, wiping her eyes, as Belara appeared. She felt her cheeks burn with embarrassment as she slid closer to the fire.

Their host was holding four mugs, a large pitcher tucked into the crook of her arm. Belara smiled at Nessa, a soft sparkle in those gold eyes that left Nessa wondering how old Belara really was.

"You have your mother's laugh. I haven't heard it in a long time."

"*What?*"

A jolt of cold fear ripped through Nessa's stomach, and she scrambled backwards until she collided abruptly with Dagorn's leg. The comforting weight of his hand fell on her shoulder, and she looked over at Liv. The elf's expression was calm, though one perfect blonde brow was quirked upward.

"It's alright, little one," Dagorn breathed in her ear. "Bel is family. She can be trusted."

"I didn't mean to alarm you." Belara set the mugs and pitcher down on the stone table. "But the pieces all fell into place the moment Livia introduced herself. The White Witch of Kiriviel disappeared almost twenty years ago, and no one knew where — though there were rumors, of course. And with her return and you coming here with those two..."

Belara seemed to lose steam as she gestured to Bryn and Dagorn. Sighing, she lowered herself to sit on the edge of the table before Nessa.

Nessa stared, wide-eyed, up at Belara as she dug her nails into the rug, watching as the woman reached out to her, a gentle smile on her face. Her expression appeared genuine. Belara's hand made a move as though to brush some hair from Nessa's face, but the long, elegant fingers never touched her.

"Besides, I would know the daughter of Larien anywhere." Belara smiled wistfully. "You have your father's eyes, though."

Nessa pressed herself against Dagorn's leg when Belara suddenly rose.

"I didn't mean to scare you, Lady. Your secret is safe with me. I give you my word on my husband's grave; I shan't tell a soul."

Nessa blinked twice in order to process what had just happened. Belara knew. And worse, she had known who Nessa was simply by looking at her. Keeping her identity a secret was not going to be easy if one glance was all it took.

Could Belara be trusted? *Don't be silly*, she scolded herself. Of course she could. Dagorn had said so, and she was running a Guard's safe house along with his estate. That kind of loyalty wasn't found easily. She glanced between Bryn, who didn't seem at all bothered or surprised by this turn of events, and Liv, who had maintained a calm expression throughout the entire conversation. Liv finally gave her a small nod.

"Uh...thank you, Belara...for your hospitality and...for not telling." Nessa was certain she sounded horribly stupid, but at least she'd tried. Belara let out a short laugh.

"Child! This is a safe house. Nothing leaves these four walls without my permission — or gets in, either." Belara rose to her feet. "Now, drink. I'm off to bed, but ring if you need me."

"Thank you, Bel," Dagorn said warmly.

Belara vanished amidst a cloud of confusion and utter relief. Nessa and the others stared after her for a long moment.

"Is she always like that?" Nessa asked, blinking.

"Usually," Bryn answered.

"She's a loyal and fierce lieutenant." Dagorn sighed. "We can trust her."

And that was the end of it, mostly because Bryn started passing out drinks. Nessa slumped back against Dagorn's legs, grateful for something else to fill her belly — and, perhaps, punish her liver.

Nessa glanced up at Liv, raising her eyebrows questioningly.

"Are there age limits on drinking here?"

"What?" Bryn scrunched up his nose, looking horrified at the mere thought.

Liv shook her head. "No."

Nessa took the mug in both hands. The liquid inside swirled dark red, smelling like spicy cherries, and she took a tentative sip, her mouth puckering slightly as fruity smoke washed over her tongue. A hint of warm spice hit her as she swallowed, and for the first time in days, her shoulders relaxed.

She realized she was practically nuzzling into Dagorn's leg, and her cheeks blushed an adorable shade of pink as she adjusted her position on the floor to lean against the stone table instead. She took another sip of the wine, sneaking a glance at Dagorn. He hadn't moved, but instead was smiling softly at her.

She needed to calm down.

She let her mind stop. All she had to do was simply sit on the floor and exist for a little while. The sound of the fire became the dominant soundtrack, interspersed with Bryn and Liv chatting quietly in Vaerin. Dagorn, feet propped on the table behind her, had returned to thoughtfully chewing on his long pipe between sips of wine. A few stray thoughts entered Nessa's mind, but she couldn't hold onto them for long.

Her entire body ached, a deep, steady tired her bones would never be rid of. The heat from the fire washed over her skin, helping her strained muscles to relax. Then again, that could have been the wine. She held the mug in her lap with both hands as she stared at the flames.

They hadn't built a lot of fires when she was a kid. On warm summer nights, her adoptive dad would insist on lighting the fire pit in the backyard, and he and Nessa would make s'mores, mountains of them. He would fill the night with stories and poems, each frightening tale blocking out another twinkling light of the San Francisco skyline. Then Nessa would refuse to sleep for fear of the raven at the door and end up in her parents' room.

There hadn't been many fires after that happened a few times.

"Ness!"

"Hmm?" She jumped when Liv said her name, and her head swiveled to the side in time to see Liv sigh. Nessa bit her lower lip, raising her eyebrows uncertainly.

"Why don't you head to bed? You look like you could use the rest," Bryn suggested. He made his way to his feet and sauntered over to Nessa, gently taking her empty cup.

Nessa nodded and moved to push herself up, but her muscles felt like taut cables; ready to snap with every movement. Wincing, she plopped back onto the floor.

Bryn offered his hands to her and she took them as he helped her to stand. She nearly collapsed again, but Bryn held onto her long enough for her to steady herself. She took a deep breath.

"What time should I get up?" she asked.

Liv gave her a nod. "Rest as long as you need."

Nessa could have cried in relief.

She slowly made her way back to the sleeping room. Shutting the door gently, she collapsed at the edge of one of the beds. She thought about changing her clothes, but realized she was simply too tired to put on the proffered nightgown. She did take off her shoes, however.

The pillow was stuffed with actual down feathers; she'd never slept on a real down pillow before. It was pokier than she imagined, but she didn't care. It was a *bed*. Sleeping in a bed was normal. Eating a full meal was normal.

Nothing else about this whole affair had been normal.

She should have thought about everything that had happened. She should have thought about new worlds, kingdoms, mercenaries, and not knowing what her life was going to be like from here on out.

She closed her eyes instead, and sleep claimed her.

Chapter Nine

Baths, an Unexpected Luxury

The fire danced happily, casting a warm glow on the three faces in the room. However, none of their expressions looked particularly warm. The flickering light sharpened Dagorn's strong profile, his pensive brows canting downward. He gently chewed on the end of his pipe, removed it to speak, and then placed it back in his mouth without saying anything.

Bryn leaned forward to pour more wine into his mug. His hands trembled, but not in fear; the set of his jaw and the fire in his gaze gave him away. Resetting his face into a calm expression, he turned to refill Liv's cup.

Liv hardly noticed her brother. She was staring into the liquid, as if she might find the answers to the cosmos at the bottom.

Dagorn removed the pipe from his mouth again.

"Have you had any rest, Liv?"

"I need to know where we stand." Liv's eyes snapped up to meet Dagorn's. She looked drawn and pale even in the golden light of the fire, her shoulders slumped over her mug.

"You also opened the Veil less than two days ago, and *brought someone with you. That takes a lot of power," Dagorn pointed out calmly. He looked over her head to beg Bryn for assistance.*

"It must be strange to be home, Li Li," Bryn tried gently. He draped an arm along the back of her chair, glancing sideways at his sister.

Liv deflated. "I am relieved, and I am not, all at the same time. I know what our return must mean."

"Yes." Bryn nodded. "A lot has changed since you went away."

"Like Nessa." Liv threw Dagorn a teasing look, and he tossed one right back.

Bryn ran a hand down his face. "And the landscape. Holm has fallen."

"What?" Liv turned to him, eyes wide and jaw slightly slack. "How? When?"

"It started about four or five years after you left." Dagorn visibly slumped, the grey hair at his temples seeming to grow more prominent as his eyes stared at nothing. By some terrible magic, he had aged twenty years in a matter of moments. "They took Hadriar by surprise. Elvar sent troops, including Bryn and myself. It wasn't enough. We held on for a few years, but between the famine and the nightly raids, it was only a matter of time."

"Menhir destroyed the Watchtower of Thomane." Bryn's voice could have cut through stone.

Liv grew pale. "How?"

"They took out one of the lower pillars during the final battle of Dreburn." Dagorn swallowed hard. "No one in the tower survived."

"Including the council?"

"Including the council." Bryn nodded. "We evacuated the city with the help of the Nolael. The people survived, but Holm is gone. Menhir took all the food stores and the farms on the plains."

"So now they have a way to feed their army." Liv groaned, running a hand down her face. "At least for a while. When did it fall?"

"About ten years ago," Dagorn replied. "The extra stores from Holm have long since run out, and they are desperate for more. Guards along the northern border have sent us what information they can, but our spies are no longer as numerous as they once were, and the information we do receive is getting less reliable. We heard from Bylur less than a fortnight ago that Menhir was preparing for a big move on the southern territories. We fear Galidel will be their next target."

Liv looked horrified. "Galidel is well within Calebrir's borders."

Dagorn sighed. "Not as much as it used to be. Now it is on the northern border of the Kingless Lands. We've heard nothing of them since. Sadly, we must assume the worst."

Liv leaned forward. "What about where we are now? Who rules?"

"No one and everyone," Bryn replied. "Menhir has a hard time keeping hold of the land. The people keep rebelling, thanks to Belara and her network, but no one really knows on any given day what's actually going on. Rebellions, outlying tribes, even the Nolael protect some regions from Menhiran forces. The original governing systems were all destroyed when Menhir conquered their lands and replaced them with their own people. And where freedom has been won, reliable systems have yet to be reestablished. Not to mention there's the constant threat of being reconquered."

"These lands are essentially permanently kingless. Survival has become more important," Dagorn added. "If you have a crown, you're a target."

"Except for Koen. Kiriviel remains well hidden." Bryn saw his sister relax.

The words suddenly grew muffled, and everything began to fade away into black...

***

Nessa woke with a start. She felt a brief flare of panic when she didn't recognize the dark wood above her, then she remembered. Avani, Calebrir, the portal…oh, and a militaristic kingdom wanted her head.

She lay there a moment longer, just to feel the sun on her face, the warm light blazing nearly golden. Then slowly, she pushed herself up to peer out of her little window. The sun sat high in the sky; it had to be well past noon.

Reluctantly, she pushed herself up and stretched, her entire body feeling sore, each muscle wound tight like a screw. She did a few yoga poses she remembered from her classes at the student center, the familiar movements helping her to move without cringing.

Her body may have been exhausted, but her mind was buzzing as she tried to remember her dream. Something was eating at the back of her brain, something she should know. She had felt this way once before, but when had that been? Midterms? No, more recently. She tried to concentrate. There had been a fire, and it had been warm. A carved rock...no. A stone?

She gave up when her spine finally popped into place.

Nessa glanced over at Liv's bed. It was still made, but her pack had been moved. Had she slept at all? Nessa hoped she had. She glanced at her shoes, decided no, and padded out barefoot to join the others.

Liv, with customary perfect timing, was already shoving a mug into her hands.

"Morning. Drink this."

Nessa scrunched her nose slightly as she looked at the dark green liquid, its heat radiating through the ceramic of the mug. The silver ring on her right hand made a light tapping noise every time she adjusted her fingers. It was a simple thing, with lily of the valley flowers etched into a silver band; a sweet sixteen present from her adoptive parents. She had forgotten she still had it on.

"What is it?" Nessa sniffed the mug dubiously. The liquid smelled bitter.

"It is like coffee."

"Oh, thank the angels."

Nessa set herself down next to the stone table as she drank. The drink did taste bitter, sort of like coffee, but also grassy, and a dark, earthy taste coated her tongue after she swallowed. It wasn't entirely unpleasant, but she didn't love it either. Liv handed her some honey, which made the drink marginally better. Maybe she would learn to like it.

She glanced up when Bryn appeared at the top of the stairs. He smiled widely when he saw her up.

"She wakes!"

She could already feel herself blushing. "What time is it?"

"It is midafternoon," Liv answered.

The elf reached into a small basket sitting on the table and pulled out a piece of cheese. Nessa did the same, spying a couple of odd fruits she would have to try later. One was spiky like a pineapple, but bright green.

"Oh." She broke off a piece of cheese. "Sorry I slept so long."

"You needed it." Dagorn was sitting in the chair across from her, a cloth and a blade in his hands. "So did Liv, for that matter."

Liv waved the pointed comment off with an impatient gesture.

"How are you feeling?" Dagorn leveled Nessa with a steady gaze.

"Better," Nessa answered. "It's strange, though. I feel like I woke up in the wrong room on vacation."

Dagorn arched a brow. "What?"

"That will pass," Liv assured her calmly.

Nessa watched Liv reach for a wooden comb on the table. Next to it sat some ribbons and a pile of pins, and she watched as Liv ran the comb through her snowy hair. Liv's hair was very long, though she rarely wore it down. Now, it could have been white flame sprouting from her head. It looked good. Like, *really* good.

...Was Liv's hair damp?

"Liv said you have a few questions."

Nessa looked back over at Dagorn when he addressed her, and nodded.

"I do." She shrugged, finishing off her cheese. "I just...seem to only have more and more with every answer I get."

"Well, we have a surprise for you, *lebiet*!" Bryn preened, and Nessa tilted her head at him.

"A good surprise?"

"I hope so." Bryn was grinning like a loon. "We drew you a bath!"

Nessa squealed. "Where!?"

A bath! With soap! Oh God, she could be clean! Her mind swam excitedly with visions of sinking into scalding hot water and soft-smelling soap, bubbles and scrubbing and clean skin.

"It's in front of the fire downstairs."

Before he could even finish, Nessa had hobbled to her feet. Mug and two fruits from the basket in hand, she marched herself straight down the stairs. She could feel the others grinning after her.

The water was hot and fragrant and smelled like the wildflowers Nessa had seen in the garden when they arrived. It might have been some kind of oil, or maybe the petals that were floating in the water. She wondered if maybe she should hurry, but decided against it. Who knew when she'd be able to have another bath?

The roaring fire wouldn't allow the water to cool. She had all the time in the world.

The first half hour was spent drinking her coffee-like substance, eating the prickly fruit and stretching her muscles as best she could in the hot water. She felt them groan and pop until finally her shoulders relaxed and her back no longer ached, her entire body letting out a deep sigh of relief.

The next ten minutes were spent deciding how to clean her hair. Through her many stories of Victorian romance — a true guilty pleasure — Nessa had learned that old-timey soap and hair didn't mix. Still, she needed something to make it not smell like river.

How could she clean her hair without shampoo? The only thing she had was a bar of soap. She finally elected to just dunk her entire head underwater and scrub as best as she could without soap. At least that way it would smell like flowers instead of algae.

She had scrubbed herself from head to foot at least three times before she finally relaxed against the side of the tub. The soap smelled like the same wildflowers as the water. Half the bar had vanished by the time she was done, but she still couldn't make enough suds for a proper bubble bath. Perhaps she shouldn't have used so much, but she couldn't regret it. She was *clean*. Well, mostly clean. What she wouldn't give for a hot shower with shampoo, but here in Avani, this was as close as she was going to get.

She stayed in the tub until she had more wrinkles than a prune, and when she did eventually get out, she dried quickly and dressed even faster, having washed her underthings in the tub and left them by the fire to dry. They were still a little damp, but the world was right again. She was clean and so was her underwear.

It was twilight when she finally returned upstairs. Bryn, Liv and Dagorn all froze when she entered the room, and Nessa glanced at Bryn, who stood behind his sister. Liv was leaning in close to Dagorn, who appeared to be backing away from her. Liv straightened when she saw the newly-clean Nessa at the top of the stairs.

"Did I interrupt?" Nessa asked, though she didn't really need an answer.

"No, of course not," Dagorn replied, a little too softly.

Nessa didn't miss the glare Liv shot his way. He was smiling at Nessa, but his face looked a little green, so she decided not to push it, electing instead to collapse into the chair across from him. She looked up at Liv, brows furrowed.

"How do you wash your hair?"

She saw Liv sag, her tense expression melting into an amused smile. The elf took the wooden comb from the table and moved behind Nessa's chair, producing a small tin of lavender-colored powder. She rubbed it all over her hands, then ran her fingers through Nessa's hair. The powder worked like dry shampoo. All Nessa had to do was brush it out.

Nessa noticed that Dagorn kept chewing on his pipe and staring at nothing in particular, while Bryn sat watching him expectantly. She felt like she was sitting in a shaken-up soda bottle and the lid was about to pop. She knew she had interrupted something; she could *feel* the tension in the air. The relaxed atmosphere of the previous night was gone.

She sat, waiting, as Liv twisted her hair around.

"Nessa," Dagorn began. "Liv said you have some questions."

Nessa wanted to nod, but Liv still had a firm grip on her hair, and she knew the consequences for moving while Liv was working. If she moved at all, Liv would take away her book.

Never mind that she didn't have one at the moment. The fear still lingered.

"Yeah, more than a few of them, I think."

"Pins," Liv requested.

Nessa retrieved a handful of pins from the pile on the table and handed them to Liv one by one. The elf would hold out her hand in Nessa's peripheral vision and then pluck them from her fingers. As was tradition.

Dagorn put away his pipe. "Maybe I can answer a few of them."

"Where are we going?"

"Galidel," Dagorn answered. "It is a border city of the Calebrian kingdom."

"We are on our way to see a wizard called Alaron," Bryn cut in. "It will be a long ride since he's on the other side of the Black Wood."

"Which is my cue to go speak to Belara about the horses," Liv sighed, even as her fingers trembled in Nessa's hair.

Nessa felt a final tug on her hair as a hand gently squeezed her shoulder, and she turned just in time to watch Liv disappear down the stairs, a worried expression on her face.

"So we're going to see a wizard, and then to Calebrir?"

"Essentially." Dagorn nodded his approval. "Alaron is needed by the king to advise and defend Galidel. If we can convince him to join us."

Nessa bit her lower lip as she looked down at her fingers. They had twisted together into a knot in her lap.

"And I'll be…I'll be okay until we get there?"

"Of course!" Dagorn smiled softly at her, and Bryn placed himself in the chair beside Dagorn.

"Unless there's a handsome young thing you need to—*ouch!*"

Dagorn kicked Bryn sharply in the shin. Bryn, ancient and mature creature that he was, kicked him right back.

"Are you sure you two aren't brothers?" Nessa asked.

"I'm more mature," Bryn pointed out as Dagorn threw a piece of fruit at him. He ducked, picked it up, and threw it right back.

Nessa shook her head, dodging Dagorn's poorly aimed return fire. Bryn shook his finger at Dagorn in a scolding manner.

"Don't waste food."

"I'll waste you," Dagorn threatened.

"I'd like to see you try."

"Liv and I will take bets." Nessa wiggled her eyebrows at Bryn. "Smart money is on her breaking you two up."

Bryn and Dagorn eyed each other sullenly.

"She has a point," Bryn admitted. Dagorn nodded.

"So, what is Galidel?" Nessa got them back on track. "I mean, why is it so important to Menhir?"

"Galidel is a fortress city on the northern border of Calebrir's territories. It sits by the Pass of Gelmar," Dagorn explained. "Which guards our main supply line."

"So, Galidel protects the pass?"

"And a key entrance into Calebrian territory," Bryn confirmed.

"And we're looking for a wizard to help defend it? An honest to gods and angels wizard?"

Bryn and Dagorn both appeared confused.

"What's an angel?" Dagorn asked.

Nessa sighed. "Never mind."

Chapter Ten

The Bonding Properties Of Cartography

Nessa had never given much thought to wood grain, but now, she considered the pattern on the bedpost a close personal friend. She *should* have been asleep; beside her, Liv's breathing had steadied what seemed like hours ago. Her body ached with an unknown weight and still, all she could do was stare at the ceiling.

Her head felt too full. Not to mention every time she closed her eyes, she saw something she'd rather not. The Bear, broken glass, a growing puddle of blood slowly seeping into grout lines on a tile floor, reaching for her…

All cheery and soothing things to dwell on while trying to find sleep.

Normally, when she was this restless, Nessa would simply read until her eyelids grew heavy. But there was nothing to read here. Nothing besides wood grain. Certain authors had believed it to be a delicate and beautiful ancient language, but after tonight, Nessa couldn't see the appeal.

Just for something to do, she rose from her bunk. Curiously, Liv, who slept notoriously light, did not stir. Perhaps the last few days had simply been too much. They certainly had been for Nessa. She was starting to see things. For instance, she could almost imagine the stone around Liv's neck was casting a faint emerald glow. She made a point not to look directly at it.

Quietly, she slid into the common room, only to stop dead.

"I'm sorry, I didn't mean…" She stumbled over her words, quickly attempting a doomed retreat.

"It's alright."

Dagorn sat at the low table, his long pipe smoldering in his hand. In the firelight, Nessa could see the stone tabletop littered with papers, some even scattered about the floor in small piles. Multiple quills and inkwells sat in the middle of it all, a small mound of quill tips resting at Dagorn's elbow. He set his current quill down to lean back, giving a puff on his pipe.

Nessa somehow felt she was intruding on a personal matter, and she felt her cheeks grow warm as she clasped her hands together. *Don't touch. Not anything*.

Still, Dagorn smiled at her with kindness, his eyes weary.

"Is there anything I can get you?" he asked.

"Uh, no. I, uh, I couldn't sleep."

She rocked back and forth on her heels, wishing for a glimmer of confidence. This was her *father*. Was every conversation with him going to be like this? Was she always going to grasp for things to say? Feel her rapid heartbeat against her ribs and look at anything else but him?

...The wood grain on the floor matched the bedposts.

"Neither could I."

"What are you doing?" She would drag this conversation kicking and screaming through the brambles. She was quite determined.

"Making adjustments."

Dagorn chewed the end of his pipe as his eyes flitted over the papers. After a little more nervous gnawing, he asked, "Would you like to see?"

Nessa nodded and made her way over to the stone table with a new lightness to her step as Dagorn quickly cleared a place beside him, shuffling papers away and even tossing a few into the hearth. She could see scribblings of landscapes amongst the rest of the papers; there were rock formations and outcroppings, trees above strange fauna, pressed flowers, and depictions of mountains, all scattered between messy and heavily slanted handwriting. *The Dark Wood, southern edge*, *King's Victory* (on a plant), *Nightblossom* beside a drawing of petals, *Everwinter* below a small village.

She gently picked up a piece of paper and lightly touched an image of a misty lake labeled *Vaerin's Looking Glass*.

"Did you make all these?" she asked, her eyes raking over the piles and piles of papers. Each drawing looked like a faraway place in a fairytale. Mountains and forests and lakes, rivers and streams, all scattered about the table. They were wonderful in every sense of the term.

In the firelight, Dagorn's ears burned red.

"I like to keep careful notes of my travels. I also have the ability to remember most of what I see."

"Seriously?" Nessa's head shot up. "You have a photographic memory?"

Dagorn looked like a deer in headlights. "I don't know what that is."

"What? Oh, right." Nessa put a hand to her forehead. No cameras, so no photographs. This was going to take some getting used to. "It, uh, it means you always remember everything you see. Everything."

"Then yes, I suppose so. It's part of my blessing. I must say, it comes in handy when the time comes to adjust the map."

"The—"

Nessa paused mid-question when her eyes fell on a large map spread across the table. The leather was faded and smoothed in certain parts, no doubt from repeated folding over the years. A waving coastline in the south curved off the map in a wide arc to the west, while a series of interlocking mountain ranges ended the eastern border and jagged cliffs fell to a northern sea. Two great rivers made a Y-shape, converging into one larger body toward the northern end of the map. Forests and lakes dotted the scene, mixed with unfamiliar symbols and languages.

Nessa leaned close, nose nearly to the table. "Is this Avani?"

"Most of it," Dagorn replied. "I haven't made it to the western coast yet. No one ventures there since the gods sunk the kingdom of Urystin below the sea to save it from burning."

"What? Like Atlantis?"

"What's an Atlantis?"

She cleared her throat. "Right."

Her eyes fell back to the map. She could feel Dagorn staring at her again; it was an odd kind of stare, resting somewhere between caution, adoration, and curiosity. *Soft* was the first word that came to her, but that still fell short. She didn't know how to feel about that stare.

"Would you like to see where you were born?" Dagorn asked, sounding like he was speaking around something in his throat.

Nessa nodded, and Dagorn leaned over the table to pull the southern coast closer. A finger gently tapped a roughly triangular symbol that rested half in the sea.

"Calebrir. The Mother City, some call it."

"Why?"

"Well," he began, "it was the heart of art and culture before the war broke out. After, it became the heart of the League."

He saw the confused look on her face and continued, "The League of Thirteen is an alliance of all those left who oppose Menhir. Most joined for the protection Calebrir provides." A pause. "And the food." Another pause. "And iron." Yet another pause. "And trade." The next pause was a rather short one. "Upon reflection, Calebrir holds an empire in all but name."

Nessa's stomach twisted slightly. "I've never heard of a *kind* empire."

"King Elvar is a fair ruler." There was a heavy silence filled with the unsaid before Dagorn spoke again. When he did, there were long pauses between his words, as if he were choosing them very carefully. "I've been told he can be exceptionally thoughtful, and never fails to do right by his people."

"It sounds like you don't like him much."

Dagorn's response was a sly smile. Pride and joy bubbled up in Nessa's chest, and she found herself returning it.

"Are you always so perceptive?" he asked.

"Only with people," she replied. "On most days, anyway. I was way off on Liv, though."

A warm chuckle erupted from Dagorn's chest. "I believe she prefers it that way."

He moved his hand closer to Nessa's, smoothing out a wrinkle in the map, and Nessa held very still, her uncertainty turning to fear. Dagorn quickly pulled his hand back, clearing his throat.

"I'm glad you trusted her."

Nessa gave him a small nod and a cautious smile. Trusting Liv had kept her safe, but at the cost of everything she knew. Had it been worth it? Well, she had finally found her birth father, whom she lost all her words around every time she tried to speak. Plus, she wasn't kidnapped or dead, and she'd found a new, magical world. A magical world, admittedly, that she knew nothing about, filled with dangerous creatures and an entire violent kingdom that wanted her, though she didn't fully understand why. She had left her home, all her friends, her dreams behind, the moment she'd trusted Liv.

No, that wasn't fair. Liv had protected her, had kept her safe her entire life. Liv was there for her when no one else was. Nessa's fate had been sealed the moment Jon Snow's evil twin entered Ollie's. And *he* wouldn't have been nearly so accommodating.

"Nessa…"

She jumped and turned to Dagorn, who was chewing thoughtfully on his pipe.

"I know this must be hard on you, but I…I would like to help you in any way I can. I'm not sure what…or if you even want…" He quickly shoved his pipe back in his mouth, prompting a small coughing fit.

The tension popped like a bubble, and Nessa giggled as Dagorn's cheeks turned red.

"I feel the same way," she told him. "I don't know what I don't know, and I know I'm going to look like an idiot if I ask. I don't even know what to ask you about."

"I could tell you something, if you like."

"I would like that."

"See this?" Dagorn pointed to the triangle representing Calebrir, half in the water. "I drew it that way for a reason. Calebrir is built on a very unusual spot. The entire city is built as a spiral, the highest point being the king's castle at the very center. The city has never been taken because every high tide, the sea rushes in to surround the city. Only small, shallow-bottom ferries can make it through."

"That's really smart, actually." Nessa smiled. "Then the rest of the food comes from the farms on the other side?"

"Yes, but with a route to the ocean from within the walls, the city is practically siege-proof." Dagorn was vibrating subtly with excitement, a smile forming on his face. "There is direct access to endless food and water. And no army can trudge efficiently through a meter of water."

"Are you always so into battle tactics?" Nessa asked with a short laugh.

Dagorn cleared his throat before sheepishly shoving his pipe back into his mouth. "It's a…beneficial part of my blessing, to understand a lot of history and battle strategy. It gives what I see context."

"Wait, what?" Nessa asked, her brows set in a deep furrow. "Your *blessing?* What do you mean, 'what you see'?"

"Ah." Dagorn pressed his lips together so hard they nearly disappeared. "Well, I am…you see…there's a legend of…hmmmm."

The pipe ended up shoved in his mouth again, and Nessa ground her teeth, fighting the urge to smack the thing from his hands. Perhaps a lecture on the dangers of smoking was in Dagorn's future.

His very near future.

"Little one," Dagorn began, "there is a legend in Avani of the three Visiril, ordinary beings blessed by the gods who made our world." He suddenly looked nervous. "Did Liv tell you any of this?"

Nessa shook her head no, and Dagorn let out a long puff of air, his shoulders slumping as he chewed on his pipe. Nessa was reminded of a goldfish, the way his mouth kept opening and closing.

"Why don't you tell me the story about the gods first?" she suggested, wanting only to ease his suffering. "I always love a good story."

Dagorn smiled, soft and genuine.

"The Great Mother had two daughters, Thera and Vaeril. Her daughters grew lonely through eternity, so the Great Mother made them lovers, Arelen and Gaelin. Together, through the magic of words and will, the sisters and their loves created a home for themselves. Thera's love was for all things green and growing, so Arelen gifted his wife the sun to watch over the garden she loved so much. When the sun set, Vaeril would shatter the last sunbeams into thousands of pieces to create the first stars. That way, the darkness would never be absolute. The stars grew lonely, so Vaeril gifted the moon to her children to keep them company. And in this way they formed the world, and the races that inhabit it.

"When evil was released into the world, the gods knew they could not stay, for evil seeks power, and their presence would only invite more trouble for their creations. They were heartbroken and each decided to appoint one being in their stead, a guardian of the world they had so lovingly created. Gaelin went first and chose to bless those who had a will similar to that of the gods. He bestowed the blessing of magic, and thus the first wizards came to be. However, this gift was not foolproof, for will and a thirst to extend it often lead to bad ends. Because of this, a wizard must endure a test of heart before they come into their full power, to know they are worthy of it.

"The other gods were more careful with their gifts. Each remaining god chose one being per generation to bless. Vaeril's blessing is of the night sky, for the night sees the world as it is, and the truths often hidden by darkness. Thera bestows the blessing of the earth, for the earth sees how things may grow to be or how things will decay with the changing seasons. And Arelen's blessing is of the sun. The sun has seen everything of the world but knows not what each new day will bring. The god and goddesses created stones for their guardians to help guide them, one from a drop of sunlight, one from the light of the full moon and one from a leaf of the First Tree. These three god-touched beings are the only ones trusted with the ability to touch the pure magic of Avani, the remnants of the gods' will that shaped this world. They are known as the Visiril."

Something tingled at the back of Nessa's brain. Had she heard that word before tonight? The story sounded so familiar, but she couldn't think of where she might have heard a similar one. Her fingers found the deep blue stone at her throat as she worried at her lip with her teeth.

"Why are they called Visiril?"

"In Common, it translates to *Dreamer*."

A spark flashed at the edge of Nessa's memory, but she couldn't turn quickly enough to catch what it was. Like water, it trickled away between her fingers, leaving only droplets of thought.

"Wait…ar—are you…*god-touched*?" She suspected she already knew the answer, but she still needed to hear him say it.

"Well, some would say so."

At least he had the decency to look uncomfortable. She shook her head, trying to get her thoughts to fall into place. It was like shaking a jigsaw box, and then opening it and hoping to find a completed picture.

…The odds would probably have been better with the jigsaw.

"You have magical god powers?"

Dagorn chuckled. "Not exactly like that. I was given the blessing of Arelen. I have Dreams — well, *visions* is a better word, I suppose. I have visions of the past. The Dreams are stronger if someone I care about is directly involved, but they don't have to be. I see battles, catastrophic events, strategy meetings, treaties… Anything that will help me protect Avani."

Nessa blinked. Her father had visions of past events. Visions. Of the past.

Visions.

She pinched the bridge of her nose and let out a deep breath, grateful she was already sitting down. Still…

"It's not the strangest thing I've heard in the past few days, honestly," she admitted. "On Earth, people who have visions are either called 'prophets,'" she said this while making quotation marks with her fingers, "or just plain crazy. And they always want your money."

"The Dreams do make me feel crazy some days," Dagorn agreed. "My vison could be from five hours ago or five hundred years ago. I never really know when they actually take place."

"That's why you need to have so much context," Nessa realized.

"Exactly," he replied proudly.

"Are powers like that, um, well, genetic?" She prayed for a *no*.

"What does genetic mean?"

"Uh…" Right. Modern Earth science. "Does it run in families? Like blue eyes."

She had her dad's eyes. That little thought liked to keep intruding.

"Oh, well, sometimes, but it's rare."

Nessa released a relieved puff of air and slumped against the table. Dagorn smiled.

"See this?"

He offered his right wrist to Nessa, and she leaned forward to examine the bracer. Secured into the dark leather and laces was a clear, round stone, larger than a quarter but smaller than a silver dollar. The crystal appeared to be liquid fire, a frozen drop of pure sunlight flickering red-orange and gold even though Dagorn held perfectly still.

Nessa lightly ran her fingers over it. "It's warm!"

"It usually is," he said. "A stone like this marks the Visiril and their blessing. It is part of the magic of Avani. The stone never leaves me."

"Do they all look like yours?"

"No." A sly grin formed on his lips. "Liv's is green."

Nessa thumped her head on the table and swore, rather impressively.

"Seriously?!" she growled, her head aching more fiercely than ever. Which of course had nothing to do with her banging it on a table just now.

"She's a *god-blessed assassin elf?*" she nearly moaned. "Who can see the future?"

Don't freak out. Well, she would later, but right now Nessa didn't have the energy left to sustain even a mild panic. At this point, a lizard person could pop out of the ground asking her to tea and jam and she would simply reply *no thank you*.

Dagorn gently placed a hand on her shoulder and squeezed. "You get used to it."

Nessa, mustering up all her dramatic energy, flopped her cheek over onto her father's hand.

Neither of them moved for a long moment. She found she liked the silence and the warmth. It was starting to become familiar.

"Why don't you try to rest on the sofa?" Dagorn offered. "I myself find being alone troublesome when I have a weary mind."

It didn't take much for Nessa to agree. Her head felt too heavy to support, bogged down with god-blessed beings, unsiegeable kingdoms and strange, captivating landscapes.

She didn't fall so much as plunge into a blissful, dreamless darkness.

Chapter Eleven

The Gift Horse and Its Awesome Teeth

Nessa eyed the creature before her warily. Large, dark eyes stared back, daring her to try anything. Oh sure, it *looked* docile and sweet. Some people even believed these things were majestic.

More like moveable mountains of mischief, if you asked her. This one towered over her, though that wasn't exactly a major accomplishment, and she jumped back as it snorted at her.

Liv almost laughed. "It's just a horse, Ness."

"Exactly. It's *big*, with a mind of its own, killer hooves and an untrustworthy middle."

Dagorn grinned, tightening the straps on the saddle. "I believe that is the exact definition."

Nessa released a deep sigh of resignation. There was no getting out of this one.

Their little group had woken with the sun, Nessa last of all. She had returned to consciousness reluctantly, and on the sofa, with Dagorn's coat draped over her. However, no one had said a word besides 'good morning.' Liv had handed her another mug of the coffee-like drink — which she called *kefe* — with lots of honey, mentioned something about lessons and left it at that.

Nessa had had no idea said lessons would be on horse riding; she'd never even seen a live horse before today. Sure, there were movies and television, but nothing had prepared her for the sheer size of the animal before her. It could have snatched an apple off her head, easily.

Bryn had actually attempted the same trick earlier, but she'd thwarted him by discovering his one weakness. Who knew elves could be ticklish?

Nessa knew how to drive a car, and Albert Everette had insisted her first vehicle be a stick shift, reasoning that she would be able to drive pretty much anything from that point on. It had been miserable at first, the lurching so bad that poor old Albert threw up from motion sickness, but he'd been right.

Horses, however, didn't come with a gear box. She'd be less apprehensive if they did.

"You won't be by yourself," Dagorn said soothingly. "I'll be with you."

"I'm sure she finds that a great comfort," Bryn chortled. "You were thrown your first time and broke your arm."

"You spooked the horse," Dagorn accused.

"I did not!"

"You did."

"On purpose," Liv added.

Nessa glared at the two smirking elves perched on the fence. "Why exactly are you two here?"

"Moral support," Liv deadpanned.

"We took bets." Bryn beamed. "I have five coins on you falling within twenty minutes."

Nessa moaned and put her face in her hands. "I'm going to die."

"Oh, do not be ridiculous," Liv told her. "I said two hours."

"Liv!"

"Alright, alright!" Dagorn waved a hand. "Shoo, you two. Don't you have other things to do?"

Bryn and Liv answered *yes* and *no* at the exact same time. Bryn looked offended. "I want to see if I win!"

Nessa arched a brow at him. "Did you seriously make a bet with someone who can see the future?"

Liv's expression slid from appalled, to sly, to proud in a matter of a seconds, her laughing grin spreading all the way to her eyes. Nessa hadn't mentioned her conversation with Dagorn the night before, but her friend's 'blessing' was definitely something they were going to have to talk about. She wanted to wait until they were able to speak freely, however, preferably with some of Belara's wine.

Bryn opened his mouth, a finger poised to prove her wrong, thought about it, then closed his mouth.

"Well, *ilisc*."

Liv's head fell back in a mischievous cackle.

Dagorn chased them off quickly after that. Nessa couldn't say she felt any better about her impending humiliation, but at least she wouldn't have an audience.

But Dagorn turned out to be a very patient teacher. First, he introduced Nessa to the horse, whose name was Maylin. He taught Nessa how to pet her, how to brush her mane and lots of other little things to help her become more comfortable with the creature. It wasn't until afternoon that he finally helped her into the saddle.

Dagorn instructed her on proper posture as he led the horse around the enclosure, though Nessa wasn't sure which was greater, her terror or Maylin's irritation. The mare seemed to know she was too good for her current rider; however, her loyalty to Dagorn prevented her from doing anything about it.

Along with the treats.

Lots and lots of treats.

Dagorn sat behind Nessa to teach her how to handle the reins, gently guiding her hands to feel the required pressure. It didn't take her long to master the correct posture and the correct hold, but her commands stayed too gentle.

Dagorn showed her again how to be firm on the reins. "You can be less accommodating."

"What if I pull too hard and she bucks?" Nessa asked.

"Don't worry. She'll tell you before it gets to that point." He gave Maylin a loving pat. "That's why I started you on May. She's a clever one."

"When did you learn to ride?" Nessa bit her lip, guiding Maylin into a turn that was only a turn if one squinted. Very hard.

"As soon as my feet could reach the stirrups." Dagorn adjusted her hands. "Squeeze your knees. There you go."

Maylin finally started to head in the direction she wanted, and Nessa smiled.

"You know, they really aren't so scary once you realize they're basically just giant dogs," she said. "When I was younger, we had a little Scotty dog. He always terrorized our neighbor's cats, but otherwise, it isn't so different."

"How so?"

"Well," Nessa paused to carefully guide Maylin around the next curve, "they'll both do tricks for treats."

Dagorn chuckled behind her. "Well spotted, little one."

Nessa did not fall off the horse once all afternoon, though there was one incident that teetered close to disaster. Luckily, Dagorn had fast reflexes and Nessa tended to crush whatever was in her hands when she was startled. The unfortunate side effect of rescuing Nessa, though, was that Dagorn himself lost his balance and ended up face down in the mud.

He said it was worth it, though. Since Nessa hadn't fallen, he'd won the bet. Nessa wasn't sure if she should be impressed, annoyed, or touched.

With the sun about to kiss the horizon, Dagorn offered to take the reins. He had something he wanted to show her before supper, he said. She happily relinquished control of Maylin, and Dagorn set them off at a quick clip, leaving Nessa to clutch at the mare's mane with her father at her back.

Something almost thrilling took over as the horse rose and fell beneath her. She could feel the evening wind in her hair, smell the grass and dirt and see the twinkle of what looked like fireflies around them. Putting out a hand, she watched it soar through the twinkling lights, the tall grasses bowing away from them as they cantered through. Startled birds fluttered away, and her eyes followed them up into the lavender sky.

There, on the horizon, rose a wall of gray stone, covered in inky vines. Evening light trailed through openings that had once been windows, and stones lay scattered on the lawn. The grand manor slept, forgotten and empty.

Dagorn seemed almost giddy, dismounting before Maylin had even come to a stop. He helped Nessa down, grabbed her hand and rushed her up the broken steps to the ruined manor.

"Where are we?" Nessa asked.

"I was raised here, little one."

With effort, he pushed open the rotted double doors. Inside stood a once-grand entry with a Y-shaped stair, but Nessa was already being pulled into another room. This one was larger, with floor-to-ceiling windows on three sides and a painted floor that was nearly impossible to make out under the layers of dirt. And something else.

"Is that…ash?"

"Yes." Dagorn sounded pained. "When I became lord of this land, my enemies tried to force me off. Menhir tried to hit me where it hurt most. Some of the manor remains untouched, but the house has sat empty for quite some time."

Nessa arched a brow at him. "Not the manor type?"

"I much prefer the carriage house." He smiled. "I have warm memories there, but this room…"

His eyes searched, seeing things Nessa could not, then suddenly, he brightened. Taking her hands, he led her into the middle of the floor.

"Imagine it. A grand ball! The floor gleaming, women in dazzling jewels and soft fabrics. Torchlight and music, this entire bay of windows open to let in the cool evening breeze!" Dagorn spun her around like a giddy child. Nessa giggled, thrilled to finally see some genuine joy from her father.

"The chandelier glittered!" His light-hearted tone turned sour in an instant. "And I could hardly stand it."

Nessa laughed as he spun her out. Pushing her hair out of her face, she found him staring grimly at the floor.

"I was young," he said. "I was awkward. I knew how to fight battles, how to campaign and make speeches, how to wield a sword with either hand, but *dancing*… Well, that was a step too far."

"Who taught you how to dance?" Nessa asked.

"Bryn," Dagorn groaned, and she snickered at the mental image. "You can imagine."

"My adopted dad taught me." Nessa led herself in a waltz. "He loved old films. Said no man can be truly charming unless he can dance. Swore by it since it earned him a wife."

"I got better, once I stopped stepping on Bryn's toes." Dagorn sounded defensive.

Nessa snorted, but he spun her around all the same, her bright laughter filling a room that had been silent for far too long.

Dagorn arched a brow. "Do you prefer to laugh at my plight, or are you going to let me finish the story?"

"Continue."

"Well, it was terrible. I had just begun to make a name for myself, and every lord wanted to have a word, give a bit of advice for the field though none of them had been to the front lines in their lives. Or they wanted to use me to sway my mentor to some cause or another.

"It was awful. I decided the party could continue without me, so when the coast was clear, I ducked behind a curtain, right over there." He pointed to a corner window. "I thought I'd escaped, until I felt something against my back, and I heard, 'Get your own curtain!' And that, my dear Nessa, is how I met Larien, your mother."

Nessa's jaw hit the floor. "That may be the cutest thing I've ever heard in my life."

Dagorn laughed. "She was the most beautiful creature I'd ever beheld. Though still very young, there was a maturity, a grace in her that I've never seen since. I apologized profusely."

"How did she take that?"

"Well, of course I had to do the chivalrous thing and rescue a damsel in distress." He flashed a mischievous grin. "We ran away together that night, the first time of many. It would be another three years before she would become my wife, but I knew the moment I saw her behind that curtain."

Nessa smiled at him. "You are a romantic."

"Little one, I am a guardian of the realm, trained in battle from childhood."

"You're a sap! All hard outer edges to hide the squishy middle!" Nessa accused.

"Little one…"

"Don't deny it!" She flapped around dramatically. "My ada is a romantic!"

Nessa paused. *Ada.* Why had she said that? She knew that word. It meant something. It made her chest warm, almost giddy, but why? A thought tumbled to the forefront of her consciousness.

"That's what I used to call you, isn't it?" she asked hesitantly. "Ada?"

Dagorn smiled softly. "It is. When you left, you couldn't say your first syllables yet."

The phrase *my ada* had made him turn sentimental. Nessa smiled to herself. She liked saying *my ada*. There was so little in the world she could claim as her own, it was nice to know she had at least one thing.

"Can I call you my Ada?"

Dagorn swallowed hard, eyes turning misty. "If you wish."

"Aww!" Nessa teased him to hide the lump in her own throat. "Sap!"

"Well, don't spread rumors." Dagorn patted her head. "My men must see me as fierce. The court doesn't like me much, anyway; I can't have that I'm a…what did you call it? Sap? I can't have that getting out."

"So, is Bryn going to try to teach me to dance?" she teased.

"I think he has claimed the honor of teaching you archery, actually."

"Oh." Nessa was horrified. "Oh dear. No innocent window will be safe."

"I shall warn the staff."

"Thank you."

Dagorn helped her guide Maylin back to the stable as the fireflies danced around the horse's legs, and Nessa chewed her lip as she mulled over the events of the day. The good news was, at least she hadn't fallen off the horse. But there was still something she was curious about. Something Dagorn had said offhandedly. She finally gathered up the courage to ask him about it once they reached the stables.

"…What?" Dagorn blinked owlishly at her. In his shock, he had frozen in place, the brush half raised in the air. Maylin snorted in irritation, and Nessa hid her smile as she reached for the feed bag, giving the poor creature some oats as an apology for the pause. The horse snorted appreciatively.

"You said the court doesn't like you. Why?"

Dagorn blinked, smiled, and then snorted, much like the mare.

"Well, some of them don't believe I'm nobility."

Nessa cocked her head. Dagorn owned land. And not just land, but an entire estate. Not to mention he was blessed by a god. Did it take something else?

"Are you?"

Dagorn's head bobbled side to side, and Nessa found herself smiling a little. She'd done the same thing, often.

"Yeeess." The word was drawn out, tentative. "But not by blood."

Nessa shook her head in confusion, running her hand gently down the mare's neck as Dagorn continued to brush. "I don't understand."

"I suppose… Well, I suppose I am nobility in the same way you are from San… Franti? Francisco! San Francisco."

Nessa's brow settled into a deep furrow. "Wait. You're adopted?"

Several things swirled around Nessa's chest, but she couldn't put a name to any of them. Dagorn nodded, holding out a brush.

"Make yourself useful, will you?"

"I fed the horse!" She rolled her eyes, but took the brush anyway. Dagorn grabbed his own and showed her which direction to stroke as Maylin stamped, her tail swishing cheerfully.

Nessa gave the horse a playful little scritch. Horses were far less scary now that she saw Maylin for what she was, a big diva dog. Give her enough treats and she'd do anything for you.

In his own time, Dagorn began the tale.

"My father had more courage than wealth. He joined the Calebrian forces after I was born. During the Battle of Neame he saved the life of a Guard, Mias, though it cost him his life, and when Lord Mias came to pay his respects to my mother, he found me. Barely five years old, trailing mud and twigs on my mother's floor and longing for faraway places and adventure. He saw a way to repay my father's courage, so I was apprenticed to become a Guard."

Nessa chewed her lower lip. Lifted from a normal life to one of dangerous adventure; she vividly recalled what that was like. Though Dagorn's introduction admittedly seemed far less traumatic.

"What about your mother?"

Dagorn let out a deep lungful of air, weighed down with the memory of days long past.

"I think she knew she was dying."

Silence hung heavy between them, her chest aching the longer her father stayed quiet. She couldn't have that, so she nudged him with her shoulder in the most affectionate way possible. Dagorn snapped back with a soft almost-smile.

"She passed away that midsummer, right before I was given my blessing."

"I'm sorry."

And she was. Nessa knew what it was like to have your world shattered, to have to reweave the fabric of your life in a new way. The holes were less noticeable, but they'd always be there.

"Thank you, little one. But the ending turns happy." He smiled and tapped her nose, which made her smile. It was just such a dad thing to do. The part of her that was still a teenager cringed inside, but the child told her to be quiet and enjoy the affection.

"I was apprenticed to a Guard, an honor higher than most noble titles, and it changed the course of my fate. Upon Mias's death, I discovered he had named me the sole heir to all his lands and titles. That led me to your mother, and later…to you."

"Do I get a title, then?" Nessa snickered. "Can I be Lady Awesome Sauce?"

Dagorn's bewildered expression made her burst out laughing, burying her face in Maylin's flank. The horse wobbled slightly, and Nessa muttered an apology to the poor thing as she continued brushing.

"Sorry. That was a joke."

"Ah. Well... You do have a title. Several, actually."

"What?" Her heart blocked her throat. "But you're just a lord."

"Your mother outranked me in every way, Nessa, but especially in title."

Nessa hadn't realized she'd stopped brushing the mare until Maylin neighed in annoyance. She jumped, then continued, her knuckles turning white on the brush.

"What was hers?"

Dagorn froze, blinking, and tossed his brush aside. In a flash, he had pulled Nessa from the stall.

"Sit," he told her, pointing to the ground.

"I don't like it when you start conversations that way."

"Apologies. All the same, it's for the best, I think."

Nessa's heart skidded around in her chest. "Maybe let's walk instead."

Dagorn chose the path between the stables and the manor, taking the long way around the back to the garden Belara meticulously kept. The glow of twilight had only just begun, the enflamed sky promising a clear night.

The pit in Nessa's stomach had opened and swallowed her pattering heart, and she clenched and unclenched her fists in preparation for more world-shattering news. She had really hoped she'd be used to this by now. Dagorn strolled next to her, his hands carefully clasped behind his back. Nessa's were twisting anxiously together at her front.

"Nessa, little one, this may be difficult for me to say… I'm not quite sure where to start."

"How about the middle?"

He smiled broadly. "Ah! In all my days I've never heard that before."

"Refreshing, isn't it?"

"Hmm," he agreed. "Little one, because of my bloodline, your grandfather refused his blessing for a union between your mother and I. Yes, I was nobility, but only on a technicality. I was common blood and, well, according to her father and the court, unsuitable for your mother. But Lari was her own woman and proclaimed that the court could not rule her heart. We were married in secret."

Nessa gasped. "I'm a secret marriage baby?!"

How romantic!

"Yes. And when we found out you were coming, it meant our marriage could no longer *remain* a secret."

Nessa snickered. "Oh, I bet that went over well."

Dagorn outright laughed at that. "I honestly thought I was going to be beheaded."

Nessa's snickers devolved into horrified laughter. Luckily, Dagorn continued before she made herself look like a madwoman.

"As fortune would have it, a wizard came to my defense. Alaron of the Wilds, Keeper of the Seven Circles. The very one Bryn and I were on our way to see when we received Liv's message." He let out a deep sigh. "He argued that we had to make any heirs unarguable lest the line end, so you grandfather was forced to recognize our union as legitimate."

Nessa snorted. "I bet he hated that."

"Immensely." Dagorn preened slightly.

In that one expression, Nessa saw the dashing romantic hero Dagorn must have been in his youth. The soft fall of dark hair, eyes the color of summer, the rugged features hiding the squishy center. The brief window to the past closed as quickly as it had opened, and Nessa found herself sorry for its loss.

"To please the court, conditions were set. Your mother's titles and all those she would inherit would pass to her heirs alone. Never to me."

The warmth inside Nessa's chest melted into ice, and she turned her face toward a flowering bush beside the path. The blooms smelled exotic and spicy and burned like a sunset. She took a deep breath, steeling herself for the worst. It was coming.

Dagorn took a step back.

"Nessa," he began gently. "Remember, you have us, Liv and Bryn and myself. No one expects you to do this alone."

Nessa swallowed hard. She turned back to her father, her shaky voice barely a whisper. "I don't like it when you start conversations like that."

"I apologize." Dagorn picked the bloom she had been admiring. Staring down, he twirled it between his fingers, his shoulders rising and falling with every breath.

"My little one." Dagorn gently tucked the bloom beside her ear. Nessa held his gaze, determined not to be afraid.

"Your mother, Larien, was the only child of High King Elvar, the crown princess and sole heir to the Calebrian throne."

Nessa swallowed hard, the air getting trapped in her throat. She choked a little, closing her eyes to stop the world spinning. Sweat appeared at her temples as her hands shook.

Princess? No. *Crown Princess*. What even was that? No. She couldn't be royalty. No. She was a *waitress*. Unremarkable. No. No!

A steady rushing filled her ears with a heated *thump, thump, thump*. Her fingers found something, and she crushed it in her grip.

"Breathe, child."

She gasped. "Uh—wh—*no*."

She fell forward onto Dagorn. He caught her by the arms and lowered her, ever so gently, to the ground as the world spun around her. She blinked, but it did nothing for the sting in her eyes.

"Nessa…"

"You have the wrong person!" she told him, her eyes rounder than saucers. "I curse! A lot! And—And I don't know a—any of the kingdoms here! And I—I turned down captain of cross country be—because it would have been too much and—and—and Kendra wanted it more…and I can't! I can't—I can't take care of a kingdom! I—I killed a cactus because I didn't water it! I—I…"

Dagorn grabbed her, hard, wrapping her in his arms as Nessa buried her head in his shoulder, her tears falling onto his coat. Breathe, she had to breathe. What were the counts? Seven, four, eight? No.

…Princess! Sole heir! No, not her. Anyone but her.

"I've got you. It's alright." Dagorn rubbed circles on her back as she collapsed into fits of violent shaking. Then, very softly, he began to sing. He wasn't very good, all breathy and trembling, but it was a tune.

Nessa listened, forcing herself to focus on the words she didn't understand. Every tripping syllable and flow of melody pulled her closer and closer back to sanity, and she gripped Dagorn's coat until she could have sworn she was tearing the fabric.

The hand on her back sat heavy, callused and warm. The circles moved clockwise; up, then down, Dagorn's breath hitching with each new phrase of the song. He smelled of leather and sweat and hay.

Finally, her body fell limp against his shoulder, exhausted.

"Sorry," she mumbled softly.

"No." Dagorn shook his head. "You have endured so much in the last few days."

"What's that song?" she asked. "It sounds…like I know it, but I don't."

"It's the story of Vaeril, who created the stars. Your mother used to sing it to you."

"Oh."

They sat like that for a long time, the shadows growing long as the twilight finally gave way to nightfall. The stars began to appear overhead, draping father and child both in cool silver light.

"Dagorn…I'm not…I'm not going to be a good princess. I can't lead."

"No one expects you to." He shook his head. "Your life is yours. And when this is all over, if you choose to return to Earth, we will find a way to get you there."

No. There could be no going back, but Nessa appreciated the attempt nonetheless.

"Okay."

Dagorn brushed her hair from her hot face. "Do—Do you feel up to supper?"

"Mm-hmm."

"Well, then…"

He helped her to her feet. "I have found," he told her conspiratorially, "that there are very few things a fine wine and a good cheese do not fix."

Nessa almost smiled.

Chapter Twelve

Just One More Thing...

The ill-fated first archery lesson came the next morning, after two hours of riding practice. Nessa learned she wasn't nearly strong enough to thread a bow, but was at least a *kind* of a shot with one.

Unfortunately, that kind was atrocious. Half the time she couldn't get the arrow threaded, and when she did, it usually fell out before she could get the shot off. The one time she did actually manage to shoot, she swore she heard a cat screech in the distance — or that might have been Bryn's laughter, she wasn't sure. Bryn remained jovial and encouraging, all the same.

It wasn't long after the rogue arrow incident that Nessa excused herself for food and another one of Belara's baths. She knew those would be hard to come by once they left, so she wanted to take advantage while she could.

In the afternoon, Dagorn took her back to the ruined manor house. The library had once been grand, all soaring ceilings and pointed arches, with a glass dome for a ceiling and a massive fireplace. Now the dome was gone, the once-lush carpets had been ruined by the rain, and the sparse collection of books remaining was beyond repair.

"Bel saved most of the manuscripts," Dagorn offered, attempting to cheer his crestfallen bibliophile. "Hid them in the wine cellar."

Ah, two of Nessa's favorite things. They seemed fated to go together.

Which was how Nessa found herself at twilight, sitting alone in the gardens and reading a book. She'd tied her hair into a messy bun and hidden herself amongst the colorful flowers she'd come to love so much. At this point her very skin smelled of them.

Liv knelt at her side, trowel in hand while she quietly pulled weeds. The flowers appeared to rejoice at her attention, nearly sighing in relief, and when Nessa asked her about it, Liv told her she missed the turning of the soil. It had been far too long since she'd gotten her hands dirty.

"What are you reading?"

Nessa glanced up to see Liv staring at her, her stormy eyes glittering in the dying light.

"The Fall of the Illiovet Forest." Nessa snapped the little book shut. "Though I'm not sure if it's true or not."

The tale spoke of a forest that held miraculous powers of healing, until a mad king drove it to destruction. The place sounded magical, where elves could capture starlight and weave it into precious jewels and cloth and healing potions. Some were given to a magical tree, though the story never stated the purpose.

"That one is real, I am afraid." The storm raged in Liv's eyes, but she quickly covered it, wiping her hands on her apron. "It fell almost six hundred years ago. Now, commoners call it the Black Wood, and stay as far away as possible. Corruption like that…"

"Corrupts absolutely?" Nessa guessed. Liv nodded solemnly.

Nessa caught sight of something she'd never seen in Liv before. There was a deep, eternal sadness hiding in the corners of her friend's eyes that made her suddenly appear much older than she looked. Like magic, though, Liv shook it off.

"Walk with me," she requested. "My back is due for a rest."

She led them through the gardens at a leisurely pace. At one point, they passed under some flowering arches, and Liv reached up to brush her fingertips against the leaves. They seemed to sigh and turn into her touch.

"Ask your questions, Ness. I know you have them."

Nessa snorted. "Is that part of your gift?"

"No." Liv smiled. "I just know you."

Liv shoulder-checked her affectionately, and Nessa gently smacked her back with her book.

"You're a Visiril? A Dreamer that can see the future?"

"I do have the gift of Thera, yes." Liv nodded, running her fingers lightly over the green stone at her neck. "What I see is different than your father, though. I see only possibilities, while your father sees certainties."

Nessa arched a brow. "What do you mean? If you see it, then shouldn't it happen?"

"Somethings are certain, yes. Large things, like the harvest or a storm, are certain. Smaller things, like what questions you will ask, are less certain because you have not decided yet."

"So, what you see is always changing?"

Liv nodded. "It can. It is what makes things so frustrating. I do not always know if what I am seeing is accurate. Or if it is, how long it is accurate for. I can be more precise when the vision is about someone I know well, or care for, because I am more connected to them."

Nessa nodded, letting the idea sink in a moment. Liv saw the future, but only whatever future they were headed toward based on current decisions. Make a different decision and the future changed.

"Do you have visions all the time? Or just when you sleep?"

"Just when I sleep." Liv shrugged. "But while I am awake, I do have a greater sense of where I need to be."

"Which is why you always have such good timing!"

"Like the last night in my apartment. I knew you were going to wake up," Liv confirmed.

"Did you see—"

"No," Liv growled. "I did not. I spoke to your father about it. They must not have expected to actually find you, and had no real plan for when they did."

"So…because no one made a decision, you didn't see anything," Nessa clarified.

"Precisely." Liv sighed deeply. "Though, I confess, I am not sure I would have wanted to."

"Why?"

"Our abilities, the gifts of the Visiril, come from the fabric of Avani itself. The ancient magic that makes Avani work is woven into our very beings. Anything we do with our magic stays with us," Liv explained. "Every vision I have becomes a permanent part of me. I can recall it with perfect clarity for the rest of my life."

"Is that specific only to you?"

"We all can do it. I know it has been a curse to your father. He often Dreams of your mother. As for me, well, I have had enough reminders of my failures. I do not wish for any more."

Nessa pursed her lips. She nudged Liv's shoulder affectionately, plucking a flower from a nearby tree to twirl between her fingers. Liv tried not to smile, but failed.

"Nessa, that night at my apartment, what woke you?"

Nessa tilted her head even as she spun the flower in her hands. What had woken her up? She remembered being scared; something had seemed so off, so wrong, that it had woken her.

She shrugged. "Bad dream, is all."

Liv's voice grew quiet. "What about?"

"Uh..." Nessa closed her eyes, letting her fingers slow their flower twirling as she sifted through her thoughts from that day on Earth. It seemed so long ago! It was after Snow had scared her at the shop, and she'd dreamed...

He'd been in it.

Nessa inhaled. She could almost smell the wood smoke. There had been a fire, and...

"Nessa!"

Nessa opened her eyes. The flower she'd been twirling in her hand was still spinning, but now the bloom was floating above her fingers.

"Ahhh!" She shrieked and jumped back, the flower falling into the dirt at her feet. Looking up, she found Liv grinning like a loon.

"What—"

"I knew it!" Liv declared, fist pumping the air. "Your father owes me ten coin!"

"Liv!"

"Nessa, you are it! You are the missing Visiril."

Nessa blinked at her. "I—what?"

"There are only three of us at any given time." Liv began pacing, talking fast, her hands flying as she spoke. "Past, present, and future. We knew about me and your father, but present has been missing for nearly twenty years! We are all connected and Vaeril's gift was just gone! We could not feel it, and now you—"

"Wait, Vaeril's gift...I could...*can* see Avani as it is?"

It wasn't the craziest thing Nessa had learned about herself this week. What was one more oddball thing?

"I thought, with the way the land reacted to you the moment you returned, it was a possibility, and your stone..."

"My stone?" Nessa clutched her pendant protectively. "What about it?"

"Nessa, I was there the day it found you."

"What?!"

Suddenly, she remembered. She had been five, and her parents had taken her to an outdoor flea market in a park near their house. Lilly Everette's mother, whom Nessa had called GiGi, sat on a nearby park bench and watched Nessa as she ran around a three-tiered fountain in the middle of the plaza. The summer sun was shining so brightly it hurt her eyes, beating down on the old woman and the child.

"Be careful, lovie!" GiGi called. "I would *hate* it if you fell in!"

GiGi had believed everyone needed a little rebellion in their lives, and encouraged the same for her grandchild. Nessa, throwing caution to the wind, slid right over the edge of the fountain and into the water, and GiGi made a show of dramatically rolling her eyes even as Nessa giggled and splashed.

"Oh dear, now I have to come in after you!"

Nessa held her breath and dived below the shallow water, opening her eyes to see something shining on the bottom. She needed it. She needed the shiny thing more than she needed oxygen in her lungs. Reaching out, she grasped something smooth and warmed by the sun.

She popped up out of the water, dripping, to find a necklace in her hand.

"Oh, did you drop that, lovie?" GiGi was suddenly beside her. "Here. Don't want to lose it!"

GiGi dropped the necklace over her head, and it had stayed around Nessa's neck for nearly fifteen years. She'd never thought to take it off.

Now, her fingers unconsciously followed the swirling silver setting.

"You were there?" she asked Liv.

"I have always watched over you. Even when you could not see me."

"Why?"

"You were mine," Liv said softly. "I brought you to Earth, and back here, because I can connect to the pure magic of Avani; it is a very unique skill. Usually, anyone other than a wizard must use power that has already been shaped by where it is drawn from: the rivers, the stones, the leaves. But Visiril do not need to do that. I am one of the few beings in Avani who can open the Veil and take you through."

"So you brought me to Earth because no one else could," Nessa said.

"I brought you because I love your mother and father." Liv held her eyes and hands. "They are family to me. I have known and loved you since before you were brought into this world. I love your family, and your family is mine. That is why."

"You're just trying to make me sentimental, so I don't panic when you start talking about training."

"Is it working?" Liv asked with a grin.

"A little bit," Nessa choked out. She flung her arm around Liv's shoulders, giving her a little squeeze. "I'm going to be rubbish."

"Beginners usually are. Don't worry. I'll be with you every step of the way."

Chapter Thirteen

Practical Magic

Just as she predicted, Nessa's first training session had gone poorly. The technique she needed to master was similar to meditation, requiring quiet thought, focus and dedication — which was made difficult by the fact that Dagorn and Liv kept bickering over who owed who more coin. By afternoon, Nessa had given up, gone on a run, and returned to another steaming hot bath.

Belara had certainly cemented herself as one of Nessa's favorite people.

She was toweling off her hair in her bunk when Liv appeared with a large pack, setting it down on the bed with a heavy and ominous *thump*. Nessa paused a moment in wringing out her damp hair to give Liv an epic dose of side-eye. Given the last few days she'd had, that pack probably contained a forgotten relic of immense power that could only be destroyed in the fires of Mount Apocalypse. And it was going to take them until next year to get there.

"What's that?" she asked, like an idiot.

"Clothes for you," Liv replied.

Nessa relaxed, continuing to work the towel through her hair. She didn't remember having this much of it, or it being this long. Getting carted off to a magical land couldn't make her hair grow.

...Could it?

The question, she decided, was one she could leave unanswered. Just like the question of why her achy muscles didn't feel as achy as they should. When she had run hard in San Francisco, the twinges and spasms had lasted days. But here, even after a push like the one she'd made in the wilderness earlier, she couldn't feel the twinges nearly as painfully.

Perhaps it wasn't as hilly here. That was what she was choosing to believe, anyway.

"Well." She gave up with a sigh, tossing the towel over her robed shoulders. "Am I going to look like a Khaleesi after this?"

Liv's deep sigh conveyed both exasperation and disappointment. Nessa felt the same, but only because she had witnessed the series finale.

"No, think more... Oh, what was it called? The Witchling?"

"The Witcher?"

"Yes."

Nessa's memory abruptly flooded with images of a handsome, fit actor clad in very well-fitting leather pants. A wistful expression crossed her face, then decided to camp there awhile.

Liv snapped her fingers.

"Sorry."

The other girl grinned like a wolf. "It is understandable. I watched it too."

"Do I get two swords?"

"Absolutely not."

Nessa nearly melted in relief. Craning her head over Liv's shoulder, she found piece after piece of clothing spread out on the bed. Most were brown, or sun-faded blue, or an approximation of white if brown ever decided to emulate it. A blue mass of something that felt like leather but wasn't looked like it might have been a corset or a short tunic. It was cool to the touch, but much softer than Earth leather, and the smell was wrong. The laces, meanwhile, were probably meant to be some kind of medieval torture device. She recognized a shirt and pants, but the rest was completely foreign. What went on first?

She arched a brow. "Where did you get all this?"

"Dagorn uses his estate as a refuge for Guards and those fleeing Menhir's wrath. He keeps a lot hidden in the cellars below the old manor for just that purpose. Food, clothes, some weaponry, herbal medicines... Which reminds me, I need to make another batch..."

Liv tossed Nessa a piece of blue something, and it smacked her in the face, leaving her fumbling to catch it. It was the not-leather tunic. The small, scale-like pattern could have been embroidery, but some part of Nessa didn't believe that.

"That belonged to your mother." Liv's hint of a smile and head tilt made it clear she was pleased. "It is made of dragon hide. Nearly impenetrable."

"Okaaaaaay." *Do not think about* dragon *hide. Just don't go there right now.* "I thought Belara owned part of the estate?" There. Land ownership. Much safer.

"No, it is all Dagorn's." Liv's head disappeared deep into the bag, muffling her next words. "Much to the court's dismay."

Nessa lifted the edge of the bag to peer at her. "Because he's not 'true nobility'?"

Liv froze for a long moment, then popped out like a startled meerkat. "He told you about that?"

"Yes." Mild curiosity compelled her onward. "And why I inherited all my mother's titles…and what those titles were."

"And?" Liv arched a brow at her.

"And what?" Nessa countered.

"Off with your robe," Liv instructed instead of answering. Nessa rolled her eyes at the deflection, but complied.

Liv began helping with her new clothes. "How do you feel about it?"

"Can we at least get me dressed first? I don't know what half of this is."

Nessa had no idea one person could wear so many layers. There were undershirts and stays and lots of things she didn't even know the names of. By the end, she was wearing a pair of brown riding boots, dark pants, a sun-faded blue skirt that she kept hitched up, and a loose shirt that had possibly once been white. The neck sat too wide on her shoulders, but the corset-like dragon armor kept it in place. She had to admit, her butt looked fantastic.

It was when Liv was helping her with the bracers that the elf finally perked up.

"Still have your sweet sixteen ring on, I see."

"I like it." Nessa tightened the laces with her teeth. "Bit of Earth and all that."

"Are you finished avoiding my original question?"

"No. Still avoiding."

"Ness!"

"What do you want me to say, Liv?" Nessa fixed her with a look. "How does one typically react to finding out they're a god-touched heir to the throne?"

"Panic, typically." Liv sounded far too calm in her admission.

"I mean, yeah." Nessa went to flap her arm, but Liv held it still to finish tying the bracer. "I figure I can deal with that bit once I'm not being hunted down by vicious mercenaries from a rival kingdom."

"It is always good to take things one step at a time," Liv agreed. "But…"

"I hate it when you do this."

"But you are the one who has to live with it," Liv pointed out. "Can you even admit it to yourself yet?"

"You mean that I'm a pri—" Without meaning to, her throat swallowed the word, so she tried again. "That I'm a…a…"

Liv gave her a knowing look.

"Fine!" Nessa deflated. "I am having a little trouble with it, okay?"

She slouched onto the edge of the bed, running her hands through her damp hair. Her chest constricted at the thought. An entire kingdom, full of people, whose happiness and safety would be her responsibility. How was this ever going to work? She had no idea how this *place* even worked. Heck, she hadn't even known Avani existed a week ago, and now she had to run part of it?

Liv gave her arm a little squeeze and sat down beside her. "No one expects you to stay, Ness."

"I know, but…" Nessa gestured out the window. "How…there's so many people counting on me…and I can't just…"

"I will take you back," Liv offered. "Once this is over and done, if you wish, I will take you back."

Nessa gave her a sad smile. "I know you would, Liv."

But Liv wouldn't stay on Earth. Nessa knew that as well as Liv did.

She let out a long breath.

"Dagorn said the Visiril are protectors of Avani." Nessa chose her words carefully. Protectors. Not soldiers, not weapons. The gods or the universe or whoever ran things, had looked down on a world at war, a world full of swords and arrows and armaments, and sent down shields. "Knowing that, how…how could I leave?"

"Your *life* is back on Earth."

"Yeah. Yeah, it is. My parents, school, the coffee shop… And I miss it. Every damn day." Nessa's throat swelled closed. "I feel like…I *need* to stay. I need to try to help if I can. And if me staying away from Menhir helps, I'll do it."

Liv blessed Nessa with a little, loving smile.

"In times like this, you remind me so much of your mother," she said. "She gave everything to her people. The one time I ever saw her be selfish was her choice in a husband."

"I don't think Ada minded too much."

"No, but the court practically imploded."

Nessa laughed, and Liv pinned her with a glare until she quieted.

"I worry about you, Ness, taking on too much, too soon."

"Liv." Nessa took her friend's hands in hers. "I'm going to be okay. Really. It may take a while, but I'll get there. Just promise you won't leave me alone, okay? I need my big scary assassin elf to help me."

"I am not an assassin." Liv preened, but smiled anyway.

***

The next day, Nessa woke with the sun.

Neither her birth status nor her godly gifts had been discussed for the rest of the previous day. Instead, at supper, Dagorn had kept the conversation light, he and Liv explaining some of the plants he had sketches of in his journals. The purple flower Nessa had taken such a liking to could apparently serve as a fever reducer and anti-inflammatory in addition to also smelling nice. Now it made sense why the baths were helping so much.

Liv kept looking expectantly between Dagorn and Nessa, as though watching their faces would reveal the details of any private mental distress. That was, until Bryn told a wild story of their youth, which resulted in Liv smacking her brother's arm no less than seven times. Dagorn suggested there'd be a mark in the morning, to which Nessa agreed, but bet that Bryn would never admit it. They put a drink on it.

And in the light of the morning, she found she could breathe normally again. The dust of the previous day's revelations had not quite settled into place, but it was closer to being where it needed to be. She wasn't safe, but she wasn't drowning anymore, either. It felt like treading water in the open ocean; madness, but it was manageable for now.

Strange how she'd thought *college* would be difficult to adapt to.

She stretched the same as she had the day before, running through her old cross-country routine till her spine snapped back into place. It seemed her muscles had finally settled.

When she finally emerged, Bryn and Liv were sitting before the fire and rummaging through their packs, a piece of cheese sticking from Bryn's mouth as he frowned at his bundle. He chewed off a portion before returning the cheese to its original position.

"Morning."

A chorus of *good morning*'s and a grunt from Bryn was all the response she received, though Dagorn pulled a mug from beside the hearth and handed it to her. Her silver sweet sixteen ring made little *clinks* on the ceramic as she took it. It was a comforting noise.

Liv glanced sideways at her. She had always known where Nessa was in the apartment because of Nessa's mug clinking habit. It had been easier than putting a bell around her neck — which Liv admittedly had considered once or twice.

Nessa, for her part, took no notice.

"How's your arm, Bryn?" she asked slyly, the mug halfway to her lips.

"I am in perfect health, thank you."

Dagorn couldn't miss the smug look Nessa tossed his way. He narrowed his eyes at the elf Guard.

"Liar," he accused.

"Well," Bryn sighed. "I like her more than you."

"Traitor."

"Are you surprised?" Liv arched a brow at Dagorn, watching Nessa hide a grin in her mug as she preened.

"You still owe me a drink."

Dagorn swore under his breath, and Bryn chuckled.

Nessa looked down at her mug. "Thank you, by the way, to whoever put a boatload of honey in here."

"You're welcome," Dagorn answered.

"Still owe me a drink."

"And she never forgets a debt," Liv sighed.

Nessa smiled at her green coffee-like drink, though it faded as her eyes fell on the basket of rolls and cheese on the stone table. Taking a piece of cheese, she chewed it over thoughtfully.

"Ada, I've been thinking..."

Liv and Dagorn locked eyes.

"Whatever it is, don't ask Bryn," cautioned Dagorn.

Bryn didn't even look up from his pack. "It's because I'm usually right."

Liv smacked Bryn's arm in response. He held up his hands up in defeat, and Liv shook her head, turning her attention back to Nessa in lieu of dealing with her brother. Nessa could only roll her eyes.

"Liv said you sent me through the Veil to protect me, that she was the only one who could do so because she is a Visiril."

"That is true, yes."

"But so are you. Why didn't you take me?"

Dagorn froze, running a hand down his face. "It's not that simple, I'm afraid."

"Nessa, do you remember how I explained the magic of Avani?" Liv asked.

Nessa nodded, lowering herself into a chair. "Yes. Each race has a place of power formed by the filter it comes through."

"Well done."

"Some think this was a system put in place by the ancient gods, the Elar," Dagorn began.

"The four main ones?" she interrupted, leaning forward in her chair. Nessa had always loved fairytales; it never occurred to her that one or two of them could be true. Then again, her life itself was turning into some kind of twisted fairytale.

...If she came across a fae prince in a ditch, she was going to leave him there.

"The Elar are the children of the Great Mother, the giver of life." Dagorn came over and sat down next to her. "Thera and Vaeril, the goddesses of the earth and the sky, and their husbands, Gaelin and Arlen."

Nessa nodded as Dagorn paused to glance at Liv and Bryn.

"Every race tells it a little differently," Liv piped up. "Our tales focus mostly on Vaeril and Gaelin."

"Why?" Nessa furrowed her brow.

"Vaeril created the stars and the moon while Gaelin created the vastness of the sky. The High Elves believe our race was created through the tears of lonely stars that fell deep into the forests of the east, so they are considered our patron Elar."

"Not that you think highly of yourselves or anything." Nessa couldn't keep the teasing out of her voice.

Bryn shook his head. "Not at *all*."

"So," Nessa began, "if Vaeril is the stars and moon and Gaelin the sky, and Thera is the earth, is Arlen the sun?"

"Arlen created the sun to watch over his wife's garden," Dagron clarified with a little smile. "Elves have a much stronger connection to their places of power than humans do. Our source was lost before living memory."

"I can not only pull power from the pure magic of Avani, but I can also pull it from the forest around me as well as myself," Liv explained.

Nessa nodded. "That's the other thing that's been bothering me. If you had to be that powerful to get through the Veil with just me, how did Menhir send an entire company of men to Earth?"

The three Guards in the room froze still as statues. Nessa's eyes darted between them as a chill ran down her spine.

"What did I just say?" she asked.

"There are other ways, surely?" Liv turned to Bryn and Dagorn in horror. "They wouldn't..."

"They have," Dagorn answered sadly. "Often."

"What?" Nessa asked.

"Rumor has it, they have a wizard," Bryn added.

"They cannot have a wizard!" Liv exclaimed.

"Hello!" Nessa waved her hands. "Can we stop talking in code, please?"

"Sorry," the other three chorused together. Dagorn sighed, moving to light his pipe.

"Little one, there are other magics in this world, some so dark they are forbidden. But in the last few years, what is forbidden in Calebrir has become common practice in Menhir. After the Elar created the races, man turned greedy. As soon as the first son spilled the blood of his father, true evil was released into the world. That is why the Elar granted the Visiril their powers, to help protect and heal Avani from this wicked magic and the fall of the races. It is a magic drawn from the life force of others."

Nessa's jaw hit the floor. "Wait, wait, wait. You're saying they *killed* people to open the Veil and find me?"

"Likely." Bryn gave a shallow nod. "Or a wizard sent them through."

"It can't be Alaron," Dagorn declared. "He's a few shingles short of a roof, but he's a good man."

"Isn't he the one who married you and Mom in secret?" Nessa asked.

Bryn preened. "Yes. I served as best man."

Dagorn glared at him. "I needed witnesses."

"And secret keepers," Liv added. "What about Ekey?"

"Ekey has been missing for nearly twenty years. Something about business in the West." Bryn waved a hand. "I'd put fifteen coin on Wulfric. He was always just arrogant enough, the prick."

"And the fourth?" Liv asked.

"Still hasn't been found," Dagorn sighed. He saw Nessa's confused expression and continued, "There are meant to be four wizards at a time: one for the north, and one each for south, east, and west. There hasn't been a wizard born in the north since the war started. Ekey vanished into the west, Wulfric left the east to journey north, and Alaron now keeps to the Kingless Lands. He's old enough that he says the solitude is better for star reading, or something of the like."

"Why hasn't there been a wizard in the north since the war started?" Nessa asked.

"There's no more magic in the land," Bryn explained. "That's why Menhir would love to have one of you lot. You heal the land back up with Avani's magic, they get their crops and their power back and can continue this war endlessly."

"Heal the land?" Nessa asked. "I thought corrupt land was corrupt?"

"Dreamers are the only ones who can harness the pure magic of Avani," Liv clarified. "Some believe it is because of their connection to the Elar. Their power can purify the land — or destroy it."

"A Visiril on the wrong side can cause devastation," Bryn agreed. "One tale has a Dreamer destroying an entire kingdom and dropping it into the sea practically overnight."

Nessa furrowed her brow at her lap. All that power was inside her, right now? How was she not a bomb that could go off at any time? Menhir obviously had no problem doing whatever it took to get what they wanted. How could she outrun people like that?

She looked up when Dagorn left a kiss in her hair. "All the more reason to keep you secret, little one. There's no telling what kind of damage Menhir could do with you."

"You'd burn the world first," Bryn accused.

"Quite happily too, I think," Dagorn agreed. "I'd do anything."

"I'd like to avoid world burning," Nessa told him. "If you don't mind."

She played with her pendant thoughtfully. If the Menhirans got ahold of her, not only would they have leverage to use against their greatest enemy, but a weapon as well. She could have the power to sink Atlantis inside her, and Menhir would use that to their full advantage. All those people, all those families…

The ruins of Brandel flashed through her mind, and she shivered.

No. She would not allow that to happen.

Thundering footsteps drew their attention to the stairs, and a panting Belara appeared, her eyes wide. There was a piece of paper clutched in her hand.

"Menhiran battalion," she gasped. "Three miles north."

Chapter Fourteen

Back to the Running

Nessa hadn't even made it to her feet before Bryn, Dagorn and Liv were moving.

"Get your things. We are leaving."

That was the last thing Liv said to her in Common before the Guards all started a tense discussion in Vaerin, their voices layering over each other so fast Nessa couldn't tell who was saying what anymore. She should have felt left out, but she was already dashing into her room. She was packed in a flash, but getting dressed proved to be more difficult; she fell over twice trying to get her boots laced, her trembling hands certainly not helping. The instant she emerged from the room, Liv grabbed her arm and started helping her with her bracers.

"We have a little bit of a head start," Liv began, and Nessa noticed that her friend's fingers were trembling slightly. She clenched her hand into a fist, so tightly her fingernails left marks in her palm, and took a deep breath before speaking.

"How much?"

"Not enough for my taste," Bryn cut in. "Separating will be our best course. Nessa, they've already seen you with Liv, so we can draw the battalion west while you and Dagorn head south to the pass at Kearfell. We'll meet you at the ruins of Dreburn in three days."

The plan had already been decided, it seemed. Nessa glanced between Liv and Dagorn.

"Are you sure this is a good idea?" she asked Liv, her stomach twisting violently. Something wasn't right, but she wasn't sure what or why. A niggling part of her brain screamed at her not to let Liv out of her sight, which was silly. If Liv got in trouble, what could Nessa realistically do about it? Swing a stick at an entire kingdom of warlords? Reluctantly, she swallowed down her concern.

"Everything will be fine," Liv reassured her gently, though Nessa could tell she was trying to sound more certain than she actually was. Still, she nodded instead of questioning.

Suddenly, Liv patted Nessa's cheek in a very motherly gesture, and Nessa blinked up at her, unexpectedly struck by the fact that Liv had been protecting Nessa her entire life. She had brought her through the Veil. Liv had known her even before Nessa had known her adopted parents.

She was family.

"Dagorn will take care of you. I promise."

"But who's going to watch your back?" Nessa gave her a cheeky smile. "Bryn clearly can't be trusted."

Liv's lips twitched. "*Redel rella.*"

With that, Bryn and Liv disappeared down the stairs, and Nessa heard the front door close with a *thunk*. She bit her lower lip, suddenly feeling very alone.

Dagorn laid a hand on her shoulder. "They'll be fine."

Nessa pursed her lips, but nodded all the same. She didn't actually believe him. "Yeah. Sure."

"We wait five minutes, then we go."

He was cut off as Belara appeared at the top of the stairs, holding a bundle of blue-gray fabric in her hand. She offered it to Nessa.

"You will need this, child. It will hide your face."

"Bel…" Dagorn's voice was soft.

"Hush, you." Belara waved him off. "I loved Larien too, if you recall. If I can help her daughter, I will."

"Belara, I can't." Nessa shook her head. "You've done so much for us already, and…"

"You hush as well." Belara draped the cloak over Nessa's shoulders, smiling softly. "You have her heart, child. Don't lose it. Go now, and stay safe."

"Thank you." Why would her throat suddenly not let her speak?

Belara patted her cheek with a last, sad smile. "Go."

She stepped aside as Dagorn took Nessa's hand, guiding her down the stairs and out of the cottage. Nessa glanced over her shoulder at the happy little cottage as they disappeared into the trees, her last inkling of safety slipping away.

She held tight to Dagorn's hand as the terrain grew rougher under their feet, pulling them up, then suddenly down, or sliding sideways, the soft grass littered with leaves that hid sharp stones. Dagorn kept glancing back to make sure Nessa was still attached to him, while Nessa did her best to keep up with his much longer stride, her pounding heart spurring her forward. She tried not to glance behind her, but she could feel phantom soldiers breathing down her neck. It didn't look like anyone was following them, but looks were deceiving here; more than once, she thought she saw a shadow darting behind the trees.

Apparently, Dagorn saw the creeping darkness too, and drew his sword without breaking stride. He cut an imposing figure with his blade flashing in the dark; he didn't move with the same ethereal smoothness that Bryn and Liv possessed, but instead with the grace and confidence of a trained fighter.

Nessa, by comparison, looked like a drowning fish.

Still, they ran.

It seemed like an eternity before they slowed their pace even a little bit, and Nessa never let go of Dagorn's hand, clutching it so tightly she was afraid she was hurting him. She noticed that he gently squeezed back occasionally, usually when she began to shake.

It grew darker than Nessa thought was possible for mid-afternoon, the forest growing thicker and thicker with trees and low brush. Finally, Dagorn guided them off the path, where the chance of being spotted was lower, but the footing was more hazardous. His steadying hand kept Nessa from falling more than a few times.

Nessa kept her eye on Dagorn's sword, continually poised for a fight. The thought made her stomach twist. How close was the battalion now? A mile? A few feet? How had they been found so quickly? She was getting tired of not having any answers. And of running.

Dagorn finally paused long enough for her to catch a breath, and she gasped greedily, her lungs grateful for the air. She had no idea how long it had been since they'd started off, too preoccupied with not falling on her face. Sheathing his sword, Dagorn spun to face her, looking her over as he gently lowered her hood to get a better look at her flushed cheeks.

"Are you unharmed?" he asked desperately.

Nessa only nodded. She didn't yet have enough air to form words. She could feel her heartbeat twitching in her legs, which fought not to wobble when Dagorn released her.

"Then we'd best keep pushing on."

"What about Liv? And Bryn?" she asked through her gasps for breath. They could have been captured, or dead, and she and Dagorn would never know until three days from now. When she focused on the thought, a horrible sinking feeling opened up in her stomach. Something was wrong, but she couldn't quite put her finger on it. "What do you think..."

"They will be fine," Dagorn told her calmly, though he didn't appear calm. "They can both handle themselves quite well. Our best option is to meet them at the pass."

She looked down at Dagorn's hand clutching her own. It looked so small in his callused palm. She didn't know how, but someone knew who she was and that she was here. Perhaps the mercenaries from the coffee shop had friends? Ones who realized *something* had happened, since the others hadn't come back?

But that didn't matter now. What was known was known and she was going to have to deal with it. She looked back the way they'd come, half expecting to see shapes forming in the shadows, but she saw only trees.

"Nessa…" Dagorn caught her attention. He licked his lips nervously. "It's going to be all right. But if we meet anyone, we'd best not use our real names."

"What? Oh, right." Nessa nodded. "Okay, that's a good idea. Makes sense."

It would allow them both to stay inconspicuous. She gave a final nod, trying for a joke, only to fall slightly short of merry. "Still father and daughter, yeah? I'm a little too young for you."

Dagorn tried to give her a smile as Nessa crushed his hand in hers. Her one security, Liv, was gone, so she was going to hold onto Dagorn for all she was worth. She would be completely lost without his help. Besides, he was scarier than anything else in these woods, right?

Dagorn glanced down at her white-knuckled grip, releasing a deep breath.

"It's going to be alright," he told her gently. "Come, we'd better get going." He gave her a reassuring smile, and Nessa gripped his hand even harder.

Their relief lasted only moments, until the sound of galloping hoofbeats reached their ears.

Nessa's heart leapt into her throat in panic. That sounded like a lot of horses.

An awful lot.

"Run." Dagorn's eyes were as wide as hers. "Run!"

They took off over the hill at a dead sprint, Nessa keeping a tight grip on Dagorn's hand. The Guard's head swiveled as he searched for a way off the disused path, but the foliage proved too thick for them to push through. They were stuck.

"Ada?"

Nessa glanced behind them to see the first horse appear over the crest of the hill, and as Dagorn followed her gaze, she heard him swear. They were losing ground, fast. She gripped tighter onto Dagorn in fear, pushing them forward.

A horse and rider leapt onto the path before them, cutting off their escape. The horse reared up on its hind legs with a whinny as Nessa released a scream, and she reeled back, but Dagorn quickly pulled her into his side, wrapping his arm protectively around her. The rider came into view just as the others appeared around him. Dagorn drew his sword, but, surprisingly, kept the blade pointed toward the ground.

"Are they…" Nessa began quietly.

"No," Dagorn whispered back. "These are not soldiers. Stay calm and follow my lead."

She nodded, looking up to see the riders circling them as they eyed her and Dagorn suspiciously. No, these were not Menhiran soldiers. There was no uniformity to their clothing, though every single one of them carried a weapon of some kind, men and women alike. Several colorful packs were slung over each horse; in fact, they seemed to be carrying everything they owned with them.

"State your name and business."

The voice came from the man on the lead horse, which seemed far less terrifying now that its hooves were not trying to squash her. The rider was a large man, larger even than Dagorn, with shoulders were broader than a tree, shoulder-length hair, and a short beard the color of sap. The beads in his wild hair matched the earring hanging from his left ear, while his layered clothing — all of it sporting varying levels of wear and tear — didn't seem to match. The fabric had once been bright and colorful, but now was sun-faded. Nessa noted that everyone around them seemed to be in a similar state.

"I expect the same from you." Dagorn straightened, holding his chin high, and the leader paused for a moment, then nodded. Nessa felt Dagorn release a breath. He gave her hand a quick squeeze for reassurance.

"I am Mias." The name came off Dagorn's tongue as easily as his own. "And this is my daughter."

"Alice," Nessa supplied. Dagorn, though his blade was still pointing toward the ground, nonetheless placed it between Nessa and the burly leader. His gaze seemed to be daring anyone to try anything.

"We were traveling to the safety of the Southlands when we ran into a Menhiran cavalry camped in the valley. We took the long way around to be certain to avoid them," Dagorn explained.

The horseman eyed Nessa. "I can see why."

She tried to shrink as far under her hood as possible, and Dagorn turned her away from the group of riders, pushing her behind him. She gripped the back of his cloak as tightly as she could as Dagorn held her against his back.

"If I had a daughter as lovely as yours," the rider continued, "I would keep her as far from Menhiran soldiers as possible."

Nessa huddled against Dagorn, trying desperately to become even smaller. The tip of Dagorn's sword rose slightly.

Then, to their surprise, the horseman smiled, pressing a fist to his chest.

"But I mean you and your child no harm. I am Brandir. As long as you are no friend of Menhir, you may be a friend of mine."

"That is kind of you," Dagorn answered. He licked his lips, thinking for a moment. "Might we join you and your…companions?"

Yep, they were bandits. Nessa had never known Dagorn to pause or sound uncertain before. But honestly, she would be choosing her words carefully, too — if only her throat would open up long enough for her to speak.

"Any man kind enough to not call us thieves may ride with us." Brandir burst out laughing with a loud boom, turning to the man next to him. "Fetch them a horse."

They watched as a brown mare was brought over to them. Dagorn helped Nessa into the saddle, and she quickly realized that this horse stood much taller than Maylin. Dagorn swung easily up behind her, taking the reins in a loose grip.

"Just relax," he told her. "I won't let you fall."

She almost toppled off a moment later, but true to his word, Dagorn caught her effortlessly. He kept them toward the back of the riding party to avoid any unnecessary glances, trying to distract her by whispering riding instructions into her ear as they rode. She tried to focus on something besides the imminent threat of Menhir for the first hour of their ride, and was just about managing it until her tailbone began to hurt.

So she shifted focus.

"Dagorn, are they…bandits?" she whispered.

The sun began to set over the horizon, the shadows of the forest growing longer and darker with each passing moment. The brief glimpses of sky Nessa could see had changed from blue to flaming orange and pinks; night would soon be upon them.

"Yes," Dagorn whispered back. "Watch what you say around them."

"I'm sure they're saying the same about us." Nessa glanced back at her father for a moment, but she couldn't take her eyes from the horse for long.

Dagorn squeezed her hand reassuringly. "Whatever happens, just stay close. I won't let them hurt you."

Nessa nodded. "I know."

And she did.

Her pendant grew warm against her skin.

Chapter Fifteen

Friends in Low Places

Nessa found their new companions quite charming, for bandits. Most had ready smiles and infectious laughs, at the very least, and she enjoyed their songs even though she couldn't understand any of the words. Dagorn had to translate, relaying the tales they told of ancient battles, honor, and lost loves.

They stopped in a clearing just before the sun had fully set behind the trees. The camp held nearly forty members of the caravan, mostly families. A few young men around Nessa's age paid her every attention and offered little besides bad one-liners, though a single glare from Dagorn sent all of them running. Only four young children, three girls and a boy, played around the fires. One of the women had a newborn that was being passed between the women to coo over.

Nessa was suddenly handed the child as they set up camp, and after a moment of pure shock (and a smirk from Dagorn), Nessa gently cuddled the little boy against her side and rocked him until his mother returned. She saw Dagorn smile softly to himself, though he didn't say anything.

Soon, all the little girls had taken an interest in the pretty young lady and were asking her question after question while playing hide and seek in her cloak. They wanted stories.

And Nessa happily obliged.

"Once upon a time, in a faraway land, a young prince lived in a shining castle…" she began, as all the children sat transfixed. She smiled to herself as she wove her tale, happy that she could at least spread her love of nerd lore to this world. Their mothers didn't mind, either. It kept the children occupied while dinner was cooking.

Dagorn eventually shooed the little ones back to their mothers, placing himself next to Nessa with a very manly plop. He handed her a bowl of hot…something.

Nessa raised her eyebrows. "Do I dare ask?"

"Just eat," he teased, taking a spoonful himself. He blinked, his nose scrunching as his eyebrows did a quick jump. "Perhaps closing our eyes would help."

Nessa gave him a half-smile of amusement before taking a spoonful herself. The consistency could only be described as dreadful, watery and somehow slimy and chewy at the same time; the copious number of spices doing nothing to hide that. Still, food was food and she was hungry, so she powered through the entire bowl, mostly with her eyes closed and fighting her gag reflex.

She only spoke once she had finished. "Where do you think Liv and Bryn are?"

Dagorn had set his bowl aside a while ago and was now smoking his pipe thoughtfully.

"I don't know." He shook his head. "But most likely, we will find them in Kiriviel. I have no doubt they avoided the soldiers. And the Nolael are in the area. Bryn and I were traveling with them before we met up with you."

"Who are they?"

"Nomads, mostly elves. They do tend to take on a few stragglers every now and then, including myself."

Dagorn suddenly paused, muttering something Nessa didn't quite catch. He had gone rigid, though he was still attempting to look relaxed and reclined, and gave her a warning look when she noticed Brandir out of the corner of her eye. The bandit chief flashed Dagorn a smile as he approached.

"Your daughter has bewitched one of our youngest." Brandir nodded to a six-year-old boy.

Nessa looked over at the little boy, who immediately blushed and ran to hide behind his mother. She couldn't help but smile.

"I will not consent to any eligible suitors at this time," Dagorn answered for her, and Nessa scooted to hide behind the Guard a little as Brandir let out a boom of a laugh.

"Tell me, Mias, to where in the south are you traveling?"

"To wherever we will be safe from Menhir's army."

Nessa swore he could have been a politician, the way Dagorn could answer without answering. Liv had the same talent. Perhaps it was a requirement for joining the Guard.

Brandir looked out over the sea of bandits gathered around the fire. They seemed content with the life they had chosen; still, his eyes grew distant, glazed over with memory. It was clearly a show of strength to hide pain.

"Why do you look so sad?" Nessa couldn't stop herself from asking. Brandir glanced at her, a soft smile on his face.

"A kind heart you have, child, to notice the grief of a man such as I," he began softly. Nessa tilted her head at him but stayed silent. Brandir settled himself with a sigh before he continued. "What you see are the last vestiges of the city of Dunale."

"Dunale?" Dagorn sounded surprised. "The last great city of Halion?"

Brandir nodded. "Yes. Oh, it was beautiful. Towers and streets of crisp stone painted in the most vivid colors. I was just a boy, but I remember it as though it were yesterday. My father was Captain of the Watch. Though the war had been raging for a long time, we were safe behind our walls, tucked away in our towers. I would steal away into the very highest ones to watch the sun set over the vineyards. We were, and still are in my opinion, the finest winemakers in all of Avani."

Nessa couldn't help but smile. Brandir spoke with such fondness of his home; she hadn't expected it of him. She could only hope she grew to love Calebrir like that.

"How old were you when the raiders came?" Dagorn asked quietly, taking her hand to comfort her. Nessa had learned about war in school, of course, but hearing firsthand stories felt different. It was easy not to think about the people affected when she memorized dates and battles. Now, the humanity — or lack thereof — was all she could see.

"I was ten," Brandir said sadly. "My father saw the Menhiran flag in the first light of dawn. The alarm woke the town, and then it was chaos. Every man in the city was called out to fight, but our army had dwindled, with many of the men having been sent off to defend the border. We were outnumbered, though we still fought like the great armies of old. We were the last men of Halion and we fought like it.

"The battle raged well into the night, as the once-green and plentiful vineyards burned red. The night sky turned black, with no stars to witness our fall, and our outer defenses broke at sundown when a blast of hot air tore through the city, ripping the flags from their poles. That was when the dragon came." He paused. "The few of us who were left fled into the hills, forced to watch our home burn to ash."

"I'm so sorry," Nessa told him. Brandir smiled softly at her.

"Thank you, child, but do not waste your grief on events that happened before your birth." He turned to Dagorn. "Menhir has taken homes from many of us."

Dagorn only nodded in agreement, and Brandir shook off his grief, his fortified smile firmly back in place.

"Let us speak no more of this. Come, eat, drink…enjoy." He clapped Dagorn on the back.

They watched him vanish, only to return with two cups of dark wine. Then he was off again, as quickly as he had appeared. Nessa pulled her knees to her chest and looked up at Dagorn.

"Was Halion a country of men?" she asked quietly. Dagorn nodded and took a sip of the wine. He blinked, making a face.

"I would recommend having only half of this." He toasted his cup in Nessa's direction. "It's delicious, though particularly strong."

"Well, he did say they were winemakers." Nessa's half-smirk reappeared as she spoke, and Dagorn returned it, his expression soft. She took a cautious sip, and cinnamon and cherries washed over her tongue, warming her body in the most pleasant way. It was the most wonderful wine she'd ever tasted, and she closed her eyes to relish it for a moment, her head falling back as she nearly purred. Dagorn smiled.

"Yes. They are clearly unmatched at their craft, even now," he teased.

Nessa blushed slightly and hid her face in her cup.

Dagorn continued, his tone soft, "Halion was a strong country of men in the early days of the war. Calebrir and Halion had been allied for centuries. I helped defend the borders before the collapse."

"And Menhir destroyed the whole kingdom?" The shock was plain in her tone.

Dagorn's face grew solemn.

"Menhir has taken three entire kingdoms of men. Only two free countries remain in Avani. One of which is Menhir itself."

"And Calebrir is the other?" Nessa couldn't hide her surprise. How had Menhir taken down three entire countries? Were they really that powerful?

…And they were after her. The thought made her want to drink more, so she did. It helped calm her heart and steady her hands.

"Are there countries of elves, too?" Nessa asked.

"There were once three great kingdoms of the elves, but now Kiriviel, or Starcrest, is all that remains," Dagorn said sadly. "One was lost long before the war began. Their king…"

The Black Wood.

The ominous pause made Nessa shift in her seat, a sudden heaviness forcing her muscles to prove they could still move. There was too much in Dagorn's eyes and the downturn of his lips to read properly, her stomach twisting into knots that sat low in her core and chilled her to the bone. How could there be a happy ending with a silence like that? Her thoughts turned to Bryn and Liv.

"They're going to be okay? Bryn and Liv?"

"I'm certain of it." Dagorn smiled reassuringly at her, and the ominous feeling dissipated slightly. The wine helped.

At that very moment, a breeze tore through the caravan, the cold air nipping at Nessa's hands and face as the flames danced with the wind, growing and swirling in a beautiful and terrifying way. She shivered under her cloak, so she slid closer to Dagorn's side and settled there quite comfortably. He was warm, large, and she was fairly certain he was safe. Well, *she* was safe from *him*, at least. That was the most comfort she'd come to hope for, here in Avani.

She sipped her wine thoughtfully as the two of them watched their new companions going about their lives. Ramshackle tents with colorful fabrics draped between them blocked their view of the horizon, while the soft glow from the fires kept the darkness at bay. Children's shadows scurried away from their mothers, attempting to ward off bedtime, but their fathers were always quick to catch them. Even Nessa's new admirer couldn't avoid the sentence forever, though it certainly wasn't for lack of trying on his part.

But even the serenity of the soft violin music and songs around the fire were not enough to soothe her nerves. Too much weighed on her mind. The Menhiran army could always be hiding in the shadows, ready to strike, and then there were her friends. She had to believe she'd see them again.

She had to.

She set her wine to the side once she had finished half her cup, but somehow, the level still grew lower and lower until suddenly she was faced with the bottom. She wasn't quite sure how that had happened.

Her eyelids grew heavy, heavier than the rest of her, and she had taken to leaning against Dagorn to stay awake. She may or may not have also been using him as a human shield to block the wind. She curled into his side, becoming surprisingly small, her eyes closed against the slight ache in her temples.

"Nessa?" She had no idea such a powerful voice could sound so tiny.

"I'm awake." Her words muffled slightly by a yawn.

The gentle wind held the kind of musky crispness that could only be found in late spring, smelling like cool water and damp earth, with the promise of heat and fire smoke. It reminded Nessa of home, and long hikes with Albert. He would tell stories by the fire to Nessa and all her friends until he was hoarse, and she would always find a way to hide under him to ward off the cold. She snuggled deeper into Dagorn's side, searching for warmth. As long as he didn't mind, she was not above using him as a space heater.

The move made Dagron clear his throat, and Nessa retreated slightly in embarrassment.

As though sensing her uncertainty, Dagorn wrapped an arm around her shoulders and pulled her against him, then after a moment, he pursed his lips and released her again. When he spoke, his voice was quiet.

"Nessa, I…"

Nessa looked up at him, her brow furrowing as her eyes grew slightly large. She could practically taste Dagorn's nerves on the cool air, mixed with wood smoke and the lingering taste of spicy wine. She suddenly and desperately wished for more wine to calm her skipping heart.

"What?"

She sat up and away from Dagorn, her back rigid. Her eyes darted around the camp, but she couldn't seem to find whatever she was frantically searching for. No one was staring at them. Could someone have heard something? Seen that Nessa was horrifically out of place?

"What is it? Have I messed up already?"

"No! No, no, no," Dagorn soothed. He moved a hand to hover over her hair, but paused just a breath away. Lowering his fingers, he swallowed hard.

"You've been…" He had to take a moment to find the right word. "Perfect."

Nessa watched his fingers flex as he rolled them into a fist and then flat again. He rubbed his palms along his legs as his throat bobbed up and down, his mouth opening twice before any words spilled from his lips.

"Nessa, I hope you haven't been…disappointed in me."

"What?" She sat up to look him full in the face. "What gave you that idea?"

"I know that for you, I've only been your father a few days, but for me… I've thought of you every day. I hope you know that," he told her.

Nessa gave Dagorn a sad smile. Oh yes, her ada was a sap.

"I looked for you," she said. "When I was old enough to be curious about my birth parents."

"I imagine the search was difficult," he teased.

"Strangely enough, no private investigator thought to check in another world." She waved a hand. "I had an aunt who gave me to my parents, then mysteriously disappeared into thin air. Now that I think about it, that was probably Liv, wasn't it?"

"Yes." Dagorn took out his pipe with a proud grin.

"I'm not disappointed that you're my father. I just hope you're not disappointed in me."

"I could never be."

"You haven't heard all my college stories." She wiggled a finger at him. "Most of them start with, 'We were drinking.'"

Dagorn chuckled, deep and warm like firelight on a winter night. He had dimples. She hadn't gotten those.

"You should hear some of my training tales. There was an awful lot of mead involved." Every youthfully questionable decision flashed visibly before Dagorn's eyes. "But perhaps we should start with safer topics."

"What's your favorite color?" Nessa asked. There. That was safe.

"Blue. The summer sky."

She had endless questions on her tongue, and Dagorn answered every single one. His early training under Mias had been happy. Mias had taught him how to ride. He'd met Liv and Bryn when he was a little older than ten. Most of the injuries in his life had been caused by Bryn and his lack of foresight. Or for love of a pretty girl. Liv had taught him herbal remedies and how to read his Dreams, as she would continue to teach Nessa once they found someplace safe. He had a weakness for tobacco from the western valleys and, of all things, cheese. He'd put it on everything if he could, he said.

She could understand the cheese obsession. She'd probably eat roadkill if you put queso on it.

Dagorn talked until his voice grew scratchy, and then kept talking. There were so many stories, so many things he wanted to share with his daughter, that he couldn't get them all out fast enough. He told her legends of their world, tales of valor and heroism and tragedy, bedtime stories that all Avani children in their cradles already knew by heart. He spoke of ancient kingdoms and famous battles, some that he'd been in and others he'd only heard of in the songs that filled the great feast halls.

And Nessa told him stories of her own. She told him about Earth, of her friends and education. She told him of her parents, how kind and good they were, and how much she missed them. She told him her favorite stories, did her best to explain podcasts and the printing press, and talked of stores filled with books, libraries where anyone could read any book at any time. She confessed to a weakness for coffee, sweets and pizza, all of which she then had to explain. She even tried to sing him some of her favorite songs — or at least, the ones she could remember the lyrics to. In turn, he sang her lullabies she almost recognized.

"…and there was Liv!" laughed Nessa. "Hauling Aisha out of the bar kicking and screaming with only one shoe on." She paused to catch her breath. "And then—then she threw her other one at the door guy, screaming, 'I'll get you, my pretty!'"

Dagorn tossed his head back as bright, warm laughter erupted from his lips, and Nessa wiped her eyes, devolving into a fit of giggles. She gasped a few times to calm herself down.

"She sounds formidable."

"She's maybe ninety pounds soaking wet."

She snuggled safely against Dagorn's side, her eyes closed though she was not yet asleep. Her head throbbed slightly, and her chest ached, as if it were too full to accommodate every feeling running through her. Something sat in the back of her brain; she couldn't quite reach it, but it was doing funny things to her stomach. What was it?

Dagorn took a few puffs on his pipe before asking, "Do you miss it?"

"Of course I do," she answered. "But it wouldn't be safe for me to go back, for them or for me. Besides, someone has to keep Liv on her toes."

"Very true, little one." He adjusted his cloak to drape over her shoulders. "Well, if you ever develop a craving, Bryn is always prepared for shenanigans."

"I think the shenanigans find me just fine on their own."

Dagorn chuckled. "That appears to be a curse I've passed on to you. Rest now, my Nessa. I'll wake you in the morning."

Nessa yawned, snuggling deeper into Dagorn and his warm cloak. "Good night, Ada."

She fell into a dreamless sleep.

Chapter Sixteen

The Tactical Advantages of a Costume Change

Nessa awoke to shouting. She scrambled to sit up, her heart pounding in her ears as the smell of smoke wafted through the air, the warm light in the sky indicating that it was past dawn.

A squeak escaped her when a hand fell on her shoulder.

"It's alright." Dagorn's pipe hovered by his lips. "Someone just came into the camp."

"Who?" Her heart flipped over in her chest.

"I'm not sure yet." He quickly snuffed his pipe, tucking it into his belt. "Stay here. I'll go have a look."

He disappeared between the tents, and Nessa shook her head. It wasn't a soldier. It couldn't be. There was no way. Solitary soldiers didn't leave their battalions.

Perhaps a scout? No, she couldn't think like that. It was probably someone like them, someone lost. Plus, wouldn't a soldier know better?

"Stop it," she told herself as she got to her feet and started to roll up her blanket. "You can't be paranoid all the time."

...Yes, she absolutely could.

She focused on loading up both her pack and Dagorn's in case they needed to make a hasty exit, munching on a piece of fruit as she waited for news. Suddenly, the yelling grew louder. She tried to see what was going on, but the tents blocked her view.

Pursing her lips, she played nervously with her pendant. Something was wrong. Well, perhaps *wrong* wasn't the correct word, more off-kilter. In any case, Nessa found herself already on her feet. She knew she should stay put. That was the smart decision. But the nagging at the back of her mind wouldn't go away.

Before she even knew what she was doing, she was marching through the camp, a little huff in her stride.

She spotted a crowd at the center of the encampment and headed that way. Children were clamoring to see around the adults, only to have their mothers scold them for getting underfoot. As she drew closer to the crowd, she heard a few words she recognized, those individual words turning into panicked whispers.

"He came just before dawn…

"He's armed! Of course, he means harm…

"What's an elf doing this far north…?

"Elf?" Nessa perked up, leaning toward the man who had spoken. "Did you say it was an elf?"

"Yes, a downright pissy one, too!"

Nessa shoved her way through the crowd, using her elbows to gain space, and finally emerged at the front to see her father deep in conversation with Brandir. They were speaking with their heads bent close together, both gesturing wildly.

Bryn was on his knees behind them.

"Bryn!"

Nessa was moving forward before she could stop herself, and Bryn gave her a half-grin despite his hands being bound behind his back. He looked like he'd been through hell and come back the same way.

"Hello, love."

"Where the hell have you been?!" she snapped.

Nessa took in his bloody nose and lip and the shallow cut above his cheek. His hair was wild, a few leaves sticking out of the ginger locks. She pushed between Brandir and her father, pointedly ignoring the look Dagorn gave her, and brushed the leaves from Bryn's hair.

The elf shrugged at her question.

"Causing trouble."

She crossed her arms like a scolding mother. "Hope you gave as good as you got."

"Always."

"Why don't I believe you?"

Bryn shrugged. "Likely poor judgment on your part."

"Alice." Brandir cut in gently, and Nessa spun to face him. "You know this elf?"

"Yes." She glanced back at Bryn. "He can be difficult, but he means no harm."

Dagorn sighed defeatedly. "Difficult is putting it lightly."

By the exhausted expression on her father's face, she would never have guessed that Bryn was the older of the two. "Brandir, he is an old friend of mine. Please, release him."

Brandir eyed Bryn suspiciously. "I've never trusted elves."

"Well, this elf doesn't trust you," Bryn snapped.

"Bryn, please." Nessa rolled her eyes. "Now is not the time to whip it out and measure."

Dagorn, Brandir and Bryn all gave her a very odd look that Nessa couldn't put a name to, so she offered a perplexed expression of her own. Brandir looked like he was fighting off a smile.

"I like your daughter," the bandit told the Guard.

"All the same." Dagorn's eyes lingered on her before he turned back to Brandir. "Bryn was traveling with us before we joined your party. I give you my word that he is harmless to you and your companions."

"Your word, Mias?" Brandir arched a brow, a small smile tugging at his lips. "And what is your word worth? When you aren't being completely honest with us?"

Dagorn glared at him, but Brandir only smirked.

"Come now, my man, of course I know you are hiding something! You've been far too polite to us. Now, don't look so affronted. Your situation is clearly not ideal."

"As ideal as yours, Brandir," Dagorn replied. "It appears you and I share the same level of honesty with each other, so I would hardly say your word is worth any more than mine."

Brandir's smirk became an all-out grin. "You make a fair point, my friend." The bandit looked over at Nessa before he continued, his eyes turning sad. "And you have something far more precious to protect than I."

Brandir looked between Bryn, Dagorn and finally Nessa, then turned to the men behind him.

"Release the elf."

Nessa let out a breath she hadn't realized she was holding, and glanced over at Bryn, who gave the men behind him a shit-eating smirk. The thought of reprimanding him crossed her mind, though she held no actual authority over the elf.

Something else niggled at the back of her mind and in the pit of her stomach. It twisted together, making her feel sick. She'd felt it last night too, but had attributed it to the wine.

"Where's Liv?"

Bryn's face fell as he looked between Nessa and Dagorn. "She hasn't shown up yet?"

Ice shot up Nessa's spine.

"Something's wrong."

Though it was her voice that had spoken, she barely recognized it. It sounded too far away, too mature. Her fingers flew to the jewel at her throat. It felt warm.

Dagorn studied her for a moment, then closed his eyes as though deep in thought, two fingers moving at his side like he was flipping the pages of a book. The longer he took, the further Nessa's stomach dropped, and she glanced at Bryn, her teeth worrying at her lower lip. Dagorn's eyes snapped open with a curse.

"We need to go."

Dagorn, thankfully, proved to be a competent tracker, as did Bryn, and between the two of them, they managed to follow the route Liv had taken. The plan to use Liv to keep the soldiers away from Nessa had worked, and all too well. The Menhirans had moved faster than either elf had anticipated, so, figuring it would be easier to lose them if they split up, the siblings had promised to meet up at dawn. When Liv hadn't shown, Bryn simply assumed she had already made her way back to Nessa and Dagorn.

They soon discovered that Menhir had gotten to her first, though apparently not before Liv had taken out about a dozen of their soldiers. They found the remains of the struggle only a few yards from Bryn and Liv's appointed meeting place, and while Nessa knew she should have felt sad at the loss of life, she just didn't have it in her anymore. At this point, she mostly just wanted to get away from the smell and find her friend. She knew they were running out of time. If the Menhirans found out Liv was a Visiril, that she could see the future, the war was as good as lost. There was no way to win against an enemy that knew your every move before you made it.

Their little party caught up with the battalion just after dark, and Nessa found herself flanked by Dagorn and Bryn at the top of a hill, looking down at an entire encampment of soldiers. Her chest and feet ached, but something kept pushing her forward. Some kind of ferocity had woken in her blood; she could feel it pressing against her ribs, filling her lungs. Perhaps it was a desire for survival, or perhaps she was finally acclimating to this new existence. Multiple attempts on one's life would do that.

Dagorn looked to Bryn. "There can't be more than forty."

"Forty-two," Bryn corrected.

"Hmmm. Not great odds, I'll admit." Even as Dagorn spoke, his eyes turned glossy and distant, his fingers making that flipping motion again.

"So it's a stealth mission." Nessa bit her lower lip. "Fighting would be suicide."

"For them," Bryn growled.

"And *us*," Dagorn pointed out.

"And you don't even know where Liv *is* in there."

Nessa's eyes settled on a singular tent, glowing like a beacon in the night. It was large, too large for a simple soldier. It looked like the ones she'd seen in war movies, the ones that usually held generals or commanders. Her gut said, *there: pay attention to that one*.

She ran her fingers over her pendant, thinking hard. Were prisoners usually kept with people of importance? Weren't there guards? The only thing she had for reference was everything she'd learned in the books she'd read, and she had no idea whether the rules would be the same here.

She couldn't take her eyes off that tent.

"We'll have to figure that out first." Dagorn shook himself slightly. "Bryn, you take the west end. I'll take the east."

Nessa arched a brow at her father. "And I'm to stay here?"

"And try to stay out of trouble."

"Right." She nodded. "Makes sense."

"We meet back here in one hour."

"And if you're late?"

Dagorn flashed a mischievous smile at his daughter, one shoulder shrugging slightly. "Wait a little bit longer."

"How many times have I told you?" Bryn rolled his eyes. "You aren't funny."

"That's your opinion."

That was the last thing she heard as her father and the elf disappeared down the hill and into the shadows.

Nessa glanced from side to side, not really certain what she was looking for. Her fingers were at her pendant again, following the swirling setting as she gazed down at the camp, her eyes drawn insistently to That One Tent. It sat towards the end closest to her, not too far into the encampment.

If Liv was in there, why was it so far from the center? Why not guard her like Fort Knox? Nessa's gut clenched. Something told her they didn't even have an hour.

It was smarter to stay here. It was safer to stay here. Menhir desperately wanted her, to use her against their greatest enemy. She should stay here.

She should.

She was crouched at the edge of the encampment before she even realized she had moved.

"This is such a bad idea," she hissed to herself.

If she was caught, Calebrir was doomed, and the war was as good as over. There would be more ghost gardens than she could count.

The solution then, clearly, was to not get caught. All she had to do was sneak into an enemy camp, find her friend, and get her out again.

Sure. Piece of cake.

Nessa snatched a uniform jacket off a nearby laundry line. It looked worn, garishly red, and a bit too large for her frame, but it would do. Passing through a shadow, she swiped a wide-brimmed hat off a log. The plan at the moment was to hide her figure, her face and her hair. If it had worked for Indiana Jones, it could work for her.

She hoped.

Drunken songs in what she supposed was Menhiran floated around her, the air smelling of smoke, roasted meat and oil. Nessa stayed well away from the firelight as she slunk her way through the camp; she knew how to remain inconspicuous if she wanted to. She had mastered the skill by sneaking into the occasional bar during her brief stint in college. Liv had taught her how.

She slipped into the back of That One Tent, a mix of terror and relief filling her chest when she found no one inside. A quick inventory of the dimly lit space didn't tell her much, either. There was a bedroll, some blankets, a little bit of food...nothing out of the ordinary.

Nessa swallowed hard. Had she risked so much only to be wrong? Her eye was drawn suddenly to a table to her left, and she tiptoed over to what looked like a workspace, her gaze drifting to the jars littering the top of the table. Something not unlike the smell of formaldehyde assaulted her nose, and through the murky water of the jars, she could make out small animals — or parts of them. She covered her mouth with her hand to keep from making a noise, several horror movies she'd have preferred to forget flashing through her mind. Papers lay scattered across the table, covered in what she assumed was Menhiran writing, and Nessa picked one up to see if she could decipher it.

As soon as her fingers touched the parchment, an overwhelming desire to burn it welled up inside her. But if she did that, whoever this tent belonged to would know she had been here. Then again, if Liv suddenly went missing, that would also be a pretty obvious clue. She decided to rip up whatever her fingers touched as a compromise.

A dark red spatter on the wood caught her eye, and she froze, a chill skating down her spine.

"Please be paint. Please be paint. Please be paint," she muttered under her breath.

She shoved all the debris out of the way, cringing as three of the jars fell from the table with a clatter, two shattering against one another.

Pausing for a moment, she held her breath, her ears straining for the slightest indication that someone might have heard. She forced her pounding heart to be silent, the sound of drunken singing, laughing and muttered growling filling the tent. Below it all, she could hear the night breeze and the crackling of the fire.

Nothing changed.

Letting out a breath, she continued to rip the papers from the table, albeit a little more carefully than before.

The red paint, as she was choosing to see it, formed a circle filled with symbols she almost recognized. The shapes were similar to the ones she'd seen in alchemy texts, but the symbols were all…*off* somehow in one way or another. Different plane, different elements, different planets.

Goosebumps crawled across her skin.

She desperately wanted to destroy the symbol, her eyes scanning the table for something, anything to wipe the awful sigil away — then she froze solid as she heard a groan from somewhere in the tent. Holding her breath, she tried desperately to get her racing pulse under control as she heard the moan again.

It sounded feminine.

Nessa swallowed hard. No, what were the chances?

"*Liv?*"

"No, it's a…mountain troll..."

"Liv!"

Nessa rushed around the other end of the table to find a figure hunched in the shadows. Liv's glazed eyes fluttered half-closed, dried blood clinging to her lips and nose. A chunk of her white hair was missing on the left side, as if part of her braid had been hacked off. Red shone against the pale skin of the elf's knuckles and wrists, which were bound with rough rope.

She took Liv's face in her hands as Liv's sunken eyes rolled from side to side. She looked like she was trying to focus on Nessa, but her gaze kept sliding away again, her pupils blown wide. Nessa had never seen Liv high, but she suspected this was what it would look like.

"Liv? Liv! Hey, it's me. It's okay."

"…Ness?" Liv sounded a thousand miles away. "What in Vaeril's name…are you wearing?"

Nessa chose not to answer.

"You're going to be okay," she whispered, as much for herself as for Liv.

Nessa spun around the tent, searching for something, anything. A weapon would be excellent right now, but of course, that was never her luck. She'd have to improvise.

She just needed something sharp. In a fit of either brilliance or stupidity, she snatched up a shard of broken jar.

"What are you doing here?" Liv swayed erratically from side to side. "You are too important…"

"Doing something stupid." Nessa cut her off as she sawed at the ropes with the jagged glass. "You know? The exact thing you told me not to do."

"You're too much like your father…wait…"

The rope snapped with a satisfying *snick*, and Liv fell backward as Nessa caught her by the shoulders.

"Hey, c'mon. Stay with me."

"But…I am with you…" Liv's head fell sideways as she furrowed her brow in confusion.

"Can you walk?" Nessa fought to squash the panic in her chest. She wasn't strong enough to carry Liv on her own.

How was she going to get Liv out of here? They were surrounded by Menhiran soldiers who knew Liv as their prisoner; she couldn't just wrap the elf in a stolen uniform. She needed a plan, or at least the vague concept of one.

That was a problem for slightly later Nessa. Right now, she had to make sure Liv could walk.

She heard Liv gasp, and spun just in time to avoid a thrown blade. It sliced harmlessly into the shoulder of her coat, landing somewhere behind her, and she looked up.

There, at the tent entrance, stood a young Menhiran soldier. He drew his sword as he approached, growling something in his native tongue.

Nessa swore.

She scrambled back, her fingers scrabbling against the ground before they fumbled over something heavy and smooth. Snatching it up, she chucked the unbroken jar at the boy's head. He tried to swipe it way with his sword, but missed, the glass shattering across his face.

Nessa jumped to her feet, already reaching for the other jars as the boy blindly charged her. She slid to the side, barely avoiding his blade, but now his body was pressing hers against the table. On reflex, she threw her knee into his groin, and he doubled over in pain as Nessa, heart racing, slammed another jar into his head, covering them both in foul-smelling liquid.

He stumbled, dropping his sword. Nessa kicked it away from him and dashed toward Liv.

"C'mon. We've got to go!" She knelt to help the elf to her feet.

"Oh, okay." Liv swayed dangerously. Suddenly, her eyes widened. "Ness!"

Without thinking, Nessa's fingers wrapped around the fallen sword. She spun, blade up, as her back collided hard against the table.

Panting, Nessa looked up at the soldier who had her pinned. His mouth hung open, his wide eyes staring at her as the dagger that only moments ago had been poised and ready to strike fell from his nerveless fingers. She took a panicked breath, then another.

On the fourth breath, he collapsed. Her hands felt hot and sticky around the hilt she held against her stomach. She stared at the boy's body, her damp eyes wide with terror.

What had she done?

Had she even done anything? No. Of course she had done *something*. She had simply turned around, and then it was over. Just like that.

A warm stickiness slid down the blade. The soldier on the ground didn't move.

The world threatened to tilt sideways.

Nessa shook her head, wiping her tears away with the back of her trembling hand. She had to get it together. It had been self-defense. He'd run into the blade. He would have killed her.

Gods and angels, he would have killed her.

She cleaned the blood from the blade with the end of her stolen coat. *Survive now. Freak out later.* She had to get Liv out of here. Both their lives depended on it. She couldn't break down, not yet.

Nessa slid the sword into her belt and covered it with the uniform coat, figuring she might need it if they ran into trouble. Whether she would actually be able to use it remained to be seen. She prayed she wouldn't have to find out.

Kneeling down next to Liv, she draped her friend's arm over her shoulder.

"Someone will notice he's missing." Nessa's voice shook.

"He was an ass." Liv's head fell onto her shoulder. "He attacked you when you weren't looking. That breaks the rules of…rules of…something."

"We need to be very quiet, okay?"

Do not look at the body on the ground. Get Liv out. Do. Not. Look.

"Okay," Liv whispered back as Nessa tucked her hair under the stolen hat and turned up the collar of the coat.

After wrapping Liv in the cloak Belara had given her, Nessa led them out the back of the tent. According to all the books she'd read, you lived longer if you used the back door. She moved as quickly as Liv's weight would allow, her muscles screaming under the strain. She told them to shut up and keep working.

Liv kept stumbling, muttering something about hair and blood, but Nessa's pounding heart wouldn't let her hear most of it. She hoped anyone who saw them would just assume Liv was drunk. They certainly smelled like it, thanks to whatever had been in that bottle.

Nessa's breath hitched as they passed the last tent in the camp. Liv's weight had her panting, her shoulder and knees burning, but she gritted her teeth and forced one foot in front of the other. They weren't safe just because they were out of the camp, plus she had no idea what was wrong with Liv. Liv needed help, and she wouldn't get it unless they made it back up the hill.

Her heart leapt into her throat when she saw two figures silhouetted at the top of the hill.

"Ada!"

Dagorn let loose a string of vibrant curses as he raced toward his daughter.

"What did you do? Why are you in a Menhiran uniform?"

Dagorn's eyes widened as he took in Liv's battered form. Placing his hands on either side of Nessa's face, he pressed their foreheads together. "When you weren't here, we assumed the worst. What were you thinking?"

"I don't know!" Nessa finally let herself breathe. "It just sort of happened!"

"Oh, she is definitely yours." Bryn feigned a smile, though the tight set of his eyes betrayed his grin. He took Liv in his arms as if she weighed no more than a doll.

"Hey!" Liv's expression formed a slow grin as her head listed back. "I know you."

"She's been drugged, or something." Nessa tossed the hat aside, her trembling hands catching on the buttons of her false uniform as she struggled fruitlessly to get it off, unable to help the little noises of frustration that escaped her. She wanted the god-forsaken thing off her as soon as possible.

Dagorn moved to help, slicing the buttons off efficiently with his dagger. His eyebrows lifted when he caught a glimpse of steel.

"Where did you get a sword?"

"Uh..." Nessa shook her head. "Found it?"

Liv laughed drunkenly, her head lolling dangerously.

"She's totally Dagorn's kid." She looked up at Bryn. "Remember when Dagorn...when Dagorn...hmmmm...."

She sounded like a metal girder had been dropped in front of her train of thought.

"We have to get her help." Nessa could feel her eyes beginning to sting. *Breathe*. She had to breathe. "She needs medicine, or a doctor or... I don't know! Something!"

Dagorn ran a hand gently over Nessa's hair to calm her. "If we can get her to Starcrest, she'll be safe there."

"Great." Nessa's hands fluttered in the air. She had no idea what or where or who Starcrest was, but if it would help Liv, she'd try it. At this point, she might as well just go with the flow.

"Let's go before an entire campful of soldiers notice their prisoner is gone."

It was another endless night of running, but for once, Nessa had no trouble keeping up.

Chapter Seventeen

When Service Workers Finally Snap

Nessa had never been more desperate for a horse.

Bryn, burdened with Liv, led their party through the woods, while Dagorn made certain to keep Nessa in front of him, his sword drawn as they ran. They were moving quickly, but Nessa kept pushing harder.

Liv's life could hang in the balance. A jet plane would not have been fast enough.

Bryn seemed to fly across the ground. No obstacle slowed him down, and his lead on Dagorn and Nessa eventually became so great they could only spot him by the flashes of his coppery hair through the brush.

Dagorn took hold of her hand to steady her as they stumbled through the rough terrain, and she kept her eyes on Bryn up ahead while her father watched the ever-thickening wood around them.

The rain started sometime in the early morning as the ground grew steadily steeper, lightning flashing twice above them before the heavens opened. The mix of water and sweat made Nessa's clothes rough and sticky against her skin as rain trickled down the back of her neck, but she couldn't bring herself to care.

Bryn pulled up the hood of Liv's borrowed cloak to offer his sister some protection. Her eyes had closed shortly after she'd last spoken her brother's name, her too-pale skin glowing against the mist. Somehow, no matter how thick the branches and the canopy above them became, the rain still poured down on their heads.

The ground's incline grew sharper until it felt more like climbing stairs instead of running. They had been climbing for hours. Mist swirled up around their legs every time they moved, leaving ghostlike wisps in their wake.

Nessa didn't see it at first. There had been nothing but fog and trees for what seemed like forever, then suddenly, there was a gate, barely visible. If Bryn hadn't stopped, she still might have missed it. The entryway was formed from the branches of two huge trees on either side, with detailed carvings shining in the rain, though Nessa had trouble discerning what the overall image was.

Bryn was speaking rapidly to a guard on the other side of a small opening in the gate. The guard looked over the four of them critically, somehow managing to look smug even though he was wetter than they were. Vaerin tripped off of Bryn's tongue faster than the rain running into Nessa's eyes, but the gate guard only responded louder and more quickly. Bryn's expression turned sour as he began to speak again, only to once more be cut off by the irritated guard. Dagorn tried to come to Bryn's assistance, but was quickly silenced.

Nessa wiped the water from her eyes and looked at Liv. She could see dark veins of…*something* starting to peek out from under Liv's collar, her body completely limp in her brother's arms. Nessa didn't know what had happened to her friend, but the lack of response made her chest ache. She thought hard, fiddling with the stone at her throat as her gut twisted, turning hot.

They didn't have time for this.

Nessa felt the flare of heat in her gut rush to her chest and her cheeks. She no longer felt the rain or the cold. How many times had she let arrogance like this slide just to keep the peace? This haughty elf was just another Mr. Lane or Melissa I'm-Head-Of-The-Book-Club Jones. How many times had she had to grin and bear it? Now her best friend's life was on the line.

She didn't exactly see red, but the color made an appearance at the edges of her vision. This smug jerk was about to find out exactly what it was like when service workers snapped.

Nessa drew herself up to her still-unimpressive full height and strode forward.

Time to put her newfound title to use.

Dagorn and Bryn paused in their speech as they felt the air around them shift. Their eyes fell on Nessa confidently striding towards them, the heels of her boots digging with determination into the mud. Human and elf both took a step away from her, seemingly without even realizing it. Dagorn recognized the spark that had been fanned to a flame. Her mother had worn the same expression more than once.

"Do you speak Common?" Nessa demanded more than asked of the face peering out at them from behind the gate. She held his eyes steadily.

"Yes." The guard blinked, and she saw him arch a condescending brow at her. She ground her teeth together. Now was not to time to fly off the handle, not yet.

"What appears to be the problem?" Her sharp and commanding tone held a hint of forced pleasantness. If it happened to sound a lot like Liv's in the same situation, that was merely a coincidence.

"You do not have permission to enter."

"What did you want us to do? Send a raven with a note?" Nessa could feel the heat in her chest turning to scalding hot magma. The guard opened his mouth to respond to such obvious ridiculousness, but Nessa barreled on, puffing out her chest.

"I was led to believe this was a *safe haven* for Guards and elves. Is that not true?"

"Yes, but…"

"Oh good! I was concerned there for a moment." Nessa turned to Bryn and Liv. She knew she was bordering on the edge of manic, but she didn't care. She had survived Melissa-Head-of-the-Book-Club-Jones for months, and right now there was more on the line than a tip and a coffee. If she could survive that entitled witch, this guard could survive her.

That didn't mean she would make the experience pleasant. Nessa was not going to let some elf with a cocky ego get her friend killed. That heat in her chest spread to her swirling gut as she gave the gatekeeper a tight smile.

"Then there should be no problem admitting the *Guards* Livia and Bryn of the House of Aeris, and Dagorn of the House of Callei. Oh, and you'll want to be quick about it. We have half a Menhiran battalion on our tail, so why don't you *open the gate,* and we can sort out the paperwork later?"

"Elves of the House of Aeris…"

"Look, Legolas…" Nessa pinched the bridge of her nose, closing her eyes briefly as her ears burned with rage. So much for diplomacy. "It's been a long night. We outsmarted the aforementioned Menhiran soldiers, found this one—" she pointed to Liv, her tone turning just left of dangerous, "—who is *very* drugged and definitely injured, fought off some guards, and practically carried her out without getting caught. Then, we ran all the way here in the pouring rain, dodging more soldiers, something we've been doing for *days*, plus avoiding all the other creatures out here that probably want to eat us."

The guard elf looked slightly concerned, but otherwise, unmoved. Nessa fixed him with a look that was full of ice and fire, her jaw clenched. When she spoke, her voice stayed eerily calm.

"Allow me to put this another way, Starshine. Standing to either side of me is a master swordsman and a master archer. And both of them will do anything I ask if I say please."

Nessa leaned forward until she was eye to eye with the elf. "Do you really think your precious *technicalities* are going to stop us?"

Dagorn had a hand over his mouth; Nessa wasn't sure if he was hiding a smile or going to be sick. She really didn't care. She would high five this guard in the face with a metal chair if she had to. This asshole was not going to be the reason for Liv's death.

Nessa straightened up again, trying to emulate Liv's intimidating bearing. She smiled tightly, her eyes blazing with barely checked anger. Her 'customer service' voice made an appearance.

"Now, be a dear and open the damn gate." Her head tilted sideways. "Please."

"Yes, my lady."

"*Thank you.*" Nessa's shoulders finally relaxed, though her expression didn't change. The door slammed shut, the gate began to move, and she could finally breathe.

"Unorthodox." Dagorn smirked. "Yet effective."

Nessa's cheeks burned with something other than anger. "We didn't exactly have time for diplomacy."

Bryn slipped in as soon as the gate was wide enough to allow his entry, and Dagorn guided Nessa in before following after, the mist and rain miraculously ceasing the moment they crossed the threshold. Nessa remembered giving the guard one final glare before Dagorn whisked her away, the gate closing firmly behind them.

Chapter Eighteen

Castle in the Sky

Nessa wasn't sure what exactly had happened.

When they'd arrived, Bryn took Liv in one direction while Dagorn had tried to take Nessa in another. *Tried* being the key word. She'd watched as Bryn and Liv were swallowed up by a crowd of elves, just barely managing to wriggle away from Dagorn to chase after them. She had to make sure Liv was going to be alright. She had to stay close to her. The last time they had been separated…

"Whoa!" Dagorn caught her before she could get far. "You need to get cleaned up and rest, little one."

"I can sleep when I'm dead."

"*Nessa.*"

The scolding was gentle, but she still flinched.

"But I need…"

"Liv is being seen to by the best healers in Avani. It's in the hands of the Elar now."

Healers? What could the healers of this land have over a regular hospital? Then again, Nessa knew Earth's modern medicine didn't have protocol for magic poison. Maybe they should have gone to see a witch, or a fairy godmother, or Lucy Pevensie.

Okay, now she was raving.

By the time Nessa managed to bring her thoughts back to some semblance of order, she was in a small room with Dagorn. The quiet startled her. After the songs and fires of the soldiers' camp, the splashing rain and gasping breaths of the woods, and even the bustling of the people in the halls of…wherever they were, actual silence seemed foreign. The lack of noise only made her racing thoughts seem louder.

"Nessa, what happened tonight?" Dagorn knelt before her. "What were you thinking, going into that camp?"

What *had* she been thinking? Had she been thinking at all? She couldn't remember making a conscious decision to stroll into the enemy camp to look for Liv; her feet had simply decided for her, as if something was pulling her there. Something had been screaming at her to *move* and the camp happened to be the direction she went.

"I—I don't…"

Her memory flicked through the night's events. She'd been on the hill with Bryn and Dagorn, then suddenly she was in the camp. She remembered her relief at finding Liv, that terrible circle on the table, then the soldier…

The soldier.

Nessa put her face in her hands, but it didn't make the memories stop.

"Are you hurt?" Dagorn asked.

"No! No, but I…"

Her throat closed up. She felt like her bones were going to rattle to bits, and her lip began to wobble. What had she done? Good God, or gods, or whatever! What had she *done*?

He would have killed her. He would have killed Liv. She'd had to. There'd been no other choice…had there? Was that supposed to make it better?

"Shhh. You're safe here, little one," Dagorn soothed.

Nessa felt him take her hands in his. She held on like a drowning man to a raft.

"There—there was a soldier, guarding Liv. I didn't mean to, he just came at me, and I grabbed something, and he just ran into it…"

Dagorn squeezed back. "You protected yourself and Liv. There is no shame in that."

"No honor, either."

"That soldier made his choice." Dagorn pressed his forehead to hers. "You know he would have hurt you, you and Liv both. I know it was a hard thing. I cannot say it was a good thing, but it was necessary."

"How could it ever be?" Tears fell from her eyes.

"Would *not* defending yourself or letting him hurt you be the right thing?"

"…No."

And somehow, that did make her feel a little better.

Dagorn let out a deep breath. He took Nessa's face in his hands, forcing her to hold his eyes.

"I'm proud of you, little one. You had the courage to protect yourself and someone you cared for. Not only that, you had enough luck on your side to rescue Liv." Kissing her forehead, he gave her a little smile.

"You also scared me within a hair's breadth of my life." He tried to laugh and failed. "Thank the Elar that you're safe. I haven't had nearly enough time with you, Nessa."

Nessa snorted. She wasn't exactly sure about the Elar, but she would thank them too. What she'd accomplished tonight was madness; even as everything was happening, she hadn't been sure how she was going to pull it off. She was damn lucky she wasn't dead.

"Don't worry. I don't ever want to do anything like that again."

"Good, though I'm sure you will at some point or another," Dagorn said ruefully. "You are my child, after all. I suppose it's my punishment."

That earned him a smile.

After washing her hands and face, plus a change into dry clothes, Nessa was beginning to feel more like a person instead of a half-drowned mouse. She tried to go find Liv, but Dagorn convinced her to lie down, 'just for a few moments.'

Her head hit the pillow, and she knew no more.

***

Nessa couldn't see anything. She shivered, feeling dampness that could have been rain or could have been something else entirely running down her forehead and the back of her neck. Her aching lungs wouldn't let her breathe as a cold tingle ran across her skin.

A bright spot came into focus, and for a moment, she thought it was a trick of her eyes, but as it grew larger and larger she finally recognized where she was. She was in the tent at the Menhiran camp. Two men stood by the ruined table, ignoring the body in the corner.

The first man appeared unremarkable, dressed in robes, but no matter how hard she concentrated, Nessa couldn't make out his face. The second towered over his companion, his broad shoulders and chest emphasized by the armor he wore. He held himself with an air of importance, like a man all eyes would turn to as soon as he entered a room. He could have been handsome, with dark hair and pale skin that shone in the lamplight, but his eyes...

There was something there. More accurately, something wasn't *there. They were dark, with nothing inside except fire. She shivered.*

He was angry.

His strong jaw clenched as he hissed at the servant, who backed away with his hands up. The other man was speaking quickly, sweat dripping from his brow despite the cold, when the boss suddenly snapped, grabbing the front of the smaller man's shirt and hoisting him into the air. The servant squeaked out quick words, his life likely depending on them, and gestured at the table with ink-stained hands.

The boss looked dubious, but slowly lowered the second man back to the ground.

His servant quickly patted his tunic, searching for something as he continued to speak. Then, with a flourish, he produced something from his pocket.

A lock of shockingly white hair…

***

Nessa snapped awake with a gasp.

"Shhh. It's just me."

Her eyes fell on Dagorn, who was sitting at the edge of her cot and gently rubbing her arm. Something nagged at the back of her brain. She had been dreaming. But what about? There had been light, and darkness…and something else. A man? No, that wasn't it. Two men? She felt like she was grasping at smoke.

"Sorry." She yawned, setting the puzzle aside for now. "Did I miss anything?"

"I thought you'd want to know Liv is awake."

"What?!" Nessa shot up, tossing her blanket aside and disappearing out the door before Dagorn could even rise from the bed.

She didn't need to be told where to go; her feet somehow knew the way. She paid no mind to the elves, who eyed with some disdain the strange human girl running through the halls in nothing more than a borrowed tunic and leggings, her bare toes slapping against the cool stone. No one tried to stop her, however. They simply got out of her way. Perhaps they thought she was crazy.

Liv was awake! She was going to be fine. Wasn't she? It felt too good to be true. She had to make sure, she had to see. Liv had to be okay. She had to be.

Nessa skidded to a brief halt before an intricately carved wooden door with two elven guards standing to either side of it, sparing them a brief glance before reaching for the handle. A guard snatched up her wrist.

"You can't go in there," he said.

Nessa yanked her hand back.

"The hell I can't," she snapped.

She shouldered her way through the guards and slammed her hands against the door. It opened so fast the handle smacked against the wall and bounced off.

There sat Liv, looking whole and healthy even with several pillows propping her up. The sunlight streaming through the windows did nothing to hide her still-too-pale skin, but there was a slight blush of pink staining her cheeks as she spoke to the male elf sitting on the edge of her bed — who had jumped up and spun around almost guiltily as soon as the door clanged open.

"Liv!"

Relief and joy flooded Nessa's chest, and she flung herself at her best friend. She clutched Liv tight, closing her eyes against the stinging.

Liv was safe. She hadn't lost her.

Liv hugged her back gingerly. "Hello, Ness."

A noise that definitely wasn't a sob escaped Nessa's throat, and she buried her face in Liv's arm to hide it.

"You're an idiot!" Nessa scolded.

"I am not the one who staged a foolish rescue attempt," countered Liv, even as she stroked Nessa's hair affectionately.

"Attempt?" Nessa snapped. "It wasn't an *attempt* if it worked!"

A soft chuckle made them both look over at the elven man. Nessa quickly wiped her eyes and sat up as Liv turned beet red.

"Sorry to interrupt." Nessa suddenly found Liv's bedsheets very interesting. "I may have been a little anxious."

"Understandable," the man said. "I will never fault you for your loyalty to dearest Livia."

Liv's ears turned pink. Nessa hadn't even known they could do that.

"Nessa, this is Koen, Lord of Kiriviel. Lord Koen, this is Nessa Everette."

"A pleasure." Koen bowed his head.

"You too." Nessa gave him an awkward smile, then turned to Liv.

"Perhaps we should change my last name to mean *awkward first meetings, but really, I'm not all that bad?*"

"That is taken, I am afraid," said Liv.

"Darn."

The sound of running footsteps in the hall made all three of them look up as Dagorn appeared in the doorway, panting. The guards attempted to keep him back, but were silenced by a look from Koen. Nessa's father took in the three of them, somehow managing to appear proud and exasperated all at once, then he bowed.

"My Lord Koen. Please forgive the intrusion."

"If you didn't intrude from time to time, Dagorn, my life would be uneventful, and honestly, far less entertaining." Koen rose and clapped Dagorn on the shoulder. "Livia was simply catching me up on your grand adventures."

"Thank you for seeing to Liv yourself," Dagorn said.

"It is my pleasure. Besides, my court would never forgive the loss of our mystic," Koen said, with a smile and a wink at Liv. "Now, if you'll excuse me, old friend, it appears I must have a strong word with my guards about their performance."

"Oh, don't be too hard on them!" Nessa interrupted. "I may have been a little manic and…well, rude."

"As you wish, dear." Lord Koen gave her a warm smile and bowed his head. "Your Highness."

Nessa half-expected him to do the same to Liv, but instead, he took her hand, lightly running his lips over her knuckles.

"Dearest Livia, I am glad for your safe return. If you require anything, simply call."

"Thank you, Koen."

Liv didn't take her eyes off him as he left.

Nessa turned to Liv, wearing a shit-eating grin, but Liv only blinked at her.

"What is it?"

"You must have seduced him with your unconsciousness and drool. Seriously, you've been awake less than an hour, and already some lord is smitten with you."

Nessa giggled as she teased her friend. It felt like taking a deep breath after swimming underwater for too long. It was such a stupid, normal girlfriends thing to do, but she *missed* having conversations that weren't about magic, or how everyone wanted her dead.

"I will feed you to my garden," Liv threatened.

"No, you won't."

"No, but I demand to know what, in the name of all the stars above, you were thinking coming after me!"

Nessa winced. "Look, that's not important right now. Are you okay?"

"I will be perfectly fine, thank you. *You*, on the other hand…"

"I don't know what happened!" Nessa tossed her hands up defensively. "It was happening before I knew what I was doing. It felt like something pulled me, like I couldn't sit still and I just had to *move…*"

Liv's brow furrowed. "You did not decide to move?"

"No." Nessa shook her head. "I just followed my gut and it took me where I needed to go."

Liv pursed her lips, then nodded. "Your abilities are starting to manifest faster than I thought they would."

"Wait, that's my Dreamer thing?"

"Since you have visions of the present, it would make sense that your intuition would be an asset," Liv clarified. "I myself often know where I need to be before I actually need to be there."

Well, that explained a lot.

Nessa stayed by Liv's side most of the morning, regaling the elf with her and Dagorn's adventures. Liv was not at all thrilled to hear about the tribe of bandits, but was at least glad their plan had worked. Well, up to a point. And it wasn't long before Bryn appeared to guard his sister and force her to finally rest.

Dagorn left Nessa to roam while Bryn watched over Liv, and after some food and a good hair brushing, she decided to wander around Starcrest.

Its streets appeared to literally be carved from the rock below, the soaring structures floating on their own with no apparent need for extra support. Intricate, swirling carvings reached up into the blue-gray mist above her head, the stone twisting and arching like delicate spider webs until the tops were lost in the clouds. Nessa longed to see the city in the sun, to glimpse the sparkle of the stone.

Green leaves and blooming flowers added pops of color to the otherwise gray landscape, the vines intertwining with the curves of the buildings. Colorful, glittering mosaics announced the streets and adorned the front of homes, most containing images of the sky, of clouds and stars and sunsets and everything else that appeared to be blocked by the eternal mist.

Everything here practically floated, including the people. The elves of the city, tall and elegant creatures, held themselves straight and proud, providing another splash of color against the neutral mass of floating stone. The men wore long, soft robes of rich hues and swirling patterns, and the women…

Every gown of shimmering fabric made Nessa green with envy. They were made from the softest fabrics, with embroidery and fine stones or leaves sewn on. Some female elves even had delicate lines of color painted on their faces to match the swirling patterns on their clothes. These elves appeared to be particularly revered; most of the others seemed to be making sure to remove themselves from their paths as they passed.

By comparison, Nessa looked like something the cat had coughed up. Her borrowed tunic and leggings had no delicate designs, and she could see the elves turning their noses up at the muddy tracks her boots left in the street. She did her best not to notice.

No one spoke to her; instead, she received sideways looks and whispers as she passed, and whenever she tried to approach someone, they quickly rushed away, pretending not to see her.

It was middle school all over again.

She finally found an isolated resting spot toward the very edge of the city. It was only a bench atop an overlook, the view obstructed by thick, churning clouds of silvery mist, but Nessa found herself relieved rather than disappointed. Here, she felt truly hidden.

"There you are!"

Nessa nearly jumped out of her skin.

So much for hidden.

She spun to see Lord Koen approaching. He was a tall, proud elf, with golden brown hair kept short and swept back in a style Nessa would associate with a World War II soldier. His strikingly handsome face, dusted with freckles, was set in a kind expression. Nessa hadn't known a jawline could be that sharp or square, nor that eyes could be so dark a blue.

"I was wondering where you had escaped to," Koen added as he settled beside her on the bench.

"Oh?" Nessa played with her fingers in her lap.

"Livia was worried. Apparently, you have a knack for finding trouble."

His tone, however, wasn't accusatory, and Nessa felt far from called out. Instead, the elven lord exuded a sense of acceptance; she could easily believe that he was wiser than the stars and fairer than a summer evening.

"I don't mean to."

"I believe it." Koen grinned. "But that, unfortunately, is something that runs in your family. Oh, please don't be alarmed. I've known your father since he was a child, and Livia and Bryn even longer. Your secret is safe with me, Your Highness."

Nessa pouted. "Doesn't seem like much of a secret."

"It will be difficult to keep your identity hidden," Koen agreed. "Anyone who knew your mother will certainly know. You look so much alike. And rumor has it, you have her spirit."

"Rumors?"

"Your—"

"Just Nessa, please."

Koen smiled, and Nessa found herself returning it, feeling as though she had passed some secret test.

"Nessa, the events of last night are being handled with the utmost secrecy." Koen sighed as he leaned back. "So, naturally, the entire city knows."

Heat rushed to Nessa's ears. Well, that explained the strange looks. They had all heard about the crazed human girl who had threatened a guard at the city gate. And of course, there couldn't be many humans in Starcrest.

"Your identity is still being speculated on, however."

"I'm sorry," Nessa told her lap. "I was, well, having a day."

"From what I hear, a week or so would be more accurate," Koen told her softly. "There is no need to apologize, child. In all honestly, I haven't been this entertained in decades."

"Well, I'm glad I'm entertaining, at least?" Though she wasn't sure whether it was a compliment or not.

"Very few of us know much of the outside world anymore. People will find their entertainment where they can."

"You mean you don't ever leave Starcrest?" she asked, shocked.

"No, not often. Kiriviel is protected. It can only be found by those who know where it is. Something the wizard you are searching for came up with, I believe."

"Kiriviel?"

"It translates to *Starcrest* in the Common tongue."

So, Kiriviel *was* Starcrest. And if Koen was Lord of Kiriviel …

Nessa felt her stomach drop into her toes.

"Wait, you're the ruler here?" she gasped.

His royal brow furrowed in mild confusion. "Everyone is always so surprised."

Nessa put her face in her hands to hide the heat in her cheeks. "I'm so sorry! I'm not crazy! I promise—"

She stopped only because Koen began to laugh. "Sweet child, there is nothing to forgive. Your courage and stubbornness saved someone who — well, Livia is a very old friend and I would miss her dearly if… But no matter."

"Your guard didn't seem to like her."

"That is his opinion."

"My father says that," Nessa agreed. "But why?"

"It is not my story to tell." Koen stared sadly into the mist, watching the swirls of silver and blue for a long moment. His eyes seemed to see nothing, or perhaps he was remembering things long forgotten. Nessa wondered where — or *when* — he was, but stayed silent for fear of interrupting.

"All I can say," he began softly, "is that elves are a rather superstitious people with an exceptionally long memory. Livia was the city's foremost mystic when we met. Most of Kiriviel believes her to be, well, tainted by association."

"Tainted with what?"

Nessa regretted the question as soon as it left her lips. Koen's dark blue eyes turned from distant to burdened, and she could feel the deep well of sadness he appeared to be drowning in. She pursed her lips together.

"It is a sad tale, and not one for today when we've already endured so much."

Nessa couldn't hide her disappointment. But she could feel Koen's melancholy from where she sat, and the desire to cheer him overwhelmed her. "Well, at least she's still here for it."

Koen smiled, looking exceptionally pleased. "Yes, she is."

***

Liv couldn't leave her bed for three days, a diagnosis she railed against and only agreed to in the face of Koen's persuasive charm. She still gave them as much trouble about it as she could, and refused to allow her bedrest to be a waste of time, demanding that Nessa continue her Visiril training. Nessa agreed if it meant that Liv would stop scaring her poor guards, for which Koen expressed his eternal gratitude. Apparently he was running out of people willing to take the position.

And so she spent her mornings sitting on Liv's bed, being lectured on her newfound abilities. She discovered that Vaeril's blessing could seep into other parts of her life besides her Dreams, and Liv said this was likely what had happened during her ill-advised (though successful!) rescue. Her connection to the magic of Avani was growing stronger, and since her blessing allowed her to see what was presently happening, her intuition was learning to react.

It was a theory, however, that Nessa was not anxious to test again.

Liv told her what having a vision felt like, how she rarely found herself occupying any physical form in her Dreams. Nessa equated it to watching a movie, with which Liv agreed. And upon waking, she said, Nessa's stone might feel odd, either very warm or comforting to the touch.

Nessa recalled the times she had woken feeling like she'd had a nightmare, but remembered nothing, and Liv confirmed that those were most likely Dreams. Nessa lamented not being able to remember them, but Liv reminded her that Dreams were a part of the Dreamer, and always would be.

"Like a photographic memory?" Nessa asked.

"Precisely." Liv nodded. "You just have to learn *how* to remember them."

"Is that why Ada is always doing that flipping motion with his fingers?"

"He has the history of the world to keep straight. He prefers to use…a mental catalog of sorts, to keep it organized."

Liv taught her a few techniques to help her remember the Dreams, which meant Nessa spent hours breathing, things eventually devolving into some kind of twisted Lamaze class. Then she tried listening to silence, or her heartbeat, which made her fidget until she nearly fell off the edge of the bed. They attempted meditation, which seemed to be working, until Nessa wondered aloud if they had dogs in Avani.

She'd lasted five whole minutes. And she still didn't remember any dream, magical or otherwise. All she knew was that she was going to lose her mind if she had to sit and breathe for one more second.

Afternoons were spent with Bryn and Dagorn. Her father had promised to teach her how to use her sword, and he intended to follow through, which at least gave her an outlet for her frustrations from the failed Visiril training. Dagorn started her out with defensive strategies, teaching her basic blocks and testing her less-than-impressive strength.

"You're smaller, so you can't rely on power to get you through," he told her. "You'll have to be fast. Your enemy won't be able to hit you if they can't catch you."

Then he made her run laps. As if life wasn't difficult enough.

Bryn, who had been watching the torture, took pity on the poor girl and suggested she learn a few dances to help with her footwork, which proved to be a marvelous idea.

Nessa had always loved to dance, and had even taken several classes back on Earth so she could go to swing nights at the YMCA with Albert. She learned the Avani dances fast, impressing even Bryn, who happened to be an excellent dancer himself.

Her sword work, however, left a lot to be desired; her first several attempts at sparring saw her smacked in the face with the practice sword. Dagorn apologized profusely every time, though it never happened on purpose, nor did he ever hit her particularly hard. It took several days before she had all the blocks down, though the bruises lasted a lot longer. Dagorn promised it would get easier.

She was waiting eagerly for that day.

At any rate, Dagorn was determined to make sure she knew how to defend herself, which she suspected was for his sake as much as her own. He even taught her a few tricks for close combat. One move in particular he drilled into her nonstop.

"When someone is coming at you with a dagger, like this—" he raised his fist up as if he were stabbing down at her "—you bring your forearm up to block it." He maneuvered Nessa's forearm into the correct place against his. "Then you push. You push *hard*, so they don't notice your free hand. That's the hand that will get you out of a jam."

"What do I do with it?" she asked.

"Take your dagger, and put it here," He indicated a space on his side just below his ribs. "And you don't take it out."

Nessa really hoped she'd never have to do that.

Her mind ached, her body throbbed, and by the time she fell into bed at the end of every day, her entire being welcomed unconsciousness enthusiastically. Koen had become invaluable; he often had potions or ointments to help with her injuries waiting for her at breakfast, a meal she often took sitting on Liv's bed. There were even fresh clothes.

Nessa never commented on the fact that Koen always happened to be in Liv's room first thing in the morning, but she had a few wild ideas.

When she felt like she couldn't take even one more minute of fake combat, Bryn whisked her away to continue her lessons in archery.

She took to it like a duck to chartered accounting.

"Bend your bow back further, *lebiet*," Bryn instructed.

"This is as far as I can go." Her bicep was screaming at her to stop.

Bryn sighed. "This is going to take a lot of work."

The first arrows she managed to thread fell from the string before she could even release them, and when they finally did leave the bow, they fell extraordinarily short of the target. In frustration, Nessa pulled an arrow back comically far, and it slipped free before she was ready.

The arrow flew gloriously, but any joy she felt disappeared abruptly when they heard glass breaking. She grimaced and turned to Bryn, who burst out laughing.

"But honestly…" He wiped his eyes. "We should probably run now."

They scrambled away like schoolchildren hiding from the principal, though on the upside, she got the afternoon off from lessons. Koen did ask at dinner that night why there was an arrow in his council room, and Nessa and Bryn shared a look, silently agreeing never to speak of it again.

Liv was allowed a walk outside the morning of their fourth day in Starcrest, and Nessa, though excited, generously suggested she take it with Koen. The two did not return until early afternoon and Liv looked happier than Nessa had ever seen her, so she considered her evil plan a resounding success.

She snuck away between her training sessions to explore the city whenever she could manage it; after all, when else would she find herself in an elven kingdom? Koen usually found her puttering around the market, or outside the city library, or simply strolling the streets and taking in all she could. He told her the story of the twisting spires of the city, how Kiriviel was arranged based on the stars they could no longer see.

When Koen wasn't with her, the elves' reaction to Nessa hovered somewhere between indifference and fascination. She didn't mind. Some of the more curious of them wanted to ask her questions, which she would answer in return for them teaching her some Vaerin.

And so, the days passed.

***

Bryn came to them on the morning of their sixth day.

"The Nolael will not come with us," he told Dagorn.

Dagorn blinked, looking surprised. Nessa, sitting on the edge of Liv's bed, took a gulp of her tea as she glanced sideways at Liv. Liv didn't look pleased.

"*What?*" Dagorn asked.

"Did you speak to Raya?" Liv suggested, her hand falling to Nessa's knee.

"She isn't here, Li Li." Bryn shook his head sadly. "And her cousin is far less agreeable."

"Chief Ayman has always helped us in the past," Dagorn cut in.

"Um…what?" Nessa asked, looking between her three companions. "What is going on?"

"I've been in talks with some of the leaders of the Nolael. Since our arrival, I've tried to convince them to assist us with the suspected attack on Galidel,"

Bryn explained. "But their chief isn't here, and negotiations with his second-in-command aren't going well."

"Why not?" asked Nessa.

"I do not see why they are so reluctant. Bryn and I traveled with Chief Ayman and his daughter, Raya, for a time," Liv told her with a shake of her head. "They have become very good friends of ours."

"And they don't treat us like we're cursed," Bryn pointed out.

"Wait, you're cursed?" Nessa scrunched her nose.

Liv said *no* at the same moment Bryn said *yes*. Nessa's eyebrows did a quick jump.

"Ooookay," she muttered. "Why don't you ask the chief directly, then? Surely he's against Menhir as much as you are."

She saw Bryn blink, then sit up. "That's not a bad idea."

"He isn't here, little one," Dagorn started, but Bryn shushed him with a light smack on his arm.

"No, no. She's right. There's no way I can get through to Cytan, but Ayman has been known to see sense on occasion."

"I know where they are," Liv spoke up.

"Bryn…"

"Look me in the eye, Dagorn, and tell me we don't need the men," Bryn challenged.

Dagorn sighed, defeated. "No, you're right."

"Always am. Then it's settled. Tomorrow, I leave with the Nolael to find Chief Ayman and convince him to join our cause, and you three will head for Erwani and Alaron."

"Is the Death Star blowing up a planet?" Nessa asked. They all stared at her, confused, and she blushed. "Alaron, Alderran…? Never mind. Who's Alaron? He's the wizard, right?"

"The wizard King Elvar asked Bryn and I to fetch for counsel, yes," answered Dagorn.

"For Galidel?" she asked.

"Yes."

Nessa nodded. "Cool."

Finally, she was getting the hang of this.

Chapter Nineteen

We Need A Code Word For Things Like This

The morning dawned bright and as clear as could be expected. Nessa hugged Bryn goodbye, forcing him to promise to return, preferably in one piece. If that couldn't be managed, she requested that he at least have most of his pieces, but admitted an eyepatch *would* look quite dashing. He only grinned and winked.

"You aren't getting rid of me that easily, love."

Nessa stood by her father, and pointedly did *not* watch Liv's conversation with her brother, which consisted of a lot of talking with heads close together and a few hugs. To her surprise and satisfaction, Koen even pulled Liv aside to wish her farewell. Nessa couldn't help but grin, while Dagorn pretended not to notice anything at all, which fooled no one. Liv returned to find both Nessa and Dagorn emphatically looking in opposite directions, and gave them both annoyed smacks on the arm.

They spent all morning trying to find their way out of the mists surrounding Starcrest, though Liv appeared to know the way well, leading them with a confident stride. Nessa kept her hand wrapped around Dagorn's for fear of being lost, which Liv mentioned casually was the very idea.

Nessa had to admit its efficacy. Without Liv, she wouldn't have been able to see her own hand in front of her face, let alone an entire small kingdom.

They didn't stop until Nessa felt the sunshine on her face again. The huge trees still surrounded the little party, though the canopy left enough open spaces between the leaves for the sun to peek through. She looked behind her to see the wall of mist had vanished. Only towering trees and long grass dotted with wildflowers met her eyes.

A few leaves tumbled to the earth. The path appeared at their feet as though it had started there all along.

Well, that was magic for you.

Liv had to sit and rest at that point. Her face had turned an unhappy color in the sunlight, a thin sheet of sweat glistening on her brow. Nessa plopped herself down beside her friend, forcing a piece of dried fruit on the elf as Dagorn paced around the pair of them like a hawk. Nessa didn't want to admit it, but the amount of time it took Liv to catch her breath worried her. They had to sit for more than half an hour before the elf was able to rise again.

Nessa chewed her lower lip when Liv wasn't looking, wondering if perhaps Liv should have stayed in Starcrest to rest. But Liv had sworn up and down that she was fit to travel, and while Dagorn and Nessa didn't really believe her, they knew neither one of them could stop her from coming with them.

Still, Nessa couldn't shake the foreboding feeling in the pit of her stomach. She ate little that day and spoke even less.

As they made their way through the forest, Nessa absentmindedly ran her fingers over her pendant. It felt cool. Liv had told her to listen to her intuition, but something wasn't adding up.

Dagorn must have felt it, too. He twitched every time a creature scuttled in the underbrush, his hand hovering by his sword.

They stopped to make camp just off the path, and Liv collapsed into sleep the second she took out her bedroll. Dagorn sat by the fire, pipe in hand, while Nessa flipped through the little book Koen had given her as a parting gift. He'd also blessed her with a set of elvish traveling clothes to go with her dragonskin armor and cloak, plus a sheath for her ill-gotten sword. The little book contained the history of Kiriviel, thankfully in the Common tongue.

She had been staring at the same page for twenty minutes.

"Does Liv…"

"Yes," Dagorn answered, pipe still in his mouth.

Nessa closed her book with a sigh, the pads of her fingers tracing the silver at her throat as she stared into the fire. A thought had been dancing just out of her reach all day. She could feel the idea of it, but every time she looked too closely, it vanished.

Her gut twisted. It felt like something was counting down, but to what, she didn't know.

"What's wrong?" Dagorn asked.

"Hmm?"

"You closed your book," he pointed out. "Something's wrong."

Her eyes fell to Liv. "I don't think letting Liv come with us was a good idea."

She hated herself for saying it, she really did, but she was barreling on before she could stop herself. “I worry she’s pushing herself too much. And something…something is coming. It’s like I can smell the rain in the air before the storm hits. I don’t like it.”

“She would not have allowed us to leave her behind,” Dagorn pointed out, though he sounded like he agreed with Nessa. “We’ll be careful with her.”

“Do we have time to be?” Nessa’s round eyes turned to her father. “I can’t stand the thought of losing her, but there’s whole families, whole kingdoms at stake, and…”

“You don’t have to think about that now, little one.” Dagorn gently kissed her hair. “We’ve always taken care of each other before, and we’ll do so now.”

“I guess you’re right,” Nessa conceded, though the feeling in her stomach didn’t go away.

“Try to get some sleep,” Dagorn told her. “The first watch is mine, anyway.”

Reluctantly, Nessa laid out her bedroll between Liv and her father, and was asleep in moments.

***

Nessa felt someone shaking her. Blinking the sleep from her eyes, she saw Liv crouched above her. She opened her mouth to speak, but Liv put a finger to her lips and crooked a finger at Nessa, beckoning her to follow.

Something buzzed around Nessa’s brain, her tight muscles making it hard to move as she shivered violently, practically tasting the unease in the air. Something was definitely wrong. Forcing herself up, she reached over to wake Dagorn.

Liv snatched up her wrist in an iron grip, and Nessa barely held in a gasp. She gave Liv a questioning look, but the elf shook her head. Nessa tried to pull her wrist away, but Liv twisted her arm hard enough to make her wince, forcing Nessa up and away from the camp. The contortions Nessa had to perform in order to grab her pack would have qualified her for Cirque du Soleil back home; as it was, she barely managed to get her hands on the bag before Liv dragged both them away into the night.

“Liv?” Nessa whispered. The twisting in her gut wouldn’t let her speak any louder. “What’s going on?”

“We must go.”

“What about Ada?”

Nessa glanced behind them at the ever-encroaching woods and saw their camp had vanished from sight. Stumbling on a hidden root, she slipped almost too easily from Liv’s grasp. Funny, why had her grip been almost painful moments ago if it was now so easily broken?

"Ada?" Liv's voice was distant.

"Yes!" Nessa growled. "You know? My father? The guy you left sleeping alone in the middle of the woods! Did something happen during your watch?"

"Yes" A pause. "No."

Cold crept into Nessa's chest before trickling into her toes and fingertips, and she found herself shivering. Every fiber of her being was screaming at her, though to do what, she wasn't sure. But *something* was making her hair stand on end and her heart pound hard against her ribs.

Something was *wrong*.

"Liv," Nessa called.

Liv didn't stop. Nessa stared, wide-eyed, at her retreating back.

"Livia!"

Liv finally stopped, and Nessa swallowed hard to steady her voice.

"Look at me."

Slowly, Liv turned, her movements becoming jerky, as though her entire body was glitching. Her usually proud shoulders were hunched, her head lax and tilted to the side, as if she had no strength to keep it upright. Liv's mouth hung slackly, her unblinking eyes staring at nothing, her gaze completely empty. Veins of inky black snaked along the back of her hands and poked out from the collar of her armor, her pale skin glowing nearly translucent in the dark.

Liv looked dead.

Nessa gasped, her hands flying to cover her mouth.

"Liv?"

"Come with me." The echoing voice wasn't coming from Liv's mouth.

Nessa shuddered and took a step back, feeling like she'd been trapped by a wicked fae from one of her stories. The lost princess, never to be seen again.

"Child." Liv's voice was at least coming through her lips this time, though they barely moved. "Come."

Nessa did what any respectable heroine in a horror movie should. She turned tail and bolted.

However, she had read enough books to know it was generally not wise to run from an immortal creature. Running, the theory went, would only attract their attention.

Unfortunately, said theory was currently proving all too true.

Liv dashed unsteadily after her as Nessa leapt off the path and into the brush, brambles clinging to her legs and scratching the back of her hands. She slid down a gentle slope, her hand flying out to grab onto a tree as she swung herself around, skidding on leaves in the dark.

Liv suddenly appeared in front of her. She swiped at Nessa with her bow, and Nessa ducked under the weapon, her boots nearly sliding out from under her.

"Liv! C'mon!" Nessa begged as she rolled to her feet. "This isn't you!"

But apparently it was, because Liv took another swing, and Nessa's forearm stung as the bow collided with her bracer. She had to get through to Liv, but how? It was hard to think clearly when Liv kept swinging a weapon at her.

Wood collided with Nessa's forearm with a *crack*, and she groaned as the vibration ran all the way up to her shoulder, rattling her teeth. At least it hadn't been aimed at her face. She ducked another swing, panting, when suddenly an idea — and the bow — hit her. Liv wasn't trying to hurt her, she realized. She was trying to wear her out.

Time to go on the offensive.

Instinctively, Nessa lunged forward, and she and Liv went tumbling to the ground, Liv rolling as they fell so that she landed on top. Nessa's eyes watered as Liv yanked cruelly at her hair, but she was still able to use her knees to knock the elf off her. They rolled again, Liv practically dragging Nessa by the hair as Nessa swung wildly at Liv's arm. Her hair finally came free and they rolled again, the struggle devolving into cheap shots and even more hair-pulling. What was going on? Liv knew better than to fight like an angry cheerleader in the girl's locker room. Mostly because last time, Nessa had actually won that one.

Nessa growled with effort and dragged Liv's bow between them. Using all her strength, she used the weapon as a wedge to shove the elf off her, sending Liv tumbling into a thicket as Nessa took off into the trees.

Dagorn. She needed to find Dagorn. But which direction had they come from? She had no idea, and while guessing didn't exactly seem like a good idea, at the moment it was the only option she had.

Slinging the bow across her back, she darted between the trees, her heart hammering inside her chest. She slid down hills, changed directions until she wasn't sure which way was up, and only stopped when her legs refused to carry her any further. Finally, she stood, panting, in the middle of a grove of trees, her eyes searching the darkness. Her rapid breath created phantoms in the air as she spun and spun, only to be met with nothing. She didn't see Liv, or Dagorn. Only the trees.

She collapsed to her knees, gasping. *Think.* She needed to think. Something was wrong with Liv; Liv had tried to *kidnap* her. She didn't know where her father was, and she had nothing but her pack, a stolen sword, and a bow with no arrows. She had no idea where Erwani was, nor Alaron the wizard. She was lost, tired, and very, very scared.

Nessa raked her fingers through her hair and swore quietly, her profanity eventually becoming a prayer.

Breathe! Think!

Things will look better in the morning, Lilly Everette had always said that. She just needed to wait for daylight. After all, she wasn't going to find her way in the dark.

Right. Morning. She just had to make it until then.

But where was safe to rest? Nessa wracked her brain, making a decision that was probably either genius or ludicrous. At this point, she didn't particularly care which, as long as it worked.

Hoisting herself into the nearest tree, she found a thick, study branch about midway up and rested her back against the trunk. It wasn't the best sleeping situation she'd ever been in, but it was better than nothing. Even with the bark digging painfully into her back, Nessa didn't fall asleep so much as pass out.

Chapter Twenty

Beware Falling Women

"Hello?"

Nessa jolted awake, her heart lodging itself in her throat. It did nothing to stop her shriek, and she tried to scramble away from what she assumed was Liv, her breath hitching in panic.

This was it. It was over.

She reached for the bow, her body tilting dangerously, but her hands found nothing but air. With a squeak, she flipped sideways off the branch, her stomach dropping as she tumbled through the air, grasping desperately at *anything* to stop her descent. Her palms scraped painfully against the bark, her hands stinging as her fingernails dug furrows into the trunk. She managed to halt her fall just long enough to think, *wow, that's a long way down*, before her aching hands finally failed. And then she was falling again, smacking into a branch on the way down and driving all the air from her lungs.

Luckily, the ground stopped her fall.

Gasping for air, Nessa put a hand over her eyes. Well, shit. That had hurt. A lot, as the pulsing ache in her hands, abdomen and back reminded her. She quietly cursed herself for being so stupid, along with the gods, the fates, a litany of Marvel villains and whoever else she felt like blaming.

"Are you hurt?" a deep male voice suddenly asked.

Liv wasn't a baritone.

The voice held an accent she couldn't quite place, its consonants sharp and its vowels slanted. It could have been a German speaking English, but there was too much French in the vowels. Nessa would know; she had been fluent in French back when she lived in a world with a France.

So, definitely not Liv. Which meant Liv hadn't found her yet. She could breathe.

...It also meant she had just fallen out of a tree in front of a complete stranger.

"Just my pride, thanks," she finally answered.

It was a lie. Her hands stung, her back ached and she wasn't even going to think about the size of the bruise that was developing on her butt. Every panicked beat of her gradually slowing heart sent fresh waves of pain to her abused body as heat flushed her face. Now that she wasn't scared, she could afford to feel embarrassed. But of course, that wouldn't do, so she settled for being annoyed.

"Didn't your mother ever tell you not to wake girls in trees?"

"No, actually. Funnily enough, the subject never came up."

Nessa looked up in order to give whoever this was a proper mouthing off, but the words died on her tongue.

The young man standing above her was everything she thought of when she pictured a dashing rogue, complete with an eyebrow quirk that made her want to punch him right in his perfectly square jaw. He appeared well-traveled; she had a front row seat to his worn, muddy boots from her position on the ground, and his many layers of clothing were faded, his skin more than kissed by the sun. In fact, he may well have taken the sun as a lover at some point and she had a *very* good time. His windswept dark hair matched his dark eyes, most of it falling in a mess around his face in a way that shouldn't have been as attractive as it was. The barely-there upturned set of his lips, slightly hidden by scruff, made Nessa realize he was making fun of her.

She quickly shut her mouth.

Smart retort. Right.

"Well, why not?"

...Nessa was not good at smart retorts.

"Why were you sleeping in a tree?" The man pointed up, his expression turning confused as he turned his gaze skyward, most likely searching for more falling women.

"So the things on the ground wouldn't see me."

"*I* saw you."

"Yes, well done," she snapped, her cheeks flushing.

Nessa quickly pushed herself up, ignoring the trembling in her muscles. Out of the corner of her eye, she saw the young man studying the bow slung across her back. She brushed the leaves from her hair to keep from having to look at him; she hadn't managed to tie it back up after the disaster that had been last night. Furiously, she combed the leaves from her locks. Since when did she have this much hair?

She could still feel him staring.

Her stomach clenched. Why was he staring? Did she have something on her face? Had she given herself away somehow? No, of course not. She reminded herself that she *had* just fallen out of a tree. Even in Avani, that likely wasn't a common occurrence.

She briefly thought about sticking her tongue out at him, but no, that would never do. Blushing, she brushed her hair behind her ear and instead drew herself up to her full — albeit mediocre — height. She opened her mouth to say something clever, but he beat her to it.

"You look like you need some help."

Nessa's train of thought derailed. There were no survivors.

She barely stopped herself from saying no. She wanted so badly to tell him no. After all, she had no idea who he was. He could have been a serial killer!

…Did Avani have serial killers? It must. Or he could have been a spy, or a mercenary. She knew Menhir, at least, had mercenaries.

Breathe.

But she needed to focus. She had to be honest about her situation: she was lost, she didn't know where she was going or how to get there, and she was separated from her father and all other forms of protection. Not to mention her best friend had somehow been bewitched into, at best, kidnapping, and at worst, murder.

Her pride stuck in her throat. "I, well, I am a little lost."

His already-quirked eyebrow shot up, though it wasn't in surprise. Nessa clenched her teeth. She could practically *hear* the condescension in that eyebrow raise.

"Where are you going?" he asked.

"Erwani."

"Well, good news, princess!"

Nessa visibly flinched. "Excuse me?" She could barely get the words out.

"You're not that lost. You're only about half a day's walk south."

"Oh." Nessa blinked. She needed to breathe. Her chest felt too tight, like her lungs couldn't expand correctly.

"Well, then. Thank you."

They stared at one another for a long moment. Nessa wasn't sure what exactly she was waiting for, but it was definitely something. Possibly it was simply to ensure that he actually left. She didn't like the idea of turning her back on him.

He pointed over his shoulder, that condescending eyebrow appearing again.

"It's that way."

"I knew that."

She hadn't.

Instead of wasting time being embarrassed, Nessa adjusted Liv's bow and started purposefully down the path, her head held high. She made an effort not to look at the man as she passed, but she could feel him staring at her back. It made her stomach churn.

Keep moving. Just put one foot in front of the other and keep going.

Princess. Why had he called her princess? Did he know? What had she done to give herself away? Was it how she spoke? Walked? It certainly wasn't her innate grace.

No. No, he couldn't possibly know. He was just some guy who woke up a sleeping girl in a tree. Gods and angels, she was never living that one down.

"I happen to be heading that way myself," he called after her.

Nessa stumbled; it was a miracle she didn't fall over entirely. Slowly, she turned to face him, her head tilted. He closed his eyes for a long moment, his handsome features set in an expression of hesitation and possible regret. One eye opened, regarding her.

"We could travel together," he suggested. "If you'd like?"

She bit her lip to keep from automatically saying *no*. After all, Dagorn had been right; it was safer to travel in numbers. Nessa had no hope of surviving another encounter with Liv if she didn't get out of these woods, and she knew it. She had to move fast, and that would be easier if she knew where she was going which she didn't. But he did. And a second pair of eyes probably wouldn't hurt. Liv might be less keen to attack if there were two of them.

She chewed on her lower lip. The guy looked like some sort of wild survivalist man who shaved with sharpened knives. He could use those same knives for serial killing.

"*And she was never seen again…*" played on a loop inside her head. This was a bad idea. This was dangerous. *He* could be dangerous, but was he more dangerous than Menhiran mercenaries? Or Liv? Was he worth the risk?

"I—yes, that might be wise."

He flashed a blink-and-you'll-miss-it grin before catching up to her in three strides.

"Off we go then, duchess."

"I'm not a duchess." Nessa's tone became a bit too stern. "It's Alice."

"Interesting name." He held out a hand, giving her a broad grin and a mocking bow. "Rinn."

They shook, and Nessa realized she wasn't touching skin, but leather. He was wearing fingerless gloves. Well, that was odd. Why would he need fingerless gloves? She shook her hand lightly, the feeling of leather on her fingertips refusing to leave.

They walked in silence for a moment, and Nessa kept her eyes on the woods around her. It all looked so very *green*. The low branches of the green trees covered in green moss hung above greener grass with green brush in between.

Surely Liv's bright white hair would stand out amidst all the green.

...Right?

Nessa had never failed to be an optimist, which was likely where that thought had come from. Liv had already proven that if she didn't want to be seen, she wouldn't be.

A twig snapped behind them.

Nessa spun around, her hand flying to the hilt of her sword as her heart launched itself into her throat and stayed there. Rinn jumped sideways, his hands flying to his belt, but he relaxed when he realized his companion's eyes were on the woods.

She swallowed hard, her breathing shaky, though her gaze remained focused on the treeline. The greens of the leaves and grass faded into still more green as the forest deepened, and she strained her eyes until her vision blurred from the effort — but there was no flash of snow-white hair.

Still, she didn't move.

Rinn didn't speak, watching the woods with his hand still hovering over his belt. He glanced back at the trembling girl, then cleared his throat with all the ease of a sunning cat.

"What happened to your party?" he asked.

Nessa jumped a mile high.

"Hmm?!"

"Your traveling party, countess."

"Oh." She forced herself to relax. "Sorry, I thought I heard something."

"You likely did."

"Not helpful," she deadpanned.

Rinn shrugged slightly, then started back down the path. Nessa quickly caught up to him.

"You didn't answer my question, my lady."

"Alice."

"Whatever." Rinn rolled his eyes. "What happened to your traveling party? A young lady such as yourself doesn't travel alone this far north. It's not smart."

"I'm not a lady."

His eyebrows jumped. "And clearly, not very smart."

"You're very rude, you know."

Nessa glared at him balefully, hoping to subdue that smirk, but Rinn only preened. His grin made her want to slap him.

Her hands itched, and she glared harder. Perhaps she could liquify his kidneys.

"So I've been told. Numerous times."

It wasn't hard to feign shock. "I can't imagine *why*."

For his part, he seemed genuinely perplexed. "Neither can I."

She wanted badly to respond but bit her tongue. Rinn seemed like the type who always needed the last word; in short, he seemed like a bit of a bastard. Perhaps if she didn't give him anything to comment on, he'd stop calling her every noble title he could think of. It made her stomach want to collapse in on itself.

She rolled her shoulders in an attempt to ease the tension, but that only reminded her of Liv's bow on her back, and *Liv*, and her hands trembled all over again.

She could relax a little once she reached Erwani; Liv would have less power once she was out of the forest. But Nessa wouldn't be able to hide there forever. The only hope she had of finding Dagorn again was to stick to the plan, and the plan was to find the wizard Alaron. And if said wizard was really so wise, perhaps he'd be able to help Liv.

It had to be a spell. Nessa *knew* it was a spell, but she wasn't certain *how* she knew that. She just did.

Her mind swirled through a fog. How did she know? A thought hovered at the edge of her mind, but every time she examined it too closely, it vanished. Was it something to do with a man? No, two men? And white. White hair…

A curtain dropped on her stage of thought. What had she been thinking about? A spell! Yes, Liv was under a spell.

And who better to lift a spell than a wizard?

She felt it again, that sense of being watched, and the hair on the back of her neck stood on end, her arms erupting in goosebumps. Rubbing at them did nothing for her unease, so she forced her lungs to function steadily, feeling eyes boring into her back. Swallowing down her heart, she glanced casually over her shoulder, but saw only green.

Out of the corner of her eye, she saw Rinn's spine straighten, the tension in his jaw racing down his neck to his shoulders. His hand was still hovering by his belt.

Nessa tried to focus, ignoring the wobbling in her gut. Her eyes fell on the leaves, which remained as still as the air around them. The woods descended into silence, without a whisper of movement, or life. No birdsong, no animals snapping twigs, and no bugs buzzing around the brush. Every sound had all but died.

A shiver ran down her spine.

"Everything alright, countess?"

"Will you stop that?" she snapped, nearly jumping out of her skin.

She could feel her annoyance with her traveling companion overcoming the roiling fear in her gut, her face growing warm with anger even as she swallowed down the tightness in her throat.

But she had to remember that none of this was Rinn's fault. He wasn't the reason Liv had gone crazy, nor had he gotten Nessa hopelessly lost. He had nothing to do with her long list of running failures, so she had to at least pretend to play nice until they got to Erwani. He was doing her a favor, after all.

"Why do you keep calling me that, anyway?"

"Because you're nobility."

Nessa quickly hid her face under the pretense of braiding her hair, unable to control the stab of cold overtaking her lungs.

Technically, everything she had told Rinn was true — and technically correct was the best kind of correct. She *wasn't* a duchess, or a countess. As long as she didn't admit the specifics, she could keep her identity a secret. The hard part would be keeping her story straight.

"Why do you say that?" she asked.

"Your hair."

Nessa moved her curtain of hair to look at him, one curious brow raised. She saw him swallow.

"I beg your pardon?"

"Your hair." His soft tone soon turned teasing. "It's clean."

"What's wrong with clean hair?"

"It means you either have the time, or money, or both, to keep it that way."

It was just her luck that Rinn was more observant than she'd given him credit for. He had spotted her all the way up in that tree, after all. Chewing this over, along with her lower lip, she tied her hair back into a braid, feeling Rinn watching her out of the corner of his eye.

"*Your* hair is clean," Nessa pointed out primly.

"I jumped in the river this morning."

"That wouldn't make it clean."

She knew *that* from experience.

A look of amusement wrestled with one of annoyance on his face, though the annoyance inevitably lost. He ran a hand over the suspicious locks in question, the disheveled look only making him more attractive.

Nessa scowled. How was that fair?

"You're lying about who you are," he pointed out. "Alice isn't a real name."

"Are you saying I'm not real?"

"You aren't denying it?" He sounded surprised.

Nessa tilted her head expectantly. "Are *you* lying about who you are?"

Rinn turned to meet her gaze, his lips quirking sideways. It wasn't his usual condescending look, but instead, there was a sadness in the corners of his eyes. He seemed almost regretful, while still enjoying some private joke.

"With every breath."

Nessa tried to give him a little smile. After all, this world was dangerous. Every world was, and anonymity was a special kind of armor; she understood that now. Rinn didn't exactly seem trustworthy, but that didn't mean she had to be cruel.

"I'm sure you have your reasons."

"I could." He shrugged. "And then there's your bow."

"My bow?"

"It's too fine a quality."

Right, he was back on why she had to be nobility. At least this time she had an answer.

"Oh!" Nessa glanced back at the weapon, as though she had suddenly found a giant stick of wood attached to her back. "That's easy. It's not mine."

"It's not?"

"No."

Those dark eyes narrowed as they looked her over again, and Nessa suppressed a grin even as her nerves skyrocketed. It felt good to bewilder him a bit, even if it was over such a little thing. Anything to humble him a touch.

However, now he was staring at her again. Did this guy ever blink?

"Hmm," came the rumble deep in his chest. "One moment."

Rinn paused in the middle of the path, and Nessa stopped beside him in surprise. What was he doing? He narrowed his eyes as Nessa shifted nervously from foot to foot. Why was he staring at her?

"What—"

She closed her mouth when he began to circle her, looking her up and down with a contemplative finger on his chin. Nessa could feel heat rising in her cheeks, though the warmth was quickly whisked away by the crisp breeze.

"Hey! Stop—what are you doing?" She stumbled away from him. "Do you have any idea how creepy that is?"

"I'm reassuring myself you won't try to kill me."

"Oh, well, if you keep that up, we'll have to see," she retorted, crossing her arms over her chest. Perhaps it would make her seem larger, or at least keep her heart from leaping out of her ribs.

"I'd like to see what you can do with a bow and no arrows," he muttered. Nessa glared.

"Stop circling me! What, were you a vulture in another life?"

"A what?"

"Never mind." She quickly found her shoes very interesting as the tension in her muscles forced her to move, leaving Rinn behind without even glancing at him. It was better than standing there, chewing on her lower lip and playing with her fingers.

He was grinning like a thief when he caught up to her. "You fluster easily."

"Or it could be I don't like strange men checking out my ass," Nessa pointed out sweetly. She knew how good her butt looked in these pants. Why lie about it?

"Who said I was doing that?" His tone indicated that was precisely what he'd been doing.

"I'm sheltered, Rinn. Not stupid."

"I will admit, I am more intrigued by your weaponry than your backside, Alice." Rinn tapped a finger on his chin. "A bow that isn't yours, no quiver, no dagger. Just some light but well-made armor and a sword."

Nessa stayed silent for a long moment. What could she say to that? That she had technically stolen the sword? Or had she actually won it? The events of Liv's somewhat pear-shaped rescue were blurred together in her mind's eye; she never had figured out what that symbol on the table meant. So why had the image stuck with her?

"Where are you from, princess?" Rinn asked.

"*Alice,*" Nessa corrected yet again, venom in her voice.

"You just seem like you aren't from around here."

"I'm not."

If only he knew.

"Then what brings you this far north?" he asked.

"I was traveling with my father. He has business up here."

She didn't think it wise to bring up the fact that their mission was to find a wizard. From what she'd been told, it sounded like Alaron preferred to remain unbothered. She didn't even know if he would be willing to help her, or Dagorn, but it was the only shot she had right now. She saw Rinn open his mouth to interrogate her further, but before he could speak, she beat him with her own question.

"Where are you from? I've never heard your accent before."

He blinked at her once, then twice before he got his voice to work again.

"My what?"

"Your accent," she said. "I've never heard it before. Your vowels are weird, and the consonants are really sharp, like they're coming from the front of your mouth…"

Nessa paused when she realized that Rinn was no longer walking beside her. She turned to face him, a question ready on her lips, but his expression silenced her.

His burning gaze tore into her, something in those narrowed eyes sending a shot of fear straight into her gut. The muscles of his shoulders coiled tightly under the collar of his coat, his jaw clenching as his fingers danced over his belt.

Nessa suddenly realized she had said a very wrong thing. Her stomach twisted sharply into knots, but she managed to keep her expression neutral.

"What?"

Rinn stared dangerously at her for a few more moments as she just barely dared to breathe. She felt like a gazelle who had just spotted the lion, and all she could do was wait to see if it was hungry.

When Rinn spoke, his tone was flat and cold.

"I've picked up a bit here and there, I suppose."

This was a test. It had to be a test.

Nessa swallowed hard. Slowly, she nodded.

"Makes sense."

It didn't.

Suddenly the tension bubble popped, and Rinn's shoulders eased as his hands flexed, then relaxed, his posture settling back into its usual loosely held grace. Nessa finally sucked air back into her lungs. Nevertheless, when he returned to her side, she gave him extra room.

"And then there's your armor," he said suddenly.

She blinked at the breaking of the silence. "My what?"

"Dragonskin armor isn't easy to come by."

"It was a gift."

She wasn't going to mention that it was a family heirloom; that would almost certainly confirm his suspicions.

"In that case, you are very fortunate in your choice of friends."

"Some might argue that point," Nessa muttered to the ground.

It *wasn't* fortunate that Liv had been bewitched into trying to kidnap her. Liv had given up everything to protect her and Avani. She'd left behind her entire world for a chance at saving it.

If the bewitchment had been successful, and Liv had managed to take her, it would have destroyed everything the elf had ever worked for. All she had sacrificed would be for naught. And for all Nessa knew, Liv had slit Dagorn's throat while he slept before attempting to take her. It would certainly have taken care of any potential loose ends.

Nessa shook her head. She couldn't think like that. Dagorn had to be alive. And she couldn't forget Bryn, still out there somewhere with the Nolael. She had allies; the question was whether she could stay alive and free long enough to find them.

Rinn arched a brow at her.

"Are you running from something?"

"Nope." Technically, she was running *to* something — a wizard, to be specific. Rinn regarded her skeptically as a feigned look of concern crossed his features.

"Lover's quarrel?"

Nessa couldn't help it. She burst out laughing, her hand quickly covering her mouth to muffle the sound. Shaking her head, she swallowed down the rest of her giggles.

"Not even close."

"Oi! You must be running from *someone*," he said indignantly.

"Why do you say that?" she asked.

"I know the look." He snapped his fingers as an idea struck him, clearly believing himself to be clever. "Escaping an arranged marriage!"

Now it was Nessa's turn to arch a brow. "Isn't that just another kind of lover's quarrel?"

He shrugged. "Well, you'd have to *like* your betrothed."

"I'm not betrothed."

"Then why do you have a ring?"

Nessa glanced down at her right hand. Her sweet sixteen present. She'd nearly forgotten. The simple silver band on her third finger had seen better days; the lily of the valley engravings, her mother's birth month flower, were now difficult to see under all the grime.

She adjusted the scarf around her neck, a little smile on her lips. Her last remnants of Earth. Neither was recognizable anymore. The scarf was already sun-faded, the blue less brilliant than it had been, and a little worn. Nessa supposed she was probably unrecognizable, too. Her ring didn't even fit on its original finger; apparently, she'd slimmed down a bit since arriving in Avani.

Well, she had been doing a lot of running.

Her fingers traced the swirls of silver at her throat as she tried to decide whether the question about her trinket was worth answering, and they fell into a companionable silence. Nessa chewed at her lower lip, sneaking surreptitious glances at Rinn. He caught her once, giving her a fox's smile, and as he turned his head, she caught a glimpse of sparkle at the back of his neck.

"You have a chain."

"To hold all my talismans," he joked, eyebrows bouncing.

"Are you a wizard, then?"

"Don't even joke about that, duchess."

"What are you heading to Erwani for?" she asked, instead of pushing. Maybe it would get him to stop thinking about her valuables, and her story.

"Just traveling."

"In the middle of a war?"

"It's always the middle of a war, Alice," he replied pessimistically.

Nessa arched a brow at him, doing her best to mimic his slumped posture. "Lover's quarrel?"

"Absolutely."

She snorted. His lover was either very lucky, or very stupid, or both. Anyone with eyes could see Rinn was attractive. A person would put up with a lot just to be able to stare at that face all day.

Nessa, however, was reaching her limit.

Off in the brush, something snapped, and Rinn spun in the direction of the noise so fast Nessa almost collided with his back, his hand hovering over his belt again. This close, she could see flashes of steel; his long fingers brushed the hilt of a broadsword, while a knife and dagger rested on his other hip. Clearly, if he wanted to kill her, it wouldn't be much of a fight. The only reason Nessa had made it this far was sheer dumb luck, and she knew it.

She put her hand on her sword and stood frozen, waiting.

Rinn finally relaxed. "That sounded big."

"I think the biggest thing out here is your ego."

"You've clearly never seen a troll." He rolled his shoulders. "They pale in comparison."

Nessa rolled her eyes so hard they nearly fell from her head. "Thank you for proving my point."

"I'm humoring you. And what is…whatever that thing is that you called me earlier?"

"A vulture?" she ventured.

"Yes, what is that?"

"Uh…" Nessa suddenly found the end of her braid fascinating. "It's a fantasy bird, I guess. Circles things that are about to die so it can eat them."

Rinn's jaw fell open.

"That sounds horrid," he muttered, disgust rolling off him in waves.

"Well, yeah," she agreed.

At that moment, the trees above them suddenly parted, allowing sunlight to blaze down onto both of them. Nessa turned her face up toward the light, her eyes nearly closing in pleasure as the warmth on her face trickled down her neck and into her chest, chasing the cold from her lungs. A gentle wind swirled around them, carrying with it a hint of damp and ozone, and she let her fingers dance across the tall brush at the edges of the path, the bobbing leaves turning into her touch as if sighing in relief.

Just exist. Just breathe.

Rinn watched her a moment out of the corner of his eye. Nessa met his gaze expectantly, but he said nothing, his expression turning curious. Finally, he shook his head, returning his eyes to the path.

The trees grew fewer and younger as they neared the edge of the wood, their trunks growing thinner and thinner. The newly bright light made Nessa blink; she really needed to invent sunglasses after this was all over. It was certainly a happier situation to contemplate than the wall of dark clouds suddenly crowding the horizon.

Piles of dark stone began to line the edges of the road. At first, they were rare, just small islands of gray in a greenish-yellow sea, but as they continued down the path, some of the islands became bars and lines, then corners, pieces of a window. Some stones were blackened under a thin layer of moss, as though they'd been singed.

The tall grasses bowed in the wind, only to reveal even more islands of rubble, and Nessa caught whiffs of rotted wood and moss amongst the ozone and damp earth. And something else, something light and sweet. That was when she saw the clumps of brightly colored flowers keeping silent watch over the stone islands.

More ghost gardens.

She released a deep sigh. She didn't think she'd ever get used to it, all the signs of a vibrant life that once was, and never would be again. That was all she'd gotten to see of Avani so far; she'd come late to the party and all the guests had gone. All that was left were torn streamers, deflated balloons, empty bottles and a great big mess. And worst of all, no one seemed interested in cleaning it up.

Nessa couldn't help but wonder what life had been like for the people here. Were there families? Pets? Had children played along the path as travelers passed by? She would never know, because now it was all gone. She knew Menhir had to be responsible, because who else could it be? How much destruction would be enough for them?

Suddenly, a stone carving just off the path caught her eye, and she paused, staring at a series of triangles and lines engraved into the cornerstone of what might have been a fence, or a home. Maybe she'd imagined it, but the lines had almost seemed to glow for a second. When she looked at the carving head on, however, the effect disappeared.

...Wait, she'd seen that sigil before. Nessa pulled on the leather cord around her neck, holding up the medallion Liv had given her when they'd first arrived. The symbols matched.

"Tired, princess?" Rinn teased.

"What's this mean?"

Nessa pointed to the symbol on the stone, ignoring the snarky title yet again, and Rinn stepped over, bending down to take a look. As he crouched next to the wall, he traced over the carving with his fingers, but never touched the stone.

Nessa lowered herself to kneel beside him, letting her own fingers brush the cool rock. Her fingertips tingled slightly, as if she'd plunged her entire hand into a bucket of ice water, and she jerked her hand away, shaking her hand with a small hiss. The tingly feeling didn't go away.

"Protection spell," Rinn said at last.

"Does it work?"

"Depends on who you ask." He nodded to the piles of rock. "It didn't for them."

"No, I guess not."

Nessa's fingers fiddled with her pendant as she thought. Well, the protection sigil *had* worked, in a way. This section of the wall still stood. Whoever lived here had clearly thought trouble was coming, and boy, had they been right. She surveyed the toppled stones with an overwhelming sense of sadness.

"Was all of this once part of Erwani?" she asked.

Rinn shrugged. "Don't know. Raids are pretty common this far north."

"To feed Menhir's army or Menhir's people?"

"Menhir does everything for its army." He pursed his lips, his expression matching his grim tone. "The people are an afterthought."

Nessa's countenance turned genuinely sorrowful. "That's awful."

What kind of country fed its army while its people starved? Though she supposed wartime rationing on Earth was a depressingly similar equivalent. Give the troops the butter and leave none for the civilians. The war needed to be won and the men needed fuel to fight it.

Napoleon had been right, armies marched on their stomachs. But did innocent people always have to bear the cost of war? Glumly, she admitted to herself that Calebrir was probably doing the same thing as Menhir.

The thought made her stomach clench. There really wasn't a good guy and a bad guy when it came to war. There was evil and lesser evil and the people involved were left to discern between the two.

"It can't be easy to see the army eat while your children have nothing. Those poor people."

Rinn was openly staring at her, his mouth agape, and Nessa blinked owlishly at him.

"What?"

He shook his head. "We shouldn't linger in the open like this."

Hoisting himself to his feet, he offered Nessa a hand up, and she took it, not sure if she was more surprised at him or herself. While his grip was strong, he didn't crush her hand — though she didn't miss how his fingers dragged over hers when he finally let go.

They continued down the path in silence, Nessa looking down without really seeing where she was going, and nearly twisting her ankle on a hidden stone buried under the dirt. She managed to catch herself, but after that, she kept a closer eye on her footing. Rinn, of course, didn't appear to be having any trouble at all. He also didn't seem the least bit bothered when his traveling companion nearly ate dirt, though he did help her up.

"Do you travel a lot?" Nessa asked suddenly, rubbing the fresh scrape on her palm. She stared at her hand instead of looking at him. Something…there had been something…when he touched her…

"Yes."

"No one can have that many lovers," she scoffed.

"In your humble opinion."

The smirk on his face, however, was anything but humble, and Nessa rolled her eyes as she shook her stinging hand.

Wait, her hand! She stared at it a moment, turning it over and over again, and spoke without thinking. "Is it because you're a thief?"

Rinn shook his head. "Such accusations."

She held her now-bare hand out to Rinn, palm up. "In that case, may I have my ring back, please?"

He glared at her. "What makes you think I have it?"

"You slipped it off my finger when you helped me up. I had it on before that, and not after." Nessa shrugged. "May I have it back, please?"

"If I did have it, and I'm not admitting I do, what do I get in return?"

"Um…well…" Nessa's heart hammered in her chest. She didn't have much to offer. He could ask for anything, but she still had the power to say no.

…Would he actually accept *no* for an answer?

"What do you want?" she asked instead.

"Your ring. I thought that was obvious."

"I'd rather have it back," Nessa said. "My parents gave it to me."

The teasing edge to his voice disappeared. "I see."

He thought a moment, fingers twiddling with one of his gloves, when suddenly her ring appeared from underneath the leather and began to walk over his knuckles like a poker chip.

"How about the bow on your back?"

Nessa bit her lower lip as she thought. Technically, the bow wasn't actually hers to trade away. Then again, she had no arrows, so it was also completely useless to her, unless her enemy happened to be an errant window. The ring wouldn't help her survive, but it was a piece of where she'd come from. That wasn't something she was willing to let go of.

"Okay." She thrust her hand back out for her ring, but Rinn jumped back, waggling a finger in her face.

"Not so fast, countess. We'll make the trade when we reach Erwani."

"So you can just stab me and take them both?" Nessa snapped. She couldn't help it, she wanted her ring back. The deal had already been struck and now he was changing the terms after the fact.

Bit of a bastard, he was.

Rinn placed a hand over his chest, feigning offense.

"Please, Alice. I'm a gentleman."

"Fine!" Nessa flung up her hands in defeat. At this point, she just wanted him to agree. She was too tired to bargain anymore; her head ached every time she thought about Liv, and Rinn's smug dealing made her crave a long sleep to escape the throbbing in her head. "Just don't lose it in all those pockets, MacGyver!"

He looked confused. "Is that another kind of bird?"

"*Yes!*"

It wasn't.

The next hour passed in silence. Nessa fumed quietly beside Rinn and made no effort to hide her irritation, her teeth grinding furiously to keep from physically snapping at him. In a feverish daydream, she pictured him tripping, getting an opportunity to kick him in the shins.

Naturally, the thief in question appeared completely unbothered by Nessa's mental attacks.

She tried harder.

"Something on your mind, my lady?" Rinn asked.

"I'm trying to make you trip with my mind," she hissed.

"And how's that going?"

"Do you feel like tripping?"

"Not particularly."

"Then not well."

Closing her eyes, Nessa took a deep breath, her chest aching nearly as badly as her temples. She ran a hand down her face in an attempt to reset her head, only to find her hand trembling. Why, of all things, was she losing her mind over a ring? It held very little value to anyone but her, and there were much bigger problems she needed to deal with. So why did she feel like crying?

"You must be upset," Rinn pointed out.

Nessa glared to prove him right, and his brows drew together curiously.

"You're quiet. It's the first time you've been quiet all morning."

"Would you prefer I talk?" If so, she hoped her tone would encourage him to change his mind.

"You just seem the type to prefer conversation to silence," he noted. "Wait, are you *pouting*?"

Nessa finally snapped. "I just had a thief steal a gift from my parents, who I'm probably never going to see again! What do you think?!"

She *really* wanted to kick him in the shins, so she kicked a stone out of her path instead. It bounced away with angry vigor.

"I thought your father had business in Erwani?" he tried.

"He does."

"But you'll probably never see him again?"

"It's complicated." Running her hands over her hair, she kicked another stone, which soared over the grass to bounce off a tree before settling right back onto the path. She stared down at her feet to hide the sting in her eyes. *Stupid rock.*

"Nothing has exactly gone according to plan lately." Her voice wobbled and she hated it. Nessa rubbed her temples. Why did her head hurt so much?

She glanced from side to side. Something didn't feel right. It felt like walking into her house and knowing someone else was there even though no one was supposed to be. The very air tasted of anticipation.

"That's your problem, duchess. Nothing can mess up your plan if you don't have one," Rinn pointed out cheerfully.

Nessa thought about conceding the point, before realizing she'd rather eat the rock she'd just kicked.

"Is that how you live, Rinn?"

"Every day."

"Sounds stressful," she observed.

"I've always managed just fine," Rinn said with a shrug.

"Until the day you don't."

The thin thread Nessa's mental state hung by jerked as a single thought suddenly snapped to the forefront of her mind.

They were being followed.

The air grew thick and heavy, sticking to her skin — and not just because of the impending rain.

Liv must have found them. But why wasn't she attacking? True, Nessa had Liv's bow, but the elf had proved herself more than capable without a weapon. So why? Unless it wasn't…

"And what about the day *your* plan falls apart?" Rinn asked.

"Strangely enough, that was yesterday," Nessa admitted.

"And yet, you're still here."

"Survive now, freak out later." Nessa's new life mantra tumbled easily from her lips, and Rinn's face turned somber for the barest of moments.

"I know the feeling, princess."

Her ring appeared again from under his glove, the light dancing across the silver. She chanced a glance at Rinn's face and saw that his eyes were scanning the thick brush around them. Maybe, if she were quick enough…

Too late, those dark eyes slid over to her, mirth twinkling in the warm depths as their owner fought to suppress a grin. Nessa narrowed her eyes.

"Now you're just being mean," she sighed.

"My apologies."

The ring disappeared again, this time into his coat.

Silence settled over them once more as Nessa kicked another stone from the path. This time, it plummeted into the grass and stayed there.

She had to calm down and refocus. This was not about her ties to Earth, or the ring. This was about surviving long enough to save Liv and save her kingdom.

Her kingdom.

Her fingertips gently grazed the blooming wildflowers beside the path. Their petals felt velvety soft, bowing to her at the lightest of touches.

Breathe in four, hold for seven, out for eight and repeat.

Much like Nessa's mood, the sky had grown dark, the gloomy gray above them threatening more than just a gentle rain. A sharp wind played with the ends of Nessa's hair, smelling of damp and ozone and a touch of cold. The rain was nearly on them. She clutched her cloak tightly.

"Does it rain a lot here?" she asked.

"Not sure," Rinn answered.

"I thought you said you'd been to Erwani before?"

"Several times," he confirmed.

"Then, what's it like?" she asked.

He shrugged. "It's a town."

Nessa rolled her eyes. "Will you just answer one damn question?"

"Not if I can help it." His grin was teasing.

"Okay, *fine*."

Nessa drew herself up to her full height, but Rinn still had most of a head on her. She couldn't tell if the look he wore was condescension or enchantment, but it was certainly not intimidation, which had been her goal.

"If you answer a question honestly, I'll answer one honestly," she finally offered, defeated.

"This is a terrible idea." Rinn shook his head, but his lips quirked all the same. "What's your question?"

"What's Erwani like?"

"Boring one to start with, duchess." He waggled a finger at her. "Why not start with something more interesting?"

"Because I don't want to stand out in Erwani. I have to know what it's like before I get there."

He raised an eyebrow. "Why so concerned?"

"Hey, I already answered your question!" Nessa poked him in the shoulder, and Rinn paused a moment, staring at her. She knew she probably looked like a chihuahua threatening a Doberman. "You have to answer mine now."

Rinn opened his mouth to reply, but closed it again after an apparently sobering thought. He looked her up and down, his brow furrowing.

"It used to be brighter," he finally said.

"Let me guess," Nessa sighed. "It suffered after the war."

"As always." Rinn shook his head. "Erwani was once a major stop on the north-south trade route. The center of the city is built around the point where the Angori and the Marsei rivers run into the Vergri."

"Uh…what's that mean, exactly?"

"The Vergri?" Rinn raised a brow in disbelief. "That runs all the way to the southern shores of Calebrir? The Great River?"

Nessa stared at him blankly. Rinn snorted and shook his head.

"Flames, princess, how do you not know about the Great River? Are you a hermit who's never looked at a map?"

She did her best to shrug it off. "I was raised in a tower. Didn't get out much."

He snorted. "And where is this so-called tower of yours?"

She waved a hand airily. "Far away from here."

"That's a lovely non-specific answer," Rinn teased.

"It was on the coast."

Technically, Rinn didn't need to know that said coast was in another realm of existence. The idea of trying to explain San Francisco to him made her brain want to implode. She'd have to skip over cars, television, and Pride parades, just to name a few.

"Ah, I thought you looked like a southerner."

She arched a brow at him. "Is that an insult or compliment?"

He shrugged. "Depends who you are."

"And where are *you* from?" Nessa asked.

"Everywhere," Rinn answered, mimicking her waving hand.

"Ah, another lovely non-specific yet honest answer," she mimicked back.

"I'm better at them than you are."

She did stick her tongue out at him this time, and Rinn glowed with pride.

At that very moment, the heavens finally opened, releasing a hard rain down on their heads. Nessa quickly pulled her hood up, but Rinn tilted his face up to the skies, letting the droplets hit his face. As he opened his mouth, she saw a trace of a grin on his lips.

She wondered if Rinn also liked pina coladas.

With a shrug, Nessa tilted her head upward as well and allowed the raindrops to fall between her lips, the taste of floral and ozone coating her tongue. She hadn't done this since she was a child. Her lungs broke free of their invisible bindings for only a moment, but it was all she needed.

"You need to come up with better games, my lady," Rinn teased. "That last one ended horribly."

"I don't see you coming up with anything better," Nessa replied.

"I don't like games." Seemingly as an afterthought, he added, "Or people."

"I'm shocked."

A lie.

The sky grew darker as morning turned to afternoon, and the steady rain became a downpour. Thunder rumbled and lightning flashed above their heads as the heavens dumped down bucket after bucket of rain, the worn path quickly turning to mud under their feet. The two elected to walk in the grass beside the trail to help save their boots, though Nessa still had to focus on not tripping or losing a shoe. All conversation ceased, as it was difficult to hear over the torrential rain.

Nessa had never been so cold and miserable. She tried very hard not to feel sorry for herself, electing instead to remain focused on her next steps. She needed to get to Erwani and resupply, and after that, find Alaron. If that didn't work, she had to make her way to Calebrir and get some help. Liv would probably at least track her southward, meaning the further they both were from Menhir, the better.

Focus on Erwani. Do that first, she told herself.

By late afternoon, the deluge had receded into a gentle dampness that reminded Nessa of the autumn rains back in San Francisco, wet, gentle, and misty. A shape began to form in the haze ahead of them; it rose up across the horizon, looming dark and imposing through the drizzle. As they drew closer, it resolved into something familiar, and Nessa's heart leapt in relief.

A gate!

She broke into a run, holding her hood up against the wind. When she reached the gate, she huddled by the wall in an attempt to get out of the rain, Rinn hovering at her shoulder as he pounded on the door. He leaned against the wall, using his forearm to support himself, and conveniently blocked most of the rain, his hair dripping onto Nessa's cheeks when she looked up at him. When had he gotten so close?

"State your business!" came the voice from the other side.

"Shut your trap, Art, and let me in! I'm drowning here!" Rinn called back.

"Oi! Welcome back, Rinn!"

Nessa gave him a look. "Charming."

He grinned back. "Always, duchess."

Much to Nessa's relief, the gate opened without further hesitation. It groaned and clanged against its hinges, but at that moment, not even the rain could dampen her spirits, and she dashed through the opening with a lighter heart. The woods were far behind her, and hopefully, that meant Liv was too.

"Rinn, you look like a drowned rat," the potbellied gate keeper told him with a grin. He appeared to be a man who thought himself very important, though likely he was the only one who believed so.

"Where did all your hair go?" Rinn asked, a shit-eating grin on his face. "Scared it off, did you?"

"Ah, shut it. Where's my coin?" the gatekeeper growled.

"If I recall," Rinn noted, his tone deliberately casual, "you still owe me forty-seven gold after our last game of Twenge."

"Curse you, boy."

Nessa had to admit, she was a little impressed with Rinn's acumen. Art, however, spat at Rinn's boots.

Rinn didn't bat an eye.

"Missed you too, Art."

Art's beady little eyes narrowed at Nessa, who quickly hid behind her hood. He nodded to her. "Who's the lass?"

Rinn stepped slightly in front of her. "She's with me."

"Poor dear."

And with a final shake of his head, the gatekeeper waved them through.

The thief and the princess rushed through the empty streets, desperate to find any protection from the wet. The wooden buildings all hunched over the muddy causeways as though conspiring about their residents; the once-grand ladies were no longer so grand, their brightly colored paint chipping off the old wood. Faded blues, greens, reds and purples dotted the buildings, with worn floral patterns of yellow, gold, and white peeking through the decay. A few sun-faded awnings poked out into the streets, the whole place looking like a gray photograph trying very hard to be colorful.

Nessa and Rinn quickly ducked under the first awning they saw, and Nessa lowered her hood, letting her damp hair come tumbling down. Rinn shook his wet locks out with his fingers, the dark waves brushing his temples and flicking Nessa with water.

She didn't care. The sense of absolute relief that filled her was finally letting her breathe, not to mention the temporary reprieve from the rain made her so happy she could burst.

She couldn't help it. She smiled at Rinn.

Rinn stared at her for a moment, then returned a small quirk of lips. Even soaking wet, with messy hair and a barely-there smile, he was the definition of roguishly handsome. Nessa found it infuriating.

She held out her hand, palm up.

"We had a deal," she felt the need to remind him.

"We did," he agreed.

Her sweet sixteen ring appeared between Rinn's fingers, and he twirled it a moment, showing off. Nessa glared at him as she removed the bow from her back, pushing her outstretched hand toward him insistently.

"You first."

"Please, princess." Rinn feigned offense, though Nessa wasn't sure he'd ever felt a genuine emotion in his life. "I am a man of my word."

Taking her hand in his own, he turned it over gently, and Nessa found herself too shocked to move as Rinn gently slid the ring onto her third finger, bowing mockingly over her knuckles.

"There we are."

He grinned like the thief he was, watching Nessa carefully as she rolled her eyes at his dramatics.

"The bow is yours." She held it out to him. "And I'm not putting it on your back for you, Casanova."

"What's a Casanova?"

Nessa's tone tuned saccharine. "He's a historic pain in the butt, just like you."

"Well then, thank you." Rinn took the bow from her and then, looking her up and down once more, he pointed up the street to a building painted a sad violet.

"Nearest inn is that way," he told her. "Tell Lyca you met me."

"Is she your friend?" Nessa asked.

"Absolutely not," Rinn answered with a grin. "But she'll take pity on you."

"Thank you, Rinn. Stay out of trouble."

"Never." He gave her a wink. "Safe travels, *Alice*."

Nessa watched him go. It wasn't long before his back disappeared into the swirling mists, and she was alone again.

Chapter Twenty-One

Emergency Swim Lessons

Nessa hated to admit it, but Rinn had been right. Lyca was no friend of his. The pretty young woman even gave Nessa a free meal for having to deal with Rinn for most of the day. Lyca claimed it was the least she could do, and Nessa certainly wasn't complaining. She didn't have money for a room, but she offered to help Lyca with the chores in order to earn one. Luckily, Lyca needed a serving maid for the night, and Nessa was more than happy to oblige. She certainly had experience serving food and dodging handsy regulars, and besides, no one ever noticed their waitress, so it was an excellent way to remain anonymous.

By the end of the night, Nessa had earned herself a bed and another hot meal as Lyca wondered aloud how such a patient young woman could possibly travel with the likes of Rinn.

"I tell ya, if Will Ashford had tried to get his hands on me, I'd've smacked him with my tray, I would," Lyca asserted. "But you, all poise and grace, you just slide right away."

Nessa nodded sagely. "I've had practice being slippery."

"Is that how you came to travel with Rinn? Being slippery?"

She shrugged. "No. Just fell into it by accident, I suppose."

With aching feet, a full stomach and a tired heart, Nessa fell gratefully onto the lumpy mattress, and was asleep almost before she kicked off her second boot.

***

He didn't seem like her type. And yet, in a way, that was *exactly her type.*

She'd nearly overlooked him. He was hard to keep track of, even with that roguishly handsome face, his dark clothes fading into the tired buildings and shadows of the predawn. He kept sliding between the sparse early morning crowd, but no one noticed him. He passed as a shadow; nothing drew any attention to him at all.

Except the bow on his back.

That had tipped her off. There was only one place that weapon could have come from. Just one, and she knew it well.

She had lost her quarry in the woods last night; how, she wasn't entirely sure. Some trick, or beginners luck, most likely.

No, she had wanted *to lose the target. Wait, that wasn't right. She hadn't wanted to lose her, but she didn't want to take...*

...What had she been thinking again? The target. Yes. She had found the target briefly again earlier. Tracking her had been easy; her prey was loud. She could have completed her task right there, but then there had been the...complication.

The thief had to be the source of the trouble; her prey had vanished the moment she entered Erwani, and even after searching all night, she could find no trace. Her frustration grew, but something else simmered below it.

Relief. But why would she be relieved? Her quarry remained hidden.

Green eyes narrowed on the man with the bow.

The Dreamer wouldn't stay hidden for long...

***

Nessa gasped as she jolted awake, her fingers flying to the pendant at her throat. As the comforting warmth seeped into her fingertips, she squeezed her eyes closed, forcing her heartbeat to slow. Why was she shaking?

What had just happened?

A Dream. She'd had a Dream.

Grasping the pendant, she tried to bury herself in the warmth, imagining it enveloping her as she forced her breathing to steady. She could feel the form of a thought taking shape in the back of her mind, and she tried to grasp at it, but it disappeared into smoke. But maybe it wasn't smoke she needed to catch. Instead, she grappled with the image the way one would a bar of soap in the bath, trying to find just the right angle and grip.

A picture started to form behind her eyes; she could see it like she could see her room, not because she was remembering it, but because she was actually there somehow. A crowd of people in the predawn glow. Some were wandering the street while others huddled round the stalls. Children were frozen mid-run across the muddy road, smiles on their faces as their parents rolled their eyes. Every person was still as a statue, while a figure clad in dark clothes moved fluidly between them. A figure with windswept hair and an infuriating smirk.

Nessa gasped out loud. "Rinn!"

Her consciousness slammed back into her head, nearly knocking her back onto the bed, and she rolled with a yip before tumbling to the floor. But by then she was already scrambling to her feet.

She laced up her boots more quickly than she ever had in her life, her racing heart pushing her to move faster as she snatched up her bag.

With a final twirl to put on her cloak, she was out thc door likc a shot, determined to find Rinn before Liv did.

***

The sun streamed weakly into the streets of Erwani, making a valiant attempt to burn through the clouds still left over from yesterday's torrent. The mud, however, refused to retreat so easily. Nessa's boots squelched as she ran, her rapid pace kicking up flying muck and almost certainly irritating more than her fair share of the locals, but she paid them no mind. Her feet knew where to go, and she let them take her there.

After all, it had worked once before.

She burst into the main square, huffing and puffing, and scanned the crowd for Rinn. The hair on the back of her neck stood on end. Stares. She was getting far too many stares.

Her shaking fingers fumbled to pull her hood over her face as her already hot cheeks turned crimson. What if she were spotted? Like Rinn had said the day before, staying out in the open wasn't smart. She ducked into the first side street she saw and waited.

The faces passed in a blur; some were smiling, others were eating, and many appeared sour about the sludge that had once been a functioning road. A woman in a white headscarf nearly gave poor Nessa a heart attack before she realized it wasn't Liv. But the elf couldn't be far off. Not if they were both trying to find Rinn.

This was a stupid idea. If Liv was looking for Rinn, then Nessa should logically be trying to get as far away from him as possible. This idiotic plan of hers was actively putting her closer to the deranged elf who wanted to kidnap her. She *knew* it was a dumb idea, and yet here she was, doing it anyway.

Stupid sense of honor.

If Liv did anything to harm the cocky thief, it would be Nessa's fault. After all, Liv was only interested in him as a way to get to her, Nessa. She had to do *something*. She had a plan.

Well, it was really more of an idea.

No, a vague concept. She had a vague concept of a moronic idea.

Nessa nearly shouted in relief when she spotted Rinn across the market, loitering about half a block down the street. He hovered quietly around busy stalls or distracted people, likely working hard at his trade. No doubt Liv was hidden somewhere nearby. Nessa suspected the elf would make her play on him soon.

Well, maybe it was time for Nessa to make a play of her own.

She slid back into the alleyway, careful to stick close to the wall, hoping Rinn wouldn't venture too far into the middle of the street. Didn't thieves need to have a quick getaway planned in case they were caught in the act? Shadows and back alleys were necessary to elude any pursuers. At least, that was what both logic and numerous D&D campaigns had taught her. But what did she know? She'd only played a halfling cleric.

She watched Rinn weave effortlessly through the crowd of people, noticing how well he blended in; no one seemed to keep their attention on him for very long. It was like he was a ghost, and even Nessa had a hard time keeping tabs on him. She tried to watch his hands, noticing that they never lingered anywhere long, though one or two gestures seemed out of place.

She had to admit, he was an excellent thief.

As Rinn drew closer to her position, Nessa steadied herself. He was a lot bigger than she was. Dagorn had been right, she'd have to rely on speed, not strength. Her best hope to get his attention was to catch him off-guard.

He was so close. Three steps…then two…one…

Nessa grabbed his arm, yanking as hard as she could, and Rinn stumbled into the alley almost too easily. And while Nessa had only really planned things up until that moment, she still wasn't expecting Rinn to be so fast.

Using his momentum, he nimbly shifted his body in front of hers, his forearm coming down across her chest. Suddenly, *he* was the one in control. Pushing her up against the wall, he used his body to pin her there. Nessa squeaked in surprise, but never lost her grip on his arm until it was suddenly ripped from her fingers.

Cold metal pressed against her throat.

"You're being followed!" she gasped desperately.

Rinn's eyes flashed in recognition, and his expression changed from murderous to annoyed, a different kind of heat flashing in those dark eyes. She obviously was not who he'd expected.

"Yes, by you," he snapped, lowering the blade. He took a step back, but kept her pinned against the wall with his arm, his lip curling back in a near-growl as he looked at the trapped girl. He was not at *all* happy to see her.

"Look, I'm trying to help you." Nessa's voice shook even worse than her hands. "I can explain in a bit, but we have to go, *now*."

"No. Explain. Now."

She winced, feeling Rinn's stern tone like a slap in the face. For a moment Nessa considered arguing, but decided they didn't have time. Honesty spilled from her lips instead.

"Someone is following *me*, and they lost me, so now they're following you and we need to go before she finds us."

Rinn's expression shifted to one of disbelief and frustration, his dark eyes hot with anger. He ran a hand through his hair, letting out a growl of annoyance.

"You have someone following you?" he hissed through a clenched jaw.

"Yes, and we need to go!"

Nessa shoved him off her in irritation. They had to *move*. If they didn't, Liv would surely find them.

She kept searching the crowd for a flash of white hair. Liv hadn't been far behind Rinn in her Dream. So where was she now?

"I specifically *asked* you if anyone was following you," Rinn growled. "You lied to me!"

"I have to lie to everyone! You're not special," Nessa snapped back.

Rinn raked his hands through his already-messy hair and gave a nasty growl, his pacing reminding her of a caged lion. He muttered something that may have been a curse.

"Who is it?"

"That's kind of hard to explain." Nessa edged back into the shadows of the alley. They had to move, *now*, or she was a dead girl. Every cell in her body screamed at her to move, her muscles coiling under her skin.

Don't sit still. Go. Run. Do something!

"She's an…old friend," she said instead.

"Friend?" The condescending eyebrow had returned. Rinn loomed not far behind her, and Nessa wasn't sure if he was coming with her or if he was planning to strangle her himself.

"Oh! Like none of your friends have never tried to kill you!"

Rinn scanned the area, muttering, "No, that job is usually reserved for family."

Suddenly, he grabbed Nessa's arm, pulling her tightly against him. She didn't even have time to scream before she felt a breeze on her cheek, and a knife embedded itself in the wall where Nessa had been standing not half a second before. Her heart lodged in her throat.

Liv had found them.

Nessa swore well enough to impress Rinn and bolted back toward the street. She couldn't hear any footsteps, nor the sound of anyone following; all she could hear was the pounding in her ears as she burst into the street, searching frantically for a flash of white as she huddled between the townspeople. *Don't let her get a clear shot.* All she saw were faces, the faces of laughing, bargaining, innocent people that she couldn't use as shields forever. And Liv could be behind any one of them.

Panic clawed at her chest and stung her eyes. She couldn't fight Liv; the elf had been trained in combat for centuries. Nessa didn't know what was worse, not being able to see her death coming, or seeing it and knowing there was nothing she could do to stop it. Her pounding heart rocked her whole frame, her eyes scanning the crowd yet again as she tried to move through it as unobtrusively as possible.

She shrieked when an arm slunk around her shoulders and pulled her down the street, an insistent voice whispering in her ear. It was Rinn.

"Tell me, and be concise."

He rushed her through the crowd of people, his strength practically the only thing keeping her on her feet. Their pace was purposeful, their heads drawn closely together; they could have been mistaken for lovers at a quick glance.

"She's an elf." Nessa's voice trembled as she spoke. "Something happened to make her go crazy, a spell or something, and I don't know what caused it or how to stop it! That's her bow you have. I took it from her when she tried to drag me off."

Rinn growled in annoyance, then raised his head and implored the heavens, "An elf. Oh, sacred flames! Why an elf!?"

He shook his head and glanced back over his shoulder, his dark eyes scanning the crowd.

"You're more trouble than you're worth, Alice."

"Like I haven't heard that before," Nessa muttered to herself.

Rinn glared at her. Nessa glared right back, and Rinn glared even harder. "How do I lose an elf, anyway?"

"You don't."

"Then you wouldn't happen to know how to break an evil spell?" Nessa snapped. "It's not like I can just kiss her, or hit her with an iron crowbar and hope for the best!"

"What kind of spell was it?" Rinn asked.

She threw up her hands. "I don't know!"

"Well, whoever cast it, what did they use?"

"I don't *know*!" she replied again, growing more frustrated.

"Then how do you know it's a spell?" he growled.

Nessa was near tears. "Because I just do!"

"That's not helpful."

"I know!"

Nessa took a deep breath, trying to keep her head clear. Panic caused mistakes, and here, mistakes meant getting carried off to a warring kingdom and used as an atomic bomb.

She took a few more deep breaths for good measure.

The crowd behind them began to rumble, Rinn's head turning to look a bare instant before Nessa's. A small group had started to draw back, swearing and cursing, their fear creating ripples of chaos as the panic spread. The initial irritated words became shouts and then screams, until finally a cacophony of horrified cries flew on the air and the crowd parted like the Red Sea, everyone scrambling for cover behind the stalls and each other. Suddenly, Rinn's eyes landed on something Nessa couldn't see.

A brief flash of white.

"Go." He shoved Nessa forward. "Go!"

Nessa bolted down the street, her heart thudding against her ribs as she skidded around the nearest corner. Rinn caught her and spun her left down the next street.

"Center of town!" he called.

"I don't know where that is!"

He pointed. "Left!"

Nessa saw a flash out of the corner of her eye. Snatching ahold of Rinn's lapel, she pulled with all her might.

Another knife whizzed just past his shoulder, burying itself nearly to the hilt in the wall.

Rinn blinked at Nessa, then the knife, then back at Nessa.

"Right, then." Sounding annoyed, he yanked the knife from the wall, cursing as the blade broke off at the hilt. "This friend of yours always like this?"

"Normally her aim is better," Nessa answered.

"Lovely."

It wasn't.

They bolted off down a dark side alley, kicking up mud as they ran. The muck sucked at their feet, slowing them down, but Nessa kept pushing. She felt a tap at her shoulder to turn left, then left again. Rinn moved to grasp the bow on his back, but Nessa stopped him.

"You can't hurt her!" she puffed.

"I'd rather not die," he countered, reaching for the bow again, but Nessa swatted his hand away.

"We just need to lose her!" she argued. "She can't control herself."

"That's hardly my problem, Alice."

Another knife whizzed past Rinn's ear, and he swore in a language Nessa almost recognized. The syllables clanged around the edges of her brain, but right now she had more important things to focus on.

Like not getting killed.

Glancing behind her, she saw a flash of snow-white hopping between the building roofs.

"Rinn! She's running on the roofs!"

That's how Liv had been keeping an eye on them; she had a height advantage. Instead of looking worried, though, Rinn's head bobbed a few times, and he grinned.

"That I can work with!"

Grabbing Nessa's arm, he practically tossed her into the nearest building, Nessa spinning like a dancer to keep her balance as they crashed through the door. She didn't question the directional change, but simply kept running.

Unfortunately, they were now in a pub, and most of the other occupants weren't pleased by the pair disturbing their day drinking. Rinn hopped across chairs and leapt over tables that Nessa simply avoided, swiping things even as they ran for their lives. Nessa never lost sight of Rinn, though he was hard to keep up with, sliding around tables like they were hurdles at her old track meets.

The patrons of the pub began to throw things at them, and she barely managed to duck a bottle that shattered just above her head. In fairness, she supposed no one really wanted a boot print with their breakfast.

They burst through the back door into the dim morning light, but Nessa barely had time to puff for air before they were across the street and crashing through another door. Flaming heat seared across her skin, a quick glance at all the iron tools and swords telling her everything she needed to know as Rinn skidded the around the smithy fire, his fingers barely skimming the tips of the flames. An angry-looking woman began shouting and waving a hot poker at their backs, and then they were out in the street again.

"Can you swim?" Rinn panted as they burst through yet another door. This place was quiet, filled with clutter and dust that made Nessa sneeze. The path they were running was the only clear space there, and it was so narrow she had to run sideways.

"Can you?" she snapped.

Rinn pushed her toward another door. "Look, can you swim or not?"

"Yes, when I have to!"

"Trust me. You have to!"

Nessa looked back at him in panic as she flung open the door to race into what she assumed was the street. However, where she was expecting ground, her foot met only air, and she spun forward just in time to see the river rushing toward her.

She was barely able to take in a breath before the freezing water crashed around her ears, the shock nearly driving the air from her lungs. She kicked to the surface, fighting the sting in her limbs, as Rinn surfaced beside her, gulping down air.

He swam toward a modest footbridge less than ten feet downstream, Nessa following as fast as she could. Luckily, the current decided to be helpful for once, and helped to push her in the correct direction, the sensation reminding Nessa more of a wave pool than a rushing river.

At least she wouldn't drown before Liv could kill her. That would certainly spoil all the elf's fun.

Rinn grabbed hold of a bridge support by the shoreline and held out a hand to her. Nessa scrambled to catch his hand, but the current was pulling her too fast. She kicked and fought against the water until she thought she might be swept away.

"C'mon!" Rinn shouted.

With one last mighty kick, Nessa grabbed onto Rinn's hand, and he pulled her to him almost effortlessly, attaching her to the wooden support while she gasped for air. As Nessa clung to the pillar like her life depended on it, Rinn hunched over her and caught her eye. Holding a single finger to his lips, he pointed up.

There, in the frigid water under the bridge, they waited.

Nessa didn't dare to breathe as light footsteps echoed above their heads. She glanced up at the wooden planks, huddling closer to the support. Liv couldn't see through wood, but that didn't stop Nessa's desire to hide.

The soft *thunk* of footsteps paused, and Nessa put a hand over her mouth to stop her noisy breathing, a rhythmic pounding only she could hear echoing in her ears. Neither she nor Rinn moved. The sound of the splashing water would have given them away.

She closed her eyes, praying to any gods or angels or Elar who would listen.

Move on. Please, just move on.

Suddenly, a flash of bright white rippled in the reflection of the water, and Nessa bit her tongue to keep from screaming as Rinn's hand moved to her back to keep her still. Her nails dug into the wooden support, hard enough to leave marks.

Move on. Don't see. Move on!

She repeated the mantra over and over as though that could make it come true, her heart threatening to choke her. This had to work. Liv couldn't see them.

She shivered hard against Rinn's hand, her eyes stinging. She needed to breathe, but was too frightened that the sound would give them away.

The white reflection jerked sideways once, then dropped away as the footsteps stumbled above their heads. A step was taken back the way they'd come, then another. There was a pause, then at last the steps continued across the bridge, their pace slow and unsteady. Finally, the sound faded into the wind.

It took several more minutes for Nessa to inhale.

Gasping, she pressed her forehead against the pillar, a swear or two escaping under her breath as she took a moment to just breathe. In for four, out for eight. Repeat.

Finally, the pounding in her chest began to slow, and she blinked when she heard Rinn move. He climbed out of the river, water dripping from his hair and his coat.

Turning, he offered Nessa his hand, and she took it, shivering as freezing water sloshed from her body onto the stone bank. She was sure she looked like a drowned cat, water puddling at her feet as she wrung out her hair.

"Are you alright?" she asked Rinn.

"Fine, no thanks to you, duchess." Rinn shook his hair out and brushed it from his face, his eyes burning. "What in the Flames are you mixed up with? Actually, no. Don't tell me."

"I—I didn't want you to get hurt."

Nessa knew she had no way to defend herself. Her mouth opened several times to explain, but the guilt wouldn't let her speak. This was all her fault. Liv would never have gone after him if not for her. In fact, Liv was only under a spell because of her. Her father might be dead because of her; Rinn had nearly been killed because of her. They were standing soaking wet in the middle of the street because of her.

She was alone. And she had no one to blame but herself.

Rinn watched her hesitate for a moment, his expectant expression quickly turning to one of frustration. Turning on his heel, he started to walk away.

"Wait!" Nessa couldn't explain why her stomach twisted so violently at the thought of him leaving. "Where are you going?"

"Away from you!"

"No, wait!" Ice coated her lungs as her feet lunged after him without permission from her brain. "Please! I need your help!"

He wouldn't even look at her. "No. Absolutely not."

"But—"

Rinn spun, coattails flying, and was in her face again in two steps, towering over her in less than a blink. Nessa jumped, suddenly terrified at how fast such a large creature could move. She winced, but forced herself not to yelp.

"You almost got me killed!" Rinn hissed. "I asked you if you were being followed and you *lied*."

"You would have, too!"

A weak argument, she knew, but the only one she could think to make. She desperately tried to hold onto her frustration to warm her chest, to bring feeling back into her dripping wet fingers. Shivering, she promised herself it was from the cold.

"No," he countered. "I wouldn't have."

"Are *you* being followed?"

"Yes!"

Nessa's mouth snapped shut as Rinn leaned over her, his eyes searching her face. She didn't look away, though she could feel water trickling down the back of her neck and down her temples. Though his eyes bored into hers, she didn't move. Her ground may not have been good, but she'd be damned if she wasn't going to stand it.

Rinn shook his head.

"Good luck, princess."

Nessa couldn't squash the panic rising in her chest as she watched him walk away. Again.

"I'm sorry, okay?!"

She wasn't certain he'd heard her, but he stopped, at least. Nessa stared at his back, her vision beginning to blur at the edges. Squeezing her eyes closed to stop the tears, she sighed, utterly defeated.

"I think we've already established that I have no idea what I'm doing."

Rinn's head rolled back as if praying to the sky, his shoulders slumping, and for a long moment, neither of them moved. Then, finally, he turned back toward her. Stepping in close, he spoke, his tone hushed.

"Where are you going?" he asked. "Honestly?"

"I'm trying to find a wizard. Alaron."

"No." Rinn shook his head. "Can't be done."

Nessa's stomach dropped into her toes. "Why not?"

No, there had to be a chance. It couldn't end here. Not now. She'd come too far.

"The way to Alaron is magicked," Rinn answered. "The wizard can only be found by those who already know the way."

Nessa shook more water from her hair to keep from screaming obscenities to the heavens. Now there were Room of Requirement rules?! How was she supposed to do this? Her life depended on finding Alaron, and so did Liv's. Not to mention the continued existence of all of Avani.

So, no pressure.

Nessa lost the battle against swearing spectacularly. Even Rinn looked impressed.

"I still have to find him, though," she admitted once she was through cursing.

"I told you, it's impossible."

"Well, I at least have to try."

It was at that moment that Nessa felt more eyes on her. Looking up, she found quite a few people in the street staring at her and Rinn. Well, they *had* been shouting at each other in full view of the public, not to mention dripping all over the street.

Great. Now she was drawing even more unwanted attention to herself.

She definitely was not cut out for this adventuring thing.

Rinn must have realized the same thing, guiding Nessa over to the mouth of a nearby alleyway where they could melt into the shadows he knew so well.

"Look," he began again quietly, "it's dangerous. And Alaron is known for being madder than a box of frogs. Just get out of town and find a place to lie low for a while. It'll be safer."

Nessa shook her head. "The elf is my friend. If I don't find the wizard, she'll die."

"So?"

Nessa could only blink at him in shock, her mouth opening and closing.

"There really is no honor amongst thieves, huh?"

"Look, princess…" Rinn paused when Nessa winced at the title. "You have to be honest with yourself. You have no idea how to defend yourself. It's dangerous out here, much more dangerous than jumping into the Angori. There are goblins, and trolls, and not all thieves are as charming as me. You. Won't. Make it. Not on your own."

"I have to try."

She knew everything he had said was true, but what else could she do? She couldn't just sit by and let Menhir get their hands on a Dreamer. Liv's current path ended in either death or slavery and Nessa wasn't sure which would be worse. Either way, she couldn't let it happen.

"You're mad."

"You think I don't know how hopeless this is?" Nessa's throat tightened as she hissed at Rinn. "You're right. The smart thing would be to get the hell out of Dodge and lie low, but I can't do that. Even if I did, I probably wouldn't make it. And if I don't at least try to fix this, I'm definitely dead. I'm royally screwed either way, so if you have any better ideas, I'm open to suggestions."

Rinn stared at her, hard, but she didn't squirm this time. Honestly, she was too tired to worry about what he saw or didn't see; she couldn't hide her shaking hands and watery eyes anymore. She was in way over her head and she knew it, but that didn't mean she was going to back down.

"I'm not taking you," he said finally.

"I'm not asking."

"Good. You're more trouble than you're worth."

Nessa almost smiled. "So you've said." She took it as a compliment, coming from a thief. "Can you at least tell me how to get to Alaron?"

Rinn paused, then swore. Something that sounded like *death wish* or possibly *stubborn girl* followed under his breath.

"First, find a dagger," he told her. "You'll need one if anything gets too close for a proper sword swing."

"With what money?" Nessa demanded.

Rinn's answering grin reminded her abruptly of his chosen profession.

"Improvise."

...She'd have to come up with a plan B.

"And second?"

"Take the east gate," he told her, and helpfully pointed in the correct direction. "Follow the path for three days. If Alaron wants to be found, you'll find him then."

"East gate. Got it." Nessa nodded, holding out her hand to shake. "Nice knowing you, Rinn."

To her surprise, Rinn took it and bowed low over her knuckles, looking almost like a proper gentleman.

"My lady Alice."

She couldn't identify the twisting in her stomach. Perhaps the title was throwing her off, or maybe it was the fact that he had used her name — even if it was fake. The bow had appeared genuine, practiced and fluid, and she realized abruptly that Rinn always moved like that. Shaking her head, she forced all thoughts of her twisting stomach from her mind.

This time, she made him watch as she walked away.

First things first, she needed to find a dagger, which wound up being easier than Nessa had anticipated. As it turned out, Lyca had one in her uncle's old trunk. The blade felt clumsy and clunky in her palm, but the steel was sharp, and she was relieved she wouldn't have to resort to thieving. She suspected she'd be awful at it.

Lyca offered Nessa a meal before she left on her journey, and though Nessa felt terrible declining, she humbly requested some supplies to take instead. She knew that with Liv still in the city it would not be smart to linger. Within an hour after her dip in the Angori, Nessa was practically dashing out of the eastern gate.

The day grew humid and hot as she walked, the plains surrounding Erwani being plentiful in tall grass, but very sparse on shade trees. However, at least the bright sun quickly dried her clothes and hair, which she promptly braided to keep off her face. She kept her face turned toward the sky.

Just keep moving.

By mid-afternoon, she had passed into the woods, the shade providing welcome relief from the heat of the day. But Nessa only picked up her pace. She didn't stop to eat, instead picking apart a piece of bread as she trotted down the path. Now that the woods had enveloped her, she didn't want to stop, knowing that if Liv caught on to her little misdirection, she wouldn't be far behind. But when darkness descended and the path blurred before her eyes, Nessa decided it was finally time to rest. Climbing the nearest tree, she settled in to sleep.

And this time, she tied herself to the branch.

Chapter Twenty-Two

Broken Promises

Dawn came all too soon.

Nessa rose with the sun all the same, breakfasting on a bit of cheese before climbing back down to the path. Two more days. She just had to make it two more days. Then, she had to hope Alaron actually wanted to be found. She didn't even know if she was setting a good pace or if Liv was lurking just around the next tree; she just knew she had to keep moving.

Mist swirled around her knees even as dawn turned into bright morning, making it difficult to follow the path. She honestly wasn't quite sure how she was actually managing it, but she tried not to overthink matters. Simply staying between the largest gaps in the trees seemed to do the trick, a nagging *something* urging her forward. It wasn't fear of Liv, necessarily. Her body simply wouldn't stop moving. For some reason, she couldn't let it, and didn't want to.

She followed the feeling until early afternoon, when she finally had to let herself rest. Quickly shoving some fruit into her mouth, she was off again within a quarter of an hour. She knew her body was going to hurt when this was all over, but she'd take it if it meant she was alive to ache.

The woods were silent. Nothing, no animals, birds, or rustling leaves could be heard. It made her want to move faster. What respectable forest was silent? Even Mirkwood had drunken elves.

...Maybe she could get Liv drunk.

No, that would never work; Nessa suspected Liv could outdrink the rowdiest of soccer hooligans. She'd never even seen Liv tipsy. Doing her best not to think about it, she kept moving.

Her heart sank when she saw it.

The road forked in two, both paths curving and bending until the trees swallowed them up. They looked amazingly similar to one another, with the same worn dirt path and the same overhanging trees, the same grasses and shadows. Even the wildflowers growing at the edges of the trail were exact copies of each other. She stared at the fork, trying to listen to her gut.

Naturally, it stayed irritatingly silent on the subject.

Nessa started down the left path but paused. No, that didn't feel right. She returned to the fork and took a few steps down the righthand path, but her stomach flopped again, leaving her back in her original spot as she frowned at the pair of paths.

Nothing changed. There was nothing to indicate where either of them led, or anything else, really. And she certainly couldn't turn back.

Her chest tightened. If she chose the wrong path, Liv would find her and drag them both back to Menhir. The war would be over, Nessa would be used as leverage against a home she'd never even seen, and Menhir would no longer have anyone in their way. She would be used up until nothing remained.

And Avani would die.

She couldn't let that happen.

Nessa took a deep breath. She didn't want to be alone; she didn't want to be used to wreak destruction. She didn't want to be hurt by someone she loved, but mostly, she didn't want to hurt her friend. When Liv came back to her senses and saw what had happened, she would never forgive herself. Failing to protect Nessa and her friends would destroy her. Nessa couldn't let that happen, either.

So she *had* to find Alaron. It was as simple as that, but how? If she chose the wrong path, they were both as good as dead. And even if she chose correctly, she could still fail if she wasn't fast enough.

Nessa ached for Dagorn so badly her chest hurt. He'd know what to do.

…If Liv had even left him alive.

Her heart skipped at the thought. No, she couldn't think that way. He was fine. Dagorn was alright, of course he was. He would find her, and everything would be fine.

Or it wouldn't.

Nessa put her face in her hands for a moment. She had to calm down and think. Panicking would not help. She took one deep breath, then two, before looking up — only to be faced once more with the same impossible decision.

She collapsed on a fallen log beside the road, her spirits plummeting. Closing her eyes, she pinched the bridge of her nose, already feeling the sting in her eyes and the soreness in her muscles. A cold panic crashed into her.

Don't cry. Survive now. Freak out later.

She had to choose. If she stayed in one place too long, she'd be caught; she didn't have much of a head start on Liv to begin with. Something twisted in her stomach as a feeling of foreboding settled in her heart. She was trying to find a wizard she'd never met on a path she didn't know running from a trained fighter who knew everything about her. Could things get any worse? Letting out the breath she'd been holding, she rested a hand over her stinging eyes and thought hard.

A horrible notion struck her then. Rinn had said the way to Alaron was magicked.

"Shit."

What if this was the test? What if Alaron didn't want to be found and there *was* no right path? Maybe he had to know you before you could find him. Dagorn could have found him because they had met before, and by that logic Liv could probably find him too, but Nessa? Nessa was up the proverbial creek without a paddle. What if there wasn't a right choice at all, and no matter what, she was doomed?

Something cold, very real, and very sharp pressed suddenly against her collarbone, and her eyes snapped open.

Jon Snow's evil twin stood above her, the tip of his sword resting gently on her chest. He smiled, giving her a little bow.

"Your Highness, it is so lovely to see you again."

Nessa blinked and gasped for air, all the color draining from her face. How had he found her? She'd left him in Syracuse! How had he escaped Liv? Plus, there was no way he could have gotten back through the Veil. She was supposed to be safe from him.

She was supposed to be safe.

Nessa trembled, her pounding heart rocking her entire frame. Leaning away from the blade, she clutched the bark below her until her knuckles turned white, air rushing in her ears. She couldn't breathe.

She'd been found. She hadn't even made it three days on her own.

The world spun, and she thought she might be sick, her face hot and her body numb. Shuddering, she forced herself not to faint.

Snow had chased her across Syracuse, hurt her friends, and pursued her through the Veil. All for Menhir. For *money*. He didn't care who he hurt, how it hurt her. Because she'd had to run from him, she'd given up everything; she'd lost her family, her friends, her school, her job… She'd lost *Earth*. She had fought so hard to stay free, to stay safe. And he had found her anyway.

Oh gods. He knew who she was.

It was over.

"Get up," he instructed.

Nessa knew her legs wouldn't hold her. Swallowing hard, she blinked to clear her watery vision, her eyes burning as she stared up at him, seeing nothing. She was trying to breathe, but couldn't get enough air in her lungs, and she gasped frantically, her heart thudding in her ears. Her mind spun, while still remaining strangely blank.

"Now, don't be difficult," he warned gently.

Nessa couldn't make herself move. He had her. Menhir had found her. She was trapped.

The world spun. Chest heaving and eyes stinging, she sat and shook apart.

He gave a dramatic sigh, reaching for her, and Nessa jolted back to reality, reeling backward with a squeak of horror. The jerky movement caused her balance to shift, and she tumbled down the other side of the log, scrambling away from Snow as he cursed at her.

Out! Out! Time to get out! Her heart tasted like bile in her throat.

The instant her feet touched the ground, she bolted into the trees, the uneven terrain dipping and rising drastically beneath her feet. She wobbled and skidded through the forest, dodging the branches that grabbed at her clothes even as her knees knocked together in terror. Her feet slid on mud and damp leaves, her legs burning with effort, but nothing would stop her blind hurtle through the trees. She didn't care about anything but getting away.

The woods before her eyes blurred and grew darker, the trees twisting as the branches transformed into the forest outside Syracuse. She wheezed for air, her throat threatening to close up. Her friends were gone. No one was going to help her this time.

Not this again. Gods and angels, please, anything but this.

Suddenly, she was tackled from behind, and she screamed as she tumbled down and down and down. Dirt and muck came loose under her fingernails as she clawed blindly at the ground, but her shaky hands only grasped grass and loose leaves. She careened down with no hope of stopping her fall, her shoulders and hips groaning with every hit. Finally, her back collided hard with the valley floor and she finally stopped, crying out in pain.

Snow instantly pounced.

"No!" Nessa kicked at him, her heart skipping several beats, but it was no use. He grabbed her ankle, yanking her toward him.

"Get off!"

She kicked and scratched desperately as Snow crawled over her, pinning her hips down with his knees. Before she could reach for her blade, he grabbed her wrists, slamming them down on either side of her head. Nessa fought to move, and found she couldn't.

"Stop. Stop it, Your Highness."

Tears fell from Nessa's eyes, her ribcage turning into a corset, constricting her lungs tighter and tighter until she couldn't help but panic. She ground her teeth together. *Fight!* Fight, *damn it!*

"Get off me!" Nearly hysterical, she tried again to pull her hands free. Snow bent down to whisper in her ear and she squeezed her eyes closed, leaning away so he wouldn't touch her. She could smell his foul breath as it ghosted across her face, and thought she might be sick.

"Shhh, it's alright. You'll like Noringuard. You'll be treated like a queen."

Nessa's chest heaved, fighting to keep the sobs from escaping. She couldn't get a full breath, her whole body trembling so badly her spine ached. She prayed the ground would open up and swallow her.

Anything would be better than this.

"I'll take good care of you, Your Highness," he promised. "Shhh, hush."

Nessa swallowed down her sickness. Think! She had to think! She wasn't just a waitress anymore, and she had overcome too much to just give up now. He knew who she was, but so did she. So, what did she know? Where was his weight distributed?

The YMCA self-defense classes kicked in with a vengeance, and Nessa jammed her knee as hard as she could between his legs. Snow grunted and fell forwards, letting out a curse when his nose smashed against the ground.

Using his surprise against him, she hurled her body to the side, and he crashed into the mud with a yelp as Nessa rolled free. She scrambled away, heart pounding in her ears and hands scrabbling at the earth as she tried desperately to put as much distance between her and Snow as possible.

Every time she tried to stand, her knees gave out, but she could hear the mercenary getting to his feet. He was coming for her. Tears filled her eyes as her stomach heaved, and there was the very distinct sound of a sword being drawn. Panic closed off her throat and she squeezed her eyes closed.

This was it.

A metallic clang echoed in the air. Then, nothing.

What was going on?

Nessa forced her eyes open. There stood Snow, straining against a gleaming piece of steel, his eyes as wide and wild as they had been that horrible day in the coffee shop. But this time, he wasn't looking at Nessa.

Standing above her, his sword braced against Snow's, was Rinn.

Rinn? What was he doing here? He had made it clear he wanted nothing to do with her.

…Hadn't he?

Rinn expertly swung his blade down and pushed Snow back, the move appearing almost effortless. He barely glanced at Nessa as he put himself between her and her would-be kidnapper; instead, he glared at the man in question, spat at Snow's feet, and raised his sword in challenge. The mercenary looked shocked for only a moment before he too brought his sword up for another go.

The air was thick with anticipation as Rinn held perfectly still, a lion resting in wait. Suddenly, Snow pounced, and Rinn met him easily, blocking strike after strike with practiced precision, their clashing blades moving too fast for Nessa to follow. She could only stare, wide-eyed.

Rinn's moves appeared graceful, calculated, and confident; he never needed to adjust his footing or stance, and he never gave up ground. No matter how smoothly he moved, he always stayed firmly planted when he struck. Snow's strikes were more about brute force; he often led with his shoulder in order to throw his full weight behind the blade. More than once, Rinn caught him off balance, but Snow was wild and unpredictable — and therefore dangerous.

Snow cursed in that strange language of his as he shoved Rinn back, managing to get in a lucky hit under Rinn's jaw. The thief stumbled, hitting the ground hard enough for Nessa to hear a *crack*. She screamed his name in terror and held her breath, waiting apprehensively. Rinn didn't move.

Ollie…Maria…

No! No, not again.

Snow grinned horribly at her, and Nessa's lungs locked, panicked tears burning her eyes. Why couldn't she move?

The mercenary approached her with a confident stride, a mocking, sickening grin on his face.

"Well, Crown Princess Nessa of Calebrir, it appears I have won the honor of your company."

Nessa swallowed down bile as he yanked her roughly up by the arm. She blindly slashed at him with her dagger, but in one fluid move, he leapt back to avoid the blade and twisted her wrist until she cried out, feeling the bones of her arm rubbing together inside the muscles. Her fingers burned, and the blade fell from her grasp, her wrist feeling as though it was about to snap.

She pulled desperately against his grip, but Snow spun her around so her back was pressed against his chest. Whimpering, she tried to throw her weight forward, but to no avail.

"Let go!" She could feel water streaming down her cheeks.

"Quiet—*aargh*!"

Snow roared unexpectedly, and Nessa threw her weight forward in a blink, ripping herself away to collapse to the ground with a terrified gasp.

Behind them, Rinn pulled her dagger from Snow's leg.

Snow spun to deal with Rinn, shouting and cursing, and Nessa flinched at hearing the same language the Bear had used. Rinn shot back a confident response in what sounded like the similar tongue as Snow swung haphazardly at Rinn, who was using both sword and dagger to block the other man's blade.

Nessa bolted up the hill, but made it only a few feet before she slid back into the valley, grabbing at leaves and dirt only for them to come away in her hands. She wiped at her welling eyes and tried again. And again. But the slope was too steep and the leaves too wet; all she did was slide closer to the battling men, her quivering knees refusing to allow her to keep her footing.

Rinn kept advancing on Snow, his sword in one hand and Nessa's dagger in the other as Snow shouted at Rinn in the Bear's tongue. The thief's responses stayed clipped, his tongue even sharper than his steel. Snow tried to circle him, but Rinn planted himself between Snow and Nessa, and no matter how hard Snow tried to distract him, Rinn pushed him back.

Suddenly, Rinn flicked his sword in a precise movement, and Snow's blade went flying. Breathing only slightly more heavily than before, Rinn pointed his sword at Snow's chest. Snow cursed and spat at him, but the thief didn't flinch.

In a flash, Snow ducked below Rinn's blades and swept his feet out from under him. The thief hit the ground hard as Snow snatched up his sword and retreated into the trees, Rinn chasing after him like a shot.

Nessa stared at the spot where they had disappeared and tried to breathe, but it would only happen in deep, heaving gulps. She couldn't feel the air in her lungs, nor the cold mud under her palms or the dampness on her cheeks. There was only a single thought.

Snow had found her.

The mercenaries had found her.

He had almost taken her. Almost dragged her to Menhir. Away from her father, from Liv…to do nothing but hurt and harm and she'd have no choice. No choice but to be used up until she was dead.

All those ghost gardens…

She closed her eyes, feeling her heart thumping in her fingertips. Instead of darkness, she saw the coffee shop: Maria and Ollie, the Bear…all the blood.

Her hands flew over her mouth to stifle her cry.

She didn't have Liv to protect her now.

She was alone.

Nessa heard footsteps running toward her. She tried to scramble up, but her legs went out from under her, her wide eyes locking on the trees. Was it Snow? Was he coming back for her?

Rinn appeared, cursing as he forced his sword back into its sheath. He ran like a furious stallion, all rage and stomping feet, as he let out a growl between clenched teeth and muttered something foul under his breath.

His gaze fell on Nessa, who stared back with wide, unseeing eyes. Immediately, his fury vanished, though it clearly took some effort on his part. Running a hand through his messy hair, he approached her calmly, his steps noiseless once more.

"We need to go," he panted. "Right now."

Nessa couldn't move.

"Alice!"

She winced, her eyes squeezing closed.

Rinn cursed. More softly this time, he said, "C'mon. Up you get."

Taking her shaking hands, he gently rocked Nessa to her feet. She nearly collapsed, but he steadied her, returning her dagger to her hip. She tried not to notice how she flinched away from him, but nevertheless, he didn't let go of her hand the entire time.

She felt half-mad. Things were happening in a haze, like she wasn't even inside her own body anymore. Everything was spinning.

"Ready?" Rinn asked.

Nessa swallowed hard, but nodded.

Survive now. Find the wizard. Freak out later.

As soon as they reached the top of the hill, they ran.

She tried not to look back.

Chapter Twenty-Three

Deep Breath

Nessa's eyes took in very little as they ran; she didn't even notice which path was the proper one as they hurtled down it. At the moment, she was lucky she even remembered to breathe. All she knew was movement; her legs pumped, her lungs inhaled, and she clutched onto Rinn, her grip like a vise.

As the shadows lengthened around them, Nessa wondered if she could stand to stay in these woods after dark. She'd certainly be found, if she stayed. Snow would find her again, or Liv.

Was there any scenario that *didn't* end with her being dragged to a warring country and being used as a weapon and a bargaining chip?

She'd been found.

The terrifying thought played on a loop in her skull.

It was over. She'd been found.

Rinn pulled them off the path, and Nessa stumbled over her own feet, a whimper escaping her lips. Rinn squeezed her hand hard, yanking her up a steep incline, and Nessa squeezed back until her knuckles turned white.

An enormous wall of stone rose up before them, seeming to come out of nowhere. Thousands of fissures covered the rock face, with old, leafy vines winding their way almost lazily through the crevices. Like a madman, Rinn started tearing the foliage away, while Nessa could only stare numbly as the world spun around her ears. Her palms found the rocky wall under the greenery and she pressed her hot forehead to the cool stone, focusing on the rough spots digging into her skin as her lungs burned worse than her eyes.

What was she doing here?

Rinn had followed her. Why?

He could be leading her into a trap. But he had saved her from…

Oh, gods and angels, she'd been found. It was over. She'd been found.

The thought wouldn't go away.

Rinn pressed a hand against the now-clean rock and said something Nessa didn't catch. The cracks in the stone began slowly filling with gold, and in a few moments, the lines had formed an angular archway. Another word from Rinn, and the archway opened.

He took Nessa's hand gently and pulled her into the darkness. The cool air made her eyes sting, so she closed them against it, feeling a hard chill at her back. It was brighter behind her eyelids, anyway.

Belatedly, she realized Rinn was speaking. He squeezed her hand, warm leather pressing against her fingers, and she blinked.

"Huh?"

It was the first thing she'd said in hours.

"I said, we should rest for the night."

Rest. Breathe. Yes.

Somehow, she ended up sitting on the stone floor and leaning against the wall. She could feel Rinn at her side, though they weren't touching. He placed a palm-sized stone between them, its angular carvings shining with bright green light that washed them both in a sickly glow.

"Alice?"

Nessa jolted back to reality, her aching body beginning to shiver as her fingers lightly brushed her collarbone. They came away flaked with old blood.

Snow had found her. It was over.

She'd lost.

Her chest felt like it was collapsing into itself; she couldn't breathe. The darkness pressed in on her temples and she curled into a ball, her head on her knees.

Breathe.

She'd been found.

Breathe!

It was over. She'd failed.

BREATHE!

This was all her fault. Her best friend was going to die because she'd failed. She hadn't been able to find the wizard. She was alone; her friends and family were gone, scattered. She'd been found and Avani would fall.

Behind her eyes, she saw Snow back on Earth. The coffee shop lay in ruins, blood creeping along the seams in the tile, the Bear looking down at her with that horrible grin on his face — and Snow, laughing.

They'd held her down as she screamed.

Liv couldn't help her now.

Nessa collapsed into wracking, miserable sobs, her breath coming in shaky gasps. She squeezed her eyes shut against the hot tears running down her cheeks, but it did no good; cold spread from her skin to her bones, settling into the middle of her chest.

Rinn's expression fell.

"Oh, Flames, don't—"

He leaned over her, but she flinched away with a squeak and he froze, looking lost. With a deep sigh, he searched through the pockets of his coat before pulling out a small flask. Popping the cork with his teeth, he took a swallow, shuddered, then offered it to Nessa.

"Here," he said. "Take a little of this. It'll help."

Nessa tried to wipe the water from her cheeks even as the tears continued to fall from her eyes.

"I didn't know about him," she told Rinn through a hiccup.

"I know." How could he sound so gentle? "Here."

Nessa carefully took the flask from Rinn, not wanting their fingers to touch, and winced when the burning aroma hit her nose. It smelled like the floor cleaner at the coffee shop.

"What is it?"

"Khava."

That could have meant poison and she probably wouldn't have cared. She took a healthy swig, the burn traveling down her throat and into her stomach. The khava tickled her nose, and she coughed.

"Holy mother—" Her curse was cut off by another cough.

"It's rotgut, but it's better than nothing," Rinn offered.

"Rotgut," Nessa agreed. Looking down at the flask, she took another gulp, but this time treated it more like a shot in order to keep the burn contained to her stomach. Grimacing, she handed it back to Rinn.

"That's awful."

"Yes." He took a long sip.

They sat in silence as Nessa stared at the floor. She felt drained, as though a vampire had sucked the life out of her. Every single part of her felt empty.

"What am I going to do?" she asked herself. "How did he even find me? I thought he was…Liv should have ki—"

Silence rushed into her mouth, choking her.

"Do you know him?" Rinn asked.

"No, but—"

Her throat closed around the words, and she flexed her fingers, only to see them trembling. Cold crushed her chest as heat prickled at her eyes.

"You've dealt with him before," Rinn finished for her.

"Yes."

Silence settled around them for a moment.

"Was it violent?"

A numbing chill flashed through her body, settling deep into her bones, and Nessa made a small, miserable noise, trying to keep her sobs in her throat as she rubbed at her stinging eyes. Rinn offered her the flask again, but this time she pushed it away.

"That's, uh, putting it mildly," she finally answered.

Rinn licked his lips. Picking up the light-stone, he tossed it absently between his hands, his gaze focused on the deep darkness before them as his dark eyes swirled with something Nessa found herself too tired to place. Instead, she remained silent, letting him think. From the looks of things, he wouldn't have heard her anyway.

Rinn's words came slowly when he finally spoke.

"There's a kind of magic that draws power from the blood. It's taboo, and usually forbidden, but it could be how he managed to track you. If he had some of your blood."

"Could he do it again?" Her voice trembled.

"No, not unless he has more of your blood."

"Oh."

Blood magic. It made a strange kind of morbid sense, to take the life in the blood and twist it to your purpose. Having only part of a person meant that you had power over the rest of them. A flash of that same *something* from earlier knocked around her brain. Two men, one holding a bright white lock of hair…

"Could…is blood magic taboo in Menhir?" she asked.

Rinn rubbed his left palm with his thumb, looking down at the leather without really seeing it.

"Any advantage is encouraged."

Nessa pursed her lips. When Liv had been captured, the tent they'd kept her in had held all kinds of things; it wouldn't be unreasonable to assume that some of the elf's blood had been taken from her. A memory emerged from the mists of her thoughts, of two men arguing and one holding up a shock of white hair. A Dream! She had Dreamed about it!

Liv was under a blood spell! The Menhirans must have cast it after she'd escaped. Liv could still be saved!

Nessa should have felt better at the realization, but she didn't. Her stomach was still twisting around in knots, and she laced her fingers together, thinking hard. Could blood spells be broken? There had to be a way. Though true love's first kiss might prove difficult.

Rinn was still speaking.

"Uh, sorry." Nessa shook her thoughts from her head. "What?"

"I said, did he hurt you?" Rinn asked.

"Uh…no. I don't think so."

Nessa wrapped her arms around her knees, her mind flicking through her narrow escape. It had all happened so fast. Snow hadn't been there and then, in a blink, he had. If she hadn't fallen backward off that log, she'd probably be halfway to Menhir right now. Her limbs simply hadn't worked right, and then Rinn had appeared, seemingly out of thin air. She remembered how the fear had choked her, how Snow had towered over her with that grin on his face, and…

…And called her by her real name.

Her stomach dropped. Had Rinn heard? Did he know who she was? He hadn't called her duchess, or princess, or any other snarky title all afternoon. Was it because he knew?

The fear tasted rotten in her mouth.

"Do we have to talk about it?" Nessa's lower lip trembled.

"No," Rinn answered. "I don't need to know. I don't *want* to know."

"Then why did you come after me? I mean, I'm glad you did, but I thought you said you weren't going to help me."

Rinn was silent for a moment. Resting his head back against the stone wall, he rubbed the back of his neck, looking annoyed.

"Sacred flames, I don't know," he groaned. "You were just so…so…"

"Well, thank you."

"What for?" he asked.

"You saved my life, you jerk." She meant it as an endearment. "So, thank you."

"Oh, that was nothing more than a little personal revenge."

"You don't like Menhir?" she asked.

"More like Menhir doesn't like me," he answered.

"To be fair, I don't think they like anybody."

"Not even royalty," Rinn agreed.

Nessa flinched, and Rinn quickly snapped his mouth shut, looking away as Nessa suddenly found her lap to be the only thing worth studying.

"Thank you," she said quietly. "All the same."

"You're welcome, Alice."

Nessa felt her body finally beginning to give out as the cold fear drained from her muscles, leaving her aching and exhausted. Slowly, she slid sideways along the wall, only to be stopped by Rinn's shoulder. It took all her energy to keep her head up.

Rinn rummaged through her bag. Strange. She didn't remember setting it down. She barely even remembered how they'd gotten here.

"You should eat," he told her.

"Not hungry."

"Eat," he urged.

"Where are we?" Nessa asked instead.

"Answers are for people who eat," Rinn replied in a singsong voice.

"Fine!" she conceded with a huff.

He placed something in her hand. It looked like a piece of dried fruit, or a more colorful piece of beef jerky. She watched him take a bite of his own morsel, his face contorting in horror. He stared at the food, perhaps trying to will it into something more palatable, but the jerky proved too much for even his mental prowess. With a defeated sigh, he forced down the rest.

Nessa understood as soon as the taste hit her tongue. She didn't know how something could be tough and slimy all at once, but whatever this was managed it. To top it off, the delicacy lacked any kind of taste at all except an unpleasant sour note that lingered after she swallowed. She stuck her tongue out, disgusted.

"What *is* this?" she asked.

"I think it used to be fruit, but at this point, best not to ask."

Nessa plugged her nose and forced the rest down, then chased it with a shot of khava. The rotgut tasted better than the food.

"Okay, will you tell me now? I ate."

"We're under the Dwarmin Hill," Rinn finally answered. "It'll be a nice shortcut to your wizard. Shave off about half a day."

"Hill?" Nessa glanced up into the ever-expanding darkness above them.

"It's a very large hill."

She blinked up into the inky black, her fingers tracing the deep, straight lines carved just below where she sat. Angular lines in patterns that might have been language or simply design flowed up the wall behind their heads, flecks of shine glimmering within the cervices. Nessa couldn't tell if the color was gold or green or both. Pillars soared and vanished into the darkness above them even as piles of rubble lay at their bases. Planks of wood and pieces of fabric, its pattern long since faded and worn away, had settled like dust into the corners of the cavern.

The shadow of memory loomed large all around them.

"Who used to live here?" Nessa asked.

"Ancient dwarves. They collapsed most of this tunnel section during the Last War. It stopped the elves from following them east."

"The what now?" she asked.

"The Last War of Wealth?"

Rinn looked at her like she was insane, so Nessa responded the only way she knew how. She stared back, doing her best impression of a deer in headlights.

"You really don't know any of this?" Rinn asked, looking skeptical.

"My tower was *very* tall."

"Flames, Alice!" Rinn shook his head. "Sometimes I wonder if you just dropped out of the sky."

"It was a tree, if you recall."

Rinn almost smiled then, an amused rush of air escaping his mouth.

"A thousand years ago, dwarves and elves fought for the wealth of the land: gems, precious metals, anything that could lead them to the pure power sources of Avani. But in the end, no one got anything except a land soaked in blood and an eternal grudge."

"The elves destroyed the tunnel?"

"See, that would be a terrible strategy." He'd started twiddling with the light-stone again. "Dwarven tunnels run all over Avani. If the elves had been able to use them, they'd have had a straight shot into the dwarves' territory, so the dwarves collapsed their own tunnels. Figured they'd rather destroy all their hard work then let anyone else use them, elf or otherwise."

Nessa contemplated the place, picturing a bustling city. She could almost see it: brightly colored stalls filled with dazzling trinkets, dwarves packed into the square, men meeting for business and women stopping to gossip. Merchants shouting to passersby to sell whatever they had glittering before them as delicious smells wafted through the air. A carousel of noise and color and scents that would be unmatched anywhere else in Avani.

She felt a pang in her chest at the loss of something so grand.

"It seems like all I get to see here is the ruins of what used to be," she said sadly. "Like I came after the party was over. Like all that remains is the memory of joy, and I'm left trying to piece it back together."

Her words made Rinn pause and stare at her with that same curious look from earlier, but Nessa couldn't even bring herself to be nervous. Instead, she chewed her lower lip until it was sore.

"Okay, Alice," Rinn began, "from what I've gathered about your situation, I know you can't tell me much. But if I'm going to get you to your wizard, I need to at least know one thing."

Nessa's stomach twisted painfully as her body started to shake all over again. "I told you, I didn't know about him!"

Rinn put his hands up, his tone gentle. "I know, I know. It's alright."

Nessa nodded, pursing her lips to keep the tears in her eyes where they belonged. Taking a deep breath through her nose, she tried to calm down. "Okay."

"Right," said Rinn. "Is anyone waiting for you? At the wizard's?"

"Uh…" She trembled as she thought of Dagorn.

Don't think about it too hard. Don't wonder about Dagorn, and definitely don't think about Liv killing Dagorn in his sleep. Don't think about losing the father you just found. Don't think about losing all your friends. Don't fall into despair.

Don't go there. Just don't.

"I hope so." She won the battle against her rising panic, but only just barely. "I don't know what happened to my father."

"Will your father be able to keep you safe, if you find him?"

Nessa nodded even as she curled in on herself. She couldn't think about the way Rinn was looking at her right now, all dark eyes and a serious expression that might have been concern.

Finally, he sighed. "Get some rest. I'll take watch."

"Shouldn't we keep moving?" Nessa asked.

"It's not safe to travel these tunnels at night." Rinn reclined back into a sprawl, his hand resting loosely over one of his knives. "We aren't the only ones down here, you know."

"That's not comforting."

"It's not meant to be."

Nessa wanted to fight him, to argue, but found herself too exhausted to even try. Instead, she curled up on the cold stone with her pack as a pillow, and fell asleep just as Rinn began to sing.

Chapter Twenty-Four

The Plunge

Eyes. Thousands upon thousands of eyes stared at the unfamiliar light in the darkness. The light. *They hated light to begin with, but this was worse. This light meant humans had come.*

Fools, the pair of them. Intruders were not welcome here...

***

Nessa jerked awake with a start, her fingers flying to the stone at her throat. A gentle warmth crept into her fingertips.

Wait, didn't that mean…

Well, shit.

What had Liv said to do? *Calm, focus. Just think of nothing and answers will come*. She closed her eyes, trying to slow her heart. *Concentrate*.

What had she seen?

Let the images form…

Eyes, so many eyes.

Nessa's eyes snapped open, an impressive curse on her lips.

"Well, that's not very ladylike," Rinn teased, his expression half quizzical and half curious. A small dagger danced between his fingers, but it paused in its motion when he saw the roundness of Nessa's eyes.

"We have to go." Nessa wanted to scowl and curse some more, but they didn't have time. Those eyes were almost on them! She leapt to her feet, but Rinn caught her arm.

"Whoa," he said. "It's not safe to travel at night, Alice. I told you that before."

"No, but there are…" What? Eyes? She paused, wracking her brain for the word. "…*Things*, creatures coming."

"Creatures?" he asked in disbelief. "What kind of creatures?"

"With eyes!"

"With *eyes*?"

Great. Now he thought she was a crazy person. Oh gods, he probably had even before now.

"I don't know, but they are coming!" Nessa tried to shake him off, and Rinn, being a gentleman, let her go, giving her a mischievous grin.

"You don't know? Well, that's hardly cause for alarm, then."

"Rinn, I'm serious," Nessa pleaded. "We need to—"

She shrieked as a creature leapt out of the dark with a hiss. Startled, Rinn let his blade fly, and there was a groan and a horrible smell from the darkness. Drawing his sword, he quickly spun Nessa behind him, and she pressed her back against his.

More and more of the things came popping out of the shadows, letting out ear-splitting howls, the sound a high-pitched cacophony that seemed to rile up all the others. It echoed off the cavern walls and enveloped the pair, making it impossible to tell how many of them surrounded Nessa and Rinn. It could have been twenty, or hundreds. Their trusty little green light had winked out before it could illuminate the entirety of the horde.

"Goblins," Rinn breathed.

"Right, of course." Nessa ground her teeth. "It can't be anything easy, like a unicorn, or a puppy."

Nessa decided right there that goblins were disgusting things. They ranged from waist high to at least two feet taller than herself, and their eyes were huge, probably from centuries of living in the dark. None of them had hair; otherwise, there was little uniformity to the horde. Some had arms that were too long, causing their knuckles to drag across the ground, while others had larger yellowed teeth than the rest of them. Still more had bowed legs from constant crouching, and from what Nessa could see poking out of their rusted armor, the dirt from the cave tunnels had permanently stained their skin a sickly brown and mushroom green.

"Just stay calm," Rinn told her.

The goblins were closing in around them; Nessa didn't think calm was going to help them much. A goblin lunged forward and grabbed her, dragging her away from Rinn with a painful tug, and she stumbled into the mass of creatures as the horde screeched victoriously.

She started flailing immediately, kicking and thrashing as she tried desperately to free herself. Her elbows and knees seemed to be making contact, but they kept pulling at her hair. She managed to fight her way upright, but her struggle only seemed to excite the creatures, the noise in the tunnel growing louder as dust began to drift down from above.

Suddenly, a leather-clad hand grabbed hers. Rinn! Nessa quickly unsheathed her dagger and swung it in a wide arc. The goblins jumped back just as Rinn pulled hard, freeing her from the pack.

Rinn quickly pulled her against his back as the goblins drew closer. They were going to attack again; Nessa could tell from the crazed look in their eyes. They were actually enjoying all the chaos and mayhem.

"*R'saz!*"

Rinn's voice echoed around the cavern like a church bell, everything and everyone freezing in place as Nessa gripped him tighter, her chest heaving for air. This was not the Rinn she knew. In fact, he appeared more commanding than she ever could have believed, standing straight with his head held high. She had seen glimpses of this Rinn when he'd fought off Snow, but now he was in full view.

...Had his shoulders always been so broad?

Chancing a glance at Nessa out of the corner of his eye, his courage seemed to falter as he stared at her a just moment too long. But in a flash, he fixed his mask and turned to address the goblins, his voice ringing firm and solid through the cavern. Whatever the strange language was, there was no doubt it was his native tongue; it spilled from his lips as easily as flowing water. Something about the words seemed familiar, but Nessa couldn't quite grasp the memory.

A single goblin came forward, snarling at Rinn the entire time in the same language. It looked horribly annoyed and offended. Rinn did his best to interject during what was apparently a rant, but it didn't seem to be going well. They argued, snapping back and forth at each other, until finally Rinn held his hands up to calm the frantic creature before running them down his own face. He turned to Nessa, who was still pressed against his back.

"Give me your necklace," he ordered.

"What?" she demanded.

"Your necklace. We need to give them something to show we aren't threats. He wants your necklace," Rinn explained calmly.

Nessa blinked at him, reaching for the clasp before she realized.

"It doesn't come off."

Rinn glared at her. Clearly, he didn't believe a word of it. Nessa herself had never actually thought about it before, but the chain had no clasp. She had never needed one; the pendant had always rested just below the hollow of her throat. Even when she was young, it had never been any longer and it never grew any shorter even as she grew taller. The jewel always gleamed pristinely, the setting never needing to be cleaned. It had always just…been there, and Nessa had never questioned it. Why had she never thought about it before?

"Alice…" Rinn hissed.

"It literally cannot come off," Nessa hissed back.

Rinn made a face, one that looked like he was barely holding in a growl. Flexing his jaw, he ran a hand through his hair and cursed quietly. He reached under his shirt to finger the gold chain around his neck, and was about to pull it off when Nessa had a thought.

"Wait."

She grabbed his arm, and he gave her an expectant look, releasing the chain around his neck. Reaching under her own shirt, she pulled out the silver charm Liv had given her.

"Would this work?"

Rinn's head bobbed in a nod. "It's precious metal."

He raised his eyebrows as Nessa passed him the charm without another word. Keeping a hand on his bicep, she watched as he offered the medallion to the goblin chieftain, a few brief but intense words passing between the goblin and the thief. She held her breath.

Finally, Rinn murmured something that sounded like assent and lightly bowed his head, glancing at Nessa out of the corner of his eye. She followed suit and bowed as well.

And that was that. The goblin horde disappeared one by one out of the reach of the light, their grotesque faces slowly fading away into the darkness, but Nessa still didn't relax until she heard Rinn release the breath he'd been holding. Only then did she finally turn to him.

"Told you so."

Rinn glared, and Nessa scooped up her pack so she wouldn't have to notice. "What did you tell them?"

Looking exhausted, he rubbed the back of his neck and began to gather his things. "That we were harmless." His jaw set in a hard line. "We had to pay him tribute, to honor our hosts."

He straightened, torch stone in hand, and glared daggers at her. "Why doesn't your necklace come off?"

Nessa's stomach dropped into her toes. "It just doesn't."

Abort! Abort!

"What *did* you give them, then?" Rinn's tone held a harsh bite.

Nessa shrugged. "Some charm. My friend gave it to me, to keep me safe."

"So that *was* a protection charm." Rinn sighed, exasperated. "We better get going before they realize we didn't give them anything of real value."

He led them down the tunnel at a quick clip, holding the torch stone high. Apparently, the incident with the goblins had him spooked. Nessa stayed close, nearly jogging to keep up with his long stride. Rinn pulled an unlit torch from the wall as they moved and whispered a word to the glowing stone, then touched the stone to the torch. The torch burst into flames.

"It doesn't bother you?" He turned to look at her, finally slowing his pace to an aggravated walk. Nessa fell into step beside him, raising an eyebrow.

"What?"

"What you heard me saying back there. It doesn't bother you?" Rinn sounded genuinely shocked, even perturbed.

"Well, I didn't really feel like being taken captive by goblins. Did you?" she replied.

He had to be teasing her. He was a thief! Why would he be worried about lying? Or about how she felt about him? It wasn't like her overall impression of him had exactly been spotless before.

"No," said Rinn, looking confused.

"Then I don't see why anything you said should bother me."

For a moment, he looked at her like she was crazy, then finally shook his head.

"So, why doesn't your necklace come off again?" One of his eyebrows arched gracefully, some of his previous frustration clinging to his words.

Nessa sighed in exasperation. "Look, Rinn. I would have given it to you if I could've, but it doesn't come off." She lifted her hair to show him the back of her neck. "It doesn't have a clasp."

"Then take it off over your head," he snapped.

"I can't." She demonstrated. The chain wouldn't allow the pendant past her chin.

"Well, you couldn't have been born with it on," Rinn growled, looking annoyed again as he inspected the jewel a little more closely. Nessa drew back.

"Look, it just stays there! Okay?" she bit out.

She started to stomp away, but paused when she realized Rinn was no longer beside her. Turning back, she saw him frozen and staring, his face contorted into an expression of horror. Her heart plummeted into her toes. What was it? More goblins? This was not the time for them to stop.

Suddenly, Rinn swore. Profusely.

He ran his hands through his mass of hair, a low growl rumbling from deep within his chest. Nessa wasn't sure if it was directed at her or himself, but his glare abruptly snapped to her, and all of a sudden she found it difficult to breathe. A fire burned in his gaze, so intense it made her stomach do a flip, and she swallowed hard, suddenly terrified of those dark eyes.

Rinn was on her in two strides. "You're a Visiril, aren't you? A Dreamer."

It wasn't a question. He knew.

Nessa felt ice churn in her stomach, freezing her heart in place, but she swallowed down her shaky breath and tried to control her trembling.

"Don't be ridiculous."

"You —"

"No!" It came out too loud.

Nessa clenched and unclenched her hands, trying to release the tension in her chest. It was too late. He knew. A common thief knew who she was, *what* she was. And she certainly couldn't trust him. Who knew what he'd do with her now that he knew her secret? It would be so easy for Rinn to betray her, to sell her to the highest bidder.

He swore again, shaking his head.

Nessa ran a hand down her face to hide her terrified eyes. There was no getting around it; he had figured it out.

Well, good for him. What did he want, a damn medal? Denying it would only strengthen his belief. No matter what she said, he would believe what he wanted.

Gods, she was in so much trouble.

"Don't be an idiot," she muttered sullenly.

She glanced at him out of the corner of her eye. He definitely knew; she could tell by the look on his face. He wasn't really even here with her, but lost in his own thoughts. Probably trying to figure out how best to sell her out. All the while, she was left standing there like an idiot as the sheer terror made a permanent home in her chest.

He could destroy her. He could destroy everything.

Nessa glanced up at him, her eyes burning, and swallowed hard in panic. She didn't have the strength to push it down anymore.

"You can't tell," she breathed. "Please…"

Rinn put a hand up, silencing her.

"Let's just get you to your wizard." His tone was quiet.

No. He couldn't just walk away from this! There was too much at stake. She grabbed his arm to stop him, and he blinked, then blinked again, his eyes falling on her shaking hand. All the fire in his gaze vanished abruptly.

"Promise me." The fear and desperation laced her words, her entire body shuddering. "Promise me you won't tell! Please!"

"Alice, who would I tell?" Rinn's tone remained uncharacteristically soft. "*I* don't even want to know."

"You won't tell?"

Rinn sighed, running a hand down his face. He opened his mouth to speak, when suddenly a screech echoed down the tunnel. They whirled around to search the passageway.

Out of the dark came a wild clamor; it started out soft, but grew and grew until it surrounded them entirely. The floor began to tremble, dust raining from the walls, and Nessa's grip on Rinn's arm tightened.

The goblins were coming.

"Run." Rinn passed Nessa the torch and drew his longsword in one move. "Run!"

But she couldn't get her feet to move. She stared at the blade, at the angular runes carved down the middle in softly shining gold, until Rinn nudged her, hard, and she snapped back to reality.

The two took off down the tunnel, and Nessa held the torch high, at first seeing only stone walls and floor. But then gradually, at the edge of the ring of light, came the hundreds of yellow eyes, glowing in the dark.

"How far to the other side?" Nessa asked, panting.

"Not far," Rinn answered, adjusting his grip on his blade. "Especially if we keep outrunning them."

"And how long can we do that?" Nessa demanded.

As if to answer her question, a goblin leapt out at them, and Nessa quickly swung the torch, knocking him into the opposite wall where he crumpled to the floor like a rag doll. She held in a gasp as Rinn helped her jump over the prone form.

"Nice arm."

He actually sounded admiring.

Their hurried footsteps echoed off the stone walls until the squeals and squawks of the goblins grew louder than the pounding of their feet. The walls trembled violently with the sound of the goblins' charge; Nessa could feel dirt and grime trickling onto her head. She looked up just as the ceiling began to crack, sending small stones raining down on them. The cracks grew larger, chasing them, as the goblins drew closer, and Nessa glanced over her shoulder, only to have Rinn yank her down. An arrow whizzed over her head.

"C'mon!"

Rinn urged her forward through a small opening into a soaring cavern, then threw his arm across her chest. Nessa gasped as she nearly toppled straight into an endless darkness that threatened to swallow her whole, her arms flailing until she was finally able to grab onto Rinn.

The path veered to the left along the edge of the drop, revealing a great staircase of stone about ten yards across. It descended about three stories down, before ending in a rope bridge that led to an opening on the other side of the canyon. Nessa's eyes widened in terror.

"You've got to be kidding me," she breathed, eyeing the bottomless darkness as Rinn took her arm and gently led her down the narrow path. *Don't look down. Don't look down. Don't look down*. Air rushed in her ears, her face growing uncomfortably hot. Heights! Why did it have to be heights?

Nessa's heart pounded in her ears as she and Rinn ran carefully along the ledge, the edges chipping away under their feet. Chancing a glance behind her, she saw the goblins less than twenty feet away. She brandished the torch at them, hoping to keep them at bay, but one leapt at her.

With a mighty swing, Nessa sent him tumbling over the edge. But the others were getting closer. There were just too many to fight.

"Rinn!" Nessa cried.

Rinn turned to see the goblins right on their tail. His eyes widened.

"Hold on!"

He grasped hold of her arm so firmly that she thought she would likely bruise and pulled her against him, wrapping his arms around her waist. Nessa grabbed onto his shoulders as he spun them around, swinging her out over the darkness below. She would have screamed, but he was setting her down on his other side before she even had time to draw breath.

Then suddenly, the goblins were on them. One lunged forward with a cry, blade upraised, and Nessa called out in alarm. Rinn spun, blocking the attack and running the creature through with one swing, but Nessa didn't even have time to be relieved as two more immediately replaced their fallen comrade. Rinn put a hand on her back, encouraging her forward.

"Faster! Faster, princess!"

He blocked one goblin strike and jammed his shoulder into a second, and Nessa watched the creature stumble before falling into the cavernous darkness below. Rinn swung his sword again, taking off another goblin's head, then pushed the body as hard as he could into the rest of the horde, tripping them up enough to gain a few more feet.

"Go! Run!" he ordered.

Nessa pushed herself onto the stairs as the stone below rumbled, the entire cavern threatening to shake apart. She stumbled to her knees, just barely managing to catch herself before she tumbled all the way down. Rinn helped her up, and she didn't let go of his hand as they flew down the staircase. They heard a massive groan and creak, as though the mountain itself was struggling to hold its own weight, and looked up to see rocks shaking loose from the ceiling, the cave crumbling around them.

Boulders hit the top of the stairs, crushing the path and sending the few goblins unlucky enough to be hit flailing into the dark abyss below. Luckily, it also prevented most of the rest from following them, but Nessa was sure there had to be another way around. The stairs shook as she and Rinn flew down them two at a time, Nessa keeping a tight hold of Rinn's hand.

A dozen of the more intrepid goblins stayed hot on their tail, one even jumping over their heads to try to cut them off. Nessa hit him in the chest with her torch, and he burst into flames as he fell backward, knocking into two others who had also made the jump. In a panic, all three lost their footing, falling from the stairs and into the darkness. A small blade flew past her arm and into the chest of another goblin as Rinn clasped her hand once more.

Another tremor shook the cave, and more stone broke free from the ceiling, pelting them with stony debris. Nessa stumbled, clutching onto Rinn for dear life.

"Look out!" he called suddenly.

Nessa dived backward, narrowly avoiding being crushed by mere inches. The stairway before her collapsed, crumbling away into the darkness below.

Looking up, she saw Rinn getting to his feet on the other side of the gaping canyon. She braved a glance over the edge. Damn, that was a long way down.

"Alice!"

Nessa turned to see that two goblins had jumped onto her little section of stair and were racing toward her, snarling.

"Jump!" Rinn ordered, opening his arms.

Nessa backed up a few steps, her heart pounding in her ears. Gods and angels, this was a bad idea. *Don't think. Just go!*

She ran, launching herself off the edge of the stone, and for the briefest moment, she flew over the bottomless pit. Then she felt herself start to fall, her stomach pitching as wind rushed through her hair.

Suddenly, Rinn had his arms wrapped around her.

"I got you."

He set her down gently as her heart pounded.

"Thanks. Thank you." Nessa's voice shook.

He quickly nudged her in front of him again, and they flew down the last few steps before taking off across the bridge at a dead sprint. It swayed dangerously from side to side, but they couldn't stop. Nessa gripped the coarse rope, knuckles white, and propelled herself onwards.

She saw Rinn pause once his foot hit solid stone, then he swung his sword twice. The rope bridge snapped, then collapsed into the darkness, taking three goblins with it.

"That'll slow them down," he panted.

The two dashed through the tunnel, hearing the faint cracking of the stone and the echoing battle cry of the goblins thundering all around them. Rinn led the way through the twists and turns of the unfamiliar labyrinth, while Nessa could barely keep track of which direction they were going. All she could do was hold on to Rinn and run.

"We're almost there," Rinn called over his shoulder.

They rounded a corner and Nessa spied a faint sliver of light. A door! The large stone stood slightly ajar, tempting them with possible escape. But they were never going to fit through that miniscule gap.

Rinn rushed over to it anyway, bracing himself against the cave wall to push the door open further, and Nessa dropped her torch to help, taking the other side and digging her heels into the ground as the goblin cries grew louder and louder. They were getting closer.

"Hurry," Rinn groaned.

"What do you think I'm doing?" Nessa snapped.

An arrow suddenly flew past her head, and Nessa ducked, letting out a shriek. She whirled around and saw the goblins had arrived, when suddenly, Rinn dashed past her, sword gleaming.

"Get the door open!"

He charged the goblins head on, cutting them down where they stood as Nessa braced her back against the wall and her feet on the door. Growling with effort, she pushed as hard as she could, Rinn's sword flashing as goblins fell around him. More arrows flew over Nessa's head, and a sting ran down her arm, making her cry out.

Rinn spun and ducked with effortless ability, the sword seeming more an extension of his arm than a weapon. The blade flashed fiercely in the small sliver of light, and some of the goblins backed away, shouting angrily in their own tongue.

With a final yell of effort and a mighty push, the door yielded the barest of inches. It was all they needed.

"Rinn!" she called.

Rinn spun, taking the head off yet another goblin, and saw Nessa waving him on. He bolted for the door, expertly sliding through the opening Nessa had created, and then the only sound was the anguish of the goblins behind them as the bright sunlight drove them back into the mountain.

Chapter Twenty-Five

The Frying Pan Was Safer

And just like that, they were out. The land around them sloped steadily and steeply downward, tall grass covering the ground. A few trees dotted the landscape, giving them enough space to see the sun just beginning to set, the sky painted pink and orange and red against the few clouds in the vast expanse. They didn't stop running until they made it to the base of the mountain, bathed in the safety of the sunlight.

Nessa fell against a tree, panting from exhaustion. She looked up at Rinn. He sheathed his sword, then leaned against the same tree to steady himself.

"I haven't done that since…" He trailed off, looking up at her as he caught his breath. "You aren't paying me enough for this."

She didn't know why, but she burst out laughing at that, while Rinn stared at her as though she were insane. Nessa, still laughing, braced her back against a tree and slid down to the ground. She shook her head.

"I'm not paying you at all."

A miracle happened just then: Rinn's usual expression of wry amusement boiled over into laughter, deep and rich. Nessa looked up at him, a smile on her face. She wasn't sure if she was more grateful to be out of those tunnels or for the first genuine emotion she'd seen so far from her traveling companion.

His laugh was doing funny things to her stomach.

Rinn finally relaxed a little and dropped to the ground next to her, his laughter fading.

"You all right?" Nessa asked.

He shrugged. "Few cuts and scrapes. I'm fine. And you, duchess?"

He was still teasing her. She wanted to smack him, but perhaps not as hard as before.

Nessa nodded. "Same."

She saw his eyes fall to the scrape on her arm. "Lucky for me, goblins have terrible aim."

"Their eyesight was never particularly renowned," he agreed, his eyes moving back to her face. "That's why they hate sunlight. Their eyes can't take it. Besides, you've had practice avoiding the arrows of your elf friend."

She gave him a mischievous smirk. "I solved that problem by taking her bow."

"Have you got your breath back?" he inquired. Nessa nodded. "Then we'd best push on. Alaron's is only a few hours off."

"So anxious to be rid of me?" Nessa teased as Rinn rose to his feet. She did the same, ignoring his outstretched hand. Brushing herself off, she adjusted her pack.

"You do tend to get into trouble," he pointed out.

"And you don't?" Nessa asked.

Rinn feigned offense to the question. "Oh, never."

A thief never getting into trouble? That was rich.

The teasing smile suddenly vanished.

"Down!"

He yanked her to the ground with him just as a dagger embedded itself in the tree behind them, a blade flying from Rinn's own hand even as he stayed crouched over her protectively. Nessa had no idea what he had even aimed at.

Then suddenly, she caught sight of a shadow moving between the trees. Her breath hitched. Was it Liv? The form slowed, resolving into a large shape.

It was a man.

Rinn swallowed. "Stay down."

He nudged Nessa behind a tree and sprang to his feet, drawing his sword in a flash. In the sunlight, the blade appeared almost aflame. Nessa peeked around the tree to see Rinn charging at seemingly nothing. Another blade flew through the air, but he easily knocked it away with his sword.

"Your aim *was* always terrible," he taunted.

A deep voice came suddenly from the trees.

"She's pretty."

There was a soft *thud* as the other man stepped into the light, and Nessa slowly rose to her feet, still safely out of sight behind the tree. Something nagged at her. She'd seen the man before, she knew it, but she couldn't remember where.

The newcomer was dressed in what might have been nice traveling clothes at one point, but now were a little worse for wear, even patched in some places.

Still, he carried what looked like a small arsenal; in fact, he practically bristled with weapons. He towered over Rinn, his broad shoulders squared at the thief. Something about him felt empty, and dangerous, as if he were burning from the inside out.

The huge man drew his sword, matching Rinn's stance, and Rinn shifted his weight between his feet as he adjusted his grip on his sword.

The stranger suddenly launched himself at Rinn, who blocked the strike easily and darted to the side. His attacker followed quickly, but Rinn had successfully turned him away from Nessa.

Nessa knew two predators facing off when she saw it. The other man stood a head taller than Rinn, with broad shoulders and bulging arm muscles. He looked like he could easily snap Nessa in half.

The man circled Rinn, the thief matching his movement step for step as they studied each other. He lunged again, impossibly fast for a man his size, and Rinn blocked him again with a flick of his blade.

They went back to circling. This time, it didn't take long for the other man to lunge, Rinn blocking him yet again before the man retreated. He grinned, spitting foreign words at Rinn in a deep growl.

Nessa suddenly realized that she had heard those words before. The Bear had said the exact same thing to her.

This man was from Menhir.

Cold fear crushed her lungs, her fingernails digging into the bark beneath her palms. *Not this again.* Grinding her teeth, she focused on the ache in her jaw as electric buzzing flooded her veins. She carefully moved her hand from the tree to the hilt of her ill-gotten sword, the leather warm under her palm.

The Menhiran charged, and Rinn dodged below the strike, his sword arcing back toward the man. His attacker spun to face him and the dance began anew, the blades flashing like lighting against the setting sun, moving too fast for Nessa to follow.

Strike, dodge, spin, parry.

The Menhiran kept snarling at Rinn in that same harsh language, but Rinn remained silent, his dark eyes hard. Nessa could see the stern set of his jaw as Rinn bared his teeth at the other man, and something twisted in her stomach as she realized his movements were growing stiff.

His attacker managed to swipe Rinn's feet out from under him, and the thief hit the ground hard. Before he could get up, the Menhiran jammed his heel onto Rinn's sword hand, and Nessa heard a loud *pop.*

Rinn groaned in pain.

Kicking the blade from Rinn's hand, the man pressed his foot to Rinn's chest, pinning him in place. Rinn tried to reach for the weapon, but didn't get very far.

Nessa bit her lower lip. Rinn was a tough guy. She'd just seen him take on an entire cave of goblins without batting an eyelash. What was different about this man that had Rinn acting so timid? She may not have known him long, but she did know one thing.

He wasn't the type to let go of his weapons.

The Menhiran stood above her thief, a gloating smile on his lips, and Nessa swallowed in terror. *C'mon, Rinn. Get up*. She knew he could. He had to.

The mercenary brought his sword up, blade poised above Rinn's chest. His smile was tinged with madness, the insanity flashing in his dark eyes.

"*Hey!*"

Nessa crashed shoulder-first into the mercenary's side, knocking him away from Rinn. She clutched at his sleeves as they rolled across the ground, and the man shifted his weight so he landed on top of Nessa, pinning her down. The dagger in his hand flashed above her for an instant as he drove it down toward her body, and Nessa threw her arm up to block the strike, just like her father had taught her. She pushed up with all her strength, her eyes fixed on the cool metal intent on ending her life.

At the same time, she dug her fingers into the earth beneath her, flinging a handful of dirt in her captor's face. He reeled back on reflex, giving her the opportunity to shift her hips and throw him off with a grunt of effort. She scrambled away from him as he glared balefully at her, wiping the mud from his face.

"Little whore," he growled.

"Let's keep your mother out of this," Nessa snapped back.

He was on her in a flash, Nessa just barely managing to get her sword up in time to block his strike. The metal rattled in her hand, but she didn't drop it, though her knuckles turned white on the hilt. She aimed her boot into the Menhiran's shin, and he cursed, hopping back.

He swiped his blade at her head and she ducked just in time, her body remembering what to do even if her head couldn't keep up. She backed up, drawing him away from Rinn, and the Menhiran chased after her. He swung again, and Nessa barely managed to escape the blade, which buried itself in the tree behind her. Keeping low to the ground, she tried to kick him backwards, but he grabbed her foot, pulling them both down.

The stolen sword went flying as her head collided hard with the ground. Her vision swam, stars flashing behind her eyes, and she fought her ringing head as she tried desperately to find her dagger. Too late, something was moving above her before she could draw. She squeezed her eyes closed.

The sound of metal clashing on metal echoed in her ears as the world finally began to steady, and she opened her eyes to see Rinn standing above her. He was pushing the Menhiran back, his sword whirling in his left hand and his injured right behind his back. Nessa caught a glimmer of silver out of the corner of her eye and skidded over the leaves to snatch up her own sword, launching herself back into the fray.

Rinn handled a blade just as well with his left hand as with his right, and every time the Menhiran turned to regroup, Nessa was there to prevent a retreat. Abruptly, he seemed to decide Nessa would be an easier target, coming after her like a lion on an injured gazelle. It took everything in her just to block his strikes.

Her foot slipped on a hidden tree root, and she fell heavily to the ground. Thinking quickly, she kicked out at his ankles, bringing him crashing down to her level.

Then without warning, her attacker slumped to the side, a thin line of red appearing at his dark hairline. Nessa glanced up to see Rinn standing over her, blood on the hilt of his sword.

She panted hard, trying to slow her pounding heart. Her eyes stayed fixed on the Menhiran for one breath, then two. He didn't move.

"Are you alright?" Rinn asked.

Nessa nodded. "Yes. You?"

He nodded too. Her eyes lingered on the cut above his left eye, but she refrained from comment.

Gazing down at her, he grimaced and sheathed his sword. With a heavy sigh, he muttered, "I hate doing this."

He squeezed his eyes closed, rubbing his injured hand, and Nessa could hear the sickening *pop* as he pushed his dislocated fingers back into place. He barely winced (though the sound was enough to make Nessa cringe), shaking his hand out once he was finished.

"You are insane," he said.

"Never said I wasn't."

She tried to make light of the situation, looking down at their attacker. He had to be at least three times her size, she noted. "Who is he?"

"Remember how I said I was being followed?"

Nessa's mouth fell open as she looked at the behemoth on the ground.

"What exactly did you *do?!*"

Instead of answering, Rinn gave her a lopsided, roguish smile, and she shook her head. Sheathing her sword, she turned her eyes to the twilight darkness around them. It wouldn't be wise to remain this close to the goblin tunnels after nightfall. She frowned as her eyes fell on the Menhiran soldier.

"We should go before he wakes up."

"I ought to ensure that never happens." But Rinn sounded far away, unable to stop staring at the man on the ground.

"What about the goblins?" Nessa asked. "Rinn, it's almost dark. I don't think they're going to give up on us so easily."

Nessa watched silently as Rinn growled, combing his hands through his hair. She forced herself to breathe, to stay calm, and swallowed hard. She'd never seen Rinn so worked up.

"He saw you. With me," he snapped. "If I don't kill him, you're a target—"

"I'm already a target," Nessa pointed out. "Biggest one there is, in fact."

She stepped close to Rinn, grabbing the lapels of his coat to get him to stop moving, and he froze, turning to stare into her worried eyes.

"I'm not telling you that you shouldn't," Nessa told him gently. As much as she hated saying it, that guy on the ground *had* tried to kill them. Still, she didn't want to be the one hurting anyone. "I'm saying, we don't have much time."

Rinn nodded. He looked at the man on the ground, then back at Nessa.

He knew everything about her now, or nearly. Rinn knew what she was and how bad it would be if she were caught — and he had also saved her life, multiple times now. A thief he may have been, but he had nevertheless proven himself to be a man of honor. This was not her decision to make. It was his, and she trusted him.

What a strange thing, to trust a thief.

Rinn sighed, growled, then sighed again.

"Let's go, princess." He sounded like he knew it was a mistake. "With our luck, your elf friend will be showing up again any minute."

Rinn took her hand, and together, they disappeared into the twilight.

Chapter Twenty-Six

Wizard School Dropout

Nessa had never been more grateful to see the sunrise.

She and Rinn had run through the night, zigging when she expected to zag, and zagging when she expected to zig. They hadn't stopped, except to hastily patch each other up, nor did they speak. Nothing needed to be said.

Nessa finally let herself breathe when she saw beams of light breaking through the canopy above, and only then did they allow themselves to slow to a walk. They passed whatever dried fruit they had between each other just to keep themselves going, Nessa occasionally glancing at Rinn out of the corner of her eye.

"How's your arm?" Rinn asked.

Nessa glanced at the bloodstained handkerchief Rinn had wrapped around her arm hours ago. He'd put some tangy-smelling goop on it that had stung like blazes, but it seemed to be working.

"Fine. How's your hand?"

"Perfect." He waggled his fingers at her, and Nessa found herself grinning.

"Are we almost there?" she asked, both excited for and dreading the answer.

"Two hours, tops," Rinn replied.

They walked in silence for a moment, Nessa watching Rinn as he fiddled with his blades, and he tilted his head at her as she spun a blade of grass between her fingers. He only tilted his head like that when he was thinking.

She happened to do the same thing.

"Say, duchess, have you thought about what happens if this doesn't work?"

Constantly. But did she have a plan for that? Absolutely not. This was it. This was her one shot.

"What do you mean?" she asked, fighting for calm.

"If the wizard won't help you, if your father isn't there, what then?"

"I don't know." Nessa chewed her lower lip. "This is pretty much all I've got."

"And if this doesn't work, where would you be safe?"

"Nowhere, really." She felt her chipper mood darkening to one of apprehension, her stomach churning. "I think probably as far south as possible."

Rinn nodded.

"I'm going to be headed back this way in three days' time. If for some reason things don't work out, meet me at the edge of the forest. I'll take you south."

"Rinn —"

"I know a few people who sail the Vergri. It'd be no trouble."

Nessa felt herself warm, heat dusting her cheeks. Of course it would be trouble, she apparently attracted it like flies to honey. Plus, there was no doubt in her mind that these so-called 'friends' weren't exactly respectable.

On the other hand, it'd be one hell of a party.

"Thank you, Rinn. For everything."

The thief fixed her with a smolder. "Don't mention it, my lady. Seriously, I have a reputation to maintain."

Nessa laughed.

The sun had barely kissed the horizon when they emerged from the thickest part of the forest, the grass shimmering dark green as it brushed against their ankles. Colorful flowers hugged the bases of the scattered trees, and before them an adorable stone and plaster cottage sat at the top of a small hill. Blooming vines crept up the chimney, overflowing onto the moss-covered shingled roof.

"It's not what I expected." Nessa tilted her head. "I was picturing a creepy tower, maybe a dragon."

"Alaron is rarely what anyone expects." Rinn flashed her a small smile. "Well, princess, this is where I leave you. I trust you can make it the rest of the way on your own?"

"I should hope." Nessa let her soft gaze fall on Rinn's face, and she smiled. "This spot? In three days?"

"Sunrise on the third day," Rinn agreed. "If I don't see you, I'll know to move on."

He held out a hand to her. "Good luck, Alice. Stay out of trouble."

Nessa took it. "You too, Rinn. And thank you. If we ever meet again…"

Rinn winked. "I'll be sure to run very far in the other direction."

"Jerk." It was an endearment, because she smiled.

She gave him her hand, and Rinn bowed low, brushing a soft kiss over her filthy knuckles. Nessa felt her cheeks heat all the way up to her ears.

"Stay safe," she wished him.

"Always, princess."

With that, she watched him disappear into the trees — and then, taking a deep breath, she marched up the hill to meet her fate.

The cottage seemed to grow bigger as she approached. At first, it looked like it was only one level, then two, and now it was somehow wider than when she'd first seen it. White smoke puffed from one chimney — no, it had three chimneys. No, two, with black smoke.

...Best not to look at the cottage, she decided, as a sprawling garden appeared on the lawn before her. A small wooden gate surrounded a large vegetable patch, with bright flowers lining the cottage wall.

She grew distracted by the pink smoke erupting from one of the chimneys, while the third stack appeared to be releasing blue sparks. Even for a wizard, this wasn't exactly subtle. She stuck to the path in the garden just in case, the one that led to the garden fence.

Her eyes fell on a purple-flowered bush growing next the gate, and she stopped dead. Lavender! It was lavender!

How had lavender gotten to Avani? Or maybe the question was, how had lavender gotten to *Earth*? She lightly touched the tips of the violet flowers, inhaling deeply. Lilly Everette loved lavender. Albert gave her a bottle of lavender perfume every Christmas.

Nessa's chest ached, and she steeled herself with a shake of her head.

"You tiny menace!"

She jumped. The prim and proper — albeit annoyed — voice had come from the garden. Carefully, she stepped through the gate, resting a hand on her dagger.

"Oh, you better not be in the lettuce crop, you wily—" The phrase was followed by a *thump*, a spectacular swear, another *thump*, and finally a less spectacular swear.

Nessa was following the grumpy voice around a crop of tall bushes filled with pink berries when a distressed squeak caught her by surprise, and she turned to see a small nose sticking out of the brush. The nose was attached to a small blond hedgehog.

"Hello, you," she cooed at the tiny creature.

"*Where did you escape to, you tiny menace?!*"

Nessa jumped, then side-eyed the hedgehog.

"He's not talking about you, is he?" she asked.

The creature squeaked indignantly and crawled toward her, still pleading its case as the branch dipped dangerously, threatening to pitch the hedgehog to the ground. Nessa lunged forward, her hands cupped, and by some miracle managed to catch the little thing. It squeaked its thanks.

"C'mon." She cradled the hedgehog in one arm. "You can come as long as you don't poop on me."

A pointed squeak.

"Hey, you run from a thousand goblins and see how clean you are," she said defensively.

This time the squeak sounded questioning, but she waved it off.

"I'll tell you about it later."

Nessa rounded the corner to see the rump of a very skinny man waggling in the air. She pursed her lips, trying to keep her giggles in her mouth.

"Where are you, you little—"

The man tried to stand up, and his head hit a branch with a *bonk*.

Nessa couldn't help it. She snorted, her free hand flying over her mouth, and the man spun, his piercing blue eyes falling on her. His short, sandy-blond hair stuck up every which way, probably because of the mud, and he was so thin, he looked as though he'd disappear if he turned sideways. The expression on his angular, middle-aged face (which was covered in dirt smudges) changed to one of shock.

"Um, are you alright?" she asked.

"What, my dear…no," he answered.

"You aren't?"

"Oh! You little cretin!" he raged.

He rose to his full height, towering over Nessa. Mud encrusted his hands and bare feet, and the pale planes of his chest were decorated in streaks of muck — which happened to be the only thing he had on.

"Oh good lord!" Nessa's hand flew to cover her eyes, but the mental image refused to leave.

"What's the matter?" the man asked, sounding confused.

"Could—could you put something on, please?"

"What?" He looked down. "Oh, dear! Yes. You are young enough to be bothered by such things."

Nessa chose not to comment. After a moment, she chanced a peek through her fingers and saw that the man was now wearing an oversized shirt. She lowered her hand with a relieved sigh and opened her mouth to speak, but the hedgehog squeaked loudly.

The man held out a hand, and she took a step back, perhaps a little too quickly.

"Have you already managed to sway this lovely girl to your devilish ways?" he asked the creature in her arms.

Nessa looked down. "The—the hedgehog?"

"The very same."

"Oh."

She handed the hedgehog back to the apparently crazy man, and he placed the tiny menace on his shoulder. The creature squeaked at him, sounding annoyed.

"Really? All the way down?"

"Um, I'm sorry to interrupt, but I'm looking for a wizard?"

"Oh, are you, now?" The man broke into a grin. "And here I thought you'd come all this way for tea!"

"I'm sorry." Nessa twisted her fingers together. "I need some help, and I'm trying to find my father…"

He nodded. "Yes, I know. He's been wearing a hole in my floor for two days."

Her heart stuttered in her chest.

"He's here? Dagorn…"

"Yes, Your Highness, he's here." The man bowed low, the back of his shirt riding up to reveal his rump as his nose nearly scraped the dirt. Nessa tried not to look.

"Alaron of the Seventh Circle, at your service."

The relief that washed over Nessa was so overwhelming she actually laughed out loud, nearly collapsing to the ground then and there. Alaron glanced up, hearing her giggle.

"Nessa, of House Callei." She returned a little bow of her own. Odd how natural the introduction seemed. She'd never said it out loud before.

"Now, let's get you in the house. Hedgerton here told me there's a story to be had about goblins."

Nessa had taken off running before the wizard could finish; she bolted up the hill, lungs burning and constricted. Her frenzied hands grabbed hold of the door and flung it open with a bang.

"Ada!" Her voice wavered, and she spun, searching. "Ada!"

Dagorn appeared at the base of the stairway. He stood frozen, staring at her.

Nessa beamed.

"Thank the Elar," Dagorn breathed.

Nessa was immediately scooped into her father's arms, and she clung back just as hard, burying her face in his shirt.

She'd made it.

A sound somewhere between a sob and laugh escaped her lips.

"Aww."

Dagorn and Nessa looked up to see Alaron standing in the doorway, the sappiest of expressions on his face. The hedgehog squeaked happily at them as Nessa wiped her eyes, though it did nothing to clean the dirt from her cheeks. Dagorn kissed her hair.

"Nessa, are you alright? I woke and found you and Liv gone. I searched and searched, but I couldn't find you. I thought…"

Dagorn frantically scanned Nessa for injuries, holding up her bandaged arm.

"Al, do you—"

The wizard was already handing Dagorn a jar of…something.

"Dare I ask?" Dagorn inquired.

Alaron shrugged. "Best not."

"I'm fine. Honest." Nessa collapsed against her father's chest. She could have curled up and slept right there on the floor. "I really, *really* would like a bath and some sleep. Then I can tell you everything."

"Oh, say no more!" Alaron piped up.

The wizard moved to snap his fingers, but Dagorn stopped him.

"Al, my friend, we discussed this."

"Oh yes, correct. No magic on the daughter." Nessa suspected that Alaron had in fact remembered Dagorn's instructions perfectly and simply elected to ignore them.

Dagorn nodded. "Correct."

"Of course."

"Food." Dagorn gently guided Nessa toward the fire. "Sit. I'll get you something."

"I could…"

"That's quite alright, Alaron. I don't want you accidentally poisoning my daughter."

"That happened *once*."

"Twice," Dagorn corrected.

There was a pause.

"What was the second time?" Alaron asked.

"Nuremir."

"Ahhhh, yes."

Nessa finally allowed herself to look around. To her right stood a large arched opening, which led to an even larger room. A massive fluffy rug lay in front of a roaring fire, the tips of the flames taking on hues of blue, green and violet to remind her that this was indeed a wizard's home. The mantel was covered in wax-encrusted candlesticks and half-used candles. She spotted several plush chairs amidst piles and piles of books, while dangling crystals cast rainbows of light across the walls.

To her left was another large arched opening, through which she could see a kitchen, with herbs, pots and jars hanging from the ceiling. The long wooden table in the center of the room was covered in parchment and ink and what looked like thousands of broken quills, and in the sink, sponges merrily scrubbed plates all on their own.

If Terry Pratchett could have seen it, he would have been a very happy man indeed.

Nessa settled herself on the large rug in front of the fire, melting so far into the softness surrounding her that she practically became a princess puddle. Every muscle in her body cried out in joy. She had finally stopped moving.

She could hear the muffled voices of Alaron and Dagorn in the kitchen as she closed her eyes, letting the heat from the magical fire dance across her skin. She could almost feel it moving along her arm, like a curious little creature.

Wait, there *was* something moving.

Nessa sat up abruptly, only to be met with the tiniest of squeaks. The hedgehog sat on her chest, its little nose twitching. She smiled.

"How did you get down here?"

The creature squeaked in response, and Nessa released a little laugh, using a finger to gently stroke its quills. She was rewarded with a purr of delight.

"Hedgerton!" Alaron entered the room, now clean and dressed in grey and brown robes. "I told you not to disturb the guests."

"Hedgerton?" Nessa giggled, then addressed the creature. "May I call you Hedgy?"

Another squeak of approval, and Alaron smiled as if Nessa had just passed some sort of secret test, offering her a glass of wine. Nessa took it with a smile.

"Thank you, Alaron."

An air of pride shrouded the wizard as he smiled at her, and Dagorn appeared with a plateful of food, passing it to his daughter with a kiss to her forehead. She offered the first morsel to Hedgy, who nibbled on the cheese appreciatively.

Alaron waved a hand dramatically. "Now, regale us with your adventures, child. I must admit, even I am a tiny bit curious."

Nessa took a deep breath and began. She started with Liv waking her in the middle of the night and how she hadn't seemed herself, the words spilling from her mouth like water bursting from a dam. She had to take several gulps of wine to calm herself down, reminding herself that she'd made it. There was a chance to fix this.

She hesitated when she got to her wakeup call in the tree, shoving food into her mouth to give herself time to think. Why was she hesitant to tell them about Rinn? He was only a simple thief, one who had helped her get to this point. Would Dagorn try to go after him anyway? No, her father was a general, not a cop.

She compromised and told them a fellow traveler on the road had helped her get to Erwani, glossing over her mad dash through the city and narrow escape in the Angori. Alaron grinned knowingly and commended her on her ingenuity, and Nessa blushed as she admitted it had been an accident. Rinn's story would remain his to tell.

She paused after she left Erwani and stared into her wineglass, which had somehow refilled itself. Hedgy crawled up to her shoulder, and Nessa reached up to pet him as he nuzzled into her neck, reminding herself that she wasn't trapped and lost in the woods anymore. She was here, safe. She snuggled Hedgy closer to her.

"I got stuck. There was a fork in the road and I didn't know which path to take. They both looked the same, and…"

"Ah, my apologies," Alaron cut in. "They looked the same because they *were* the same. You father informed me of the situation upon his arrival, and of course, I promised to help you along. Whichever path you chose would have led you here."

"I never got the chance to find out. One of the mercenaries from Earth followed me through the Veil. He found me."

Dagorn's hand dragged over his mouth as his eyes widened, his crow's feet growing prominent.

"Ness—" His voice cracked.

Nessa sat up so she could rest her head on her father's knee, letting him stroke her hair as she cuddled Hedgy in her lap.

"I'm okay."

It was only partly a lie.

"You must have been so scared." Dagorn's voice wavered. "And I wasn't there."

Nessa looked up at him. "Don't do that. I didn't realize Liv had left anyone alive to follow us. You couldn't have known."

"How did you escape?"

Nessa licked her lips. "I got lucky. But he's still out there."

"You are safe here, dear," Alaron told her. "My wards are superb."

"Thank you."

She stumbled over her discovery of the dwarven tunnels, making her escape from the goblins sound far less exciting than it had been in reality. All the same, Hedgy let out a few squeaky gasps, which she appreciated. She skipped over the battle with Rinn's shadow entirely, ending with her run up to the garden and her discovery of Alaron swearing profusely at a hedgehog.

Alaron narrowed his eyes with a knowing smile, and Nessa chewed her lip at the look he was giving her. She knew she wasn't the best liar in the world, but she wasn't *technically* saying anything untrue, merely choosing what to omit.

The wizard rose, rubbing his hands together.

"I believe you mentioned something about a bath," he told her. "I think that can be arranged."

Nessa pushed herself up eagerly, but stopped when Dagorn caught her hand. He kissed her knuckles, making her smile at her sap of a father.

"I'm so thankful you're safe, little one."

"Same here, Ada."

"Awwww!"

They both turned to see Alaron with another lovesick look on his face. Nessa arched a brow, and the wizard blinked several times, as if only just realizing they could hear him.

"Oh, ignore me!"

Nessa couldn't suppress a small laugh. Madder than a box of frogs, indeed.

"Bath?" she asked hopefully.

"Yes, right. This way."

Alaron grinned at her like a loon the moment he got her alone. Then again, most of his grinning since Nessa arrived had been of the lunatic variety.

"That was quite a tale."

Nessa shrugged. "Wait till you hear the one about how I got to Avani."

"I'm more curious about what you left out." The wizard side-eyed her. "Why didn't you tell your father about Rinn?"

Nessa nearly stumbled, looking up at Alaron's smug face with wide eyes.

"Oh, child, someone had to lead you here. Into the dwarven tunnels, at least. Doors like that can't be found unless you know they're there."

"But how did you know it was Rinn?"

"Details," Alaron answered, waving a hand airily. "Why didn't you tell your father about him?"

Nessa tried to act nonchalant. "He's a thief."

Alaron leered. "And you think your father wouldn't approve?"

"It hardly matters." Nessa shrugged, even though it actually mattered quite a lot to her.

Alaron narrowed his eyes. "How did you find him?"

"Annoying."

The wizard chuckled, sounding surprised. "My, that was not the answer I was expecting."

"Did you think I'd swoon over the first thief I met?" Nessa tried to tease.

"Isn't that supposed to be…oh, what's the phrase? Shipping it?"

Nessa's head snapped around so fast she heard it crack.

"Where did you hear that?!" she gasped.

Alaron grinned proudly. Without explaining further, he opened a door with a sweeping gesture. Inside sat a copper tub, filled with steaming water.

"A bath, just as promised, and there's a change of clothes on the windowsill. Come down when you're done, there's a love."

And then he was gone again.
The soap smelled of lavender.
…Now he was just showing off.

Chapter Twenty-Seven

'Stressed' Spelled Backwards Is 'Desserts'

Nessa took a deep breath, then another, trying to focus. She'd dabbled in mediation exercises now and again, mostly during her failed training sessions with Liv. Albert had also been a big proponent of clearing one's mind before taking on a task, though he usually did it with the morning paper and a cup of coffee.

She straightened her back, rolling her shoulders to force herself to settle.

"I can still hear you pacing," she accused.

One eye crept open to glare at Dagorn, and he threw his hands in the air, as if in apology.

"Are you *sure* you had a Dream about it?" he asked.

"Yes!"

After a bath and a long sleep, longer than she should have allowed herself, Nessa and Dagorn had talked at length about what was wrong with Liv. Nessa was convinced Liv was under a spell, but citing a Dream she couldn't fully remember was hardly sufficient evidence. So, here they were, nearing the third hour of Nessa's failing attempts at remembering anything specific.

Nessa sagged against the floor, rubbing her aching temples. It did little to soothe the pounding behind her eyes.

"Perhaps," Alaron chimed in, "if you could recite something you know by heart? It may spark something."

Nessa paused, thinking. What was something she had memorized?

"It was a nice day. All the days had been nice. There had been rather more than seven of them and rain hadn't been invented yet..."

"Hmmm…no, no, no." Alaron waved a hand in the air. "Something else. Something you can put more *feeling* into."

Nessa closed her eyes again. More feeling? What held more feeling for her than Neil Gaiman and Terry Pratchett? She had literally thrown the book across the room when a certain angel had been discorporated. Albert had laughed, but warned her not to put a hole in the drywall.

Digging deeper into her memory, she thought of the horror stories her adoptive father had told around the fire every fall. *Frankenstein* or *Dr. Jekyll and Mr. Hyde* she didn't know well enough, and *The Raven* didn't seem appropriate, nor did *Dracula.* Besides, Albert Everette was the one who had those memorized, not her.

Then, she remembered, and her chest ached. Lilly Everette wasn't one for traditional lullabies, but that didn't mean she'd never sung Nessa to sleep.

"*Yesterday…*"

Nessa rolled her shoulders, murmuring the familiar Beatles lyrics under her breath. It felt almost like she was being rocked to sleep again as the rhythm lulled her into the quiet space behind her eyelids, the scent of lavender filling her nostrils.

The warmth in her chest twisted, lights dancing in the darkness behind her closed eyes. Slowly, they began to form into an image.

She was in the tent where she had found Liv. Her stomach rolled. The light dimmed as the image fuzzed a bit around the edges, and the two arguing men came into focus. The larger man was holding the smaller one up by the neck. He had dark eyes, and she realized with a start that she *knew* those eyes.

It was the man who had attacked Rinn.

She swallowed down her panic. Rinn was far away from here, far away from that man; she couldn't do anything to protect him. Right now, it was time to protect Liv.

"There were two men arguing, after I got Liv out." Nessa swallowed hard. She could *feel* the chill in the air, hear the soldiers' songs, smell the smoke from the fires. Goosebumps prickled her arms. It was like she was living it all over again. Every part of her wanted to recoil, but she forced herself to breathe. *Do the courageous thing and courage will come.*

"What do they look like?" Dagorn's voice seemed to come from far away.

"One is tall, broad, and sharp. He's a soldier, or at least carries himself like one. The other one is a small, bookish type, wearing robes."

She mentally 'froze' the frame, zooming in on the servant. He was holding something important, something she'd missed before. Bright white strands stuck out between his fingers.

"He has a handful of Liv's hair!"

Alaron swore loudly, and Nessa jumped, her eyes flying open as what felt like a huge rubber band snapped against her forehead. She shrieked in pain, falling back on the floor. Moaning, she rubbed her forehead, her temples throbbing.

"Oh, sorry. My bad," Alaron said apologetically, kneeling down to help her sit back up.

Hedgerton scurried over to squeak worriedly at Nessa. She gave him a small smile of reassurance and gently petted his head.

"I'm okay, Hedgerton."

It was only half a lie.

"Al." Dagorn's brow furrowed as he practically wore a hole in the floor with his pacing. "If the Menhirans have a lock of Liv's hair, they probably have some of her blood, too."

"My thoughts precisely." The wizard tapped a finger to his lips. "Blood magic will wreak havoc on her body. The pure magic of Avani will fight against the dark sorcery, try to purge it. With the body fighting itself, it will wither quickly."

"So how do we break a blood magic spell?" Nessa asked.

"And prevent them from doing it again?" Dagorn added.

"Well, I'm assuming that controlling an entire person would take a lot of blood." Nessa glanced at the wizard, who nodded in approval. "Which means they probably don't have enough for a second try."

Dagorn's brow furrowed in confusion. He opened his mouth to ask a question, but Alaron beat him to it.

"First we must break the connection." He gave Nessa a wink only she could see. "It's doable. Difficult, but doable."

"But why did she go after Nessa?" Dagorn asked. "They already know Liv is a Dreamer. Why not just take her?"

"Ah, that's the good bit." Alaron rubbed his hands together with knowledgeable glee. "Liv is fighting, if I know her at all — and I flatter myself that I do — and mind control isn't as black and white as one might think. Orders such as 'bring the Dreamer,' which seem very direct and straightforward, can slip into something similar but not quite the same with enough resistance and stubbornness, not to mention her pure magic is likely attempting to run interference. So, 'bring the Dreamer' becomes 'bring *a* Dreamer,' she conveniently forgets that she is one, and goes for the nearest other one."

"I was sleeping between you two that night," Nessa remembered. "I was closer to her."

"I must commend you, dear child." Alaron produced three glasses and a pitcher of wine from seemingly nowhere, and Nessa realized being a wizard came with perks she had never considered before. She wondered how much enrollment in wizarding school cost.

"The fact that you managed to make it here alive, with Liv chasing you," he continued, "is likely the only reason Menhir doesn't have the upper hand at the moment."

Nessa sighed, accepting the wine with a smile. "Glad to be of use."

"Excellent, then we should have no problem breaking the spell on Liv."

"Alaron," Dagorn warned.

The wizard waved him off. "She'll be perfectly safe." He thought for a second. "Well, mostly safe." A pause. "Probably."

"No," Dagorn said.

"Sixty percent," Alaron assured him, waving his hand again.

"Absolutely not."

"Sixty-five percent?"

"No," Dagorn snapped.

"I'm sitting right here, you know," Nessa growled at the men arguing her fate right in front of her. "If it will save Liv, I'll do it."

"Nessa…"

"No." Her voice was soft, but commanding. "If there's anything I can do to prevent Liv from dying, I'll do it. And everything will only get worse if Menhir gets ahold of her. For everyone, not just us. I can't let that happen. I just…can't."

Dagorn sighed, his eyes softening as he gazed at her. He leaned forward to gently kiss her forehead.

"You have your mother's heart, little one."

Nessa felt her chest swell with pride, and she gave her father a small smile.

"Not to mention Lari could always convince you to let her do anything," Alaron pointed out.

Dagorn glared.

***

Nessa spent the rest of the day resting; Alaron had told her she would need it in order to perform her part. And she tried, she really did, but her nerves just wouldn't let her sit still for long. Alaron attempted to teach her a few more words in Vaerin, but her constant pacing was wearing a hole in the rug, which the poor rug had done nothing to deserve. Finally, she went outside and wandered through the garden until the heavens above opened, sending down a gentle but steady rain.

Which was how Nessa came to be reading by the kitchen hearth, a tiny hedgehog snuggled into her neck. Hedgerton had become her constant companion, and she welcomed the company, even if he did scamper all over the pages. Really, she was only pretending to read. The words kept blurring on the page, each letter becoming nothing more than a blob that held no interest for her. Her thoughts kept turning to Liv.

And to Rinn.

Alaron appeared at her side as late afternoon faded into early evening. "I can *hear* you thinking."

Nessa jumped, then gave him a sad smile. "Sorry."

"Don't be. Not enough people think, or think properly, if you ask me." Alaron set the scrolls he was carrying onto the table across from her. "What are you thinking about?"

"My friends, mostly," she answered sadly.

Alaron's face turned soft, radiating a warmth and kindness Nessa hadn't yet seen from him.

"They'll be alright, child." He patted her hand. "Now, would you feel better if I gave you a task?"

"Yes, please."

Alaron handed her a card, and Nessa took it gingerly, her eyes flying over the words as she attempted to decipher its secrets. Flour, water, milk, eggs…

It was a recipe.

She glanced up at Alaron, who beamed. Smiling back, she rose from her stool and went straight to work.

There was something therapeutic about the familiar motions, the stirring and kneading and thumping of the dough. Nessa hadn't had the luxury of baking from scratch since she'd arrived in Avani. She'd made chocolate crinkle cookies for her going away party in San Francisco, right before she shipped off to college, plus the chess squares for midterms, and the chocolate-covered peanut butter balls to celebrate her new job. And the sticky buns, just because. And the cake, because Liv had wanted some.

Stress baking happened to be a coping mechanism that worked to everyone's benefit.

Dagorn entered the kitchen, pipe in hand, looking none too surprised to find Nessa elbow-deep in flour. He smiled, the pipe between his teeth as he joined Alaron at the table. Nessa barely even noticed him.

Ever so quietly, she began to hum, a light, bright melody. It was a song Nessa had heard often on the radio, but she never bothered with the lyrics. Sometimes, words got in the way of the fun part, which was butchering the melody to her heart's content. Admittedly, she was a better baker than a singer, but that was alright. Singing didn't produce raspberry tarts.

She muttered a few of the lyrics she did know under her breath.

"*Dining at the Ritz, we'll meet at nine…*"

Dagorn stared at her for a long moment, his expression torn between joy and utter heartache.

"Her mother used to do that," he told Alaron softly.

Alaron pulled himself from his scrolls with difficulty. "Hmm? What, dear boy?"

"Hum. Lari used to hum while she cooked," Dagorn said, sounding wistful.

"I wasn't aware she knew how."

"Lari would run away to the kitchens when duty became too much." Dagorn watched his daughter with haunted eyes, remembering. "Learned quite a few things. I never thought I'd hear it again."

"A world away, she found her mother's heart." Alaron grinned. "Or so it seems."

Dagorn couldn't answer.

***

Supper was had and the biscuits were a resounding success. Nessa humbly accepted the praise with a blush and a quiet *thank you*, and afterwards fell sound asleep on the fluffy rug in front of the fire with Hedgerton curled close.

The next day, the wizard offered her a box of recipes to choose from, and by early afternoon, the entire kitchen was alive with mouthwatering smells. Small cakes and tarts littered the table, though not nearly as many as there should have been due to Dagorn's thieving. Nessa gazed over it all, feeling proud and just a touch embarrassed at how far overboard she'd gone. She wrapped a few of the pastries in a cloth to pass along to Rinn.

After all, what man didn't like food?

The morning of the third day, Nessa woke before the sun, dressing quickly and quietly so as not to wake the slumbering hedgehog by the hearth. Snatching up the treats she'd set aside, she headed for the door, but paused by the hearth, seeing her sword and dagger glinting in the dull predawn light.

She stared, feeling a niggle at the back of her mind, as though something was telling her to take them with her. But that made no sense. Rinn surely wouldn't hurt her. He'd had ample opportunity to do so, and yet he always came through. She trusted him.

...Now there was a thought to unpack later.

She took the blades anyway, strapping on the belt as she opened the door and slid quietly out into the morning chill.

The sky looked angry and clearly didn't want anyone to cheer it up, a small gap of bright sunlight the only thing standing between the treetops and a line of dark, purplish clouds. It looked increasingly likely that today wouldn't turn out like Nessa had hoped. Alaron had promised her a tour of the gardens, which was supposed to involve a crash course on the various — and numerous — poisonous plants he kept so she could avoid accidentally putting them in her cooking. However, he had offered them to her freely if she ever felt like doing it on purpose.

The wizard had indeed proved to be a few dice short of Yahtzee, but her fondness for him had grown almost against her will. She had come to realize that Alaron was only as mad as the world around him; he had seen the crazy of the world and simply adjusted his personality to match.

She reached the treeline just as the sun began to peek over the treetops. As she stopped, she turned to look at the sunrise. It seemed…dimmer, somehow. Nessa glanced down at the dagger on her hip, the niggle at the back of her mind beginning to tap dance.

Something was wrong.

Nessa studied the forest before her. *The woods are lovely dark and deep, but I have promises to keep, and miles to go before I sleep…*

The part at the end had always made her wonder if the sleep Frost referred to was meant to be of the temporary or the permanent variety. But in the end, she supposed it didn't matter. She had promised to meet Rinn here and meet him she would.

Hand hovering over her dagger, she strode into the trees.

It crossed her mind to call out for Rinn, but for some reason she didn't. Instead, she continued slowly on the path, never dreaming of veering. These woods belonged to Alaron, who tended to not understand what was considered life-threatening simply because it was needed for research.

All was quiet. No snapping twigs, no animals rustling in the trees. Even the leaves seemed to have stilled in anticipation. She didn't like the suspicious silence.

Rounding a bend, Nessa stopped dead.

…Which was exactly what she was going to be in a moment if she wasn't careful.

Before her, right in the middle of the path, stood Liv. The elf swayed in a non-existent wind, listing dangerously to one side. She looked awful. Her usually pearlescent white hair hung limp and tangled around her face, and her eyes rolled glassily in their sockets, looking but not seeing. Nessa would have thought she was high if it weren't for the dark veins creeping across her skin. They spiderwebbed out from the corners of her eyes, continuing down her neck and under her tunic. Larger spots of inky darkness snaked over the backs of her hands and stained her fingertips.

Liv was cracking apart, little by little.

In front of the elf, on his knees, was Rinn. Nessa could see him straining against the cords that bound his wrists as he bit down hard on the gag in his mouth, which was no doubt there to prevent him shouting abuse. His dark eyes glared at Nessa as if to say, 'Run, you stupid thing!'

Nessa straightened instead, a hand on her dagger.

"Hello, Liv."

What could have been the vague idea of words spilled from Liv's lips. "Come with me."

Nessa shivered. This wasn't Liv. This wasn't the same person who had saved her in Syracuse, who had given up their life for her.

No, this was someone else.

"No." She kept her voice and stance firm. "Liv, you know what's happening to you. You know this is wrong."

"I will kill him," the thing using Liv's body said.

"I know you've been fighting." Nessa took a cautious step toward her friend, her eyes flitting between Liv and Rinn. He tried to shift, his muscles straining against something she couldn't see. She held his eyes. "Keep fighting. We can help you."

"I will—"

"Kill him, yes, you said." She crept toward Liv, trying to keep the elf's attention on her. The spell would want that, surely. *Keep Liv talking. Get Rinn out of here*. "He has nothing to do with us. You know that."

"Usss…?" The last syllable turned to a hiss on the wind.

Nessa nodded, chancing another step. "You and me. He has nothing to do with you and me, what we are."

"He isss wanted."

"Of course he is." She fought hard to sound casual. "He's a thief. But only that, nothing more. C'mon, Liv, listen to yourself. There's bigger quarry right here. You know that." She rubbed her hands together, feeling them shake. She was so close now.

"You…are…wanted." The words came slowly, as if Liv had to remember each one.

"I noticed, thanks."

Nessa glanced at Rinn. His jaw clenched as he stared up her, and she spotted a flash of steel pressed against his back.

She swallowed down her fear. It had a hard time going down and tasted a little like sick.

"Look, I'll make you a deal. How's that sound?" Nessa's brain whirled. She had to think of something, anything to get Rinn away from the bewitched elf. If she was quick and clever, maybe she could outwit this golem. "I'll come to you, quiet and easy, if you let him go. Right now. You just have to let him go."

"Or I could just take you." The cracks were beginning to spread toward Liv's mouth.

"But it'll be a fight," Nessa pointed out, her palms dripping with sweat. She clenched her hands tightly into fists. "And you're in no condition for a fight, are you?"

Liv considered, her snowy head rolling dangerously. Slowly, ever so slowly, she drew the blade away from Rinn.

Nessa pounced.

She took two lunging steps before she ducked, ramming her shoulder straight into Liv's gut. The two girls went tumbling to the ground, and Nessa saw stars behind her eyes. Rinn threw himself to the side as Liv's dagger went flying into the dirt, and the elf jammed her knee into Nessa's gut. Nessa gasped for air, clawing at the ground. She had to move.

Move! Move!

Nessa flipped them over, pinning Liv down with a knee to the chest. Squeezing her eyes closed, she pressed her palms to her friend's temples, feeling the pulsing cold of the spell in her hands.

"Let her go!" Nessa ordered.

Liv struggled, a blade appearing in her hand as she swiped up at Nessa. Nessa jumped back, nearly losing her grip, when Rinn suddenly flung himself on top of the elf, twisting her wrists and slamming them into the dirt.

"I got her!" he shouted at Nessa.

Liv let out an angry scream.

"Let. Her. Go!"

Nessa rested her forehead against Liv's, closed her eyes, and breathed, feeling Liv's skin cold and clammy against her own. She felt a tugging in her chest and followed it all the way down her to feet, her body thrumming with something she couldn't name. It was so cold it stung her clenched muscles, crashing like waves against a rocky shore and threatening to pull her out to sea.

She imagined burying herself deeper into the ground, planting her roots like an ancient oak. Something in the dark pulsed with light, so hot no one should have been able to touch it. But Nessa wasn't afraid of that burning spark. No, she wanted it, welcomed the intensity and connection. With each beat of her heart, she pulled it closer and closer to the surface.

The wave swelled inside her chest, pale blue lights forming in the darkness behind her eyes, and Liv's screams faded as each pulse pulled her deeper and deeper into the earth. Or was it the sky? She couldn't tell. All sensation had fallen away, leaving her with only the crashing waves of light behind her eyes and the flaming roots that anchored her deep into…something.

Suddenly, everything imploded, rocketing her back into her head from wherever she'd been. Her chest felt like it was aflame, her palms burning. She held on to Liv for dear life.

A voice that might have been hers ordered, "*Release her!*"

Energy rushed from Nessa's toes to her skull, and she shrieked as she was flung abruptly off Liv to collapse backwards to the ground, her head slamming into the dirt with a sharp flash of pain.

She hardly noticed. She was falling through sky, then water, and then there was nothing but stars and she was flying, tetherless, through the void between pinpoints of light. It was warm.

Nessa was set gently down inside a vessel. It had fingers, and toes, and hair. And it had a head. Slowly, she became aware of the roaring ache in the temples of the head in question, one that was rapidly migrating down to the rest of her.

That's right. She had a body, and it *hurt*.

Swearing under her breath, she opened her eyes.

"Take it easy, duchess."

Rinn knelt over her, and she noticed that the tips of his fingers were tinged with red as he helped her sit up. She stared for a moment at his eyes, which were usually dark brown, but now seemed edged with…gold? Like a…a…

Nessa rubbed the side of her head.

"Are you okay?" she asked instead.

"You didn't pay me nearly enough for that," he told her.

"Oh, you're fine."

Nessa crawled over to Liv, whose eyes were closed, her face a milky white. She placed a hand on her friend's forehead. It was cool, the black veins now barely reaching her jaw. Were they receding? With shaking hands, Nessa placed two fingers on Liv's neck.

Her breath caught. *Please don't be dead. Please don't be dead. Please don't be dead.*

A gentle *tha-thump* thudded against her fingers.

Nessa breathed, thanking all the gods, angels and possibly a few Marvel superheroes.

"She's alive."

Thunder suddenly cracked across the sky and Nessa jumped, huddling closer to Rinn. She was grateful he stayed silent when her aching head fell on his shoulder.

"You're bleeding," he told her instead.

He held out a dark swatch of cloth, and Nessa glanced down at the heel of her right palm. The cut was small, but it was bleeding plenty. Taking the fabric gratefully, she held it to her hand.

"Thanks."

"Did you know that was going to work?"

"No." Nessa gave him a little smile, a slightly crazed look in her eyes. "But that's been my last couple of weeks."

Fat droplets of water began to patter down onto their heads, and Nessa gently pulled Liv to sit up against her. The elf was freezing! She wrapped her cloak around Liv to keep her dry and warm, hoping it would help at least a little.

"She'll be fine, I'm sure," Rinn told her, sucking his bleeding fingers. "I take it your wizard decided to help you?"

"Yeah." Nessa let the rain fall on her head, exhaustion overtaking her as she slumped against her unconscious friend. Perhaps the cold water running down her hot face and neck would help ease the throbbing in her head. "Sorry about all that."

"It's not the first time a pair of doe eyes has gotten me in trouble, duchess."

Nessa shrugged. "Still."

She gave him a grateful smile as the rain soaked through her clothes, the fabric rubbing coarsely against her skin. Her hair plastered against her forehead and cheeks and dripped onto the rest of her, but she still didn't think she had it in her to move.

Rinn blinked and shook himself. "I'd better go."

"Oh! What's the rush, dear boy!"

Rinn visibly winced at the sound of Alaron's voice, and Nessa jumped as the wizard in question suddenly appeared, crouching beside Nessa and Liv. He grinned, already drenched by the rain as thunder rolled above their heads.

"Hello, Nessa," Alaron greeted her.

Rinn's eyes snapped quickly to her before finding something, anything else, to look at. She still noticed.

"You did exceptionally well, child." The wizard beamed. "And I'm so glad you brought a friend."

Nessa shook her head. "We aren't friends."

Alaron just waved it off. "Acquaintance, then."

He was grinning like a loon who had just discovered an exceptionally good fanfiction. "Rinn, be a dear and help us to the cottage, would you?"

Rinn closed his eyes, letting the rain kiss his face as he took a deep breath. Alaron had already scooped Liv into his arms and was waiting impatiently. Nessa stood, only for the world to swirl abruptly around her head. She stumbled sideways, the earth suddenly deciding to tilt upward, but Rinn caught her before she splashed down into the mud. Nessa wrapped her fingers in his shirt.

"Oh yes, be careful there," Alaron told her. "Your head will be a bit muddled after you pull from Avani's pure power for the first time. Next time will be easier."

"Excuse me?" Nessa blinked up at the wizard, Rinn's grip on her waist the only thing keeping her on her feet. "I did what?"

"Hurry now!" Alaron was already marching away, Liv in his arms. "The rain is getting worse, dearies!"

Rinn cursed at the wizard's retreating back, and Nessa looked up at him, rain pouring down her face. She shivered.

"That could have gone better."

Rinn shook his head, little droplets flying from the ends of his hair. "Can you walk?"

"I…may need a little help."

"I have to do everything for you, duchess," he teased, tossing Nessa's arm over his shoulders. Nessa inhaled the smell of ozone and worn leather as his face dipped close to hers, just for a moment. She saw his Adam's apple bob, then he fixed his gaze straight ahead.

"Thanks for the rescue, by the way."

Nessa smiled softly at him. "You're welcome, Rinn."

It was slow work getting back up to the cottage, Alaron having already gone ahead with Liv. It wasn't even eight in the morning and already Nessa was exhausted. She felt ready to go back to bed and sleep for a week, if only the world would stop swaying and tilting.

The entire garden looked strange, as if every plant had its own unique phosphorescence floating off the stems and leaves. Everything had its own color; some were bright teals and purples, others whites and pinks and golds. It made her head hurt.

She squeezed her eyes shut, and when she opened them again, the sensation was gone. It was a garden in the rain, nothing more.

Rinn kicked the cottage door open as Nessa finally managed take a little of her own weight, the rocking of her vision easing from a rowboat in a hurricane to a mere tropical storm. At least they were finally dry.

"Easy, Alice." Rinn gently lowered her into the chair that had miraculously appeared in the entryway.

Strange. It hadn't been there earlier.

"What happened?"

Dagorn appeared in the hall, rushing to his daughter's side with the fury of a tornado. When had he acquired such a stern voice?

"I'm okay, Ada." Nessa gave her father a little smile as he knelt before her. "Just a bit tired."

"*What. Happened?*" He took her face in his hands, searching her over, and she quickly hid her bloody palm in her lap.

"Uh, I think I broke the spell on Liv?"

"How?"

"I don't know." Nessa wanted to shake her head, but she didn't want her mental hallway to start spinning again, like a funhouse that wasn't actually all that fun. "Al said something about Avani's power?"

Dagorn closed his eyes for a moment, his expression somewhere between shock, disbelief, and murder.

"Where's Liv?" Nessa asked.

"With Alaron."

Dagorn glared daggers at Rinn, and the thief blinked, shook his head, then quickly pressed his back against the far end of the hallway, searching frantically for an escape.

He didn't find one.

"And who is *he?*" Dagorn hissed.

This time, Nessa didn't hesitate. "He's a friend."

Strangely, Rinn didn't offer a response to that, only ducked his head and retreated into another room, his metaphorical tail between his legs. Nessa watched him retreat, feeling bewildered. How could the thief who would outlive the gods just to get the last word not have a single thing to say?

Only once she'd had a dry change of clothes, a very large cup of tea, and was sitting warm and cozy beside the kitchen hearth did she tell Dagorn everything that had happened, including the strange pulling and snapping feeling when the spell had broken. Dagorn contemplated this for a long moment.

"You felt…a connection, like a tether?" he asked, and Nessa nodded, warming her hands with her mug. Her sweet sixteen ring let out a soft *clink*.

Dagorn chewed thoughtfully on the end of his pipe. "You shouldn't be able to do that yet."

"Why?" she asked.

"Do you remember what Liv told you? About the places of power?"

Nessa nodded again.

"Well," he continued, "all that power has to come from somewhere. At the very center of it all is the power of the world, untainted. Only the Visiril have the ability to tap into that leftover bit of the first spark of magic and creation. That's what you did. It's a lot for a physical body to handle, stronger than any magic."

"Even blood magic?"

Dagorn nodded grimly. "Even Alaron's magic. Imagine a waterfall, but it only has a finite supply of water until it rains again. That's what most magic is like. Wizards simply have a larger supply. If blood magic is a lake, then wizards have an ocean. But the Visiril…we can have *worlds* if we connect with Avani's core magic."

Nessa swore softly.

Dagorn elected to ignore it. "Our magic doesn't work like a wizard's. It's different in that we don't choose the form it takes. It becomes what we need, not what we want. It binds the three of us, you, me, and Liv, together."

"That still doesn't explain what happened, though."

"I think you may have become a sort of channel for Liv, that magic somehow flowed *through* you and into Liv, and she was able to use that power to break the spell. But that shouldn't be possible."

"Glad I didn't know that, then." Nessa grimaced. "And I never want to do it again. It hurts. A lot."

"That's the first word of sense I've heard in a long time." Dagorn smiled, looking nervous, but proud. They sat in silence as he refilled and relit his pipe.

"So." He leaned back, fixing his daughter with a very parental expression. "Tell me about that boy."

Nessa blushed scarlet.

"Um…about that…"

Finally, she came clean. She told her father of how she'd met Rinn and how he had helped her to reach Alaron's, stressing the point about Rinn saving her from Liv, and the Menhiran mercenaries, and also the goblins. Dagorn's sour expression didn't change, having long since settled somewhere between accusatory and unimpressed.

"I don't care for him," he concluded as soon as she'd finished.

"You haven't even talked to him yet."

"No mere thief can hold off an entire goblin horde, Ness."

"I mean, I figured, yeah."

But Rinn *wasn't* some mere thief. A mere thief wouldn't have a Menhiran bounty hunter after him. He was either very good at something, or very bad.

"Anyway, I didn't exactly expect to see him again," she pointed out.

"Little one," Dagorn pressed on worriedly, "the only man who could even think about doing something like that is a soldier, and an exceptional one at that."

Nessa arched a brow. "Would you have been able to do it?"

"When I was his age, yes. And I did, more than a few times, but that is beside the point."

"Okay." Nessa was beginning to wonder what the point *was*, besides the unsurprising fact that her father didn't like the boy hanging around his daughter.

"What kind of soldier doesn't have an army?" he asked.

Nessa took a pointed sip of her tea. "You?"

"No! I mean, yes, a little, but…" He clearly didn't care for the smirk Nessa was giving him. "Stop that."

Nessa's raised her eyebrows, but she took pity on her poor father and elected to remain silent.

"Nessa, he's probably a defector. He abandoned his duties."

"Ada, he's a thief." Nessa shook her head. "I never expected him to be a pillar of honor."

"I still don't like him."

She shrugged. "I'm not asking you to like him. I'm asking you to tolerate him. I know you don't like it, but without Rinn, I wouldn't be here to have this argument with you."

Dagorn sighed in the face of her admittedly unflappable logic. "Fine. I'll *tolerate* him."

Nessa smiled. "Thank you."

"I still don't like him," he said sulkily.

"As you've said."

"...Do *you* like him?" he asked, sounding like he wasn't sure he wanted to hear the answer.

"Honestly? It varies from moment to moment."

Chapter Twenty-Eight

Soldier Boy

They stayed in the kitchen talking most of the day.

Nessa kept looking to the doorway. She saw Rinn pass by a few times, but he never actually came in. Instead, he would pause, glance in at her for a brief moment, then hastily move on. Alaron remained completely absent.

By early afternoon, Nessa had dug out the recipe box and enlisted her father's help in exchange for letting him partake in the fruits of her labor. He was easily swayed by the deal; Dagorn had surprisingly proved to have a secret sweet tooth.

The rain refused to ease up for the rest of the day; Nessa could hear the steady *tap tap* of it against the kitchen windows as she worked. Thunder occasionally rumbled in the distance, but faded away just as quickly.

At one point, Hedgerton scrambled in through one of the windows Nessa had cracked open to ease the heat in the kitchen and shook himself like a dog, only to have Nessa scold him for doing it so close to her dough. He squeaked an apology, which earned him a treat of dried fruit.

Kneading the dough was helpful. Nessa could pound it as hard as she liked and pointedly not think about Liv, or Rinn. She could think about the bread, not her sick friend a few rooms away, or her other friend who was lurking gods knew where. She didn't have to think about them at all.

At least, that was what she told herself.

Every five minutes.

By evening, Nessa was covered in flour, but calmer. Her nerves had forced her to produce a vast spread for dinner, including the sticky buns she was currently pulling out of the oven.

"Don't eat that!" she scolded, catching Dagorn with a biscuit sticking out of his mouth. "You'll spoil your dinner!"

Her father swallowed in simultaneous appreciation and terror.

"*Hmmmm!*"

They both looked up to see Alaron entering the kitchen, his hand on his chest. He inhaled deeply.

"That smells divine!"

"Thanks." Nessa tried to place the tray of treats on the counter, only to realize she had run out of room. She pursed her lips. "I may have gone a little overboard."

Alaron laughed. "All to our benefit, then!"

"How's Liv?"

"Still resting," he answered. "But I may tell you the rest over supper. Now, where did that boy get off to?"

"I'm sure he's lurking somewhere," Nessa called after the wizard's retreating back, but it was too late. Alaron had already disappeared. He reappeared moments later holding Rinn by the ear, and Nessa ducked her head to keep from laughing.

Alaron had spent the afternoon ridding Liv's body of the lingering dark magic. The Visiril, as an outlet for untainted magic, could become corrupt, he explained, like an oil slick filling a reservoir. It took time and care to return to full health, but with rest and a little luck, Liv would be back to normal in a few days. Nessa could not express the relief she felt at hearing this. Instead, she just grinned, slumped back in her chair, and ate another sticky bun, calories be damned.

Alaron smacked Rinn's hand away as he reached for a third sticky bun, and in retaliation, Rinn sneaked Al's own bun off his plate, casually allowing it to disappear into one of his pockets.

The wizard finally looked down at his plate and blinked, bewildered. "Hmm, I thought…oh, never mind. Nessa, child, you will have to forgive my gluttony." He sheepishly helped himself to another sweet. "These are exceptional."

"Thanks, Al."

Rinn blinked. "*You* made these?"

Nessa shrugged. "I stress bake."

Rinn said nothing for the rest of dinner. It might have been the way Dagorn kept glaring at him.

Nessa offered to clean up so Alaron could return to Liv, while Rinn disappeared as soon as he was free to make his escape. Dagorn remained behind to smoke his pipe and keep his daughter company. But Nessa couldn't sit still. She had squirmed all through supper, and now she fluttered around the kitchen, doggedly scrubbing surfaces that were already spotless.

"Nessa," Dagorn began softly. "Do you trust this boy?"

"*Rinn*, Ada."

"Rinn. Do you trust him?"

Nessa paused, drying off a dish. "I think so. Maybe not with my valuables, but still."

"Tonight, when he spoke…" Dagorn paused, choosing his words carefully. "Do you know where his accent is from?"

Nessa shook her head. "No."

Her memory flashed back to the one time she'd mentioned it, and how Rinn had stared at her like she had three heads.

"Nessa, little one, he's Menhiran."

The dish clattered to the counter. A thrill of fear ran down her spine and settled in her gut as dinner lurched uncomfortably in her stomach.

Menhiran.

Rinn…

She swallowed hard and forced her brain to kick in, to consider what she already knew. Menhir was after Rinn. He was wanted. He may have been Menhiran, but that didn't mean he was on Menhir's side; Dagorn himself had said he was probably a defector. Besides, Menhir wouldn't put a bounty on someone who was working for them. She had left that bit out of her story to Dagorn, knowing his tolerance would only extend so far.

"You think he used to be a soldier in the Menhiran army?" The calmness of her voice surprised even her.

"I know it," Dagorn answered. "Promise me you'll stay away from him."

"Ada," Nessa sighed, "I'm not going to blame one person for the faults of an entire kingdom, especially when they ran away from it."

Dagorn caught her hand as she brushed by him, looking up at her pleadingly. "Just promise me you'll be careful."

"That I can do," Nessa promised.

"Sometimes I worry your heart is too big for you, little one." Dagorn kissed her knuckles. "If he upsets you, I still reserve the right to kill him."

"Ada!"

Dagorn offered to watch over Liv for the night to give Alaron a chance to rest, which the wizard accepted gratefully. Nessa fed Alaron another sticky bun before shooing him off to bed, and only when she realized she'd wiped down the kitchen counter for the third time did she finally admit that perhaps it was time to quit.

After wiping her hands off on her apron, she hung it on a peg by the door before leaving the kitchen, the skirt of her cotton dress swishing gently around her legs as she padded barefoot along the wooden floor. The dress had clearly been made for someone much taller, leaving the hem to drag along behind her. She didn't want to ask or even think about why Al had women's clothes lying around, but she was glad he did. The constant dampness outside was preventing her regular clothes from drying.

Nessa found herself in the parlor after snatching up a book from one of the numerous piles scattered about the cottage. The room was dark, save for the warm light of the fire.

Rinn sat before the hearth. He didn't look up when she came in.

Nessa collapsed beside him on the fluffy rug, and Rinn's eyes flicked briefly to her. He had been gazing into the flames, his fingers twiddling with a spoon. The thief wore nothing more than a shirt, pants, and boots, looking practically naked without his fingerless gloves. Nessa suspected her father had confiscated his blades, but she was also fairly certain Dagorn had missed at least one.

Nessa had twisted her hair up while she cooked, but now she pulled the sticks from her thick locks, shaking her hair out. Rinn's eyes moved to her and stayed there.

"How's your elf?" he asked.

"Still sleeping." Nessa sighed deeply. "I've not been allowed to see her. Al says it'll take some time for her body to recover from the spell's effects."

Nessa ran her hands reverently over the small book she held. She had come here to read, but her mind was too exhausted to interpret words. Instead, she stared blankly into the fire as Rinn continued his spoon twiddling.

"Sorry about all that earlier," she told him.

"You're nothing but trouble, pri—" Rinn cut himself off. He swallowed and pulled his eyes away from her, his teasing smile vanishing.

Nessa chewed her lower lip, her stomach flipping. Taking a deep breath, she gathered up her courage.

"When did you figure it out?"

Rinn stayed quiet for a moment as the spoon stopped moving, mimicking the rest of him. When he finally spoke, his words were soft and apprehensive.

"That day I followed you. I heard what he called you." He paused thoughtfully. "Didn't really believe it until now."

Nessa brushed a lock of hair behind her ear, for some reason feeling her shoulders relax and her chest loosen. She was probably tired, that was all.

"Now you know why I wouldn't tell you my name."

"Rinn's my real one, in case you're wondering. Your Highness." He bowed his head, and Nessa winced.

"Nessa is fine," she told him. "Please, please, *please* never call me Your Highness ever again."

Rinn's eyebrows shot up. "Why not? It's your title."

"In case you haven't noticed, I don't exactly live up to it," Nessa pointed out. "I doubt most royalty falls out of trees and traipses across the countryside by themselves."

"I bet you'd be surprised." Rinn's smile turned a little sad. She could see it in the corners of his eyes before he shook his head. "I don't need to know any more. It's better if I don't, actually."

Nessa nodded.

"Just don't tell anyone when you're back out thie—uh…traveling."

"Oh, you won't have to worry about that, prin—" He swallowed the nickname down. "I'm not going anywhere for a while."

Nessa blinked at him. "Wh—why?"

"I can't leave."

"Of course you can." Nessa pointed behind him. "The door's right there."

"Oh, I'm sure your father would be thrilled to be rid of me." He gave her a slightly exaggerated smolder, and Nessa laughed at the sheer absurdity. Rinn's look of practiced seduction melted into a grin, then a sad shrug. "But sadly, I can't. I'm not allowed."

Nessa quirked a brow. "Allowed?"

He let out a deep sigh, then hesitantly reached under his shirt, removing the chain from around his neck. Two charms glittered in the firelight as he laid them gently in his palm. Nessa slid closer in order to see better and swallowed a gasp.

Rinn's hands were covered in scars, the long-healed wounds glistening in the firelight. Most were long, thin lines along his palms, while others were shorter, dancing up his thumbs and around his knuckles. Still others wound their way up his arms, disappearing under the cuffs of his shirt.

Nessa gently took one of his hands in hers.

"What happened?" she asked, her stomach dropping. His hands burned hotly between her own.

Rinn stared at where their hands joined, and his eyes grew distant, looking without seeing. Nessa gently ran her thumb along the longest one, which must have cut nearly his entire palm open, and he flinched — but not in a bad way.

Throat bobbing, he guided her fingers away from his marked skin and directed them to the talismans.

One was a large, antique golden ring. The setting, which looked a little strange, held a multifaceted rectangular stone the color of a flames and blood. The band had a small pattern embossed in the gold. It was scales.

Nessa very deliberately did not think about why.

The second charm was a flat metal hexagon the color of iron. Runes decorated the entire surface save for a dot in the middle, which held a small stone the color of darkened blood. This was the one he offered up to her.

"I stole this from the wizard a long time ago." Rinn let the stone catch the dancing light. "But he caught me in the act."

He paused, looking as though he expected Nessa to get in a comment about him being a bad thief, but she didn't rise to the bait. Instead, she settled for staring at him curiously as she waited for him to continue.

"Alaron let me take it," he began, "if I would assist him for one year as payment. I was a stupid, scared, eighteen-year-old moron, so I agreed, then the moment his back was turned, I ran as far and as fast as I could. I never planned on coming back, obviously. But now, because of that magically binding deal I made six years ago, I'm stuck being Alaron's assistant for the next year."

Nessa blinked at him.

"Wait, you're twenty-four?"

Rinn rolled his eyes. "That's all you got from that story?"

Nessa shrugged, and Rinn flashed her a teasing grin.

"Am I too old for you, princess?"

"I date soccer players," Nessa pointed out demurely. "Not thieves."

"What's a soccer?"

"It's a sport that involves a lot of attractive men running around in short-shorts."

The mental image proved distracting as she remembered the time she'd taken Liv to a game back in Syracuse. The elf had also enthusiastically approved of the pastime.

As she shook the image loose from her mind with a sigh, it suddenly occurred to her how close she was sitting to Rinn. Their shoulders were barely a breath away, and in the firelight, she could see the flecks of gold glittering in his dark eyes.

She swallowed hard.

"So, what is it then?" Her voice won the war for casualness. "It must be important."

"It's a charm," Rinn answered. "It keeps people from noticing certain things about me."

He let out a deep sigh. "Like my accent."

Nessa blushed down at her lap.

"I take it your father — who I'm fairly certain hates me, by the way — told you why." Rinn refused to look at her as he placed the charms back around his neck.

Nessa's heart fluttered in terror, and the thief slid away from her, tucking his treasures back under his shirt. She forced herself to swallow her anxiety. This was *Rinn*, not some shadowy threat from a faraway land.

"He suspects," she answered finally. "Is he right?"

She studied him quietly, watching as his lips flattened into a thin line, his jaw tightening. He still wouldn't look at her, and she wasn't sure if she should be scared, relieved or pitying. Instead of deciding, she scooted a little closer to the fire.

"Why did you leave?" she asked quietly. "I was told no one leaves."

"No one *can*," Rinn replied meaningfully.

"Wh—"

"If you're caught trying to leave Menhir, it's treated as abandonment, which is punishable by death. And those who do manage to get away are held accountable for Menhir's crimes by the outside kingdoms. Either way, there's no escape."

Nessa chewed her lip as she ran her hands over the book cover in her lap. Which would be worse? Staying in a kingdom that would oppress and kill you, or running away to another kingdom that would kill you for something you had no control over?

"What about innocents? Children? Surely *some* refugees would be alright?"

"It was, until Daradir about twenty years ago," Rinn answered, and Nessa stiffened. "Rumor had it that a Menhiran spy was able to sneak in with a family requesting sanctuary. It was never proven, but the damage was done."

Nessa swallowed hard, watching as Rinn began twiddling with the spoon again, making a clear effort not to look at her. How did he know all this, anyway? There was only one answer she could think of and she was afraid to be right.

"Were you a soldier?" she asked quietly, wanting desperately to take the question back the moment it hit the air.

"Military service was expected in my family." Rinn's pallor turned ghostly, the spoon stilling in his fingers. "And the army isn't exactly volunteer."

"I thought it was."

"The army is the only thing that puts food on the table." The spoon began its tumble through his fingers once more. "The people can't grow their own crops, not reliably anyway, and any land that *can* produce is owned by the royal family, of which some members are more generous than others. Even then, it's not truly enough, and the spoils of war, the tales of treasure and meat and mead, they're very alluring. If you want to survive, you have no choice but to enlist. And most of the nobles like it that way."

"I'm so sorry." Nessa shook her head sadly. "That's awful."

The spoon stopped moving as Rinn stared openly at her, and Nessa stared back, her expression giving her thoughts away. What a horrible situation to be in. Fight for a terrible country and possibly die, or condemn yourself to starvation. No wonder Rinn had chosen to become a thief.

"You're…very unique, Nessa," he told her gently.

She blinked curiously at him, heat rushing to her cheeks. He had called her by her name, her *real* name. No, it had to be the warmth from the fire.

"Is that an insult or a compliment?" She straightened up to slide away from the heat of the flames, which only served to bring her closer to him.

He shrugged. "Take it how you like."

"Thank you, then."

"You're welcome."

They fell into a companionable silence as they stared into the flames, each lost in their own thoughts. The quiet was filled with the crackle of the fire and the old memories neither of them wanted to ruminate on.

"How did you escape, then?" Nessa finally turned to look at Rinn. "If no one leaves?"

Rinn looked as though he would have flicked something into the fire if he'd had something to flick. The spoon's acrobatics stopped for a moment, then began again with increased fervor, his jaw clenching and unclenching no less than three times before he finally spoke.

"I was never meant to escape," he admitted. "I was never meant to *survive*."

Nessa bit her lower lip, her heart aching. What had Rinn left behind? What had he done? Had he tried to leave? Been caught stealing? From the sound of it, Menhir wasn't usually a country to settle for mere exile.

"I didn't know about any of this until a few weeks ago," she found herself saying.

"Your lineage?"

"Avani," she corrected, then felt the need to add to the list as she thought further. "Or the war. Or Menhir. Or Calebrir. Or any of it."

Rinn's eyebrow furrowed. "Then how—"

"Earth. I was…well…" Nessa felt her chest ache with familiar longing. "The guy you met, he showed up one day with about four other mercenaries and they tried to drag me back through the Veil. I only got away because of Liv."

Rinn looked horrified. "And you didn't know anything at all about why they wanted you?"

She shrugged, smiling sadly. "Not a clue."

"Wow." Rinn shook his head. "That tower you were raised in sounds awful."

Nessa let out a weak laugh. "It wasn't so bad! I had all the books I could read."

"Oh, well then. You've convinced me."

This time she did stick her tongue out at him, and Rinn retaliated in kind, leaving her to devolve into a fit of giggles. Rinn even smiled genuinely for once in his life.

The subject of Nessa's tower led to stories of her love of books and stress baking, and in return, Rinn told her of his travels around Avani and a few of his more successful adventures — though he emphatically refused to say anything about the unsuccessful ones, even when she asked. Hedgerton joined them eventually, having apparently been sent to supervise — a task he did a poor job of, since he promptly fell asleep in Nessa's lap.

By midnight, Nessa had made herself comfortable on the fluffy carpet. She rested on her back with Hedgerton tucked into her side, trying not to move so as not to disturb the little guy. Rinn rested his back against a chair, one leg stretched out in front of him while he used his other knee as an elbow rest, the spoon twirling in his free hand.

The conversation had gone off the rails hours ago.

Rinn finished a story that ended with him clutching a priceless relic and nursing a broken nose, with only one shoe and half his pride still intact, before being accidentally covered in mud by a passing cart. Nessa couldn't hear the rest over her laughter.

"Okay, okay…" She did her best to stifle her giggles. "So if that's the worst thing you've ever stolen, what's the strangest?"

Rinn paused, eyes floating to the ceiling as he thought. The spoon tapped against his lips a few times.

"An eyeball."

Nessa shot up, staring wide-eyed as her jaw hit the floor. Rinn blinked innocently at her.

"It was an accident," he added.

Nessa continued to goggle, and Rinn's face did a complicated contortion.

"I'm not making this better, am I?"

"Not at all." She shook her head in amazement. "How do you steal an eyeball by *accident*?"

"I was traveling with this merchant for a few days along the Angori. He was a bit off, but not unfriendly. You know how rough the road can be. Anyway, when we parted ways, I swiped his purse while he wasn't looking, but when I looked inside, there was nothing in it except an *eye*."

Nessa, slack-jawed, continued to stare. "Was it…glass?"

"No." Rinn scrunched his face in disgust.

She gasped in horror, her hands flying to her mouth. "You pickpocketed a serial killer!"

"Likely," Rinn agreed, the terrifying thought suddenly becoming reality. "Though I don't quite know what that is."

They stared at each other for a long, horrified moment as slowly, the incongruity of it all began to sink in. Nessa blinked, her mind finally kicking back into gear.

She swore.

Rinn agreed.

And the dam burst.

Laughter, bright and absurd, rang through the room, and Hedgerton moaned, rolling over in annoyance at the disturbance. Nessa's hands flew over her mouth in a failed attempt to contain herself. Rinn managed to swallow the last of his amusement, but it looked as though it didn't go down without a fight.

"You swear exceptionally well for a princess."

Nessa shrugged.

"I was pretty much a barmaid in another life. Certain skills are essential in such a profession."

"Now *that* I can't see."

Nessa was suddenly overtaken by a deep yawn. She stretched, and Rinn averted his eyes.

"Why don't you get to bed, princess?"

"Liv's in the only spare." Nessa laid back on the rug, shifting slightly so both she and Hedgy were comfortable. "I'm sleeping here tonight."

Using one arm as a pillow, she closed her eyes, but she could still feel Rinn staring. Cracking one eye open, she glared at him.

"You aren't going to watch me sleep, are you? Because that's creepy."

Rinn rolled his eyes, an amused smile tugging at his lips. Ever the showman, he rose with a groan, then spun the chair around and placed himself in it, his back to her.

"Your privacy is assured, my lady."

Nessa smiled, but still kicked the chair leg in retaliation.

"Oi!"

But there was no real heat in his warning, and Nessa settled into the rug, smug with victory. Hedgy snored contently somewhere around her hip as she curled up on her side facing the fire, the heat enticing her to sleep. She yawned again.

"Wake me if Liv does."

"Of course, princess."

It wasn't long before she drifted off into darkness.

Chapter Twenty-Nine

Best Laid Plans of Elves and Men

Nessa stretched, feeling the warm sunlight on her face as her back and neck twinged and popped. She supposed that was what she got for falling asleep in a chair.

She had relieved her father of his watch over Liv in the early hours of the morning. Despite the full moon outside, there wasn't enough light to read, so she'd sat in silence, watching Liv take short, shallow breaths. It helped reassure Nessa that she was still alive.

Suddenly, Liv's eyes fluttered open, and Nessa swallowed a gasp.

Liv was awake!

And not only that, but she was also struggling into a sitting position and staring down at her bruised hands. The black veins had disappeared, leaving Liv looking far too pale, with splotches of purple ringing her forearms. Even the frost of her hair seemed dull in the morning light.

The elf's eyes stared at something thousands of miles away, a hurricane-tossed sea flashing behind them. The waves kept coming, seeming like they were nearly crushing her.

"Liv?" Nessa kept her voice soft, but Liv still jumped, startled. Nessa quietly slid to her knees beside the bed. "How are you feeling?"

Liv's shuddering breath was answer enough. Her eyes glistened damply.

"Nessa..."

Liv swallowed the rest of whatever she'd been about to say, silent tears spilling onto her bone-white cheeks.

Nessa's lungs constricted. "Hey, it's okay." She reached out and grasped Liv's hand, squeezing hard. "I'm here. It's alright."

"Hardly." Liv wiped her eyes. "How could it be? I am a Guard of Avani. I swore to protect you, and what I almost did —"

"No."

Nessa cut her off before Liv could finish, squeezing her friend's hand in both of hers. She tried to hold Liv's eyes, but the elf refused to look at her.

"It wasn't you. Never was," Nessa said firmly. "The only reason we're here is you. I know you would never hurt me."

"But I did! I was going to give Menhir a Visiril! And you—"

"No."

"No?" Liv asked.

"No," Nessa continued. "Blood magic did all that. Not you. You weren't in control."

"That's the problem. I fought, but it wasn't enough." Liv shook her head. "*I* wasn't enough."

"Didn't you just hear what I said? It. Wasn't. You. For goodness sake, Liv! Evil Menhiran mages had your hair *and* blood. And you said it yourself. You fought. You fought so hard that you *didn't* turn yourself in as a Visiril. You fought so hard you forced their orders to change."

"They had…they did?"

"Yes!" Nessa replied. "I saw it, I *Dreamed* about it. So don't you dare blame yourself for this, not for one second. Do you hear me?"

Liv still looked wretched. Nessa ducked her head, looking Liv straight in the eyes. A storm still raged behind the green, but the tempest was starting to ease, if only a little.

"You had a Dream?"

"Yes," Nessa said. "And those are never wrong, right?"

Liv attempted a smile. "Correct."

"And we got you back." Nessa beamed at her friend, relief washing over her features.

"Yes, and how did you manage that, exactly?"

"Well…" Nessa shrugged and borrowed a turn of phrase from Rinn. "I had to improvise. Now, how are you feeling?"

"Drained." Liv practically melted back into the pillows. "It was…I could see and hear everything, but I couldn't stop it. I tried. I did everything I could think of, but I was trapped inside my own body. I—"

She swallowed hard, her hand flying to her mouth.

Nessa's heart shattered in her chest. Slowly, she slid onto the bed beside Liv, wrapping the elf up in the tightest hug she could manage without hurting her. Liv tensed, then settled into the embrace, her forehead falling onto Nessa's shoulder.

"I'm so sorry, Liv," Nessa hiccupped. "I'm sorry." She felt Liv's breathing gradually even out.

"I'm alright," Liv told her. But she didn't push Nessa away. Instead, she slowly sat up, and Nessa let her go.

"Are you hungry?" Nessa asked. "I may have stress baked, a lot."

"I'm not an infant, Ness."

Nessa arched a brow, unconvinced, and Liv rolled her eyes in response. Nessa knew that age-wise, she was probably a toddler compared to Liv, but that wouldn't stop Nessa from babying her, at least for today.

"Maybe later," Liv finally admitted. "First, tell me how you got here."

"Well…"

"And about that boy."

Nessa's mouth clamped shut as Liv fixed her with a look. Trying to seem nonchalant, she waved a hand airily.

"I needed a guide! And I had to pay with something, and the only thing I had was

your bow."

"My *what*?"

"Don't worry." Nessa tried not to laugh at her friend's horrified, yet somehow still scolding, expression. "You stole it back. It's under your bed."

Liv fixed her with a glare. "Never do that again."

Nessa was a dead girl if she tried, was the unspoken implication.

"Understood."

Nessa refused to even hear of Liv getting out of bed until the next day. Liv fought her, of course, but luckily Alaron and Dagorn not only agreed with Nessa, but were able to enforce the policy. Consequently, to pass the time, Liv required Nessa to sit with her as she braided and twisted Nessa's hair into different styles while Nessa told Liv of her adventures.

It felt almost like the old days. Nessa, stressed over work and finals, would vent to Liv as they sat on the apartment floor, and Liv would play with Nessa's hair until she determined they needed tea, or something stronger. Nessa kept her adventures interesting, but left out the bits about Rinn's personal shadow. Liv was trying to heal, after all, and giving her a possible aneurysm wouldn't help.

"Let me see if I have this correct," Liv said. "You asked a boy, who had already caused you to fall out of a tree, to guide you to Erwani, and along the way you discovered he was a thief, followed him underground, and had to run from a city full of goblins. And then it turns out said thief is indebted to a wizard? *And* you gave him my bow?"

"You got it back," Nessa less-than-helpfully pointed out.

Liv shook her head. "I'm never leaving you alone ever again."

"There is one more thing." Nessa bit her lip. "And I'm fine, so you can't freak out, okay?"

"Is he a wizard, too?"

"No, but…he's a Menhiran defector."

Liv blinked, her jaw going lax. "Nessa!"

"I know! I know, but he's saved my skin twice already, and once was from another Menhiran."

"He can't be trusted."

"Liv." Nessa grabbed her friend's hand. "I was found, okay? *I was found.* One of the mercenaries from Ollie's got away and *he found me.*"

"What?! Are you—"

Nessa cut her off. "Rinn saved me. He saved my life. And I never could have made it here, never could have helped you, without him. Just give him a chance. Please?"

"Well…" Liv mused. "I won't make any promises."

Nessa tried again. "Don't kill him on sight, at least?"

"I shall refrain, for your sake."

"Thank you."

That night, Nessa returned to her fluffy rug to rest, while Rinn joined her in the parlor with a glass of wine. Apparently, Alaron had kept him working in the garden all day. He had pointed out all the poisons, but Rinn hadn't really been paying attention since Hedgerton kept scolding him. Nessa only smiled, and eventually, he congratulated her on Liv's recovery.

"I didn't really do anything," Nessa pointed out.

"So modest." Rinn raised his glass to his lips. "You're as stubborn as they come. I pity any man who doesn't see it."

"Why is that?"

"Well, after you're done talking his ear off, he'll realize you never listen to good advice."

"I give *myself* very good advice." Nessa shrugged. "Though I very seldom follow it."

"Obviously."

Rinn left her the entire parlor, opting to sleep in a cushioned chair in the hall instead of the wooden one he claimed had nearly broken his neck the night before. He said he preferred the ground to that chair.

Nessa found herself in the kitchen the next morning when Rinn finally came in. Alaron and Dagorn sat at the table, smoking their pipes; Alaron preferred a short pipe, as opposed to Dagorn's long one. Dagorn glared balefully at the thief when he entered the kitchen, but Nessa hardly noticed since she was busy pulling a fresh batch of sweet rolls from the oven. Alaron may have been a stick of a man, but he ate more than most linebackers.

"Good morning, Rinn, my boy."

Rinn glared at Alaron.

"Oh!" Nessa scolded. "Don't be a grump. I made breakfast."

"Do you always cook like this?" Dagorn asked, sneaking two pastries off the tray.

"Only during finals week."

"Finally what?"

"Never mind."

Nessa shook her head, offering the tray to Rinn. She only saw him take one, but there were suddenly three open spots on the tray. She elected not to comment.

"Thank you," Rinn muttered to the tray.

"Welcome."

Nessa froze when she spotted Liv in the doorway, looking more like herself than she had in days. Her complexion was starting to regain some color, her bright white locks braided around the crown of her head. Some small bit of her usual grace and fluidity had returned to her movements.

"Shouldn't you be resting?" Nessa arched a brow at her friend, but nevertheless offered her the sweet rolls.

"I have rested enough," Liv answered, eying the tray with suspicion.

"I thought you'd say that." Nessa sighed, defeated. "It's still good to see you up."

Liv simply nodded. She didn't take a roll, but instead glared at something over Nessa's shoulder, who spun to see Rinn standing behind her, frozen. His eyes widened slightly.

"Are you going to introduce us?" Liv's tone had turned chilly.

"Oh, um…Rinn, this is my best friend, Livia of the House of Aeris. Liv, this is my frie—uh, this is Rinn."

Rinn bowed his head a bit, swallowing hard. Liv simply narrowed her eyes. If looks could kill, Rinn would have already been on a slab.

"Hello," Liv more threatened than greeted.

"Liv!" Nessa scolded.

"Oh!" Alaron's sudden exclamation caused all of them to jump. "I'm so glad we've all met now!"

The three of them stared at the wizard, each wearing a complicated and completely different expression of perplexity.

"Seeing as you're up," Alaron barreled on, unaware, "have some breakfast and tell us what's on your mind. I can see it floating about your aura."

"I would rather wait until we are in private." Liv sat at the table, sparing a glare for Rinn.

"As you wish." Rinn snatched up a roll and left. After a moment, he came back in and took two more, before vanishing again.

Nessa fought not to smile. Apparently, Alaron wasn't the only one with an appetite.

"I had a vision last night," Liv began. "Galidel burned."

"Galidel is a city?" Nessa asked. Her memory rattled with a few mentions of the word, and she turned to her father. "Isn't that where we're supposed to be going?"

Dagorn nodded. "Galidel is a fort on the northern front. Our intelligence believes Menhir may strike there soon."

"They will," Liv corrected. "I saw it fall."

"That's impossible." Dagorn shook his head. "No one has breached Galidel's walls for over four hundred years."

"Menhir will if we don't find a way to stop them."

"Did you see anything?" Dagorn leaned forward, pipe and breakfast forgotten. Even Alaron hovered closer to the table. "How?"

Liv closed her eyes and sat back, taking a few deep breaths. "I see a great shadow over all of Galidel. The tower fallen, the gates wide open. All is covered in ash and flames. I hear a noise…a thunderous roar that shakes the stone walls down."

"Any heat?" Alaron asked.

"Yes."

"Well, that sounds like a dragon." Alaron pursed his lips. "There aren't many of those left."

"Whoa, wait?" Nessa put her hands up. "Dragon? As in, furnace with wings, giant lizard with fireballs, honest-to-goodness dragon?"

"There aren't many left, thanks to your grandfather." Alaron sounded none too thrilled with the fact. "All the southern breeds were destroyed some fifty years ago, and Menhir is hunting theirs to extinction."

"Dragons are difficult to defend against." Dagorn's fingers were already doing their usual flipping motion, his eyes glazing over. "Not impossible, but difficult."

"We must set out by dawn if we are to have any hope of warning them," Liv declared.

Nessa felt her stomach clench. "Liv, you just got better. Are you sure you're going to be alright?"

"I will be, yes."

Nessa didn't believe her, but she changed the subject anyway. "Why is Menhir going after Galidel?"

"It protects a mountain pass that leads to the coast," Dagorn explained. "If Menhir were to take Galidel, that would be it. Calebrir would lose most of their supply routes and we'd have to fight on two fronts; our forces would be split between the north and the sea to the south of the kingdom. We simply don't have the manpower to maintain that."

Nessa chewed on her lower lip in thought. From what little she knew, it sounded like the freemen of the south were already spread too thin. Opening a new front to the north would surely mean Calebrir's collapse. And how many more people would die? Starve? She didn't think the royals of Menhir would share any of the new farmland. They couldn't allow that to happen, dragon or no.

"I will join you," Alaron volunteered without needing to be asked. "I think I can help with your dragon problem, and I'm sure Rinn has never been to Calebrir's borders. It'll be quite educational."

Dagorn scowled. "He's not coming."

"Oh, don't be ridiculous." Alaron waved a hand. "It'll be good for him!"

"Al, if we show up with a Menhiran soldier, he'll be put to death. You know that," Liv pointed out.

Nessa swallowed hard. Put to death? Rinn had warned her of the negative sentiments against refugees, but to hear someone else say it was another thing entirely.

"Nonsense!" beamed the wizard. "It'll all work out splendidly!"

...Nessa seriously doubted it.

Chapter Thirty

Fulcrum

Setting a breakneck pace, they reached Galidel on the dawn of the tenth day. Hedgerton had apparently promised to guard the cottage, though Nessa wasn't quite sure how he would accomplish that. While she liked him, he was after all only a hedgehog. Then again, Alaron was just crazy enough for it to work.

Nessa had also begged Alaron to either let Rinn go or send him back to the cottage, but the wizard only refused with a knowing smile or simply changed the subject.

"*…Did your father ever tell you of the Elar?…*

"*Isn't that plant interesting? The buds make a wonderful tea, but the leaves can shut down a man's liver…*

"*Oh, don't trouble yourself, child. Trolls only eat maidens in tales, you know. They much prefer horse or dwarf…*"

It was almost maddening. Also, Nessa was growing concerned about how much the wizard knew about poisons. She didn't want to think about how he had managed to acquire the information.

Nessa had tried to enlist Liv's help, but the elf explained firmly that Rinn, no matter what he had done for Nessa, was still a Menhiran soldier and needed to be held accountable for his crimes. Nessa had countered that they didn't even know if there *were* any crimes, aside from the thieving, to which Liv had replied that that was what the trial was for.

Nessa held very little faith in any supposed trial, but had given up when Rinn seemingly resigned himself to his fate.

"No thief dies old in their bed, princess," he told her. "I did much better than I thought I would."

After that, she didn't have the heart to bring it up again.

The rest of the journey was relatively quiet; apparently, nothing wanted to interfere with a wizard, not even Nessa's usual propensity for trouble. The only real inconvenience came from Dagorn and Liv glaring at Rinn, especially during the times when Nessa would occasionally hang back to speak with him. She did her best to cheer them both up, but the melancholy mood refused to lift. The closer she got to safety, the closer Rinn came to his fate. Nessa couldn't shake the feeling that they were all marching to a fulcrum, and no one knew which way the world was going to tip.

The morning of their arrival to Galidel dawned bright and clear, a soft breeze which smelled of pine and morning dew playing with Nessa's hair. Nessa stood at the top of a small hill with her father and best friend at her side, gazing ahead at the fields of plentiful green in the fresh morning light.

In the valley, nestled between two mountains, stood a lone hill, crowned in layers of red and gray stone. A thick forest of green and black loomed on the left like gathering storm clouds, while a square wall of red rose up from the green fields, a tower marking each corner. Colorful roofs and low spires filled the inside of the red wall, with a second wall of gray stone forming a six-pointed star inside the city. This one was filled with larger roofs and taller towers, as if it were building onto the first tier.

At the very center of the star stood the third and final wall, a circle of red stone protecting the green and blue of a single massive estate with four square towers that kissed the blue sky. Clearly, this was the jewel in the town's crown; each of the towers was capped with a cheerfully waving flag of blue, white and gold.

Dagorn's smile showed what he must have looked like in his youth, and Nessa returned his look of delight. However, she couldn't keep her eyes off the grand city for long. Even from afar, it felt so alive! She could already see dots of color among the green fields: people and their carts, banners of every color. Her cheeks ached from grinning as Dagorn put an arm around his daughter, pointing to the flags atop the towers.

"It's a sun," he told her wistfully. "It means the people of Calebrir will always rise again."

"We're in Calebrir?" Nessa's eyes brightened with a hope she hadn't felt in weeks.

Liv let out a deep sigh of relief. "Her territory, yes."

Dagorn kissed Nessa's forehead. "Welcome home, Ness."

Nessa finally let go of the tension she'd been holding since her arrival in Avani, pushing her fear and anxiety away with it. Behind her, she heard Alaron shushing Rinn, saying something about letting her have her moment. She fought not to laugh.

Welcome home.

Home.

Nessa hadn't winced when Dagorn used the word. She found she didn't mind hearing it; the mention no longer sent a pang of sadness through her. Instead, she felt warm and giddy with excitement. She wasn't Nessa of Earth any longer, and she finally knew it, though of course she would always miss Earth. Sure, Avani didn't have pizza, or Tex-Mex, but it had her father and her friends, and that was enough. It was more than enough. They were finally safe.

Finally home.

"What do you think of Galidel?" Dagorn asked with a smirk.

Nessa snorted playfully. She thought of all the old friends from her childhood books who talked about roads and how if you didn't keep your feet, all the places you could get swept off to.

"It doesn't look like a bad place to land," she said thoughtfully.

"Wait till you see inside," Liv said.

"Come, little one." Dagorn smiled mischievously. "Let's go give your grandfather heart palpations."

Liv tossed her head back and cackled in pure, unadulterated joy.

The people working the fields paid them little mind, aside from a nod or the occasional smile as the strange little party passed. A few children even waved, prompting Nessa to wave back with equal enthusiasm. Liv smiled at her friend while Rinn directed his own grin toward the ground. For his part, Alaron made sure to keep the thief close, half blocking him from view at times.

Nessa's spirits rose higher with the sun, the warmth of the day pushing the lingering ache from her bones. *Home*. The word had finally begun to have a happy meaning again.

"Just wait." Liv nudged her playfully. "It gets better."

Inside the gates, Galidel burst into a kaleidoscope of color. The aroma of spices wafted through the market as children played in the street, many narrowly avoiding Nessa and Rinn. Nessa laughed as she watched them dart past, but still kept a close eye on her things.

What could she say? Knowing Rinn had taught her a thing or two.

The stalls held everything in every color she could have imagined: fruits, beads of glass and silver, furs, cloth, ink in every shade. She even spied a few books. She knew Rinn's hands must have been itching; everywhere she looked, she saw something bright and delightful. Vendors called out to them, offering food and anything else they might want.

Alaron lightly smacked Rinn's sticky fingers more than once, and Rinn dutifully passed along his ill-gotten snacks to either the wizard or one of the children playing around him. Though Nessa tried (and failed) not to notice, her attention was quickly taken up by an entirely different situation.

Everyone knew Dagorn.

Everyone.

Nessa, in her early teens, had been dragged to many work functions with Albert Everette, where people decades older than she would comment on how beautiful she was growing since they'd last seen her. She would be polite, say thank you, and once they had moved on, ask Albert who exactly that person was. The evenings always became a very specific kind of awkward.

Walking through the market with Dagorn was exactly like that, but worse.

Every guard and soldier they passed stopped to speak with him, while Dagorn did his best to keep Nessa behind him, distracting them with conversation about the goings-on of Avani. Nessa honestly wasn't sure if it was more uncomfortable to be introduced or ignored, and in the end, she elected to go hide behind Alaron with Rinn. Even Liv joined them, though Nessa suspected it was more to chaperone her and the thief than an indication of discomfort.

It was early afternoon by the time they reached the manor at the center of Galidel, though *manor* wasn't quite the right word for it. To Nessa, it looked like a small four-story castle made of the same red stone as Galidel's walls. It didn't seem too out of place from the rest of the city; perhaps the builder had been attempting to remain modest.

The inside of the mini-castle, however, was far from humble. The gray stone of the entry hall floor gleamed like a mirror, with plaster walls painted with flowers and detailed scenes in a pale blue. Tapestries shrouded the far end of the hall, and not an inch of the intricately carved wooden ceiling wasn't painted.

Nessa shrank in on herself when she realized how much dirt she must be tracking inside the spotless hall. She knew she was filthy. Her last bath had been a rinse in a stream six days ago and it had really only gotten the surface dirt.

Though the experience hadn't been a total waste. Rinn had lifted his shirt up enough for her to catch a glimpse of his toned waist, the sliver of abdomen revealing that he had the kind of hipline that made smart girls go stupid.

Some god was testing her, she was sure of it.

Beside her, the thief in question sighed, eyebrows raised.

"Subtle."

"I think it was meant to be," Nessa agreed. "May have missed the mark."

"I've seen worse." He looked around the room, shaking his head. "Far worse, actually."

"Whichever duchess you seduced likely had poor taste."

"Why do you assume she was a duchess?" Though his tone reeked of offense, he smiled nonetheless.

At that moment, two guards began heading toward them, and Nessa could see Dagorn speaking to them in hushed, yet harsh, tones. Her heart plummeted, Rinn's face falling even as Alaron hovered at his back. The thief ran a hand along the back of his neck.

"Well." Rinn snapped to attention, and Nessa felt something slip into a pocket of her cloak. "It was nice knowing you, Alice."

"You'll be alright." Nessa put a hand over the weight of Rinn's chain in her cloak. "I'll do what I can."

"Just don't go ruining my reputation."

The two guards separated from Dagorn and ordered Rinn to come with them, but before the thief could respond, they grabbed his arms and began dragging him away. He didn't fight, aside from the occasional snide remark.

"I'd better ensure they don't damage him," Alaron muttered, following them out the door. Nessa watched until they had both vanished.

Chewing at her bottom lip, she stared at the empty door. Rinn would be okay. He was a thief, after all. And she had to be honest with herself, this probably wasn't the first time he'd been to jail.

She jumped when Liv placed a hand on her shoulder, the elf smiling softly at her. Tilting her head, she fussed with Nessa's messy braid, carefully replacing the coils around the crown of her head. For some reason, the move made Nessa's stomach twist.

"What are you doing?" she asked. "What's that look for?"

"Well, your hair is a mess," Liv pointed out, replacing the last strand.

"I've been traipsing through the wild for two weeks. You should see *your* hair."

"I am flawless as usual."

And she was.

Dang it.

"And that look was for…?"

Liv softened. "Oh nothing. You just…" She released a deep sigh. "You look so much like your mother. That is all."

Nessa felt her cheeks warm. Suddenly, Liv gave one last gentle squeeze to her shoulder and smoothly turned the other girl toward Dagorn, who had appeared unexpectedly beside her. He gave a peck to her hair, and Nessa arched a brow at him.

"For courage, little one."

"Why do I need to be brave?"

Liv raised an eyebrow. "Who said it was for you?"

"Sir Dagorn!"

They all spun to see a man descending the grand stairs. Though he was older, as evidenced by his gray hair, he still stood tall and proud, fire burning behind his sharp hazel eyes. He had a straight nose, a jawline that looked as if it never unclenched and a permanent disappointed expression even when he smiled. The one he currently wore was strained, and Nessa recognized a dealing-with-Mr.-Lane expression when she saw one.

Dagorn forced his own grimace into a grin as he turned to greet the man. Putting a fist to his chest, he bowed low.

"I grew worried." The man clearly hadn't been anything of the sort. "You're nearly a week behind your appointed time."

"My apologies, King Elvar."

Nessa almost fell over. Liv, ever attentive, quickly intervened to stop a possible descent to the floor, taking both Nessa's hands in her own and squeezing. Nessa practically crushed the elf's fingers and ducked behind Dagorn, trying to breathe even as her stomach flipped painfully.

"There was a complication," Dagorn continued.

Suddenly, Alaron appeared before Nessa and Liv, causing both girls to jump. He really needed to stop doing that. Alaron bowed dramatically to the king, making a grand performance of it. If it was his intention to hide the ladies from the king with his cloak, he accomplished it perfectly.

"High Wizard Alaron of the Seventh Circle," King Elvar guessed.

"Your Highness. I will claim no such responsibility, though I know not of what you accuse me. I didn't do it."

"You never do."

The king clasped forearms with Dagorn, his eyes finally catching a glimpse of Liv. His hazel eyes narrowed, then widened abruptly, his proud expression turning to one of confusion and worry.

"Lady Li—"

Then his eyes found Nessa.

She wasn't sure where to look, so she settled for staring at her twisting fingers, feeling the heat in her cheeks race to her ears. She glanced at Liv out of the corner of her eye, and the elf inclined her head slightly. A tingle of panic raced through her. She couldn't bow! Her head was already down!

"Dagorn—"

Elvar's voice failed him.

Alaron, of course, ruined the tension by snickering. "Well, Dagorn, we finally found a way to silence him."

Dagorn's failure to swallow his own chuckle gave Nessa the courage to finally look up. The king was still staring at her. She swallowed, the temperature on her face rising.

"Um, hello?"

Nessa mentally decided that she and her brain were no longer on speaking terms. She was literally meeting royalty while dressed like a Skyrim knockoff character and stinking like a sewer rat and all she could think to say was *hello?* She put her hands over her cheeks to hide their deep crimson color.

This was going terribly.

…At least she hadn't fallen out of a tree.

Yet.

"I'm sorry if I'm doing something wrong." The thought tumbled from her mouth before she could stop it.

The king smiled, his eyes crinkling merrily.

"You're *perfect*," beamed her grandfather.

In the span of a breath, King Elvar became another person entirely. He resonated warmth and welcome, and possibly grew younger by at least ten years, the glistening in his eyes perhaps mirth or perhaps something else. He held out both hands to his granddaughter, and Nessa took them hesitantly, chewing at her poor lower lip.

"Let me look at you." He sounded breathless. "You've grown so beautifully. You just turned nineteen, yes?"

"Yeah, about two months ago." Nessa's blush ran down her neck as the king stared openly at her. He gently turned her from side to side, clutching her hands as if he couldn't quite believe she was real.

"You weren't even two when I last saw you," Elvar told her quietly. "You played with my brooch during a council meeting while you sat on my lap, and blew raspberries at Lord Narka every time he spoke."

"…Sorry?"

"Oh, don't be." The cranky old king had returned. "The bugger deserved far worse than a little humiliation from my heir."

"Oh."

"You must be tired." Elvar's eyes blinked rapidly, looking suspiciously shiny. "Please, rest awhile, then join me for dinner. I want to hear all about your adventures."

Well, if she managed to survive her embarrassment, at least there would be food.

***

Nessa had never, not once in her life, 'dressed for dinner.' 'Dressing for dinner' was something that happened in period novels, not in real life. Sure, if she had just come from a track meet, she'd shower and put on dressier, non-sweat-soaked leggings, but that was about where the parallels ended. Yet, here she was, dressing for dinner with the king of Calebrir.

She hadn't minded the hot bath in the clawfoot tub she could practically swim in, where she'd been provided with more soaps and oils and powders than she could ever dream of using. Using only half a bar of soap that smelled like the ocean felt luxurious enough; the rest of the jars remained untouched.

She stayed in the tub until Liv finally came to retrieve her, and even then, Nessa hid in the soapy water like a petulant child demanding a few minutes more. When the servants, an idea Nessa was not yet comfortable with, lamented the unused cosmetics, Nessa passed out the little luxuries to the shocked maids. Liv commented that she had likely won their loyalty for life.

The elf proceeded to twist delicate white ribbons into Nessa's dark hair, then helped her into a soft, pale blue dress with silver embroidery at the wrists and collarbones, fighting doggedly with the line of buttons that ran down the back. Liv also happened to be 'dressed for dinner' in a champagne gold gown that had no business making her look as ethereal as it did.

Nessa finally voiced the thought that had been running through her head since their arrival. "This is so strange."

"How so?" The curious tilt of Liv's head echoed in her question.

"Well, I don't think it really hit me until now that I'm…well…*royalty*. I mean, look at this room, Liv! It's bigger than your entire apartment in Syracuse!" She gestured wildly at the huge four-poster bed, the richly embroidered rugs on the marble floors, and the vanity covered in delicate jewels, all of which remained untouched by her. There were stacks of books between tall windows and window seats, and a fireplace she could fully stand in. It all made her head spin.

"Hold still," Liv commanded softly.

Nessa became a statue, but only for a brief moment, her fingers twisting together as her bare toes wiggled in the rug. Liv furrowed her brow, concern flickering in her green eyes.

"You do not like it?"

Nessa fought not to shrug. "It's just…a lot, considering. It all seems a bit…"

"Extravagant?"

"Yeah." Nessa deflated. "There's a war on. It seems almost…well, selfish."

"Your mother felt the same." Liv wrestled with the last few buttons on the gown. "There. Finished."

She smoothed down the back of the dress even as Nessa turned toward the tall looking glass on the vanity. Mirrors had been a rarity the last few weeks. Alaron had one at his cottage, but Nessa had looked very different then; a mud-streaked traveler wearing sun-bleached clothes, with strong legs and arms. She'd thinned out in some places and filled out in others since her arrival in this world, and now, dressed in a luscious gown with ribbons twisted in her hair, she looked like a fair maiden from a children's storybook.

She looked like a princess.

Nessa ripped her eyes away from the glass. She didn't really understand what the reflection showed her, so she decided not to think about it. Her eyes fell on the heeled slippers that matched the gown.

"Do I have to wear those?" She arched a brow as she pointed at the offending shoes.

Liv grinned. With a cheeky smirk, the elf raised the hem of her gown to reveal a pale set of bare toes. She gave Nessa a wink.

Nessa laughed, relief flooding her already-abused feet.

With that, Liv looped her arm through Nessa's, and they glided off to dinner.

Chapter Thirty-One

A Dungeon and A Dragon

The wine tasted like moonlight in a glass, and Nessa probably had a little too much of it. More than one cup went to wet her throat as she told King Elvar of her previous life and adventures. He appeared pleased beyond measure when Nessa mentioned her love of reading.

"Your mother was a ferocious reader. I'd often enter her room to see her reading three or four books at once." Elvar chuckled slightly. "She argued it was more efficient that way."

"And you are no better," Liv told Nessa with a teasing grin.

Nessa hid her face in her glass. "I cannot be judged by what I did to survive midterms."

Elvar sounded less pleased, however, when told the story of how his granddaughter had been discovered and had to escape through the Veil. As Nessa continued, his face grew paler and more grim, a small vein appearing in his forehead. Nessa worried it might actually burst when she admitted to entering a Menhiran camp in order to rescue Liv. It was then she knew Rinn's origins were best kept to herself for the time being.

Dagorn helped with the story wherever he could, while Alaron listened in fascination, adding his input to the parts he knew. Eventually, the story devolved into everyone completing the thoughts of all the others at the table as Elvar's head bounced back and forth between them like a very worried and undignified ping pong ball.

Once they finished, Nessa sat back, her breath easing. Elvar blinked twice in rapid succession, then drained his glass in one gulp. Giving himself a shake, he turned, at last, to Liv.

"You say you had a vision?"

Liv nodded. "Yes, Your Majesty."

"Tell me what you saw."

The stern ruler had returned, all softness gone from his expression and bearing.

Liv obeyed the king, and as the litany of details expanded, Elvar's face grew gray — except for his eyes. A cold fire sparked deep within the hazel, his mind clearly alight.

A heavy silence filled the hall as Liv finished. Nessa feared to move lest she make a noise.

At long last, Elvar spoke.

"We've suspected for some time that Menhir would attempt to strike here. Now, we have confirmation."

"Ca—Can I ask something?"

Nessa shrank in on herself as everyone looked at her.

Elvar turned soft again in a blink. "Of course, dearest."

"I keep hearing about Galidel being important." Nessa twisted her fingers together. "Supply routes and all that, but I'm not really clear on how? Why is it so essential?"

"Oh, well." Dagorn shrugged. "Galidel and the fort sit at the entrance to the Pass of Gelmar. The woods, you see, are simply too thick and precarious to march any kind of force through, unless it is in very small numbers. Without use of the pass, the trip around the Aresti Woods and the Twenin Mountains takes another three or four weeks."

"If Menhir were to take Galidel," Liv began, "they would have a straight shot to Calebrir, the Mother City."

"The farmland outside these walls and on the other side of the mountains provides for most of the households in the kingdom," said Elvar. "Without food to sustain our men, we wouldn't last half an annual."

"These mountains and hills have protected Calebrir and her territories for decades," Dagorn explained. "Menhir has never breached them. Though certainly not for lack of trying."

"The Pass of Gelmar is the gateway to our empire," Elvar confirmed.

Nessa nodded. "Oh."

A rush of cold air clawed at Nessa's throat, her fingers balling into her skirts. *Empire?* She wasn't sure how she felt about that word, or the consequences of it. Empires contained so many people: homes and families and lives. Was Calebrir taking care of them? She knew Menhir certainly wouldn't; they starved their people to feed their army. And Galidel so far appeared to be a place of abundance, of joy. It was the first place Nessa had found that wasn't marred by what had been, the lone before in her seemingly endless series of afters.

And now, Menhir was on their doorstep yet again. Even the safety of Galidel wasn't safe enough.

Suddenly, long fingers clutched at hers and Nessa held tight to Liv, unable to hide the fear in her expression.

"Well then, we shan't let Galidel fall," Alaron declared.

Elvar sighed sadly. "If only it were so simple. I've lost more good men than I can count in its defense, and none of them were facing a dragon."

"That's what you have me for," Alaron offered with a grin.

Elvar and Dagorn both blinked at the wizard.

"You'll stay to help, then?" Dagorn asked.

"Of course! Besides, my assistant is in your dungeon." Alaron took a long drink. "I would like him back, eventually. And in good working order, if you don't mind."

"That will be up for discussion at a later date," Elvar replied.

Nessa had only just met her grandfather, but to her that sounded like the issue would be up for discussion a few days past never.

She found the courage to speak up. "He did save my life. At least twice."

Dagorn suddenly found something very interesting in his lap while Al beamed like his favorite television program was on. Meanwhile, Elvar's jaw hit the table, his mouth opening and closing a few times before he could finally speak.

"What?"

Nessa swallowed her nerves along with a gulp of wine and straightened like the royal princess she was quickly learning to be.

"You heard me."

Liv and Dagorn ducked their heads as Alaron, not caring to share their discretion, snorted into his wine, chuckling. Nessa could have sworn she heard him say something under his breath about knowing he liked her.

Elvar made a noise as though he were deflating, rubbing his temples.

"And there is your grandmother's steel." He shook his head. "Very well. I promise that will be taken into consideration."

Alaron made a pleased noise, as if Nessa had performed perfectly. Liv gave her hand a squeeze.

"How many men do we have?" Dagorn asked, not-so-subtly changing the subject.

"Not as many as I would like." The grim mood settled back over them all as Elvar answered. "How much time do we have to get more?"

"Not long," Liv replied. She shifted in her seat, taking a deep breath. Closing her eyes partway, she allowed them to roll back in her head, her body going lax for a breath before she snapped back to the present world. "Two days hence, at dawn."

"So we've only one day to prepare." Dagorn sounded apprehensive.

Nessa's stomach twisted, leaving her wishing she hadn't eaten so much. She played with her pendant, gripping hard at Liv's hand. The elf squeezed back.

"Do we know who is in command of the Menhirans?" Dagorn asked.

"Not for certain," Elvar answered. "But our spies indicate Gerric Emrys was seen rejoining the garrison to our north. He would be the most likely candidate."

"Who is that?" Nessa asked.

"The son of Duke Eldric of the House of Emrys, cousin to the High King of Menhir," Elvar answered. "He's only a handful of years older than you, but he already has a reputation for ruthlessness."

"Great," Nessa breathed.

It was not.

Apparently, Calebrian scouts had discovered four battalions of Menhiran soldiers moving through the Kingless Lands, their convergence likely why Nessa and her friends had had such trouble avoiding them. Menhir hadn't moved this many men in decades, and these were battle-hardened soldiers, men who had faced death time and time again and had no fear of it.

And no doubt they had brought their weapons of war with them. Galidel's light infantry and young men might be able to hold them off, but the odds were more uncertain than anyone would have liked.

That wasn't even taking the dragon into account.

It was quickly agreed that they needed help, so Elvar sent his fastest messenger to Starcrest to ask for Lord Koen's assistance. Nessa had no idea if the elven king would make it in time, but they had to try. No one knew where Bryn was, or whether he'd been successful in locating the Nolael. All they could do was hope.

Dinner ended on a somber note full of oncoming dread and uncertainty, and Dagorn walked Nessa back to her room, kissing her forehead goodnight. It had been decided that Nessa would be kept safe at the manor, as according to the king no army had ever penetrated so far. She hadn't argued. She knew she had no place in war. With nothing but minimal training and an apparent lucky streak, she simply wasn't equipped for a true battle. Liv, Alaron and her father, however, were to lead the defense.

Nessa, lying in her too-large bed covered in too-soft sheets, found her mind racing even hours later. Her thoughts lingered on her family, on Liv and Dagorn and what would become of them, her lower lip raw from chewing. She'd been so preoccupied, she hadn't even bothered to change out of her gown. There simply hadn't been room in her mind for the thought. And when she finally did think of it, she realized she couldn't reach the buttons anyway.

Something wasn't right. Nessa could feel it in her gut. A vital piece of the puzzle was hiding under the couch, and it didn't matter because the complete picture didn't match the one on the box anyway.

With a sigh, she rose from her bed and flung open one of the tall windows, the light of the full moon kissing her hot face as she sank onto the window seat. The warm air whispered of a quickly approaching summer.

If Menhir had their way, Galidel wouldn't see another summer.

She leaned out the window with a deep sigh, soaking up the dim light. Her eyes scanned the manor gardens with their not-so-little gate, moving on to the flickering lights of the town nestled inside the second gate, then the first, and finally to the darkened horizon. She found herself wondering what all the other families in Galidel were doing now, if any of them knew what was coming.

Probably not. Even Liv wasn't sure, and she could see the future.

A sense of nervous stillness settled over her, and she breathed in the scent of warm air, spiced smoke, and moonflowers. She still couldn't quite release the tension in her gut. Another wise wizard had said it best: it was the deep breath before the plunge.

No one could possibly know what Menhir had planned, but Elvar had promised that Galidel had never been taken. Its walls were too thick, its gates too strong, its men too courageous. The people of the sun would always rise again.

A dragon might test that, though, plus there was whatever else they were missing. And there *was* something.

Nessa had heard too many *I hope*s and *probably*s over dinner for her liking. And the odds didn't seem good. They were outnumbered three to one, and the firepower, literally and figuratively, was all on the side of Menhir. Galidel had no war machines, only archers. Calebrir boasted young, untried men, while Menhir had brought hardened soldiers. What could Galidel possibly do? Hope and prayer couldn't hold gates shut.

There was nothing for it.

She found herself striding across the courtyard before she had even realized it was probably a bad idea. She decided she didn't care. She would do whatever it took to defend her people.

Her people.

Her home.

Nessa found that her slippered feet somehow knew where to take her. The guards at the door were surprisingly – or perhaps unsurprisingly, given the empty bottle dripping onto the table between them — asleep. The archway beside the uninspiring security led to an ajar door, and beyond, she found a stone spiral staircase leading deep into the earth. She followed the twisting path into the darkness, eventually emerging into a small stone room lit by a single torch. It held nothing more than a table and a few stools, with hooks holding keys and weaponry she almost recognized lining the wall closest to her. The opposite wall held a line of empty cells.

Empty, that was, save for one.

Rinn sat against the wall with his head reclined and eyes closed, one hand hanging nonchalantly off a propped-up knee. He reminded Nessa of a greaser rebel without a cause from one of Lilly Everette's old movies.

His jaw clenched the moment she stepped up to the bars, and she smiled.

"I know you're awake."

The thief immediately snapped to attention, his eyes widening to the size of saucers as they fell on Nessa.

"What are you doing here?" he asked, sounding bewildered.

Nessa shrugged. "Couldn't sleep."

She pulled up a stool and lowered herself onto it, gathering up her skirts to keep them from dragging on the floor. There was so much fabric that she dropped some, gathered them up again, and then finally gave up, letting them fall into the dirt.

Rinn stared at her, astonishment coloring his expression.

"Sacred flames," he breathed. "You really *are* a princess."

"I'm just wearing a dress." Nessa scrunched her nose to squash the heat in her cheeks. "Don't get used to it."

Rinn's smile faded as quickly as it had appeared, and he glanced down at the twisting fingers in her lap. His eyes snapped up to hers.

"What's wrong?"

Nessa sighed.

"Menhir."

"What do you need?"

She quickly explained the situation, though she knew it likely wasn't wise to be revealing all of Calebrir's key information to a former Menhiran soldier. It was entirely possible Rinn meant to betray them, and this had all been nothing more than an elaborate ruse. But Nessa somehow knew he wouldn't, and it wasn't only because he listened as she told him what was happening with a quiet intensity she'd never seen before. His jaw grew tighter and tighter the more she spoke, to the point that Nessa found herself surprised he still had teeth. He nearly fell over when she finally mentioned the fiery flying lizard problem.

"I mean, how are we going to fight a dragon?" she concluded weakly.

Her eyes fell to Rinn's hands. His nails were digging into his knees, his knuckles white. His dark eyes flashed with heat.

"Gaough shouldn't even have a dragon," he growled through clenched teeth. "Dragons are sacred. To use one for war…to soil one…"

Nessa could hear Rinn's teeth grinding together as he jumped to his feet and began to pace like a captive tiger. She watched him rake his hands through his hair, growling.

"What do you mean?" she asked, slowly approaching the cell. She wrapped her hands around the bars, the cold metal biting into the palms of her hot hands.

"Do you have any idea how much magic it would take to control a dragon?" Rinn had turned very pale, his thumb running over his gloved palm.

"Blood magic?" Nessa's voice quivered.

Her mind whirled with the possible horrors. How much pain for this spell? How many people?

"Yes," Rinn hissed. He clenched his hands together, relaxed, then clenched them again. "Dragons are creatures of ancient magic. To soil one just to make a suicide run on Calebrir is reckless and is sure to get him sent to Sedah."

"What's Sedah?" she asked.

"A frozen underworld of torment," Rinn muttered as he continued his pacing. Nessa raised an eyebrow.

"Then why run the risk?"

"Gaough may be king, but his cousin Eldric is the strategist." Rinn shook his head and continued to pace.

"Eldric?"

Rinn nodded. "He leads the army with an iron fist. Menhir must be locked in a stalemate, and you've seen the sentiment towards Menhir in the Kingless Lands. They won't get any help from the outside, not any significant help, anyway. And Gaough always had to prove to the people he was better than Gerin."

"From what I heard," Nessa murmured worriedly, "I'm not sure how much longer Calebrir can hold on. Not much was said about going on the offensive. It was just about survival."

"Plus, you're here," Rinn kindly pointed out. "Your discovery alone is proof of Menhir's growing power."

Nessa's guts twisted, her throat abruptly drying out. She nodded instead, taking a deep breath to loosen her voice.

"Any thoughts?" she asked.

"Who's leading the Menhirans? Do you know?"

"Uh…" She searched for the names in her mental files. "The son of the king's cousin, Gerric Emrys."

Rinn froze solid for a full minute, then he exploded with a spectacular string of curses, kicking at the bars.

"That good, huh?" Nessa deadpanned.

Rinn turned deathly serious. "You need to stay away from him."

"I'll be sure to avoid a guy I've never seen before. Should be easy."

She hadn't meant to snap, but her fingers ached from her grip on the bars — which was currently the only thing keeping her wobbly knees from giving out.

Rinn released a noise somewhere between a sigh and a growl. Raking a hand through his wild hair, he seemed to deflate, kicking the hay on the floor of his cell.

"You *have* met him before," he said darkly.

Nessa looked at him curiously, her memories whirling. She'd met Gerric Emrys?

Suddenly, her eyes widened.

"Wait, you mean…" She leaned forward through the bars, her voice a hushed whisper as her heart pounded against her ribs. "Your shadow?"

Rinn pursed his lips and nodded. Nessa's jaw dropped.

"Saints and angels, Rinn! What did you *do?!*"

"Depends who you ask." Rinn attempted to flash a cheeky grin, but his heart clearly wasn't in it. "Look, if Gerric is leading the charge, he has something up his sleeve."

"You mean besides a dragon?"

Rinn shook his head. "That's not his plan. Gerric is subtle. He never faces an obstacle head on. Prefers to come at them sideways."

Nessa nodded, her heart thudding in her throat. Sideways? How could they be hit sideways? Maybe Liv or Dagorn would have an idea.

"Would he be the one controlling the dragon?" she asked.

"No." Rinn shook his head. "Gerric never had any real talent for magic."

"That's good for us, I guess." Nessa chewed her lower lip, then stopped, wincing, when she realized how sore it was. Rinn seemed to soften.

"You'd better get back, princess. It's getting late."

She didn't want to, but she knew he was right. "Thank you, Rinn."

Nessa wanted to touch his hand, but she didn't move, giving him a soft smile even as he shook his head.

"Thank me after it's over. Now go."

Nessa tried to make her smile seem reassuring. She swallowed down another offer of thanks and, with a nod, she left.

She had a feeling they would see each other again sooner rather than later.

It was a feeling she was still getting used to.

Chapter Thirty-Two

Be Prepared

Nessa couldn't find her family all morning. Elvar had appointed her a shadow of her very own, a tall, skinny guardsmen named Chavet with an intimidating long scar across his left eye. His presence, while she understood its purpose, proved to be the single most annoying thing in the universe. She would speak to him and get no answer, though she occasionally thought she heard a disapproving huff from the general vicinity of his mouth. She'd been starting to worry he didn't speak Common, until she wanted to visit Alaron. Then the answer was a solitary *no*.

She finally managed to lose Chavet when she ducked into the kitchens, as Satu, who ran the place with a precisely crocheted fist, was the embodiment of a mother hen. She did not abide guardsmen, fools, or any other useless bodies in her domain. Luckily, she took a liking to Nessa, who would happily pound any dough into submission, and was more than happy to put Nessa's stress baking skills to good use.

Nessa found the little group who tended the kitchen to be some of the most wonderful people she'd ever met. She told them her name was Alice and that she was visiting nobility, and they welcomed her with only minor trepidation. After a batch of sweet rolls, the welcome became far more enthusiastic. An elderly baker, Rauna, told Nessa all about the old days, and about her two sons and four grandchildren. Nessa tried not to look too excited when Rauna started telling stories about the former princess, Larien.

"She was a gentle soul, sometimes too gentle for royal life, if you ask me, which no one ever does." The woman rocked gently back and forth, twisting the dough with a wistful smile. "The princess would often hide in here to escape a lesson or two, poor dear. Sometimes, and this was more often, she would hide here just to sneak out with that handsome young Guard of hers. And we all know how that turned out, don't we?"

Nessa couldn't stop the smile that spread across her lips. "Yes."

"You watch out for those handsome Guards, young lady." Rauna waggled a finger at her. "You're far too pretty to stay out of their notice."

"I don't exactly think Chavet will be a problem."

Rauna laughed out loud.

Nessa borrowed a trick from her mother's book and, with Rauna's help, managed to give Chavet the slip that afternoon. Behind the enormous cooking fireplace, hidden by large sacks of grain and dried fruit, was a small servant's hall, easy to miss if you weren't looking for it. It led to the dining hall, which opened out into the courtyard, and from there she was able to make her way through the gardens and around the manor toward the stables.

The long stone building rested against the manor's defense wall. Her grandfather had told her the stables originally served as the guardhouse until it became too small to hold the whole garrison. The number of men had increased due to the intensity of the war with Menhir, so a new, larger guardhouse was built on the other side of the complex shortly after her birth. Nessa had visited the stable last night, but now, in the light of the late afternoon sun, she could see bits of moss growing on the gray stone roof. A single door stood wide open as a chestnut mare pranced out into the daylight.

Liv was standing outside, waiting for her.

"You are late," the elf told her with a smirk. "You should have been here ten minutes ago."

"Sorry to keep you waiting." Nessa tried to give her a smile, but it floundered on the rocks of uncertainty before being swept away entirely.

Liv studied her, face falling. "I can see we need to talk." She turned to the open door. "Dagorn!"

Dagorn trotted out, worry written across his face until he saw his daughter. Then he smiled.

"Hello, little one."

"Hi Ad—"

Not in public.

"Uh—Dagorn."

He kissed her hair reassuringly. "Don't worry, we're quite alone."

"Hi Ada!"

He chuckled even as Nessa wrapped her fingers in her sage green skirts. Today's gown had pearls embroidered at the square neckline and a silver belt.

Elvar had insisted she have a princess's wardrobe, though she would have been much happier in simpler clothing. Perhaps with a hemline she didn't trip on constantly, or even functional pockets. Her hem was already covered in a layer of dirt and grass from her escape across the courtyard, and Nessa made a mental note to apologize to Marin, the lovely young girl who did the laundry. Perhaps she could invent the miniskirt. That certainly would give her grandfather a heart attack, plus allow Marin some relief.

Dagorn waved them in. "Come inside. We'll have a bit of privacy; except for the horses, and they are excellent secret keepers."

The clang of the doors closing echoed off the stone roof, the torches that lined the solid walls serving as the only source of light in the stable. Few stalls held any actual equestrian occupants, leaving the place feeling hollow. Nessa suspected the horses were all being prepared for tomorrow.

Tomorrow, when the fate of Nessa and her family would be decided. There would be no more running. No more hiding. Menhir would invade and they would have to do their best to survive the onslaught.

And the dragon.

Nessa wasn't sure what a dragon actually meant. All she knew were the stories from Earth, and all those painted dragons as maiden-eating, fire-breathing engines of destruction. Plus there was an entire invading army to deal with, along with Rinn's warnings. Nessa's lunch pitched in her stomach.

This could be their last night together.

She pushed the thought down along with her lunch.

Liv's voice suddenly cut into Nessa's rambling thoughts. "Before we begin, I need you to promise me one thing, Nessa."

"What?"

"Whatever happens tomorrow, please do not get involved." Liv's tone was firm. "Stay inside where it is safe."

Nessa scoffed, though she swayed a little unsteadily. "I'm not dumb enough to run into a battle I'm not prepared for, Liv. At least give me that much credit."

"Of course I do!" Clearly, though, she did not. Liv's hand fluttered a moment before she huffed and grabbed Nessa's hands, hard. "It's just…well, I know you and your father, and I know how you both can be."

"On this, I share Liv's opinion," added Dagorn.

Nessa looked at the worried faces of her father and her best friend. They had only just found each other again, and now she could lose them both at dawn. A cold, heavy shiver traveled down her spine and into her toes. She squeezed Liv's hands.

"Well." Nessa swallowed hard. "I'm fairly certain I wasn't built for war. I'll do my best."

Relief washed over Liv's face, and Dagorn leaned down to kiss his daughter's hair. Nessa inhaled the smell of worn leather and hay.

"Thank you," Liv said. "Now, what do we need to discuss?"

Nessa chewed her lower lip, winced, and let out a deep sigh. Her fingers fell away from Liv's as she began to pace around the stall.

"I went to see Rinn last night." The words spilled out before she could stop them.

"Of course you did," Liv deadpanned. Dagorn put a hand over his face, and it looked like he was swallowing a groan.

Nessa barreled on, telling them what Rinn had said about the dragon and Gerric Emrys. The end of her tale left Dagorn pinching the bridge of his nose, and she could see the fingers at his side doing that flipping motion again. His eyes still did not open.

"Sideways, you say?" Liv's tone remained calm, but a current of fear and wrath trembled just below the surface.

"Yeah. What do you think that means?" Nessa asked, twisting her fingers in her skirt. She was probably ruining the fabric, but she didn't care.

"It could be any number of things."

"You don't know?" Nessa asked.

"No." Liv shook her head. "The future is not set in stone. It is always changing and shifting, effects of countless decisions. It can be truly maddening."

Liv swallowed, her eyes going distant for long while. Finally, she shook herself and continued, "Some things grow more certain as the moment draws near, but if a decision is not made until the last minute, even I am blind to it."

"What about the forest?" Nessa asked. "The Aresti Wood?"

"What about it?" Liv asked.

"Can an army come through it?"

Dagorn shook his head. "It's too thick. No force has ever succeeded, and many have tried. To attempt it would be madness."

His fingers continued their flipping.

"And what about from the west?" Nessa asked.

"All open," said Liv. "We would see them coming, just like we would from the north. And of course, there is no way for them to come from the mountains themselves."

Nessa chewed her lower lip, now only slightly recovered from the previous night's thinking. In the south, Galidel was guarded by the mountains, and the forest to the east was its only other hidden front. North and west were vast open plains with few hills. Any approaching army would be spotted.

And there would be nowhere to hide from a dragon.

"We're missing something, Liv." Nessa started to pace again, her forgotten hem dragging in the hay. "I know we are. I can feel it."

Sideways. There was that word again.

"If you say we are, then we must be." Liv watched her a moment. "Dagorn? Any insight?"

"I'm looking." His hand went to cover his eyes. "The only vision I've had is of Daradir, and you know how often I have that one."

Liv nodded solemnly. Nessa collapsed against the stable wall, pressing the heels of her palms into her eyes.

"What about Bryn?" she asked. She couldn't keep the desperation out of her voice. "Or Koen?"

"We have heard nothing from either of them." Liv's eyes rolled back into her head as she slumped against the wall. After a moment, she snapped back to attention. "Koen will be here, Vaeril willing."

"Well, there's that at least," Nessa muttered to the floor.

Dagorn quit flipping his fingers and shook himself. "I fear we are as prepared as we can possibly be. We must simply hope that it is enough."

Hope.

She would try to hold onto that.

Chapter Thirty-Three

Always Label Your Keys

The sky glowed a pure azure in the predawn light. Nessa was trying not to look at it, nor at the army that had appeared on the plains outside of town seemingly overnight.

Smoke floated through the air from the already-burning fields. Not even the bells in their towers dared to ring, an ominous quiet resting over Galidel.

The city was holding its breath.

Outside the stables, Nessa stood staring up at Dagorn and Liv, who were both covered in heavy armor. She trembled, twisting her fingers and chewing her lip until it bled. What could she say to them, if they might be the last words they ever exchanged?

Nessa opened her mouth several times to say what she had practiced the night before. She had promised herself she'd be brave, that she wouldn't cry. This had to be done to protect Galidel, to protect her people. But all her courage flew straight out the window the second Nessa saw her father's face.

With a hiccup, she launched herself forward, wrapping Dagorn and Liv in her arms as hard as she could. Tears trickled from her eyes as she forced herself to breathe.

"Just come back, okay?" Nessa prayed to whatever gods were listening.

Dagorn kissed her hair, clutching her back just as tightly. "No dragon could keep me from you, little one."

Nessa held on tight, trying to memorize the faces of the people she loved, how they felt in her arms. It wasn't fair! She had just found them again; how could she lose them now? She swallowed the fear down and held on, as tightly as she could.

All too soon, the moment ended and the next had to come. Nessa stood by the gate, watching her family march off to war as the first rays of morning sunlight kissed the hills. Dagorn and Liv held their heads high, their commanding voices soaring over the troops as they faded from view.

Don't forget to breathe.

She didn't want to go back to her room, so she went to sit in the gardens of the courtyard as the sun rose higher in the perfect blue sky, oblivious to her fear. In the quiet of the morning, she could hear the drums and horns echoing off the mountains. She wasn't sure what was worse: waiting for the battle to begin, or seeing who or what was left when it did.

Chavet came to stand beside her, but Nessa still didn't move. She kept her head tilted toward the sun, her eyes closed.

The sound of a battle horn made her jump.

"Have you ever been to war, Chavet?" She already knew he wouldn't respond. Chavet had said only two words since his assignment to her, and both of them had been *no*. Though there'd also been a few non-committal grunts sprinkled in.

"More than I have cared to, Your Highness."

Nessa blinked up at him, her eyes wide and round. "How much trouble are we in?"

"Permission to speak freely?"

"Granted," Nessa replied.

"May I?" He gestured to the stone bench, and Nessa quickly slid over.

"You know, Your Highness…" Chavet's body bent and twisted oddly as he moved to sit. His knees didn't seem to want to bend. "Truthfully, we'll be lucky to make it through the day."

Nessa's heart plummeted.

"But," Chavet added, "we always are, war or not."

"I take it you've lost a lot?"

"I don't know a man who hasn't," he agreed.

"Does it get any easier?"

"No, Your Highness."

"Nessa," she offered.

"I cannot do that," he admitted.

"I understand."

Another non-committal noise. Nessa turned her face back to the sun, trying to draw courage from its warmth.

"I don't know if…" She lost the words and tried again. "I can't…I…" Swallowing down the lump forming in her throat, she buried her face in her hands.

"You know, Your Highness, I've always wondered."

"Wondered what?" asked Nessa.

"Who war is harder on, those fighting, or those left behind. On the battlefield you at least have a certain amount of control over your fate. But at home, you're simply waiting and hoping, and that's all you can do. Both require courage, but the quiet courage is harder to muster, I think."

Nessa tried to give him a smile. "Thank you, Chavet."

He almost smiled back. "I will be annoying you again soon enough, Your Highness."

Chavet took Nessa to the kitchens when black smoke clouded over the sun. A shadow hung over the band of usually merry cooks, and the little group, with Chavet hovering outside the door, could do little to keep Nessa distracted. The sounds of shouting and the clashing ring of metal echoed through the empty halls, while nothing she did could drown out the sound of those drums. She shuddered so hard at every loud *clang* that no one dared to even open a door too quickly around her for fear she would snap.

One young woman, Goodwin, set a tray down too hard on the table beside her, and Nessa leapt up with a shriek. Chavet charged in, only to find Satu rubbing her back as Nessa sat with her face in her hands, gasping for air.

It was going to be fine.

Her heart still failed to slow.

…What if it wasn't?

Satu handed the rattled girl off to Chavet and instructed the guard, in the sternest tone possible, to take the poor thing to her room. She even sent Nessa away with a little flask of something for her nerves. It tasted like cinnamon and burned like good whiskey.

But her room high in the tower was no better. Nessa paced, picked up books, put them back, fiddled with hair combs and pins, moved pillows here and there and continued to wear a hole in the very expensive-looking rug. Her stomach twisted as cold rushed through her chest, her thoughts filled with everything and nothing all at once. The weight of it all pressed hard into her temples.

Chavet brought her a plate around midday, which she refused to touch. Well, she touched the bread, at least; she'd ripped and picked at it until it was nothing but crumbs. Every thump, every clang, every bang sent her running to her balcony to look, only to decide she didn't actually want to know and go dashing back into her room. And the pacing would begin anew.

Nessa finally dressed herself in her traveling dragonskin armor just to have something to focus on. She relaced her bracers twice, then took up her sword and practiced her fundamentals to give her nerves somewhere to go. But after nearly shattering her vanity mirror, she decided it was probably safer to sheath her sword and pace.

Picking up her dagger, she began to fiddle with it. What was that trick Rinn was always doing?

And suddenly, a thought struck her like lightning.

Sideways.

The word had been knocking around in her head for hours, but perhaps it wasn't quite the word she needed. A sword wasn't always the best weapon. There was no hiding a sword, even a plain one. But daggers! Daggers were small and easy to hide, better for close combat.

Maybe the word she needed was *subtle.*

Everything finally clicked into place.

Nessa flung open the doors to her balcony and dashed out, sliding to a stop at the balustrade. She turned to look northward, her heart in her throat. Scores of men flooded the fields outside the first gate, soldiers dressed in blue and silver lining the walls against the sea of red and bronze. Billows of smoke rose from the watchtowers and the crude catapults dotting the field. Colored clouds and a tower of sapphire and bright red light rose at the edge of her line of sight.

Alaron.

Arrows flew through the tainted sky, the acrid smell of flames and copper singeing her nose. The drums rang as the scream of metal on metal carried on the breeze.

The Menhirans were trying to knock down the front door.

Somewhere amidst all the destruction, Nessa's family was fighting. Her lungs nearly collapsed inward at the idea, but she ripped herself away from the thought, turning her eyes east to the Aresti Wood. She stared, though the wind stung her eyes and she had no idea what she was looking for.

With all the attention on the front door, no one was paying attention to the one at the back. This battle wasn't a suicide attempt to take Galidel.

It was a distraction.

Nessa leaned down as far as she could over the balustrade, the lush green and black of the forest making the shadows seem all the darker. Trying to steady her breathing, she narrowed her eyes.

Breathe.

Focus.

Calm.

There! Between the trees, the shadows moved, and she watched in horror as figures emerged from the forest and began to scale the first wall. Nessa frantically scanned the town, only to see a steady line of shadows, like ants at a picnic, already dodging between buildings and dropping down behind the second wall of gray stone.

"Chavet!" she called, as another man reached the top of the second wall.

Suddenly, a hot wind slammed into her chest, and she stumbled and fell, groaning when her shoulder hit the floor. She rolled away just as a massive shadow blocked out the sun.

Her stomach plummeted.

"CHAVET!"

Nessa scrambled into her room as fast as her limbs would carry her. A bright light flashed outside her windows, blinding her, just as a mighty *BOOM* ripped through the air, shaking the stone below her feet. She tumbled to the ground, a thunderous noise that could have been an avalanche or something else entirely surrounding her. Rage and pain swirled in the air, and heat. So much heat.

Nessa covered her ears and screamed.

All of a sudden, Chavet had his arms around her, and Nessa attached herself to his armor like a limpet. The royal guard held his shield above them as stone, books and tapestries came tumbling down around them, the floor littered with shattered bottles. If she hadn't known better, Nessa would have sworn it was an earthquake.

"Up, Your Highness!"

Together, they struggled to their feet, and Nessa looked back at her room just in time to see the balcony collapse.

Leaning on each other to stay steady, they raced down the stairs two at a time. A roar that sounded like thunder colliding with a racing train rang though the stone, the very foundations shaking with the force.

Nessa tripped and fell to her knees. Her palms stung, but she kept them clamped over her ears anyway, her heart aching with anguish and terror.

The dragon had arrived.

She practically slid down two of the stairs as Chavet tried to pull her along, and she finally ripped her arm away and wobbled to stand her own. Chavet guided her past him, and they ran for dear life, Nessa's heart lodged in her throat. She had no idea how it could possibly be beating so fast. They flew down the steps, Chavet steadying her every time the stone tried to send them tumbling.

They made it to the ground floor just as they heard the roar of collapsing stone, and dust stung her eyes as Chavet pulled her away from the rocks careening down the stairs.

The tower was gone.

"Your Highness."

It took Nessa a second to realize that the gruff, raspy voice belonged to Chavet.

"The stables."

What? The stables?

Of course! The stone roof! But she couldn't go. Not yet.

"What about the kitchens?" Nessa demanded.

"Your Highness…"

The ground below their feet shuddered with another powerful roar, the sound of drums echoing threateningly. They were out of time.

"Chavet, listen to me. Menhir has sent men through the Aresti. They've already breached the second wall, I saw them! You have to spread the word. Grab anyone you can and mount a defense. We'll need as much time as you can give us."

"My orders are to see you safe," he protested.

"I'm giving you new ones." Nessa's voice came so firm and steady, she almost didn't recognize it as her own. "We'll barricade ourselves in the stables. Save everyone you can."

"Yes, Your Highness."

"Thank you."

With a last nod of respect, Nessa raced off to the kitchens, her heart thrumming like a hummingbird's. She knew she should be scared, but she simply didn't have time for fear. Her tightly coiled muscles sprang to life, and she realized this was the moment she'd been waiting for all day without knowing it.

This was it.

Nessa skidded into the kitchens, only to find that the back wall had collapsed. She swallowed down the lump in her throat, coughing against the dust in the air.

"Satu! Rauna! Goodwin!"

Goodwin huddled next to the pile of rubble, sobbing, and Nessa grabbed her by the shoulders. Poor Goodwin's eyes were wide and bewildered, like a horse ready to bolt.

"Goodwin, get to the stables! Now!"

"Alice—"

"There's no time! Go!"

Apparently, *go* was the magic word. Goodwin grabbed the arm of another woman and they dashed for the exit as Nessa started to shove anyone out the door she could lay hands on. Satu started directing the women on the best route to go, while Nessa herself had to chivvy some of the younger girls who were too scared to move out from under the tables. Satu set them off in groups and insisted on going last, refusing to leave until the kitchen was empty.

Nessa turned to run when she heard a groan. Looking down, she saw Rauna half-buried in the debris.

"Rauna!"

Nessa dived down next to the old woman and frantically started tearing away every stone she touched, her hands trembling with nerves. One of her bracers had come loose, she noticed, but there was no time to fix it. She spotted a line of red dripping from Rauna's hairline.

"Rauna, are you alright?"

"I've been hit by worse, child," Rauna muttered. "What happened?"

"A dragon. And Menhir. We need to get to the stables." As Nessa bent down to help the woman to her feet, she saw Rauna's eyes dart to the left, then widen.

Nessa spun, drawing her dagger in one swift arc just in time to block the blade aimed at her back. The Menhiran soldier growled as she dodged another strike, jamming her heel into his kneecap. He hopped back with a howl, but it gave Nessa all the time she needed.

"Go, Rauna! The hearth!"

Her free hand grabbed the first thing it touched, which happened to be a frying pan. She swung with all her might, the metal making a loud *clang* as it collided with the soldier's head. He crumpled instantly, and Nessa didn't wait for him to hit the floor. She was already bolting through the servant's passage into the courtyard.

Nessa glanced up when the sun disappeared, catching a glimpse of a massive, lithe body blocking out the sky. The creature's tail undulated, long and pointed just like its neck, the rectangular snout trailing smoke. Ram-like horns curled from scaly temples, but the most terrifying part was the massive wings, wider than any airplane she'd ever seen. The creature's black and red scales glowed, as if it were a hot coal.

Time to go.

Nessa fought her way through the crowd she'd sent to the stables, heading instead in the opposite direction. They needed a new plan, and she was in over her head.

She burst into the guardhouse to find utter chaos, men and boys rushing around half-armored and half-armed. Another roar caused the building to tremble, the wobbling floor sending Nessa careening into the doorframe to stay upright. No one noticed her in their panic.

She grabbed the first boy to pass her.

"You, get to the front. Get a message to the king. Tell him the manor has been breached."

"Who—"

"Don't ask questions. Just go!"

The boy paused for only a breath, then nodded, racing out the door.

Nessa took the stairs two at a time as she flew down into the dark, yanking the laces of her bracer closed with her teeth as she ran. There was no time; she could hear the shouting above her. Her panic faded as she descended, giving way to the rushing in her ears. The charge had already begun, and fighting on two fronts would spread their forces thin. They were going to need every hand they had to get out of this one.

Those boys upstairs had no experience. The only thing they knew to do was follow orders. They needed someone to lead them, someone who knew what they were getting into. Nessa didn't know what else to do. She certainly couldn't lead an army; she'd never fought a battle before.

But luckily, she knew someone who did.

"Rinn!"

Nessa skidded across the floor as she reached his cell, snatching the keys off the table as she went. Why were there so many? And of course, none of them were labeled. One that said *yes, I open Rinn's door, thank you* would have been so nice.

Rinn popped to his feet in shock, his hands wrapping around the bars as if trying to tear them down so he could run to her. He stared as Nessa started shoving keys into the lock as fast as her shaking hands would allow.

"What are you doing here?" he demanded.

"Breaking you out of jail. Duh."

"Are you mad?!"

Still, he didn't try to stop her. The roar of battle rattled in her ears, the screech of metal on metal reverberating through the floor. Another howl vibrated the stone around them as the shaking timbers sent dust billowing through the air. Nessa wiped it impatiently from her already-irritated eyes. Time was running short.

She gripped the key she held more tightly to keep it from slipping from her sweating fingers, her face and ears growing hot. She needed Rinn out of this damn cell, *now*.

Not that key.

Next one? No.

She forced her hands to steady.

"Rinn, I need your help."

"You *are* mad."

"I'm not." The frantic pitch in her voice begged him to contradict her. "My parents had me tested and everything."

She jumped as a thunderous crash drowned out even the dragon's roar. The sound had come from the top of the stairs. Nessa let loose a litany of curses that would have made a sailor blush and bowed her head over the keys, praying for salvation.

"What's going on?"

"Gerric." She couldn't seem to get enough air. "You were right about *sideways*. A second squad came through the Aresti. Came out of the wood like demons…"

She swore again as the seventh key didn't work. She could hear pounding footsteps. They were growing louder.

Don't look back. Keep going.

"The outer wall is about to fall…"

Rinn suddenly grabbed her waist and slammed Nessa hard against the cold bars. She gasped in air to scream but didn't have time before Rinn snatched up her dagger, plunging it forward.

Wide-eyed, Nessa held perfectly still, her fingers frozen mid-turn on the key. Fear held her throat closed, the heat spilling down her side shocking her hypersensitized skin. Terror and disbelief fought for dominance as Rinn clutched her tightly for a breath, then another. He had…had he…?

The thief held her gaze.

His eyes were a warm, spicy brown, the color of dark rum.

Slowly, the Menhiran soldier collapsed to the ground behind her as Nessa let out a breath, the key finally turning in the lock. It popped open with a *click*, and Rinn jumped out, tossing Nessa back her blade.

"Thanks for that," she said quietly.

Nessa glanced at the soldier. Dark blood pooled from his gut; the strike had been expertly placed. She had his blood on her, but his blade had never touched her. But she couldn't think about that now; she couldn't think about who he'd been. All that mattered was that he would have killed her, and she had to survive. She spun away to grab Rinn's weapons from the wall.

"How many men? In the second wave?" Rinn demanded as he rushed to put his armor on. Without a thought, Nessa began to help him, her fingers flying over the straps. She didn't even have to think about what she was doing anymore.

"Two hundred-ish, probably more. I didn't exactly have time to count."

Trying to focus on the armor and getting out of there rather than how outnumbered they were, Nessa tightened a shoulder strap with possibly too much vigor and Rinn rocked on his feet.

He arched a brow at her. "Are you this gentle with all your lovers?"

"Yes."

Nessa pulled Rinn's chain from around her neck and dangled it in front of him, the ward-charm and the gold ring glinting in the dim light. Raising a brow, he grinned proudly and snatched it up.

"Noted."

Taking up his sword, he stood tall, his blade poised and ready. He looked complete again.

"How much time to we have?" he asked.

"Not much," Nessa answered.

Drawing her own blade, she rushed toward the stairs, Rinn hot on her heels. "We have to get the civilians to the stables before the guards close the gates."

"On it."

Nessa took the stairs two at a time while Rinn took them in threes, quickly overtaking her to cut down a Menhiran soldier with two swipes of his blade. She pressed her back to the wall and didn't stop to watch the soldier tumble down the stairs, hearing chaos erupt the moment Rinn reached the top. She swung her blade the moment she entered the room, an enemy blade skittering away from her. Another soldier ducked behind his shield, and in a flash, Rinn grabbed her forearm, spun her behind him and struck low. Nessa's sword flew up to block another strike, her body arching backward over Rinn's. She braced herself against his back and kicked out, hard. It was over in one more swipe.

They stood back-to-back, spinning in tandem as though this were a coordinated dance and not a battle. Nessa always knew, somehow, exactly where Rinn was. After their foray in the goblin tunnels, this felt almost easy. Rinn spun her into him at the last moment just as a soldier lunged, then spun her back out in the next instant. Nessa hip-checked the Menhiran, who tumbled down the stairs – all the way down, judging by the noise.

Silence fell for a beat.

"Prisoner!" came the outcry.

"Well observed," Nessa snapped, placing herself in front of Rinn. Her blade warded off the young squire who had been absolutely no help moments ago. It took her a moment to gather enough breath for a full sentence, her heart pounding painfully against her ribs. "I grant him a reprieve until the battle is finished."

"But…" The boy pointed, and Nessa felt her temper flare. They didn't have time for this.

"No buts, kid. Get the women and children to the stable. That's an order."

The kid stared at her, pale-faced, and Nessa felt panic rise in her chest.

"Now!"

The terrified squire scurried out the door, Nessa and Rinn at his heels as bells rang out from the towers above. The bright sunlight assaulted her eyes, and she blinked as they watered. Shouting roared in her ears, the hot wind pulling at her clothes and hair. She fought not to cover her nose to keep the smell of smoke and rot at bay, swallowing down her heart. It tasted a lot like bile.

If Menhir took Galidel, they had their entry into Calebrir and the war would be over in a matter of weeks. Menhir's sneak attack had breached the inner walls, and no one on the front lines knew. The only fighters left behind the wall were, like herself, young and inexperienced. Trained military men against some light infantry was a recipe for a massacre.

This was a battle she knew they couldn't win. They were outmanned, outnumbered, and outplanned.

Time to make an all-out stand.

Nessa's people were at stake, and even if they couldn't win, they could still stall, at least until the main army could rally back to the city. Hopefully, that would be enough. The endeavor was foolish, but what else could they do? They had to get to the stables, outlast a dragon, regroup, and hold the fort, literally. And she had to do it; there was no one else. She had to at least try. It was both that simple and that hard.

Taking a breath for courage, she dove headfirst into the fray.

Nessa tore through the chaos like a madwoman. Here, there was no proper footwork, no perfection of position, only survival. Her blade flashed in the sun, blocking and striking with wild abandon as sweat dripped down her face, her palms growing damp.

The Menhirans may have been more experienced, but Nessa was faster and lighter in her dragonskin armor, Rinn at her side. They danced around each other effortlessly, Nessa blocking and dodging, wearing out the enemy before Rinn struck the final blow. Blades swirled as smoke, screams, and blood filled the air. The echoing bells faded, swallowed by the sounds of battle.

The books never described it like this.

"Alice!"

Nessa spun to see a horse and rider racing toward her, the sharpened point of a spear glinting menacingly in the sun. The rider twirled the weapon once and hurled it through the air just as Nessa dodged to the side, a rush of air blowing past her arm.

The angry horse kept coming, but she was faster. She hurled her body backward, rolling to get clear of the stomping hooves, then pushed herself up, ignoring the sting in her shoulder and the roar of the dragon over the battlefield.

The rider fixed his eyes on her as the thunderous noise of hooves filled her ears, and Nessa stumbled back, only to collide with something solid. She spun to see the rider's spear embedded in the ground. A mad idea flickered in her mind.

She scrambled to her feet, ripping the spear from the dirt with one mighty tug. Unfortunately, the point broke off in the ground, leaving the end dull and round.

Okay, new plan. It was almost a baseball bat, right? She assumed the position, holding the eyes of the rider intent on grabbing her.

With a hefty grunt, Nessa swung for the fences, and the staff shattered against the rider's chest plate with a *CRACK*. He tumbled backwards off the horse as she leapt out of the way, his cry abruptly cutting off as his neck collided with the ground.

She didn't have time to enjoy her victory as a large *BANG* reverberated through the air, the whine of metal on metal making her cringe. Women and children cried out in warning and fear, and she saw the guards pulling the stable gates closed.

Time was up.

She was never going to make it.

"Alice!"

She whirled to see Rinn swinging effortlessly onto the back of the riderless horse, and knew the plan even before their eyes met. Nessa ran toward the stables, half an eye behind her and half looking ahead at the gates as the gap between the doors grew smaller. They had one shot at this. She couldn't miss.

Rinn lowered his hand.

"Now!" he ordered.

Nessa jumped, and Rinn clasped her forearm, hoisting her from the ground with a growl of effort. She planted one foot on top of Rinn's in the stirrup, balancing precariously between badass and disaster. Rinn yanked her toward the horse and Nessa grabbed onto the saddle horn for dear life, pressing herself against the horse's flank and burying her face in Rinn's thigh. He tightened his grip on her forearm, refusing to let her fall.

Breathe. Breathe. It's okay.

"There's a child!"

Nessa's head shot up at the urgency in Rinn's voice. A few yards ahead of them, a small boy crouched, whimpering, on the ground. He couldn't have been more than two. The soldiers didn't seem to be paying him much attention, and the poor thing kept falling as he tried desperately to escape the battle.

Nessa turned wide eyes to Rinn. "We can't leave him!"

"I knew you'd say that."

The thief guided the galloping horse toward the child, effortlessly switching his sword from side to side to protect himself and Nessa from the onslaught of Menhiran soldiers. He seemed to be guiding the horse using only his knees.

Nessa stayed pressed tightly against the beast as they raced toward the child. They couldn't come back for him if she missed. A child's life depended on her timing. If she fell, they were both dead.

"Give me some slack," she called above the chaos, sliding her fingers from Rinn's forearm to his palm. "And don't let go."

She couldn't hide the fear in her eyes.

Rinn held her gaze. "I won't."

Nessa nodded once to build up her courage, then let go of the saddle and swung out over the ground, half her body flying. One hand stayed tightly clenched in Rinn's as her free arm scooped the little boy up at the very last second. In one fluid move, she pulled him to her chest as Rinn yanked her against the saddle, holding them both tightly.

"Shhh, shhh. It's okay, sweetie, I got you," Nessa whispered into the crying child's hair, his little arms clenched around her neck. "You're going to be okay."

Rinn spurred the horse forward. Speed would be their only savior now; they had no way to defend themselves without letting Nessa and the child fall. The scream of the rusty gates whined in her ears, and she buried her face in Rinn's leg, curling tightly around the child. If they didn't make it, she didn't want to see.

Wood and metal slammed together with a clang of thunder, and for one blessed moment, there was silence. Then Rinn's voice was murmuring softly in her ear.

"It's alright. We made it."

Nessa slid limply to the ground with the child still clutched to her chest, her knees buckling under her weight. They'd made it. She could breathe — for now.

The air stank of heat, sweat, and fear, and she desperately wanted to cry, though she wasn't sure whether it was in relief or sorrow.

A woman screamed and rushed forward through the crowd, and Nessa jumped, startled.

"Toma! Toma! Oh, my baby!" The woman snatched the crying child from Nessa's arms, nearly sobbing with relief. Nessa took a moment to watch as the mother cried, cradling her baby to her chest. Suddenly, Rauna appeared, a bandage at her hairline, and wrapped her arms around the crying mother and child.

"You're alright now. You're safe. Oh, my baby," the woman wept into her son's hair. She looked gratefully up at Nessa, her eyes red and swollen. Rauna saw Nessa, and immediately flung her arms around her as she stumbled back in shock.

"Thank you. I owe you not only my life, but the life of my grandson," she sobbed. "I don't know how we can repay you."

Nessa wiped her eyes. "Stay alive. That'll be enough."

Rauna let out a little laugh. "May the Elar and the Great Mother bless you, child." She gave Nessa a kiss on the cheek.

Nessa watched Rauna and her family disappear back into the crowd, staring without really seeing. A muted snarl echoed down through the stone roof as dust trickled onto their heads, the building's foundation shuddering. Families huddled together inside the once-empty stalls.

How many people had made it into the stable? How many had they left out on the battlefield? How many parents were gone? Children? Were they all to perish here? Trapped?

This couldn't be it. This couldn't be the end.

"I do not love the bright sword for its sharpness," she breathed like a prayer, "nor the warrior for his glory. I love only that which they defend."

Tolkien had said it best. *Fight for the love that is behind you.* That, she could do. She would not let her people fall, not without a fight.

"Pretty," Rinn said from behind her. "You make that up yourself?"

"I do read, Rinn." Nessa tried to give him a smile and failed. His hand hovered over her shoulder, but he never touched her.

"You alright?"

Nessa nodded. "You?"

"I assure you, princess, I've survived far, far worse." The hand hovering by her shoulder moved to rub his neck.

"I don't doubt it." Nessa sighed, taking in the terrified mass of people before her. She counted maybe fifty soldiers, most of the crowd consisting of women, children, and men who had seen too many winters. Altogether, they couldn't have numbered more than a hundred. She spun to face Rinn.

"How long do you think we have?" she demanded.

They jumped as a massive *BANG* echoed through the air, both of them whirling toward the gate. The wood whined and groaned, but did not give in.

Rinn's voice rose in pitch. "Not long, apparently."

Nessa swore. They didn't have time for a plan. Time to improvise.

"You!" Nessa grabbed hold of the nearest uniformed man, and he paused to stare at her, wide-eyed. "Is there a way to get the women and children out?"

"We are trapped…"

"Bullshit! Is there a way?"

"…Uh, maybe?" volunteered a new voice.

Nessa spun to see a soldier swaying at her side, a mess of blood and bandages where his left eye should have been. He couldn't have been any older than she was.

"Possibly, through the storage tunnels." He stumbled, but was steadied by the soldier Nessa had grabbed. "They lead into the mountains. There may be a way out from there."

"What are your names?" Nessa asked. Another loud *crack* snapped around them. This time, it was followed by worried cries.

"Alistair, of the House of Hurlin," said the one with the injured eye. "And Indrid, House of Colde."

"Alistair and Indrid, who is in charge? Where's Chavet?" Nessa fought not to lean back into the warmth of Rinn behind her; instead, she clenched her fists, trying to hide her shaking. What could they possibly do now?

"Dead," Indrid answered. "He fell raising the alarm."

Cold fear rushed through Nessa. She swayed, and Rinn's hand found her shoulder.

Another *CRACK* issued from the other side of the gate, and the shouting of the surrounding crowd grew louder. Cries of panic and fear rose, spreading even to the soldiers, most of whom were huddled together and jumping at every bang. Everyone wore expressions of terror, their eyes wild and features pale. Some cried. Some held each other. All appeared entirely beaten.

Nessa glanced up at Rinn. He had slumped slightly, looking tired and broken. They had already overcome so much.

"We can't give up now," she told him with a slight shake of her head.

"What's left?" asked Rinn, sounding hopeless.

Nessa didn't have an answer.

Grinding her teeth, she wracked her brain. She had no idea what to do, but she couldn't let them know that; she couldn't let their last hours be fearful. If this was the end, she was going to make it a good one.

The cries gradually tapered off to sniffles and whimpers as Nessa searched the terrified faces of the crowd, feeling her chest tighten. Her eyes stung, the fear in the air so thick she could have cut it with a knife. She took a breath, then forced herself to stand tall. Back on Earth, she knew, there were princesses who had become generals in their people's hour of need.

It was time she do the same.

Words could be powerful magic. Words could destroy, but they could also create. How many times had she heard that from Lilly and Albert? Words could chase away the darkness, could weave stories that could hurt and heal and inspire. She just needed the right ones.

"Help me up." Nessa grabbed Rinn's arm and clambered up onto a nearby wooden table. Below her, the huddled pockets of soldiers argued over tactics as another crash sounded at the stable door.

"Hey!" Nessa waved her hands, but the soldiers paid her no notice, continuing to argue amongst themselves. Exasperated, she put two fingers to her lips and let out a high-pitched whistle. The entire stable jumped a mile high as silence finally fell.

Nessa took a deep breath and, for the first time, addressed her people as their leader.

"I know you are afraid," she began quietly. "Menhir has come to destroy us, to destroy Calebrir. I know you are afraid, because I'm afraid, too."

She paused, feeling the pounding of her heart rocking her frame, then let her voice grow stronger, louder.

"And this," she gestured toward the door, "this is scary! But we are still here. We are not destroyed yet."

Nessa could feel her muscles winding tight as she searched the crowd for Rauna, Satu and all her friends from the kitchen. The stable had gone silent, save for the bang of the Menhiran army at their door and the dull roar of battle outside.

Nessa thought of the heroes she'd read about, of lost kings who had regained their thrones, abused children who brought down governments, ancient soldiers who protected galaxies and brave barricade boys who had died too young. The stories filled her heart, lent her the courage she needed so she had hope to give away.

Her voice rang out, strong and clear, through the air.

"We are still here! We are still standing! We still hope, and Menhir cannot crush it! The day may come when all memory of Calebrir will fade and the kingdom of the sun will be forgotten, but it is not this day! On this day, we will show Menhir *why* we are the people of the sun! We will remind them of our light, and they will be *blinded by it!*"

Shouts of agreement echoed throughout the stable, a few fists rising into the air. Her head spun with the rush as she pressed on, thanking the Elar she had *Return of the King* memorized.

"Our story will long echo in the halls of kings!"

More excited shouts rang out around her.

"We will fight to the last!" Nessa spread her arms wide. "On this day we stand! We rise!"

"We rise!" they bellowed back as one.

"Rise!" she roared.

"*Rise!*"

"*RISE*!"

The stable erupted into thunderous roars and chants.

"RISE! RISE! RISE!"

Nearly gasping under the weight of the adrenaline, Nessa let reality settle back around her. She'd done it, she'd given a speech Tolkien himself would have been proud of. The troops were rallied. Now they just had to deliver.

"Alistair! Indrid!" she called, and the two soldiers snapped to attention. "Get the mothers and children out. The elderly, anyone too hurt to fight, get them to safety."

Nessa turned to address the crowd. "If you wish to fight, grab a weapon and whatever else you can find. We're forming a barricade!"

Slightly organized chaos erupted around them, and Rinn appeared miraculously at her side, helping her down from the table before he flipped it over to add to the barricade. The thief wore a mischievous grin.

"Did you come up with that all on your own, or did you read about that, too?"

"Oh, shush, you." There was no heat in Nessa's reprimand. "It worked, didn't it?"

In no time, the barricade was built, out of anything they could get their hands on: tables, chairs, broken shields, carts… Anything and everything was piled before them. The people standing with their princess were a mix of green soldiers and civilian men and women, but even armed with shoddy makeshift weapons, Nessa would take loyal hearts over career soldiers any day. She knew not to underestimate a person with a cause to fight for.

Rinn lined up the few archers they had at the back of the barricade, where they stood proud, arrows nocked and ready. Nessa and Rinn crouched hip-to-hip behind a wall of shields, a mob of spears, pitchforks, hoes, scythes, and anything else that was long and pointy at their backs. Some of the kitchen ladies were even armed with pans and rolling pins, ready to lay down their lives for their kingdom.

The gate was beginning to cave in with every hit, and Nessa fought not to flinch. Little by little, the gap began to grow, and she had no idea what was waiting for them on the other side.

This was it. She could die in the next few moments. Her people could fall, Menhir would win the war, and all their sacrifices would be for nothing. Every home would become a ghost garden.

She could feel her heart rushing in her ears, the taste of bile filling her mouth, but she swallowed it down. She needed to have courage. It was the only way she would see her family again.

Her sword trembled in her hands.

Suddenly, Rinn's hand came to rest over her knee, and she glanced over at him, her eyes wide. She hadn't realized how close they were. They were connected from hip to ankle and shoulder to elbow.

His eyes held the softest expression. Nessa had never seen him look like that before.

Rinn had gold in his brown eyes, she remembered suddenly.

"There's something you should know," he began, "if things don't go well."

"Okay…" Nessa prompted, terror gripping her chest.

Rinn looked serious for a moment, then his lips twitched upward. "You look very fetching in mail."

A hysterical laugh burst from her lips. What an absurd thief he was! She was so grateful for it.

"Thanks, Rinn."

The gate groaned, snaps and pops sounding under each loud bang. Splinters of wood fell away as sunlight trickled in around the chains holding the doors together, the iron handles moaning. It wouldn't be long now.

She wasn't the only one trembling. Rinn's jaw flexed so hard she could hear his teeth grinding together, the brief heartbeats of quiet echoing with heavy, terrified breathing. A buzz of anticipation filled the air around them, and Nessa matched her breathing to the chaos.

BANG, breathe.

Bang, breathe.

Screwing her courage to the sticking place, she took a deep breath and held it, just to feel the air in her lungs. She tightened her grip on her sword as the ramming grew louder.

Bang!

Bang!

BANG!

"Whatever comes through that gate," she called over the noise, "remember, you are the children of the sun! We are the people of Galidel, and *THEY SHALL NOT PASS!*"

The gates flew open.

It was time to go to war.

Chapter Thirty-Four

Mind Your Footing

Time slowed to a crawl as the doors banged open, a wall of heat crashing against her face. Shadowy soldiers backlit by bright sunlight and fire charged toward them.

One step.

Then another.

Arrows flew above Nessa's head, the very air rumbling in her ears as a flash of flame exploded beside the door, its fiery tendrils reaching for her. The arrows found their marks, sending the first wave of invaders tumbling down. More followed, however, death at their heels.

Nessa gripped her sword until her knuckles ached as more arrows flew around them.

"Now," Rinn breathed in her ear.

Time slammed back into place, and her voice cut loud and clear through the chaos.

"*Charge!*"

The wall of shields rose with a shout, hands bracing Nessa's shoulders as their makeshift militia surged forward, a rallying cry for Calebrir on every lip. Her shield shuddered hard in her hands, but she refused to let go, even as Rinn winced beside her. They lowered their stances as one and shoved.

Above them, the bells clanged.

Nessa's heels slid against the floor. Grinding her teeth, she pushed with all her might, borrowing strength from the hands at her back. The mass of citizens moved as one, a steady boulder that refused to be worn away amidst the waves of enemy soldiers.

"Spears!"

Like lightning, the spear tips of the men at their backs jabbed between the shields. They were moving faster now, hardly meeting any resistance as more arrows flew above them. The path grew steadily clearer.

They emerged into the sunlight as one, and the Menhiran soldiers' eyes grew wide as the wall of shields split open to unleash the fierce Calebrians, all roaring like beasts of the wild. Weapons clashed, but the enemy fell away, their courage deserting them at the unexpected resistance. Nessa and company chased them outside the manor gate, where the Menhirans finally turned to make a stand.

Nessa and her little army realigned themselves, Rinn remaining faithfully at her side with his shield over both their heads. Nessa shook off the shattered remains of her own shield, gripping her sword with both hands. She glanced over at Rinn.

"Still here?" she panted.

"Are you kidding? Things are just starting to get interesting."

Nessa almost grinned. Raising her sword, she addressed her people.

"They want us to burn?! *Then let them burn with us!*"

Cries and weapons rose, and the charge began anew as Nessa and Rinn launched themselves side by side into the battle. A soldier went for Nessa, but she slid under him like she was aiming for home plate, Rinn following up with a single swing the soldier never saw coming — and never would.

Nessa refused to stray from Rinn's side. At times, they would grab onto each other, spinning themselves this way and that to protect each other's backs. Sweat poured down her face, her cut lip stinging and nostrils burning with a horrid smell she didn't care to identify. She could only keep moving, her sword flashing in the early afternoon sun.

"*Dragon!*"

Nessa felt the heat before she saw the flames, and she clutched tightly to Rinn at the very same moment he grabbed her arm, hurling them both against the defensive wall. She held her breath, screwing her eyes tightly shut as heat and flame painted the sky. Flames licked at the other side of the wall, a roar causing the stones at their backs to tremble before the fire vanished, as swiftly as it had come. The roar faded into a different sound altogether.

Horns.

Nessa's head popped up, and she stared at a shocked Rinn, her wide eyes questioning.

"Elves!" he gasped.

Hope threatened to burst from Nessa's chest, her eyes scanning the battlefield. There! She could see, faintly, a line of white coming from the west.

Silvery pale armor sparkled against the gentle hills as banners of soft green snapped in the breeze. The horns sounded again, the sky darkening under a hail of arrows.

Nessa nearly collapsed with relief. "Koen!"

Suddenly, a wave of elves crashed into the men standing before them. Sucking in gulps of air, Nessa watched as they carved a path through the enemy with their double short swords, long curved blades, and pointed shields. One elven soldier came to stand over the pair, offering them a hand up. Nessa recognized the night-blue eyes instantly.

"You called for aid, Your Highness?" Koen gave her a charming grin as he helped her to her feet. She couldn't stop herself; she flung her arms around his neck.

"I've never been so glad to see anyone in all my life!" Nessa felt like her smile might actually split her face in two.

"Watch out!" Rinn shouted suddenly.

Koen fell to the ground even as Rinn planted himself over him and Nessa, sword raised above his head to block the sudden strike. Nessa crouched next to Koen as a line of red appeared at his shoulder.

"Koen!"

"I am alright, child."

They looked to Rinn, who was bracing himself, his face glistening with sweat as he strained against the attacking blade. The broadsword was attached to an even broader man with dark, mad eyes. Nessa's throat closed in horror, all the air leaving her lungs as she stared, wide-eyed and trembling.

Towering over Rinn was Gerric Emrys.

Gerric gave them a crazed smile.

"Well, well," he snickered, and Nessa shivered in fright at the menace in his deep voice, "imagine my luck, finding old friends here."

Koen put himself between Nessa and the frenzied general. "Quickly! Go!"

He shoved Nessa up the gray stone stairs at their rear and followed immediately after, Rinn hot on his heels. Rinn's sword flashed against Gerric's, keeping the monster at bay as they climbed. As their blades locked once more, Rinn shoved his foot into Gerric's gut, sending him tumbling back down the steps.

They took the stairs two or three at a time, jumping over the broken ones as rubble slid beneath their feet. Rinn nearly stumbled, but Koen caught him just before he could fall over the edge into the battle below. Nessa could see Gerric, back on his feet and following, madness in his eyes as his massive broadsword flashed. He shouted something at Rinn, but the other man didn't take the bait.

Finally, they reached the top of the wall. Nessa gasped for air, Koen's hand on her back the only thing keeping her from toppling over. She spun, heart lodged in her throat as she searched desperately for her thief. Rinn appeared breathless and wild, but unharmed.

"Get her out of here!" Rinn shouted to Koen. "I'll hold him off!"

"Rinn, no!" Nessa cried. She couldn't leave him. Not now! Her eyes burned.

"Go!" he ordered, an edge of panic in his voice.

A roar like a crashing freight train exploded over them, and the stones below their feet crumbled. Nessa collapsed with a yelp, her fingers clutching at the quaking stone. A deafening wind rushed past her ears as her lungs filled with smoke, and she coughed, squeezing her eyes shut against the dust.

And then, just like that, it was over.

She opened her eyes.

Half the wall had disappeared, and so had Koen and Rinn.

Bile rose in her throat. She tried to call out, but only coughed out mud. She spat to rid herself of the taste, of the grit between her teeth, then scrambled to her feet, gasping.

And found herself face to face with Gerric Emrys.

Nessa leapt back, her eyes widening in terror. He was grinning.

"Well, if it isn't Rinn's little companion," Gerric cooed. "I believe we have business to finish."

She adjusted her grip on her sword, mentally stringing together a slew of curses. Gerric was twice her size, and his blade looked like it could snap hers in half with one swipe. She'd have to be smart here.

Sideways…sideways…

"How did the goblins like you, Gerric?" Nessa attempted bravado and failed. She tried again. "You must have fit right in. You smell like one, at any rate."

"You little—"

"Let's not mention your mother again."

She lowered her stance, frantically searching for an out, but it was no use. She was trapped on the wall. Gerric was blocking the path before her, and behind her was nothing but bodies. There was no place to hide, no way out. She was trapped.

Before she could ready herself, Gerric lunged, the force of his blade against hers rattling her teeth. She skipped back a few steps, but he followed, taking a swipe that she only just managed to duck. Snatching up a fallen shield, she shoved it along the ground like a sled toward the mad general. The sharp edge slammed into his ankle, and he stumbled, buying her some time.

Nessa raced along the wall as arrows whizzed past her head, smoke filling her lungs and stinging her eyes. Her legs burned from the effort, but she kept going. There had to be another way down.

She turned a sharp corner and skidded to a halt.

The wall before her had completely collapsed. She peered over the edge, finding only a long drop ending in a pile of rubble. It looked to be nearly ten feet across to the other side. She'd never be able to make the jump.

She swore and turned back the way she'd come, ash and soot filling her vision…

When out of the billowing smoke came Gerric stalking towards her, an insane glee radiating from the battered soldier. Her heart raced, threatening to jump out of her chest.

Still, she stood her ground.

Shit. Shit. Shit.

Gerric lunged, and Nessa managed to block three strikes before he stepped back and began to circle her again. He had done this with Rinn that day in the woods, she remembered, assessing his prey, so she adjusted to meet him head on. He lunged again and she dodged, but he hooked his foot around her leg and she tumbled to the ground with a hard *thud.*

Nessa saw stars when her head collided with the stone, managing to recover just in time to see Gerric stabbing down at her. She rolled, barely avoiding the blow, and tried to kick him away, but he merely twirled his sword and struck again. She rolled out of the way again even as the wall shook below them.

The men on the field beneath began to shout.

"Dragon! Dragon!"

Nessa looked up to see the creature swooping in low for another pass. Her heart raced. What was more dangerous? Gerric or the dragon?

Sideways.

She needed to hit him where it hurt.

"I see your aim still hasn't improved," Nessa taunted.

Gerric growled, insane anger flashing through his eyes. Enraged, he made a reckless grab for her, and she struck.

Nessa yanked down hard on his breastplate as her feet pushed up against his gut, and Gerric flew over her with a yell. His back hit the stone and he kept rolling, nearly careening off the wall. He managed to grab hold of the edge at the last second, his feet dangling in the empty air.

Nessa gulped, rising to a crouch as she sheathed her sword. Her body froze as a cramping ache rippled through her bones, and she sucked in heaving gasps of air, trying to fill her desperate lungs. Something hot, sticky, and metallic trickled down her lips. But none of that mattered.

She stared at the wild-eyed commander. Gerric's eyes bulged as he scrabbled for a handhold, his fingers clawing at the smooth stone. He searched frantically for anything to pull him up from the edge, but there was nothing.

His eyes met hers for a split second, then he disappeared over the edge.

Nessa paused, terror and relief fighting for dominance in her chest, and she winced as she pushed herself to her feet, her shaking fingers carding through her disheveled hair. Had he fallen? Had she really…?

Breathe.

Hot air blew into her face. Was he actually…? There was only one way to find out, but she didn't want to look.

She had to, though. She had to know. Carefully, she made her way over to the precipice and looked down.

Gerric seized her ankle and yanked.

Nessa fell.

Hot air billowed around her as her hair ripped from its braid. Her arms spread wide and she braced her legs apart, reaching frantically for something, anything to grab onto. But she found nothing.

The ground rushed toward her.

She shut her eyes.

And collided hard with something fiery hot.

Nessa's fingers wrapped around cool metal even as the wind was knocked from her lungs. By some miracle, she managed to not let go as she pressed herself against the undulating form beneath her, her eyes closed against the hot, stinging wind. Gasping, she peeked through one eye to see dark scales below her.

She shut her eyes again, letting loose a litany of curses.

The dragon vibrated with a roar, and she squeaked in terror, hiding her face in her aching arms. It spun in midair, and she screamed, forcing herself to open her eyes. She clutched at the beast's collar, squeezing with her knees as her stomach pitched and rolled. This was worse than the roller coaster at Six Flags. No safety bars, for a start. Her breath caught when the dragon looked back at her, its eyes slitted, like a snake's, and burning gold. It seemed to look without seeing.

Nessa looked down at the collar she held onto. Strange symbols covered the metal, seeming somehow familiar, though she was sure she'd never seen them before. Suddenly, she spotted one she *knew* she knew. It had been on the table in the Menhiran camp!

The creature roared, shooting straight up in the air, and her fingers burned as the collar suddenly turned hot, the body below her feeling more like an oven than an animal. The heat in the air above its skin was so intense it warped her vision.

"Stop!" she called to the dragon. "Please!"

Don't look down. Don't look down!

Nessa trembled despite the heat in the air and squeezed her eyes closed, listening to the rapid beating of her heart. The world spun upside down.

Just hold on!

Her stomach flipped into her toes, and she forced herself to listen only to her heartbeat in her ears, focusing her entire self on the rhythm. She felt something building inside her chest, each *thump* of her heart filling her with a buzzing energy, like waves upon a shore.

She'd felt this before.

The dragon righted itself, and Nessa pressed her cheek to the scales. There, right there, she could hear a deep, steady *tha-thump*. She tried to match her breathing to the rhythm as her body shook like she had a fever, sweat dripping from her palms and brow. Calm, she needed to calm down. She reached for her roots, for the tether within herself, the buzzing energy growing stronger with every breath and heartbeat.

Nessa felt her entire body twitching with energy. It tore through her aching muscles and made the hair on her arms stand straight up as the space behind her eyes prickled, her head throbbing. There was nowhere else for it to go.

And so, she did the bravest, stupidest thing she could think of. She took her hand off the collar and splayed her fingers across the dragon's back, directly between its heaving wings. She gathered all that energy, the buzzing and the crashing waves and the tether and the aching and the twitching, right in the middle of her chest and held it there for a moment, just breathing.

Then, with a scream, she pushed it all out at once.

The dragon erupted in a thunderous roar as Nessa felt something snap between her shoulder blades. The sting ran down her spine and blazed across her temples, her body shuddering as everything within her emptied in a rush. Her vision swam as the last of the current left her body, a *SNAP* like a massive rubber band to the heart knocking her back. And then she was falling, through darkness and stars and light until suddenly her back hit something solid. She shrieked, but by virtue of her fingers wedged under the collar, she managed not to fall.

Nessa slumped against the dragon, gasping for air like a drowning woman as the creature shuddered beneath her. It shook its head, finally catching sight of the shaking girl holding onto it for dear life.

She could feel something sticky and hot dripping from her nose as she blinked, trying to get her eyes to focus. Her vision had gone funny, an eerie colored light shimmering off the dragon's rippling scales. The sky above was swirling together with blacks and blues and whites like a Van Gogh painting as darkness threatened to overtake her, when all of a sudden there was a hot wind blowing in her face. She shook her head, meeting the gaze of the largest eye she'd ever seen.

"What just happened?" Nessa asked the dragon.

A small grumble was her only response. The rumbling went on, changing in pitch and tone as if the creature were trying to speak. She thought about responding, but found her mouth too dry for speech. All she could do was hold on tighter to the collar, just in case it suddenly decided to eat her.

The dragon gently banked, careful not to toss Nessa around any further, and she slowly slid forward to sit up, keeping a tight grip on the collar with both hands. Below her, she saw the battle lines of Menhir, their catapults at the ready. The dragon circled above, swooping lower each time.

Nessa pressed herself back against the beast as the dragon went into a sharp dive and released a torrent of fire directly onto Menhir's soldiers, its throat glowing like hot embers. The flames spread across the field, engulfing the catapults in a tower of flame, and Nessa could see the confusion and panic on the faces of the soldiers ducking for cover. The dragon let out a roar as it swung back up into the open sky.

Nessa gasped in joy and absolute terror. "Well done, dragon!"

The creature rumbled in satisfaction.

She grabbed back onto the collar and instantly regretted looking down as the dragon flattened out its flight for a moment. Nessa gently stroked the scales around the collar, and the dragon seemed to purr as it circled around for another pass.

This time, it came in low, and Nessa pressed her whole front against the dragon's back to avoid the arrows flying overhead. She still made an effort to keep her eyes open to watch as its great hind claws tore through Menhir's war machines like paper, flames billowing in its wake. The soldiers fled.

The Menhirans fought to turn their remaining catapults around as the dragon and Nessa flew over the fields. Nessa held on tight, not daring to look down or let go, as they spun and dived, the dragon painting the field in flames. For her part, Nessa tried very hard not to throw up.

The dragon finally paused, hovering over the battle to survey the damage. Pillars of smoke wafted into the sky, turning day into night as tides of red pushed against a sea of blue speckled with silver. Catapults and weapons lay strewn across the battlefield, stones and arrows flying through the smoke as flashes of color erupted from below.

The dragon let loose a mighty roar of vindication.

They dove once more, spinning through a column of colorful smoke, and Nessa glimpsed Alaron less than twenty feet below her, green and pink flames jumping between his fists.

"Al!" Nessa called, just as the dragon spat a ball of flame into the smoke. The fumes burst into balls of fire, a blazing tornado of color roaring into the sky.

And then they were past it, rising up to meet the sun.

Suddenly, the sound of horns blasted over the chaos, and Nessa and the dragon both turned toward the hill on the southwest plain. In the light of the setting sun, an army appeared, flying flags of every color imaginable. The horns sounded again as the dragon flew closer.

Below, Nessa could see a sea of men and women mounted on horses, all wearing different armor in browns, blues and silvers. She spotted a familiar mare rearing up at the front.

Brandir!

Beside him, elves readied their bows. The horn trumpeted once more, and she saw a strawberry-blond rider on a white horse racing ahead of the army, a battle cry on his lips as he waved a familiar bow in the air. Nessa gasped.

"Bryn!" Her hands flew to her mouth, and she nearly fell, her heart plummeting to her toes. She quickly grabbed back onto her new friend.

Don't let go of the dragon.

"Bryn!"

The horns blew. The dragon roared in harmony with the new arrivals.

They took a collective deep breath.

And then, as one, they plunged forward.

Bryn's army thundered down the hill, and Nessa held on tight as the dragon dove with them, its wings shielding the riders below. The ground shook with the force of the approaching army, the thunder of hooves crashing through the air. The dragon snapped and growled, and Nessa braced herself against the onslaught, muttering prayers under her breath as she clung tightly to her new friend's back.

Nessa could see Menhir's men falter as they faced the fresh charge, their eyes widening. They quaked visibly at the ferocity of the men and women racing toward them, all thoughts of bravery and valor forgotten in the face of Bryn's army and their madness. The unstoppable force was about to meet the immoveable object.

Bryn's army washed over them with a cacophony of metal and screams just as the dragon let loose a mouthful of fire. The Menhirans scattered, and Nessa held on, begging the dragon not to drop her. As the dragon flew upwards in a wide curve, soaring into the air, she closed her eyes to let the wind dry the sweat on her brow.

Suddenly, the dragon jerked sideways, and Nessa felt a stinging shock rip across her right side. She screamed and pressed herself against the beast, blinking open her watery eyes to see black smoke dissipating.

Magic. That had been magic. She turned to see a vast ball of black smoke and lightning coming straight for them.

"Look out!" Nessa screamed.

The dragon turned, spouting fire at the last second, and the ball of magic burned as they dove directly through the fire in the sky. They were struck again, this time from the back, and the dragon twisted in the air, roaring painfully. Nessa's fingers started to slip on the collar as bright red blood spilled over the dragon's scales.

She didn't know how to help. If the dragon was done, so was she. A fall from this high up would mean her death, but she didn't know what to do. She searched her brain, finding nothing. All she could do was hold on.

She saw it coming a moment before she screamed. "Left!"

It was too late.

Black smoke and flashes of magic engulfed them, and Nessa shrieked as acid ripped through her muscles. She squeezed her eyes closed, pain, white and hot like she'd never experienced, tearing across her chest. The air left her lungs as the dragon reared back, its blood slicking her fingers.

Nessa fought the fuzziness in her brain as the dragon desperately flapped its wings, straining higher and higher. She tried to make herself move, to hold on, but her body could only tremble in exhaustion.

The edges of her vision began to haze, the world growing dark.

She heard a voice murmuring apology after apology and realized it was her own.

"Just go. You're free…you're free…I'm sorry…just go…"

The dragon streaked through the air as Nessa's fingers slipped from the collar.

Wind rushed around her as the world faded to black.

Chapter Thirty-Five

Who's Gonna Clean This Mess Up?

The first thing Nessa heard was the gentle crackle of flames. The air tasted like grass, salty smoke and intolerable heat. A steady, thumping ache split her head in two, the acidic throbbing spreading all the way to her fingertips and toes, and she groaned, her voice rough as sandpaper.

After a moment, she opened her eyes, and then wasn't really sure she had. This couldn't be right. She had to be dead. She *had* to be. She'd fallen off a *dragon*, for goodness sake.

…Gods and angels, she'd ridden a dragon!

She finally moved, and the pain galloping through her was enough to prove she was alive. Death couldn't possibly hurt this much. She felt something wrapped loosely around her body, something that had scales and rumbled gently.

Slowly, Nessa crawled toward a sliver of light. Her palms split and bled, and she hissed at the sting as she poked her head cautiously out of her shelter, her eyes watering against the twilight. The field before her was charred and singed, bits of ash swirling through the air like snow. She braced a hand on the mighty creature at her side and hoisted herself up to stand on wobbly legs. The dragon's breathing went ragged under her palm.

Nessa's overworked heart lodged in her throat. "No! No, no, no, no!"

She stumbled to face the dragon. It lay sprawled on the blackened dirt, its golden eyes following her. It rumbled once, gently, and Nessa was horrified to see dark blood staining its side.

Her eyes stung, her throat bobbing as she swallowed. It wasn't fair. The poor thing didn't deserve this. It had been taken and controlled and hurt. It didn't deserve to live and die in pain.

"You saved me," she hiccupped. "You saved me, and you shouldn't have…you didn't have to…you didn't... Thank you. I can't… Oh, you poor thing. I'm so sorry."

She fell to her knees and leaned against the dragon's head, gently stroking the scales along its nose as hot, sorrow-laden tears fell to her cheeks.

This never should have happened, she thought.

There wasn't anything she could do. The dragon had saved her, and now she could do nothing to help it. She cried, gently petting its head and feeling altogether utterly useless.

Suddenly, the beast turned its head to her and Nessa jumped, sitting back on her heels as the dragon gently nudged her chest with its snout. Her chest began to feel warm, like sinking into a hot bath; it spread to her fingers and down to her feet for a moment, then it all melted away. The dragon let out one last breath, the fire leaving its eyes.

"Poor dragon." Nessa pressed her forehead against the scales. "Rest well."

It was a long moment before she could bring herself to do anything else.

Nessa forced herself to move, though her body wasn't too happy about it. Every part of her groaned in protest, and she stumbled as the world tilted and spun, closing her eyes until the feeling passed.

Finally, she blinked smoke from her eyes and looked around. The battlefield before her smoldered, pillars of fumes rising from dying flames. She never wanted to relive the smell that assaulted her nose: a putrid mix of coppery blood and sweet decay with a layer of burnt flesh on top. Soldiers scavenged the dead, some burning the bodies where they lay. Nessa couldn't tell the color of the uniforms in the dying light.

Galidel stood in the distance; she could see the collapsed portions of outer and inner wall from the mix of colored stones. One of the inner watchtowers had crumbled to rubble, stones strewn across the city. Galidel looked singed, broken, and tired, but still proud. Still alive.

What had happened? Where was Liv? And her father? Rinn? The thought sent a chill through Nessa, and she trotted off in the direction of the collapsed gate as fast as her aching muscles would allow. She slid to a stop just outside the gate, bent over and gasping for air.

Three men wearing Calebrian uniforms were sitting on the ruined stones next to the gate, sharing what Nessa hoped was a victory pint. At her appearance, the three of them scrambled from their seats, one even knocking over his pint in his haste to reach her. She felt like hell and knew she must look it. One soldier hovered his hands at her side while another offered his arm for her to take as she wobbled unsteadily. She grasped onto it gratefully.

"What happened?" she gasped, her throat raw and tasting like smoke.

"Galidel still stands," answered the one she whose arm she held. "Sit. Please, sit. We'll get you some wine."

"We won?" Nessa couldn't quite believe it. All her breath left her in a rush. "The Menhirans are gone?"

"For now, yes."

It was over. They'd won. They were still here.

Her knees buckled, and a second soldier quickly caught her before she could fall, the first still holding tight to her arm. Relief bubbled up in her chest, spilling from her lips in a hysterical giggle, and her eyes watered as the giggle abruptly turned to gasping cries. The first soldier gently patted her hand as they lowered her to sit, and the second handed her his pint while the third told her to calm. She forced herself to breathe.

In and out.

It was over.

In and out.

"I'm okay." Nessa shook her head after a few minutes, a slightly hysterical smile still on her lips. "I'm okay."

"Miss, who can we try to find for you? Your husband?" the third soldier asked.

"Where is General Callei?" Her heart started pounding again and she jumped to her feet. "Where is he?"

"Miss, please. You need to rest—"

"*Where is he?*"

"We don't know." The first shook his head. "The commanders, wounded, and honored dead are all up in the castle."

Wounded? Honored dead?

Nessa took off at a dead sprint. She scrambled over the rubble, caring nothing for the ache in her bones as fresh panic ripped through her veins, pushing her forward. Buildings, parts of them anyway, lay strewn about the streets, bits of charred and burned flags drifting on the breeze. Ash covered the whole city in a menacing blanket, and she had to dodge survivors gathering what they could from the wreckage. Still, she kept running, faster and faster until she was skidding through the manor gate.

Soldiers and civilians alike gathered on the green, some huddled tightly together in little groups. Others sat around small campfires with bowls and cups, and still others tended the wounded. Each face was covered in ash and soot and looked exactly like the one next to it.

Her eyes stung as she strained to tell who was who. She didn't see anyone she recognized, not Dagorn, or Liv, or even Alaron. She wasn't sure if she should be relieved or worried.

"Ada!" she called, as loudly as she could. "Ada! Ada!"

She spun around the gathered, searching frantically. Her eyes flew over face after face after face, but she couldn't find the one she needed. People were starting to stare at her with unreadable expressions, and one young man pointed openly, whispering to his companion. Nessa rushed past him without another thought.

"Ada!"

Suddenly, the crowd rumbled, people muttering and pointing as a deep voice sounded over their heads. It was yelling something Nessa couldn't make out over the growing clamor when suddenly, the crowd parted. A large man covered head to toe in grime and blood was pushing his way through the group of soldiers, all of whom sprang out of his way as if burned.

"Move! For Arelen's sake!"

Nessa gave a strangled cry of relief. "Ada!"

Dagorn wrapped her up in his arms so tightly she couldn't breathe, and she crushed him right back, a hiccupping sob escaping her lips as she buried her face in his shoulder. He reeked of smoke, blood and sweat, but she didn't care. Her father was still here. She could feel his armor under her torn hands, feel him hugging her close.

They were still here.

"Oh, my little one. My Nessa. Oh, thank Arelen and the Elar!" He pulled back to look at her, tears welling in his eyes. Kissing her forehead, he crushed her to him again, not caring who saw. "We couldn't find you, and then Rauna told us what happened and... Oh, my baby, we feared the worst. We couldn't find you. I thought...I couldn't..."

"Where is she!?" a *very* stern feminine voice demanded, sounding enraged. "*WHERE IS SHE?*"

Nessa jumped, wiping the water from her eyes, and the crowd rumbled again as a shock of white emerged, fiercer than a hurricane. Liv's hair flew wildly about her ash-covered face, the very picture of an angry fae queen. The elf's red-rimmed eyes took in Nessa, searching.

"You reckless thing!"

Liv took Nessa's face in her hands, pressing their foreheads together. Nessa smiled and exhaled a sniffle.

"Liv!" she nearly laughed.

"You are going to be the death of me." Liv finally released her with a smack to the arm, then paused, thought about it, and smacked Nessa again. Pain shot up her arm, and Nessa winced.

"Ow!"

"If you EVER—"

"Trust me, I have no intention of doing that again."

"Little one, what happened?" Dagorn kissed his daughter's hair again.

"How about what happened to *you?!*" Nessa demanded. "You look like hell!"

"Later," he told her. "Let's get you fixed up first. Then we'll talk."

Dagorn and Liv took Nessa inside the manor, her father keeping a protective arm around her the whole time. The soldiers in the halls scuttled out of their way like terrified children, all of them staring wide-eyed as they passed. Nessa could hear them whispering behind their hands as the trio went by. She was sure she looked like the embodiment of chaos, but they could also have been gossiping about Dagorn, or Liv. Surely, they weren't interested in *her*.

...Right?

Liv glided past them into what had once been the front parlor but was now serving as a makeshift hospital. It was filled with people running around with bowls, bandages, and rags, but no healer approached them as Dagorn rushed Nessa to a private room just off the parlor. Inside, Koen reclined on the floor, propped up by a mountain of pillows. The elf king's face was the same color as his clean linen robes.

Bryn, who was sitting on the edge of a desk and getting his arm wrapped by Alaron, beamed when he saw Nessa. He waved a hand in Koen's face.

"By the stars, Koen! Look at this beautiful young thing!" He laughed, squeezing Nessa's shoulders affectionately. "Returned victorious from her ride atop the fearsome beast!"

Koen blinked blearily. "Liv does look remarkably lovely."

Bryn looked a little sick at the thought. "Not what I meant."

"It's Alaron's potions. Can make people go a little funny for a bit," Dagorn whispered in Nessa's ear.

"There is nothing wrong with my potions, Gornie."

The wizard gave Nessa a wink, and she offered him a relieved smile, filing her father's embarrassing nickname away for later. To Nessa's surprise, Alaron hugged her, his arms so long they could nearly wrap around her twice. The man had the wingspan of a condor.

"So glad to see you back on solid ground, child." He squeezed her tightly. "You served as an excellent distraction."

"Glad I could help," she remarked sardonically.

"Come. I have someone who wants to see you."

Nessa's heart leapt into her throat as Alaron led her back through the parlor and into another side room. It was dark, save for one window, and there, sitting with his back against the wall, was Rinn. His eyes were closed, and he was covered head to toe in blood.

Nessa almost choked.

"Gods and angels!"

Fear gripped her chest as she knelt next to him, one warm dark eye cracking open at her screech. The corner of his mouth twitched.

"'S not mine," he told her, looking exhausted. His shoulders shifted slightly. "'M fine. Just tired."

"What happened to you?"

"Uh…broke a blood curse." Rinn's eyes blinked open, then closed again. "Your elf lord got himself into a tight spot."

Nessa let her forehead drop onto his shoulder. "Thank you."

"So…" Rinn turned to look at her. "I'm guessing it was you everyone saw on that dragon?"

"What can I say?" Nessa shrugged. "It was an accident?"

Rinn snorted. "You're nothing but trouble, princess."

"To be fair, I *was* thrown off a wall," Nessa pointed out. "The dragon just happened to be in the path of my fall."

Rinn blinked at her. "You were thrown off a wall?"

Nessa released a puff of air. "Your shadow doesn't like me much. Besides, I kicked him off the wall first, so I guess it was only to be expected."

"I fear Gerric Emrys will continue to be a problem," Alaron muttered darkly, handing Nessa a vial. Neither of them bothered to ask how the wizard knew who Rinn's shadow was. He probably wouldn't have answered anyway.

Nessa winced as she tried to grip the cork, her fingers unable to move without her eyes watering in pain. Her palm tore further as she tried, blood streaking her skin. Rinn offered his hand, and she passed the vial to him. He pulled the cork out with his teeth, then handed it back.

It tasted like cold olive oil with red pepper, and she took it like a shot, sticking her tongue out as she fought not to gag.

"What did you just give me?"

"Painkiller, dear," Al answered cheerfully.

"Oh, thank heavens."

The wizard laughed.

***

Alaron had to pry both Nessa and Rinn from the floor to take them back to Bryn and Koen's room. Al sat Nessa on top of the desk where Bryn had been and got to work on her torn hands. Liv hovered around Koen while Dagorn leaned against the desk next to his daughter.

Liv and Dagorn had been on the front lines of the battle when the first wave of Menhiran soldiers had struck, but it wasn't until the second charge that the dragon had arrived. The creature had rushed the wall, collapsing the stone in one fell swoop as Alaron used most of his energy protecting the Calebrian soldiers with as much magic as he could spare. They'd all been so busy with the dragon — which at that point had been trying to take down the second wall — that Nessa's warnings hadn't made sense until they heard the manor bells ringing.

The story was interrupted when the door opened to admit King Elvar. His worried eyes instantly fell on Nessa sitting on the desk, and his rigid posture relaxed.

"There you are!"

Nessa smiled and did little jazz hands, though the effect was ruined by the bandages. "I'm alive!"

"For which I am immensely grateful." Elvar stepped over Koen to peck her on the forehead. "I didn't know what to think once I heard the bells."

Koen whacked the king in the shins with the side of his fist. "You are being very rude. I almost died, if you recall. I do not need you stepping on me."

Elvar apologized immediately and moved to a space on the floor where he wasn't in danger of stomping on another royal. Nessa explained that she'd seen Menhiran soldiers coming in over the walls just as the dragon arrived, though she skimmed over sending Chavet to raise the alarm and her valiant but probably ill-advised evacuation of the kitchens. She did tell them, albeit in the loosest possible terms, about releasing Rinn from prison and hiding out in the stables with the other townsfolk.

"The stone roof!" Dagorn realized.

"Stone doesn't burn." Nessa shrugged, then instantly regretted it as a twinge of pain shot down her back.

At that point, Alaron cut in and told them of his battle with Wulfric, Menhir's own High Wizard. Apparently, there was some history between the two and none of it was good; at least, Nessa had never seen that particular curl to the wizard's lip before. Upon hearing the name Wulfric, Bryn pumped his fist in the air, informed Dagorn he'd told him so, and demanded his fifteen coin.

While Alaron was occupied with his old adversary, Dagorn and Liv had been fighting tooth and nail to get back to the manor. However, they'd found themselves surrounded thanks to Menhir's little side entrance. It was then that they'd heard the bells again, and Nessa sheepishly admitted to rallying the civilians and leading a charge against the attacking Menhirans. Elvar grew pale, while Bryn, to everyone's surprise, burst out laughing.

"You *are* your father's child, I'll give you that."

Liv narrowed her eyes at Nessa, who swallowed guiltily, shuddering at the furious tumult in the elf's gaze. There was a lecture in her future and it was going to be a long one. Probably with even more arm smacking.

Koen then relayed the story of his own arrival and charge into the battle, his account veering from Nessa's after the wall collapse. He and Rinn had fallen together, and the two had searched for Nessa but found Liv instead.

Their forces overwhelmed, they'd had to stand and fight. Koen had struck down a Menhiran commander who'd laid a blood curse on him with his final breath, though luckily — or perhaps unluckily, depending how you looked at it — it had been cast with blood magic.

"Were it not for him," Koen nodded to Rinn, "I would not be here."

"How do you know how to…" Nessa started to ask, but Rinn quickly ducked his head and Koen continued before she could say anything further.

"I believe his exact words were, 'Find me someone you don't need alive.'"

"Easy enough, on a battlefield."

Liv's words sliced through the air like a very sharp, very cold knife. Nessa swallowed and vowed again never to get on Liv's bad side.

Nessa picked the story back up with her encounter with Gerric Emrys, deciding to keep Rinn's history with him to herself. Everyone in the room shuddered and gasped as she recounted how she'd been tossed off the wall right onto the dragon's back, then fell into shocked silence when she described the feeling of the magical snap.

"You—" Liv swallowed. "You broke the blood magic binding on the dragon?"

"It was just like breaking it on you," Nessa pointed out. "Only, well, bigger."

"That shouldn't be possible." Rinn shook his head. "Blood magic doesn't work like that. It's a corruption, not a power."

"You shouldn't even have been able to reach the magic of Avani. You were hundreds of feet in the air!" Dagorn exclaimed.

"The Visiril *are* connected to Avani," Alaron pointed out. "Regardless of where their feet are."

"Still, that amount of power…" Dagron breathed. "After channeling that… It shouldn't be possible."

"And yet." Alaron's eyebrows jumped as he gave Nessa a pleased smile.

Nessa looked down at her lap. She wanted to twist her fingers, but couldn't fit them together around the bandages. Her teeth clamped down on her lower lip and she winced at the sudden sting, finishing her tale with the collapse of the dragon and how she had watched it breathe its last. Rinn's eyes stayed fixed on her, his mouth agape. Even Alaron looked stunned.

"The dragon gave you its last breath?" he asked.

"I…um…I guess so?" Nessa reminded herself not to shrug.

"Well…" It seemed like the wizard was about to go on, but he said nothing else.

Bryn cut in with his own tale. After leaving Starcrest, he had indeed managed to find the Nolael. With help from his old friend Raya, he'd managed to convince Chief Ayman and the rest of the company to come assist them at Galidel. He said he suspected their agreement had been more about hurting Menhir than assisting Calebrir, but he would take it nonetheless. On the way, they'd met up with Brandir and his caravan, who had also agreed to help when they learned it would bring Menhir grief.

The battle had ended shortly after Bryn led the Nolael into battle, and it was only afterward that they realized Nessa was missing. Dagorn had searched for hours and had almost given up hope when she'd arrived.

"You are quite the topic," Elvar told her. "At this very moment, my men are spreading the stories of the fearless woman who led them into battle, and of the great dragon rider. I never imagined they were one and the same…or my granddaughter."

"I never imagined any of it," Nessa answered. "I wanted to be a literature professor."

"I doubt you would have stayed out of trouble, even then," Liv teased, and Nessa snorted.

"I mean, think of the paper cuts."

She could hear Rinn rolling his eyes from across the room.

Chapter Thirty-Six

Governing Is Harder

Rebuilding efforts began immediately. The reconstruction of the walls started that evening, and Nessa persuaded her grandfather to use the many rooms of the manor as a refuge for civilians until their homes could be rebuilt.

In the end, it hadn't taken much convincing. Dagorn told Nessa that her mother had often done the same, and Elvar could never say no to Larien. It was nice, he said, smirking, to see her daughter carrying on the tradition.

Alaron also helped the laborers along as best he could with his magic. He had a knack for levitation, and lifted Nessa into the air on a few memorable occasions — and once, even more memorably, on accident. Nessa, along with her new and now forever-loyal friends from the kitchens, often made excursions into town to pass out bread and supplies.

She was relieved to find that her identity was now an open secret. Everyone in Galidel had already known she was of noble blood, and after seeing her in Dagorn's company so often, her true lineage hadn't been difficult to guess.

Then, of course, there was her new reputation. The legend of the fierce dragon rider had spread even faster than the dragon's destruction, and little children would beg to hear the tale over and over again. Nessa quickly learned to limit herself to only recounting her adventures once a day; otherwise, nothing would have ever gotten done.

Elvar happily reported that the Menhirans had retreated to lick their wounds. For now. But Rinn swore they would be back. King Gaough did not accept defeat gracefully, if at all. The thief, though still a prisoner, had been granted a small reprieve by the king for his service to the crown, and Koen had provided the same as thanks for saving his life. Rinn was now officially under Alaron's supervision and was not permitted to leave the wizard's sight. He said it was a worse punishment than prison.

All the same, Rinn told Nessa, he was sure King Gaough wouldn't try anything so risky again. At least, not for a while. It seemed Menhir had been defeated, albeit temporarily. The fact worried her, though she tried not to show it. The battle for Galidel may have been over, but the war for Avani had yet to be decided.

Three full weeks after the battle, Nessa paced outside a set of ornately carved arched doors, chewing her lip anxiously. On the other side of said doors was the Chambers of the Court. Nobility from every corner of the empire had arrived a few days previous, every one of them wondering what Elvar had to announce. And of course, they were all eager to witness the trial of the 'captured Menhiran soldier.'

Luckily for their curiosity, both events were to take place simultaneously.

Nessa had been forced to dress as a princess should, as she was to be formally presented at court as crown princess and rightful heir. As such, she was not allowed to wear anything simple. Her sapphire blue gown had been chosen to match her pendant, with silver and pearls decorating the neckline and bodice. and she'd been strapped into the garment so tightly she thought she might faint. The hem, which had been covered in flour and dirt from a morning in the kitchens until Liv attacked it with a brush, was far too long, the jewels embroidered there dragging on the floor behind her. Resting on Nessa's head was a delicate silver circlet, with swirls and vines decorated with sapphires and pearls. Liv followed a few steps behind, twisting silver ribbons into Nessa's hair.

"Will you stand still?" Liv ordered.

Nessa stopped, allowing Liv to finally finish twisting her hair up. Liv wore her own crown of green leaves and a flowing gown of palest green, her soft waves of snowy hair cascading down her bare back.

"What are they saying in there?" Nessa asked. "They've been talking for two hours."

"Likely they are all imagining how best to kill your thief."

"He's not *my* thief, Liv."

Nessa wasn't sure if she was arguing with Liv or herself.

"Someone needs to tell him that, then."

"I'm being serious." She narrowed her eyes at the offensive door. "They can't hurt him, right? Do I have to issue a royal decree or something?"

"You have to be presented at court before you can do such a thing," Liv explained.

"Well, isn't that what this is about?"

"And Rinn's trial, yes."

"Then why can't I use my newly bestowed authority to be a bitch about it?" asked Nessa.

"Because I know you, and you won't," Liv answered.

Nessa pouted. "I hate this."

"I know," Liv answered, sounding sympathetic.

"Waiting sucks," Nessa said sulkily.

"It does," Liv agreed. The pitter patter of Nessa's heart made her chest tighten as Liv squeezed her arm.

"Nessa." Liv took her by the shoulders, forcing the other girl to look at her. "Think of everything you've done, how far you've come. Anyone in that room would be foolish to think you any less than they. You rode a dragon, for the stars' sake! You are beloved by your people already. Remember who you are."

Nessa arched a brow. "A trouble magnet?"

"Besides that." Liv smiled. "You are the future queen. Remember what I told you."

Nessa nodded. "Do no harm but take no shit."

"Precisely."

Suddenly, they looked up to see Dagorn approaching them, wearing the deep greens and blues of the formal Guard's uniform. Golden ropes draped across one shoulder, a short cape fell down his back, and his beard had been neatly trimmed for the occasion. Nessa almost didn't recognize him in all his finery.

"You almost look respectable," Liv told him with a smile.

"You know the truth of it, of course," Dagorn shot back. He kissed Nessa's forehead. "Ready, little one?"

"Nope." She rolled her shoulders as Dagorn offered his arm, and she took it gratefully. "Let's do this."

"Bryn and I will see you inside." Liv winked. "I can't wait to see the look on Lord Narka's face."

And with that, she disappeared. Nessa looked up at her father.

"Any tips?"

Dagorn snorted. "Don't be afraid. I think the other nobles can smell it."

"Right." Nessa's voice cracked. "Who's scared?"

Dagorn squeezed her arms. "The king and your people are behind you. That's more than a lot of them have."

At that moment, the doors to the chamber opened. Nessa straightened, holding her head high, and entered like the princess she was.

The room inside was round, with columns holding up an enormous silver dome. Nessa and Dagorn entered to find themselves in a pit created by three levels of seating, amphitheater-style. Ahead of them, Elvar presided over the room from a golden throne. The two thrones to either side of him, one also golden and smaller than his, and the other smaller still and silver, sat vacant.

The room was only half-full, the space and shape of the empty seats leading Nessa to believe that once a line died out, their seat remained, left to sit empty. She found herself wondering how many had been lost in battle.

She also couldn't say she found the ratio of men to women particularly encouraging.

Dagorn bowed low to the king, while Nessa did her best to curtsy. She'd never curtsied before, something Liv had discovered an hour ago and quickly given her a crash course in. As her head came back up, she could hear the hushed whispers echoing around the room.

She swallowed.

"My Lord Dagorn, of House Callei." Elvar rose from his throne to greet them. "You are welcome in my kingdom and my household."

"I thank you, King Elvar," Dagorn answered. "I am humbled."

Which, Nessa had learned, was the correct response.

Elvar held a hand out to Nessa, and Dagorn gently passed her hand to the king, who squeezed it tightly and beamed at her, turning to address the assembled crowd. Nessa took in their faces, some hopeful, some curious, and some who looked like they were going to be sick. She fought to keep her face proud and serene.

"My lords and ladies, esteemed guests, this is a joyous day for our kingdom," King Elvar began. "We have once again held our borders and protected our home. But the joy of victory cannot compare to the joy I feel today. I am pleased to announce that the future of our kingdom is once again secure."

Elvar released Nessa's hand and gestured toward her.

"After many long years, my heir has returned to us!"

A pin drop could have been heard in the shocked silence.

"May I present the daughter of my daughter," her grandfather announced, "the sole heir to my throne, Her Royal Highness Nessa Persephone Everette of the House of Callei, First of Her Line and Crown Princess of Calebrir."

Nessa's eyes searched the faces in the crowd. Some looked pleased, while others were clearly less so. A few of the ladies looked smug, nudging the men beside them. Liv and Bryn she found instantly, both of them sitting beside the silver throne.

Alaron, sitting behind the second golden throne, began to clap, and the rest of the council joined in, some more enthusiastically than others.

"Your Highness." A young man sitting in the front row rose to his feet, the applause ending abruptly. "Are you not the same warrior who rode the dragon into battle?"

"That is not entirely accurate," Nessa answered with a practiced coy smile. "I *ran* into the battle. I found myself on the dragon's back a little later."

A few satisfied chuckles echoed around her, including those of her father and grandfather. Elvar led Nessa to the silver throne while Dagorn settled in beside Alaron. Liv discreetly patted her hand.

"You did well," she whispered.

"Thanks."

"You kept your last name," Liv noted.

"It's another middle name now." Nessa gave her a sad smile. "I thought it was important."

"I like it."

Nessa caught sight of an elderly man a few seats down to her left. He wore a permanently sour expression, which looked even more lemon-puckered at the moment. Nessa glanced at him, then at Liv, then back at the unpleasant-looking man. Liv followed her eyes, sighing.

"Lord Vido Narka," she whispered. "He's steward of the southeast borders by the sea. He's a shrewd businessman, but his wife and daughters are actually the ones who get the deals made as his personality usually ends negotiations before they begin."

"I can see why."

The room fell silent as the doors opened again and the guards brought in Rinn. He gazed around the room, his eyes falling on Nessa. They did not move again.

"State your name for the court." Elvar's voice was stern.

"Rinn Aylir, Your Majesty."

"Rinn Aylir, you stand accused of being a Menhiran defector," the king continued. "And not only of defecting, but of serving as a soldier in their army. Do you have a defense?"

"No, Your Majesty."

A quiet murmur raced through the assembled nobles, and Nessa seized Liv's hand.

"Does anyone wish to say anything on your behalf?" Elvar asked.

At that, Koen rose from his seat. Glancing at Nessa over his shoulder, he gave her a conspiratorial wink.

"I would, Your Majesty."

Koen took a few steps down to the floor, turning to address the court. "I have granted clemency to this young man due to his service to me. In the battle for Galidel, I was struck by a blood curse that would have killed me. I had never met this young man before the battle; in fact, we had only met a few minutes prior, but he saved my life, at great risk to himself, without hesitation."

"And what benefit was it to him?" Lord Narka spoke up, his voice uneven and nasally, but stern. Nessa was reminded of Melissa I'm-Head-Of-The-Book-Club Jones. It had all the tone of authority without any actual substance behind it.

"None," Koen answered calmly. "Perhaps it would please the court to think of things another way. This young man knows the inner workings of Menhir's military. He knows their people, their strategy. He is a powerful resource. The more we know of our enemy, the more easily we can anticipate their movements. Perhaps it is time we move past our prejudice for the betterment of our kingdoms."

"With all due respect, Lord Koen." Narka rose, with no respect evident. "I must remind you of the reason we have our laws in place. No one wishes for a repeat of Daradir, especially our esteemed king."

Koen leveled him with a fierce gaze. "It is not wise to create rules of law based on rumors. My people have known this for thousands of years. But perhaps men, with their shorter memories, are in need of reminders."

Nessa's hand flew to her mouth to hide a smirk. She wiped it away, glancing at Liv. Her friend's face had gone pale, though Nessa couldn't think of a reason for such a reaction.

The debate continued, all about the price of intelligence and the risks of letting Rinn go; the two sides were simple enough. The argument for letting him go had some support, while most others wanted him executed as a spy. A third option presented was that they extract as much information as they could from Rinn before executing him, thus getting the best of both worlds. The thief looked more and more disheartened as the debate raged on, offering nothing in his own defense.

The room had erupted into so many differing opinions, Nessa could hardly keep track. Dagorn was whispering in Elvar's ear, glancing worriedly at Rinn, when suddenly, Lord Narka stood.

"I say let's stick him on the racks and see what he has to say."

"Absolutely not!" Nessa's stern voice echoed through the room, silencing all other voices. A sea of eyes blinked at her, some with pride and others in shock as she turned to Narka, remaining calm and proud on her throne.

"I will not allow us to stoop so low as to use the tactics of our enemy, Lord Narka, for then we are no better."

"With all due respect, your ladyship…"

"Your *Highness*," Nessa corrected. Out of the corner of her eye, she saw Elvar, Dagorn and Alaron all duck their heads together, shoulders shaking in glee. Narka turned several shades of red.

"Your *Highness*, you are new to our court. You cannot be aware…"

"Yes, I am new." Nessa rose from her throne. "Which means I can come to this argument without years of hurt and pain influencing my decision-making abilities. To be at war is to cause destruction. I have seen the effects of the war during my travels. I know the scars it has left on our people, on their lives and their families. Do not think I make any decision regarding it lightly."

Nessa had no idea where this side of her was coming from. Perhaps her father's military traits were finally starting to rub off.

"Without ceremony, I can tell you that Rinn has saved my life multiple times, and the only reason we were able to hold off the attack at the walls was because of his information, which he freely gave. He was at my side when we charged into battle and fought beside me to protect our people. I can tell you with certainty that Rinn is no longer Menhir's man. And I, for one, do not believe in condemning a man for an accident of birth. I don't believe my mother would have stood for it, either."

Silence fell over the hall, and Nessa took a breath.

"The only way this war will be won is together, through our loyalty and trust in one another and the compassion of our people."

She chanced a glance at Rinn. He was looking at her as though she were the sun bursting through thunderclouds. She gave him a little smile.

"I trust Rinn completely," she said, looking directly into his eyes. A hint of a roguish smile appeared on the thief's lips.

"Where do your loyalties lie, Lord Narka?" Nessa asked calmly. "With your kingdom? Or your hatred?"

"Well spoken, my dear." Elvar beamed at her as Nessa finally allowed her shaking knees to bend.

"Thank you, grandfather."

The debate simmered into a discussion, with the whole of Nessa's family fighting to save Rinn's life. She was a bit surprised, but apparently Rinn saving Koen's life had endeared the thief to Liv, who fought as hard as Nessa for his release. But for all their wise words and passion, she could tell they weren't getting anywhere.

It was like telling an enraged Karen that the coffee shop had never carried chicken wings, that she was looking for the place up the street, only for her to respond by screaming louder about wanting chicken wings.

Maria had had to call the cops while Nessa hid in the bakery after taking a full coffee cup to the face. And that still wasn't the worst shift she'd ever worked.

Finally, Elvar called for a vote.

"Not guilty, say aye."

Nessa could count the votes on her fingers. Her little family was not going to be enough.

"Guilty, say aye."

The entire room erupted with *ayes*, and Nessa felt her eyes sting. She blinked rapidly and Liv clutched her hand, while Rinn's expression remained blank, his eyes closed.

"It is decided," Elvar intoned solemnly.

"Yes, yes, well done." Alaron clapped impatiently as he got to his feet. "If you are all quite finished, I'll be taking back my apprentice now. Thank you."

"Alaron," Elvar began, "I'm afraid…"

"Yes, you found him guilty. Good for you lot." Alaron waved a hand nonchalantly. "I had been rather hoping you would come to your senses, but no matter."

"What's he doing?" Nessa whispered to Liv.

"Not sure. Give it a moment."

Alaron waved a finger in the air. "I'm going to invoke the law of Malodus."

Liv's hands clamped suddenly onto Nessa's arm.

"What—"

"Wizards," Liv hissed. "Wizards are blessed with magic from the gods. They are considered almost divine, like the Visiril. It is sacrilege to waste such a gift."

"What does that mean?" Nessa asked.

"It normally does not come up, since there are only three wizards in all of Avani. They are just too rare!" Liv vibrated with excitement.

"Liv!"

"Rinn has proven himself worthy by saving Koen's life, and yours. The court cannot do anything to a divinity who has proven themselves."

"Wait." Nessa's heart pounded. "It's illegal to kill a good wizard?"

"It is illegal to kill a good wizard," Liv confirmed.

But…a wizard? Rinn *wasn't* a wizard. He was only a wizard's apprentice…

"A new wizard hasn't been born in over two hundred years," Elvar argued.

"Which means it's about time." Alaron crossed his arms. "Are you going to sit there and argue with me about the boy's magical prowess? He has clearly passed his test of heart and been bestowed his full power! He broke a blood curse, for Gaelin's sake!"

Even Rinn was looking at Alaron like he was crazy…but Nessa was starting to realize Alaron was crazy like a fox.

"If you knew the boy was a wizard," Narka began, "then why let the trial continue?"

"Well…" Alaron scratched his chin, found a speck, and rubbed his fingers on Dagorn's shoulder. "You all seemed so intent on the thing. I thought I'd let you have your fun. Besides, he can't be tried for this again, according to your laws. Now the matter is completely laid to rest."

Nessa couldn't help it; she put both hands over her mouth to stifle her laughter. It was all just so *Alaron*. Lord Narka looked like he'd eaten a rodent that been run over by a wagon a few days previous, while Elvar's lips were pressed tight to hide his grin.

"Then it's decided," he told Alaron with a nod.

"But my king—!"

Nessa blew a raspberry at Narka, and he fell silent as a chuckle ran through Nessa's half of the room. Elvar had turned his back, but she saw his shoulders shake as Narka, thankfully, sat down.

"Rinn Aylir," Elvar addressed the thief, a small smile on his face. "You are free to go."

Epilogue

For Now

Nessa slipped from the kitchens before the sun peeked over the manor walls, keeping the basket she carried tucked carefully under her arm. She'd been up half the night baking with Liv, too riled up to sleep after her first day at court. Liv, for her part, had been grateful for both the distraction and the sweet rolls.

Satu, now that she knew who Nessa was, didn't change her treatment of the young lady who had proven so loyal to her and her staff one bit. Besides, Nessa didn't need to use her title to talk Satu into allowing her access to the kitchens. Her snickerdoodles could do that just fine.

Nessa could walk the path from the kitchens to the stables blindfolded now, but luckily she didn't need to, as the first weak rays of dawn were slowly turning the black grass back to deep green. The last of the stars twinkled out for a long-deserved rest before nightfall. The world was quiet and still and warm.

Silhouetted against the new morning dawn were two figures standing outside the stable, one hunched over a pack while a tall, lanky one wrangled two mares.

"Are you really so ready to be rid of me?" she asked.

Rinn straightened, flashing her a grin.

"I'm getting tired of being in mortal peril, to be honest." He shrugged. "Though I don't think wizard training is going to prove any kind of reprieve."

"How about this?" Nessa handed him a basket. "I made you a little something for the road."

Rinn took the basket, lifting a corner of the cloth to see what was inside. His eyebrows lifted.

"Did you make these?" The thief was nearly vibrating in excitement. The sweet rolls were still warm.

"Yep."

"Al's going to have to fight me if he wants any." Rinn glanced around to see if Alaron was listening. The wizard stood off to the side, appearing to tend to the horses in a very focused manner — but neither of them doubted that he was listening closely.

Nessa laughed. "Good luck, then."

"What are you going to do now, Nessa?" Rinn asked. "Done with adventuring?"

She shrugged. "For a bit. We'll be heading to the Mother City at the end of the week."

"Try to stay out of trouble," Rinn suggested, sounding as though he knew it was in vain.

"You know…" Nessa tilted her head. "I never go *looking* for it."

"No." Rinn fixed her with a smug look. "It just runs at you flapping its arms and screeching."

Nessa's hand flew over her mouth to suppress a giggle as Rinn gave her a sweet, genuine smile. It was all the thanks she needed.

"Will you write to me?" she asked hopefully.

"'Course." Rinn's voice turned soft. "I'll probably be bad at it, though. I've never had anyone to write to before."

Nessa felt heat rise to her cheeks. "I won't mind."

She glanced over to see Alaron watching them, grinning like a loon. The moment he saw Rinn and Nessa turn his way, his eyes dramatically rolled to the sky and he turned around, pointedly giving them privacy.

"He's not very subtle, is he?" Rinn asked.

"No." Nessa had to laugh. "Good luck with him."

"Thank you."

They stared at each other for an uncomfortable amount of time.

"Well, I suppose this is goodbye." Rinn ran a hand through his tangled hair.

"Yes." Nessa shuffled her feet. "For now."

"For now," he agreed.

Quickly, Rinn snatched up her hand, bowing low over her knuckles.

"Farewell, princess. Until our paths cross again."

"Goodbye, Rinn. Travel safe."

Rinn hovered over her hand, placing a quick kiss to her fingers. She felt her cheeks burn, but luckily, he had already turned away.

She watched as Rinn and Alaron mounted their horses, heading out into the fields beyond Galidel. When they reached the gate, Rinn paused, turning back in his saddle. Nessa smiled and waved, and Rinn raised a hand in farewell before they disappeared into the dawn.

Nessa sighed, blinking back the dampness in her eyes.

"For now."

How Do I Say This

Names

Nessa Everette	NES-uh Ever-ette
Livia Aeris	Liv-ee-uh AIR-is
Dagorn Callei	Dag-OR-n CAL-lye
Bryn Aeris	Br-in AIR-is
Gaough Remont	GO Reh-MONT
Belara Baerin	Bell-lar-uh Bay-rin
Mias	MY-us
Alaron	AL-uh-ron
Elvar	EL-var
Larien	Lar-EE-en
Maylin	May-lyn
Brandir	Brand-ear
Koen	KOH-en
Nolael	No-LAY-el
Cytan	S-eye-tan
Ayman	Aye-MON
Rinn	Rin
Lyca	LIE-kuh
Hedgerton	H-edge-er-ton
Chavet	SHA-vet
Gerric	G-air-ick
Eldric	ELLE-drick
Fisilmiri	Fis-il-meer-ee
Visiril	VIS-ih-ril
Khava	Kaw-va
Lebiet	le-BEE-ette
Vaerin	VAY-rin
Satu	SAH-too
Rauna	RAH-oo-nuh
Vido Narka	VEE-Doh NAR-kuh

Gods

Vaeril	VAY-rill
Arelen	Ar-EH-linn
Thera	Th-air-uh
Gaelin	GAY-lin
Elar	Eh-LAR

Kingdoms

Avani	Uh-VAH-knee
Menhir	MEH-near
Calebrir	CAL-eh-brir
Kiriviel	Keer-i-viel
Illiovet	ILL-lee-oh-vet

Rivers

Marsei	MAR-say
Angori	Anne-gore-ee
Vergri	Ver-gree

Cities

Daradir	Dare-UH-deer
Brandel	Brand-dell
Orestel	Or-es-tell
Erwani	Er-Wan-ee
Galidel	GAL-i-dell
Hadriar	Had-REE-are
Thomane	TOE-main
Dreburn	DRAY-Burn
Gelmar	GELL-mar
Kearfell	K-EAR-fell
Dunale	DUNE-ale
Halion	HAL-ee-on
Noringuard	Nor-in-GUARD
Dwarmin	DW-are-min
Nuremir	NOOR-eh-mir
Urystin	Your-ISS-tin

Acknowledgements

Dearest Reader,

Writing a book is hard. No, really, it is. Everyone thinks they can do it. I thought I could do it when I was thirteen, and I did, though it wasn't any good. That book, along with many other false starts, has since been sent upstate to a nice farm, where it will not darken my doorway again.

I would not be here without the other women in my life. I would like to thank my mother, Darra, for not crushing my hopes and dreams when she read some of my earliest works. Instead of sending me to a padded room, she encouraged my love of stories and writing. This book would have never happened without you igniting that first spark. I wouldn't be here without you. I also need to thank my Mom-Mom, Pat, for encouraging me to get out there and have enough experiences to write well, and for hitting that one mean girl in the face with a paper plate in marching band. You rock, Mom-Mom.

Next, I would like to thank my amazing, charming and incredibly sexy husband, Paul. Without your extensive knowledge of battle strategy, history and fantasy lore, the battles would have been incredibly boring. From brainstorming sessions to early edits to watching our darling children so I could write, you are as much a part of this book as I am. Your encouragement and support throughout this entire process means the world to me. Thank you so much, sweetie. I love you.

And I'm very sorry, but this book writing thing is going to continue.

I need to thank Evelyn and Charlotte, whom this book is for. Your arrival encouraged me to do the impossible, to give you everything I have, including this. Now, you always have a bit of mommy and her stories to keep with you forever. Have courage and be kind. I love you.

I would also like to thank my father-in-law Roy, who's guidance among the author and publishing world I found invaluable. And don't worry Roy, I'm keeping my day job. Thank you for all your advice.

Now, I'd like to thank Liz a.k.a. Aunt Kitty for helping to proofread this crazy story. I'd like to thank Liz further for not staring at me strangely when I asked her to read my book about magic and remaining my friend after she read it. (Book 2 is in progress. You can stop camping on my lawn now.)

And speaking of friends, I'd like to thank my tribe; Mallory, Emily, Karina and Case for keeping me sane during this entire process. And to Ms. Ronda, thank you for your unwavering support. Best teacher bestie ever!

Taylor, you make some of the most incredible art I've ever seen. I am so grateful to you for adding some truly amazing art to my book. Thank you for your talents and your heart. You are an incredible friend.

Ivy, bless you. You are an astonishing editor and I'm so thankful to you for making it look like I know what I'm doing. Thank you for all the time and effort you have put into this book. And thank you for working with me. This is going to be incredible because of you.

Thank you to my pups, Vesta and Luna for keeping my feet warm on long nights and interrupting epic scenes with their snoring.

Last, but certainly not least, I need to thank my constant companions while writing this book. They have stayed with me through thick and thin, often late into the night. They will continue to be with me as we venture on in this series.

Thank you to dry chardonnay and good bourbon.

We'll see you all back in Avani again soon.

Love,

Elizabeth

About the Author

Elizabeth Bird is a Kansas City born fantasy author. She began writing at thirteen, but admittedly didn't get good at it until her late twenties. Her love of stories grew with the arrival of her two daughters, which she blames on her darling husband. She has collected a host of skills like teaching and acting to make story time awesome for her kids. She is proud to say that after over 20 years in the making, *The Azure Crown* is her debut novel.

Follow her social media @elizabethbirdwrites or go to her website at www.elizabethbirdwrites.com

www.ingramcontent.com/pod-product-compliance
Lightning Source LLC
Chambersburg PA
CBHW060631310726
48982CB00003B/739
9798991336444